# ANTHOLOGY

## Andrew Vernon Barber

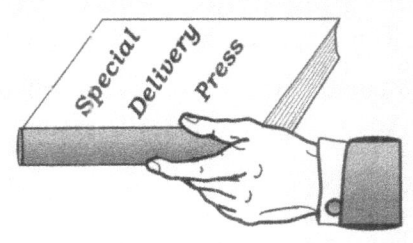

Published, March 2020, by:
Special Delivery Press, 7121 Tierra Alta Ave., El Paso, TX, 79912, (915) 600-5039

Title: Anthology
Author: Andrew V. Barber

Illustrations, Photography, Cover Design, and Layout: Andrew V. Barber

Subjects: Adventure, Intrigue, Romance, Humanity, Psychology, Growth, Potential, Humor, Satire, Music, Songs and Lyrics, Art, Poetry and Prose

LCCN: 2020933904

ISBN: 9780966970289

Printed in the United States of America

# TABLE OF CONTENTS

# FOREWORD

This book is a compilation of previous works by Andrew V. Barber which were produced, submitted for publication, and/or copyrighted, but never were published or disseminated until now. There is a variety of subject matter, styles, and formatting comprising prose, poetry, short stories, screenplay-novelette, songbook, and satirical workbook. Subject matter includes romance, adventure, intrigue, insights, military operations, spirituality, the human psyche, and offbeat humor. This volume of art, music, and literature represents material dating back to the 1960's when the author was in public school. Approximate dates associated with original works are provided as a benchmark, to reflect the maturity of the writing and the writer, the times and crises in his life and around the world, and the different personalities and circumstances that influenced and inspired creative expressions from this author. Minor revisions have been made to these works over the years, but the content and meaning have not changed, nor have the differing styles and attitudes reflected in the individual pieces. Prose and poetry selections are presented in no particular order.

I would like to thank family, friends, and associates for their support and encouragement which instilled my desire to express myself creatively. My mother, grandfather, and two great aunts were especially reassuring and instructive throughout my childhood, and my wife, son, brother, and cousin continue to be my support by believing in me and my work. I dedicate this anthology to all of them. The list of people who have been in my corner would fill this page, and it continues to grow. I will be forever grateful for their guidance and assistance in my success. I wish God's blessing on them and upon you.

Above all, I thank and praise God Almighty who is in all and above all, without whom I would have no talent, potential, or purpose. I am richly blessed with a diversity of gifts, mentors, adventures, and loved ones. The greatest gift being love, embodied through indwelling of the Holy Spirit who has spoken to me through the written word and through the living word who is Christ the Lord. His words inspire me more than anything, and my prayer is that my words and works will bring glory to his name and be an inspiration to others to grow spiritually and express themselves creatively. Experience is the wellspring of life which continues forever for everyone who believes, and this is certainly something worth sharing in any form or by any means.

# PROSE AND POETRY

## THE NAME OF THE GAME
(1999)

True or False: It's not whether you win or lose, but how you play the game? Well, in all probability, how you play the game determines whether you win or lose. However, superior sportsmanship often results in exemplary performance. That's the way it was for this year's national champions in the coed fast-pitch league.

The league originated to provide exercise and athletic entertainment for hard working adults. Thus, the league was comprised primarily of professional men and women across the country who loved the game but were not about to quit their day jobs. The majority of the spring-summer games were scheduled on weekends to accommodate members. However, participants from playoff teams often had to burn their vacation time or take unpaid leaves of absence from their regular jobs.

The most unique characteristic of this league was that each team was required to have at least four females in the lineup or on the field at all times. Thus, substitutions were according to gender. The rules were standard, with the following exceptions: no stealing of bases, no pinch hitters or runners, and blatant roughness was never tolerated under any circumstances.

The American Coed Softball League (ACSL) was only in its sixth season but it rapidly was becoming America's favorite pastime. In only five years, the league had grown from twenty-four teams to seventy-two teams divided into six regions. A team was motivated to win the majority of their twelve regular season games and make it to the regional playoffs. Then the top three divisional teams would fight it out, with the top ranked team from each division reaching the semifinals. Every team making it that far played two designated finalists in a double-header. The two teams with the best records made it to the ACSL National Championship. The champions had to win three seven-inning games of a five-game series to claim the American title. The winning team received ten thousand in scholarship money to dole out in their community; second place received five thousand. Both teams making it to the final series were provided lodging and meals at a fancy hotel; the ACSL covered room and board for playoff games as well.

The most recent season produced a number of excellent teams, so the competition was fierce at the regional playoffs. The Chicago Bulldogs had dominated the league, winning three of the first five national championships. It was no wonder they were favored to win it all again. The big surprise of the season was a second-year team called the San Angelo Killer Bees. They managed to edge out their opponents one-by-one through their excellent pitching and some creative hitting and base running. Nevertheless, the Bulldogs maintained a season average of 7.5 runs-per-game, versus the 5.5 average for the Killer Bees.

The series was held that year in Cincinnati, so the Chicago Bulldogs enjoyed home field advantage. This didn't faze the Killer Bees, for they battled diligently to tie the series at 2-2. Some terrific hitting enabled the Bulldogs to blow away the Killer Bees in the first two games. But the Bees rallied back, and via superb pitching eked out wins over the next two games by keeping the scoring to a minimum. Thus, when the night of game five neared, there was a heightened interest across the country. Everyone was talking about the League; it was in all the newspapers and sportscasts. The Sports Broadcasting Network (SBN) was receiving its highest ratings ever for the evening timeslot; they had exclusive rights due to their sponsorship.

The final game was scheduled for Sunday evening. Early that afternoon a picnic was held in Central Park which welcomed the teams, the media, and sports journalists from across the nation. Unfortunately, by game time a great number of people had come down with a form of food poisoning due to contaminated coleslaw. Five of the Killer Bees sixteen-person roster became seriously ill by game time, with another player questionable. Of the Bulldogs sixteen-member squad, only two were listed as unplayable, and conveniently, neither were starters. Sports officials suggested the game be postponed, but the pressure was tremendous from promoters, reporters, broadcasters, and City Hall to go on with it. Since San Angelo only had eleven healthy players, Chicago had to select their best eleven. Thus, endurance would be a factor, with opponents being limited to one substitution for ten fielders the entire game.

The Bees had a team meeting just prior to the National Anthem. General Manager and relief pitcher Rudy Molina gave a pep talk to generate some team spirit amongst the players, who were well aware that the cards were stacked against them. But this did not discourage Rudy; his optimism and faith became contagious, engulfing the whole team. Morale was high, despite the fact that a third of their players would be watching the game from a hospital bed.

Rudy was not scheduled to start, but the frontline pitchers were too sick to play. Thus, he would have to pitch the entire game. He had one save and one loss under his belt for the series. However, the Bulldogs had gotten wise to his changeup pitch. Chicago was able to manage three hits in the first inning of game five to take a 1-0 lead. Inning two was an improvement, as Rudy was pitching to the bottom of the order and retired the side with only one base hit. The Bees mustered only two hits in the first two innings.

Inning three was a catastrophe for the Bees. Five hits were attained and three runs scored by the Bulldogs, while the Bees had yet to score, making the tally 4-0 after three. In the middle of the fourth inning, the Bulldogs opened with a single, followed by a homer to left field. They put two more runners on base and were close to breaking the game wide open. A line drive tracking hard down the foul line might have solidified the win, but a miraculous throw by the Bees right fielder cut off the runner at home plate. Pausing after rounding third, the runner suddenly barreled towards home like a freight train. The Bees petite and young lady catcher was about to tag the runner, then ducked to avoid being bulldozed by a woman twice her size. The runner tripped over the crouching catcher and landed on home plate. The initial call was "safe" but Rudy protested, invoking the roughness rule, and bringing up the fact that the catcher had the runner dead-to-rights and contact was made by the catcher who never dropped the ball. The umpires held a brief conference then concluded that the runner was indeed out as the knee had made physical contact with the catcher's arm, and the roughing call also applied. A vehement protest from the Bulldogs manager and the entire dugout stalled the game for several minutes, but to no avail. Still, the Bees remained scoreless after four, while the Bulldogs enjoyed a commanding lead of six points.

It was time to change strategy. What the Bees were doing was not working, so they had a skull session. Rudy knew his changeup had been rendered ineffective and he couldn't rely on his arm to keep throwing fast balls for three more innings. He agreed to resurrect some old pitches he seldom threw. One was a mean curveball that Rudy had difficulty controlling because he had to throw it practically side-armed. It was a legal pitch, but few pitchers ever threw it. Another was a type of underhanded knuckle ball, that Rudy tossed maybe half-a-dozen times during the entire regular season. The team also agreed to make some modifications to their batting strategy, hoping to change the pace of the game.

At the top of the fifth inning, the Bees came to bat with Daryl Waters, a .309 hitter who played center field. He ended up walking to first base, due to an over-zealous pitcher vying for a strikeout, which he succeeded in accomplishing against the second batter. Maria, the young southpaw catcher was up next. She wasn't what one would call a heavy hitter but she had a good eye for the strike zone. Rudy signaled for the bunt. The first pitch was right over the plate and Maria bunted it perfectly, with the ball rolling down the left field line, halfway between third and home. The pitcher raced to the ball, but hesitated to pick it up, then watched as the ball died on

PROSE AND POETRY

the line, shattering his hopes that it would roll foul. Maria made it to first base with time to spare and moved the runner to second.

The next batter hit into a force out at second, leaving runners stranded on first and third. The eighth batter in the lineup was positioned there to balance the order; he was a decent hitter with a .321 average. The Bulldog pitcher knew this and elected to walk him so he could pitch to the last batter, the large right fielder named Tim who had a great throwing arm but only managed a .215 batting average. Tim got behind in the count 2-2. The next pitch hovered above the plate, out of the strike zone, but Tim swung at it anyway, and it looped over the short stop, dropping for a base hit. The runners held after one run scored. This brought Rudy, the leadoff man, to the plate with the bases still loaded and two down.

Now, Rudy was a right-handed pitcher but he was a switch-hitter. He had started batting as a lefty, because the Bulldog pitcher was a right-hander. Rudy had been burned a few times by the pitcher's inside slider, so he elected to switch to the other side of the plate. He was anticipating the slider, figuring he could step into it and line one into right field, possibly for extra bases. Rudy fought off two fast balls, placing both into foul territory, and getting behind two strikes and no balls. The next pitch was the slider, which barely caught the outside edge of the plate. Rudy stepped forward with his left foot and swung hard, landing the end of the bat solidly on the ball, his right hand slipping off the handle. He stood there motionless, observing closely as the softball sailed to the opposite field and into the stands, just inside the foul line post. It was a grand slam home run and the Bees were back in business. Naturally, the rest of the team came out on the field to congratulate Rudy. The Bulldog catcher brushed dirt over the plate and spat at Rudy's feet as Rudy nonchalantly stepped over it and dragged his heel on the edge of home base. The next hitter struck out, bringing the Bulldogs up to bat with the Bees down by only one run.

It was the bottom of the order for the Bulldogs. After walking the first batter, Rudy's curveball began to strike, and he wasted no time retiring the next three, bringing up the top of the sixth inning. It was the elect of the lineup for the Bees, but they were unsuccessful adding any points to the scoreboard and the tally remained 6-5. The Bulldogs came to bat with great determination, but couldn't add to their lead; after two hits and a walk, they completed the inning leaving the bases loaded. Before the players knew it, the final inning was upon them.

The Bees were facing a do or die situation at the top of the seventh. The lead-in batter fouled out, bringing up little Maria. Rudy and Maria had discussed their plan in the dugout. Maria would fake the bunt, expecting to draw the infield closer. Then she would swing at the next good pitch, hoping to connect and lob one into the outfield. The strategy went exactly according to plan. The first pitch was high but Maria faked the bunt as instructed; the infield took several steps forward anticipating another dying bunt. After a few high pitches that Maria ignored, the Bulldog pitcher tossed a fastball right down the pike. Maria swung as hard as she could and got just enough of it to flop one over the first baseman's head. If he hadn't been inside the baseline, he might have caught the ball which dropped way behind him for a base hit.

Brenda, who played second base, came to the plate swinging at every pitch. She landed the bat against the third pitch, knocking a ground ball down the third base line that ricocheted off the base for a single. The next batter struck out. With two ladies on base and two batters down, Tim came back to the plate. Tim was strong, but a bit slow in his swing and in running bases. Consequently, he seldom accomplished anything more than a single, and he frequently struck out. Tim's favorite pitch was above the strike zone, just like the last one he'd connected for a single. Rudy instructed Tim to look for a high and inside changeup, which the Bulldog pitcher often threw as a sucker pitch. Tim let two strikes and a ball sail past him. As fate would have it, the next pitch was the high-inside changeup. Tim took a peculiar swipe at it but landed the bat solidly, driving the ball deep into left field. The ball kept drifting back, back as the left fielder crossed the warning path. He leaped into the air trying to snag the fly, but it bounced off the top of his glove and fell over the fence for the first home in Tim's lackluster batting history.

The fielder dropped to his knees with his face buried in his glove. The pitcher threw down his mitt in disgust. The Bees had taken the lead 8-6. Rudy was the next to bat. With two down and the bases empty, he had nothing to lose so he took a huge swing at each pitch, fouling out with a bomber that took the left fielder to the wall. Now the Chicago team was becoming desperate. They had the top of the order on deck for last bats. It was up to their veteran lineup to either make or break the last inning in this the sixth world series of coed fast-pitch.

Rudy tried to go after the first batter, only to hand him a base-on-balls. The second batter, the husky female that tried to smear little Maria, drove a hard-hit ball which was snagged by the third baseman in time to make the play at first. With one down and a runner on second, the next batter connected with a grounder that blasted directly downward into the grass and catapulted high into the air. Rudy snatched the ball with his free hand and hurled it towards first, but it struck the runner who was slightly out of the base line in a deliberate attempt to shield the first baseman. The first base umpire hesitated before declaring him safe. Rudy marched over towards first and began to criticize the call, but Brenda came from second base and affectionately restrained him.

The Bulldogs now had runners at first and third, with only one down. Rudy was facing the Bulldogs cleanup man, a .373 hitter who led the league in home runs. Rudy fired his best fast ball, which screamed to the plate at sixty miles-per-hour, just catching the inside corner. The hitter slammed it down the right field line, but it landed out of play. The next pitch, a breaking ball, dropped just below the strike zone for ball one. Then, Rudy delivered his finest curve ball, which slid over the outside edge of the plate for call strike two. Hoping that the batter would chase a pitch out of the strike zone, Rudy delivered two more fast balls, but the batter wasn't biting. Full count, and the game on the line, Rudy opted to gamble. He wound up and lobbed an extraordinary knuckle ball that hovered for a second before dropping over the edge of the plate like a lead balloon. The batter took a ferocious swing, thinking that the ball was up in the strike zone. With a swing and a miss that twirled the batter around, he struck out, landing on his behind. In anger, he leapt to his feet, stomped out of the batter's box, and slammed the bat onto the warm-up deck where it shattered into pieces.

There were two outs with two onboard and the winning run at the plate, who was another consistent batter averaging .333 during the regular season. He was a lefty, so Rudy engaged him with his sliding curve ball. Rudy was able to get ahead in the count two strikes and one ball. After two more sliders that the batter fought off and fouled into the stands, Rudy knew he had to change pitches. He mustered up all the strength he had and fired a fast ball towards the high, outside corner of the plate. The batter struck it hard, but the ball sailed straight up, vertical to home plate.

Maria flipped off her mask and searched the heavens for the ball, which seemed to stay aloft forever. The Bulldogs began razzing her and insulting her, saying how she would never catch it, that she was a chicken, and that she'd better look out because the ball was bound to smack her in the head. However, Maria never lost her concentration, tuning out all the ridicule and jabber. Eventually, the ball came screaming down, slapping the butt of Maria's mitt and bouncing backwards into her chest. She cradled the ball against her stomach, while her free hand probed for the ball. Her fingers found the ball and clutched it firmly. She raised the ball into the air and began jumping up and down, as the umpire shouted, "You're out of there."

A moment of silence elapsed while reality began to set in. It was like slow motion. Rudy raced from the mound and grabbed Maria around the waist, raising her into the air. The rest of the team rushed to the batter's box where everyone hugged and patted one another. A crowd of people, including the press and a hoard of spectators began to assemble onto the field.

Meanwhile, the Bulldogs slithered away in disgust, not even taking time to congratulate their contenders.

Carole Caruthers a syndicated network sportscaster was the first reporter on the scene. She managed to separate Rudy from the rest of the mob for an exclusive interview. She began, "Please describe what it feels like to be an underdog and defeat the three-time champion Bulldogs?" "I can't begin to tell you," was the reply. "I've just been informed you were voted most valuable player; how does that make you feel?" she inquired. Rudy responded, "I don't know that I deserve that honor. It was a team effort. Everybody pulled together. There were outstanding individual performances from all ten players. I pitched an average game, giving up six runs; and I only managed the one hit at bat. Personally, my vote would go to our catcher, Maria Contreras, who was 2 for 4, and made some great plays at the plate, including the force out in the fourth, and that great saving catch to end the game. I'd say Tim also turned in a stellar performance, especially that unbelievable throw from right field, and a homer at the last to give us the lead. Furthermore, we had Victor covering third, who is used to playing outfield; he made some great snags and throws to first. Then there's Brenda, who took over at second base; she hasn't seen a lot of play during the post season but she performed admirably."

Carole interrupted, "Tell us about your pitching exhibition. The Bulldogs were all over your pitches in the beginning, but you shut them out the remainder of the game." Rudy explained, "Like I said, I had a great team backing me up. You're right. I was giving the Bulldogs my best stuff and they were jumping all over it. My changeup is my bread-and-butter. It helped get us to the finals, but the Bulldogs weren't falling for it. I had to employ some pitches that I seldom throw because I'm not very accurate with them. Fortunately, I managed to find the strike zone today." "It was an impressive achievement, to say the least," added Carole, "Striking out seven Chicago batters is something that few pitchers have been able to accomplish all season." "Well, I think the Bulldogs were a little flabbergasted," Rudy declared, adding, "You could see the look of exasperation in their faces. We managed to keep our cool and never lost focus."

At that point, several adolescent autograph seekers dragged Rudy aside, so Carole approached Maria for her analysis of the game. "Rudy Molina spoke very highly of your performance, Maria, recommending you for MVP. How do you respond to that?" Carole asked. Maria answered in her slight Hispanic accent, "Rudy is a very humble and honest man, and I give him a great deal of credit for keeping our morale high and making us believe in ourselves." Carole requested, "Tell us about the game you had today, it seems you were doing everything well: batting, running bases, and catching." "Well, it was Rudy's idea to bunt and then to fake a bunt the next time. He is really good at strategy, and that's why he deserves the MVP," Maria asserted, continuing, "I was just playing the best that I know how." "What about the play at home, when the umpire changed the call from safe to out?" inquired Carole. "Well, Ms. Caruthers, I think the umpires called a fair game, and that's all I can say," Maria concluded.

Next, Carole strode over to Tim, introducing him to the listening audience, "This is Tim Rollins, who homered in the last to thrust the Killer Bees into the lead. How does it feel to beat Chicago in their home territory?" Carole inquired. "It feels great!" Tim exclaimed. "That was some throw you made from deep into right to catch the runner in the fourth," Carole remarked. "Yeah, I guess that's why Rudy always plays me; 'cause I can catch and I can throw; but I don't get to first all that often," Tim admitted. "Well, you certainly came through today, Tim, with two crucial base hits and four RBIs," informed Carole. "It's nice of you to say that," Tim remarked.

Carole was swamped with spectators. "That's the report from here on the field," she informed, "Let's go back to Will and Smokey in the booth." "We've got Johnny Bingham down in the Bulldogs' locker room," announced Will. "Talk to us Johnny," Smokey interjected. "I'm speaking to Shawn Trafton, the Bulldogs General Manager," Johnny cried. He aimed the microphone towards Shawn and asked, "You guys started out like gangbusters, but then the magic disappeared, Shawn, can you tell us what happened?" Shawn stated, "I'd just like to say that I think the Bees were lucky, and that we got some bad calls. I'm convinced that we're the better team, and I think the rest of the world would probably agree." The manager turned away; Johnny approached a veteran player, who also turned away. "It looks like a dead end here, Will, so I'll send it up to you guys in the booth," Johnny howled.

Will queried his co-announcer, "It appears that the Chicago gang is upset, Smokey, do you think they have a point?" "I think the Bulldogs are acting like a bunch of whiners," Smokey maintained. "The Killer Bees outplayed them and that's all there is to it. It bothers me to see champions like the Bulldogs behaving as poor sports." Will questioned Smokey further, "What about that controversial call in the fourth, Smokey, did the umpires make the correct call?" Smokey informed, "You bet they did, Will. Actually, there was nothing controversial about it. Rules are rules. I feel the umpires called a great game. Nothing got past them. They were strict and they were final. If the pitch was one inch out of the zone, it was called a ball. The only potentially questionable call as I see it, was when the first base ump gave the Bulldog runner first base in the bottom of the seventh, even though it looked like interference to me." "I suppose the umpire didn't want the course of the game to be decided by a close call," Will added. Smokey continued, "You're absolutely right, Will, the Killer Bees had to earn the victory, and that's precisely what they did." "And what a great victory it was! They really showed a lot of class," Will concluded.

"Any closing thoughts, Smokey?" Will asked. Smokey summarized, "The Killer Bees are excellent champions and have exhibited the utmost in manners and fair play throughout the playoffs. They deserve everyone's respect. The Bulldogs, on the other hand, appear to be sore losers. I'm sure kids everywhere will regard the team from San Angelo as number one, and will look up to them as a model of sportsmanship." "Well said," Will interposed. "And now we must leave you with those profound thoughts from the great Jim "Smokey" Jackson, two-time American League MVP and World Series champion. It was exciting to the end, and I expect that next year's season will be every bit as dramatic. That's it for now, folks. This is Will Foster and Smokey Jackson saying so long from SBN Sports."

## MY COLLEGE YEARS
### (1975)

I often find myself reminiscing about my college years and the excitement, work, and sometimes boredom that I experienced. I can still see the expressionless faces of my instructors, the concerned faces of my classmates, and the glowing faces of my friends.

I remember having to wake up at six-thirty every morning to prepare for classes. It was difficult getting out of bed. I would always gulp down my cereal and juice, rush down the five flights of stairs in my apartment building, and hurry to make my eight o'clock class. It was about a mile walk, but it didn't seem that far. I memorized every turn and shortcut. I would wager that I could still follow my old route to the university blindfolded. I recall strolling by the dress shops, department stores, and taverns. I surveyed each building along the way, especially that ancient-looking office building called the Burgess Building. I knew there were only four blocks to the campus from there.

Sometimes these golden memories haunt me though. The journey through town plagues me when I think about it. I visualize the early morning alcoholics, the busy traffic, and that weird building.

Every day when I walked by the Burgess Building, I would stare up at it. Why did the building intrigue me so? Probably because it was one of the oldest and tallest buildings along my route. It had a very unique architecture, particularly the overhanging twelfth story. It was unusual how the top floor jutted out like that. I always wanted to go to the top and look out of a twelfth story window. I'm sure a person could have viewed the entire campus from there. Instead, I would always glance upward toward the top at full stride.

In my memory lingers the events that took place during the spring of my junior year. I had more fun that semester than the rest of my college days combined. It was beautiful that spring, and all of the girls looked sexy. I often would get the jitters watching them amble by.

With the spring came Gayle. I constantly find myself missing her smile and understanding. Gayle was the loveliest creature I had ever laid eyes on. I felt like the envy of every man in town when we were together. She had a gorgeous figure and the face of a goddess, not to mention being a most intelligent lady. I loved gazing into her eyes wondering what she was thinking. She would act embarrassed and blush when I stared at her that way. She had a mysterious insight toward life which made me believe she always knew more about what was happening than I did. I don't imagine I'll ever forget her. Never have I met a more compassionate, loving, and caring individual, not just towards me but towards all of God's creation.

Most of my friends graduated that spring. They were a year or two ahead of me because of my stretch in the Coast Guard. I'll always cherish the memory of the graduating class dance. I was lucky; I got to attend because Gayle was a senior, and I was her escort. She looked ravishing that evening. Her hair was golden, and her long blue formal contrasted so perfectly; those were our school colors as well. I was almost afraid to touch her, because she resembled an angel. I found it very hard to suppress my desires that night.

It must have cost a fortune to decorate the gymnasium for the prom. There were chandeliers, felt tablecloths, flower arrangements, and table ornaments. The band played excellently; I could have danced all night. Although, on the other hand, I suppose I may have been a little too inebriated for that.

I recall Gayle mentioning we should go for a walk and a breath of fresh air. We wandered around campus clinging closely to each other. I would have proposed to her on the spot if I thought she'd consent. We went all the way into town, walking, talking, and experiencing a powerful warmth and devotion towars one another.

I noticed a small crowd gathering in front of the Burgess Building and suggested we investigate what was happening there. We turned and approached the Burgess Building just in time to see someone leap from the twelfth story ledge to his doom. The crowd had hidden anything more that was to be seen. Gayle and I simultaneously turned toward one another, each of us expressing the same unspeakable horror. Somehow, I don't remember anything more about that evening.

After a few weeks, the initial impact of the experience left me. It was replaced by the loss of Gayle, who moved on for graduate work in another city. I took summer classes that year, following the same route, always peering upwards to the top floor of that horrid building. One day during late July, I neglected to peer upward, but looked downward. I stopped because I had seen something. It was a crack in the sidewalk over a faded stain, which must have been awfully close to where the body of the suicide victim had landed. I'd never noticed this before, but then I seldom looked down when passing that mysterious edifice.

For quite a while, I ceased to gaze to the top of the building. I chose to avoid stepping on the spot, as if it represented death itself. During my last semester, I decided to bypass that street altogether. I went two blocks out of my way just to avoid the stupid building. I returned to my original route during final exams, why, I don't know. Maybe because it was the last week that I would make that journey, which I had grown to despise. Perhaps I had overcome my fear of death. Or possibly I had finally recovered from losing my precious Gayle.

I remember the graduating ceremony. It was long and boring. I recall the senior prom. Gayle was long gone then, but Kaye was there to take her place.

❀❀❀❀❀❀❀❀❀❀❀❀❀❀❀❀❀❀❀❀❀❀❀❀❀❀❀❀❀❀❀❀❀❀

## FORGOTTEN PEOPLE

### (2001)

I was born and raised in Brooklyn, New York. My family lived in a modest home where my parents provided a comfortable living. They married late in life, having me when they were pushing forty. They worked extremely hard, but they never were too tired to be there for me. They scrimped and saved so that I could get a first-rate education. I attended New York University and then Harvard Law School.

My parents dedicated their entire lives to ensuring a prosperous future for me. I only wish they could have been there to share that future. Unfortunately, both were heavy smokers. Lung cancer claimed my mother when she was only sixty-two years old. My father suffered from emphysema for several years before succumbing to the disease a few years later at the age of sixty-seven. He lived just long enough to see me pass the bar.

During my first year as a practicing attorney, I managed to settle a few substantial personal injury lawsuits. That, along with the savings and insurance money I inherited, left me in excellent financial shape. Therefore, a year ago I began to volunteer my services as a public defender. After all my parents had given me, I felt it was time to give something back. I represented those less fortunate than I, such as addicts, derelicts, mental misfits, and the homeless. I became an advocate for the lowly, and the majority of my cases were pro bono.

As you can imagine, I interacted with numerous interesting and unusual characters. From them, I came to understand the street like I'd never known it before. I became quite a celebrity on the streets of New York City, especially in the borough of Queens. That's where I first saw Kristin, a voluptuous brunette who physically resembled my ex-wife, Marsha. I failed to mention that I was married to a law student for about nine months before we realized we didn't have enough time or love for each other.

While Kristin looked a great deal like Marsha, their personalities were as different as night and day. Marsha was serious, studious, and introverted. Kristin was constantly joking, very audacious, and enormously outgoing. Marsha liked being pampered; she was extravagant, meticulous, touchy, and picky. Kristin was forever catering to others; she would give them anything she had but was content to survive with the bare minimum.

When I was formally introduced to Kristin, she was sharing a dilapidated apartment with eight to ten transients. It was sort of a commune where everybody pitched in to maintain the place. People were frequently entering and leaving so it was difficult to ascertain exactly who lived there. Kristin originally moved in as a single tenant, being the mistress of a wealthy old gentleman, who withdrew his support when she started allowing acquaintances to spend the night.

I know very little about her past, other than the fact that she ran away from an abusive home when she was fifteen. As a teen, she maintained doing odd jobs, sometimes dealing drugs or turning tricks. Of late, she had been supporting herself panhandling, giving blood, and as a cleaning woman. Despite the mileage and the baggage, she was considerate, compassionate, and kind. Behind the dirt, grime, and smell she also was quite adorable.

I came into her life after she got arrested for possession and trafficking of narcotics. A drug pusher had attempted to trade two grams of cocaine for sex. The alleged transaction was observed by an undercover agent, who had been performing surveillance on a nearby crack house. The dealer was able to afford a fancy counselor. He claimed that she was the one trying to trade the drugs to him for money she owed him. It was a ridiculous story, but it easily would have flown by a judge if Kristin didn't have adequate representation. I intervened in her case to ensure she wouldn't get railroaded by an illicit druggist and his shyster lawyer.

In the weeks prior to her arraignment I got to know Kristin on an intimate level. In fact, we were practically inseparable. I invited her into my home, cleaned her up, and bought her some new clothes. She looked like a real lady. I convinced her to stay with me, but after several days, she became uncomfortable in the big lavish townhouse. She convinced me to stay with her awhile to "balance things out." I lasted only one night. I expect her discomfort with my accommodations must have been similar to my discomfort with hers.

On the morning of her court appearance I arrived at the apartment to take Kristin out for breakfast. I knocked on the door, which was answered by one of her girlfriends. This young woman looked like a flower child from the sixties. Apparently, her mother was one of the original Haight-Ashbury hippies; I guess the daughter wanted to carry on the family tradition. She pointed towards the kitchen where I found Kristin sitting at a table with three bearded young men. The room was clouded with a thick blanket of marijuana smoke; I could barely focus. I scolded Kristin for getting blitzed on the day of her trial and she simply laughed. I dragged her down the stairs, insisting that she have some coffee and sharpen up.

I drove her to a café downtown but she refused to get out of the car, so I bought some sweet rolls and coffee and brought them to the car. We sat, chatted, and drank coffee for a couple of hours. Suddenly, a gang member approached with a crowbar, threatening to bash in the windshield of my Porsche if I didn't give him fifty bucks. Since the car was running (I had the heater on low), I slammed it into reverse. After backing up twenty or thirty feet, I shifted into first gear and proceeded to chase the hoodlum with my car. He back-peddled through the parking lot until he stumbled into a motorcycle, which tipped over, knocking over the motorcycle beside it. At that point, four bikers sitting outside of the café promptly rose to their feet. Kristin opened her window and waved at one of them crying, "Hi Wolf," who waved back.

I sped away, feeling guilty that the poor lad was about to be beaten to a pulp. Kristin assured me that her friends would teach him a lesson but they would not kill him, which did little to boost my spirit. I was maneuvering through traffic until I was forced to stop at a red light. Kristin quickly opened the passenger door and hopped out, announcing, "I'll walk from here and meet you at the courthouse." I waited an hour, but still she didn't show. I convinced the judge to put us last on the docket so I could search for her.

I checked everyplace I could think of but she was nowhere to be found. I was combing the subways where I noticed a congregation gathered around a team of emergency medical personnel. I asked some people standing in the circle what had happened. One guy exclaimed, "Some lady just walked straight into the train." His female companion added, "She didn't appear to see the train, or hear it either." Another man, dressed in a three-piece suit, informed, "I think she might have been in a catatonic state." Another said it was an obvious suicide.

Immediately I thought of Kristin. I wormed my way through the mob to discover a gurney holding a corpse enclosed in a body bag. My heart sunk to my feet. About that time, a street rat named "Chipmunk" tugged on my arm. What a character this guy was. He had buckteeth and puffy little cheeks, which is clearly how he acquired his street identity. He was a creative sort with tall tales of adventure and intrigue. He once claimed to have attended Harvard. He was articulate and educated, and I was inclined to believe him if it wasn't for his fake Boston accent. He forced an imitation of the late president JFK every time he spoke. It was almost laughable. I asked Chipmunk about the tragedy, but he had no answers, neither had he seen hide nor hair of Kristin.

I continued my search for Kristin, hoping against hope that it wasn't her in the body bag. She wasn't at any of her usual hangouts and nobody at her apartment had seen her since morning. I ambled home after that. Court was already over and I knew it was a hopeless case. I didn't sleep a wink that night. All I could think of was Kristin. I prayed that she was alive and well. I was sitting on the front porch in the cold fog when the morning paper arrived. I flipped through several pages until I found a summary of the subway incident. The reporter indicated that the victim was much older than Kristin. The article further pointed out that the police had yet to distinguish if the tragedy was a suicide or an accident. I was relieved that it wasn't Kristin, but I was still depressed. Some poor lady had taken her life, or it had been taken from her. Either way, she was yet another nameless person who would die, and nobody would care or remember.

A month has passed since these events transpired. I am still tremendously upset. I am troubled, not only by the tragic death but also by the disappearance of Kristin. My guess is she decided it was time to move along. She's probably living in another town, with new friends and roommates. As little as we had in common, I thought we got along famously. They say opposites attract and I suppose that's true, because I believe I was falling in love with her. I know I'll never see her again and that bothers me most, for I'll always wonder what became of her.

I don't know what creates a street urchin and I don't know how to prevent someone from becoming one. All I know is it makes me sad to see them. I imagine them never experiencing the luxury of a wholesome and nourishing environment like the one in which I was reared. However, from my experience, most of them appear perfectly happy with who, what, and where they are.

In the case of Kristin, she was the happiest person I've ever known. It's a misconception that the forgotten people are underprivileged and unloved. Some are, some aren't, just as in all strata of society.

Although it's true that I get considerable satisfaction helping the needy, and the majority of them show a sincere appreciation for what I do, I doubt if I have any long-term impact on the direction or quality of their lives. Perhaps my uneasiness is due to the fact that I cannot influence them to change for the better, or to conform to my personal image of what they could be. Yet I am compelled to serve them, motivated by the altruistic rewards I suspect, which far exceed any monetary compensation. All I can do is sow the seeds of hope, which is the greatest gift that I've received from the experience and my friendship with Kristin.

## MILESTONES

(1976)

Heat in the traffic:
Stalemated by lawmakers
And growing backwards.
No experience; learning
From failing attempts to live.

Stopped by the roadside;
Left my car for Spring woodlands.
Forgot the city
In a place that won't retard
Forward movement, but provides.

Never yielding
To society, but there;
Without changing pace.
Keeping country in my heart;
No traffic lights in my mind.

# HOW I MET MAGGIE

## (1989)

I was driving to a major metropolitan airport to catch a jet plane. I was in a bit of a hurry because I was running a little behind. I was only about five miles from the Interstate, where I would have been able to make up some valuable time. I approached three guys cruising on their Harley Davidson motorcycles. They were riding three abreast, blocking the entire road. I honked several times and they merely gave me the finger and slowed down. I would try to pass and they would block me off.

We came upon a curve in the road and they opened up just enough for me to shoot through. Luckily, there were no oncoming cars, so I broke free. I guess that made them mad, because one of them sped up next to me, pulled a gun and shot out my front tire. That was a stupid thing to do, since it caused me to veer left. I bumped his rear tire and we both careened into the forest. I crashed into a tree, practically totaling my rental vehicle.

I was dazed momentarily, blood dripping down my forehead. Before I knew it, I was surrounded; the gunman was boiling mad, holding a pistol at my face. "Get out!" He shouted, "And don't try nothing funny." One of the other dudes said to leave me there but the gunman demanded, "Just run into town, tell the old lady you need to borrow my truck, and come back and help me load up the bike." I looked at his chopper. The rear wheel was badly bent. "You're gonna pay for that," he uttered. "It was your own fault you maniac," was my irritated comeback.

About twenty minutes later, the two other guys returned, one of them driving a fancy red, extended cab, long bed pickup truck. The four of us loaded the bike onto the bed of the truck. (I was forced against my will to help). The other two guys piled onto the other bike, while the crazy one motioned for me to get into the truck and drive, holding a 9mm on me the whole time.

This dude was a fat, redneck, goat-roper type who apparently played the role of tough biker on the weekends. He was about six-foot four and probably weighed two-fifty. Still, I knew I could take him if I had an opening, but I wasn't about to challenge him while he aimed that cannon at my head. He outweighed me by some sixty-five pounds and had four inches on me in stature, but I could've put him away with two punches.

He drove us to a quaint little cottage in the woods, dragged me inside, and tied my hands and feet to a chair. The woman who lived there vehemently objected, imploring "Why don't you take him to your own house?" "You know how my wife is," he answered. She responded, "And what am I, chopped liver?" She continued, "I don't want to be an accessory to one of your idiotic schemes, so turn this man loose." I added, "The lady is right. Do you want to go to jail for a first-degree felony?" "Shut up," he said as he gagged me with one of her scarves.

He began rummaging through my suitcase and then inspected my wallet. He found the two-hundred some-odd dollars I was carrying but found nothing else of value to him. "Who the hell is this guy? He doesn't even have any ID on him," he declared. The lady replied, "I've got a bad feeling about this, Donald. He may be someone important." "Come on, Maggie, don't be saying my name in front of him," was all he said.

Old Donald was about as big and dumb as they come. Little did he know that Miss Maggie was right. I was important enough, because I'd established connections with various federal, state, and local governments. You see, I work as an independent contractor performing special undercover, secret, and discreet tasks for a fee. I had just finished a six-month project involving the infiltration of a Ku Klux Klan faction in southern Alabama. I successfully gathered the necessary evidence to indict two of their leaders for murdering a black congressional candidate. I was looking forward to a vacation. I was on my way to my sister's house when this fiasco occurred.

I've got a great job. It pays well, and it's extremely challenging, stimulating and adventurous. But it does take a lot out of me. I guess I get my jollies doing dangerous stuff. It's how I vent my own aggression, perhaps. I suppose it's because I'm still bitter over my pa. He was a traveling salesman. My mom found out he had another wife and daughter in a neighboring state. When the authorities got involved, they discovered my father was engaged to yet another woman. They sent him up the river for twenty years on bigamy, fraud, embezzlement, and a host of other charges.

My mom became quite a recluse after that. I began corresponding with my half-sister. Mom really resented that and we drifted further apart. As soon as I graduated from high school I ran away from home and joined the Navy. In six years, I had become a Naval Officer with a degree in Finance. I was a Navy SEAL for four more years, where I learned quite a lot about covert operations. After resigning my commission, I started working on my Master Degree, supporting myself as a part-time bounty hunter for bail jumpers.

I was looking for more excitement when I became acquainted with a gentleman who worked for the U.S. Secret Service. He was probing for some help protecting the President of the United States who was in Tennessee campaigning for reelection. That's how I got into my current line of work. I quit college and started working for the Treasury Department. After several years I began freelancing so I could finish my Masters in Business. I've been in some tight situations before, but never have I been tied up, staring down the barrel of a gun, in the hand of a dimwit.

I knew I could escape from the chair I was tied to, even though it was reasonably solid. All I needed was an opportunity and some leverage. While Donald contemplated how he was going to get more money out of me, I began loosening the legs of the chair using isometrics. Little by little, I worked on the joints and the ropes. Finally, I got my chance.

Donald had decided to do something but I don't know what it was. All I knew is I wasn't about to wait and find out. As he reached around to untie the gag in my mouth, I jerked my feet apart separating the front legs from the chair. Then I landed a solid kick right into his groin. He dropped to his knees and I smacked him solidly on the head with the back of the chair. Then I jumped up and backwards, crashing the chair against the floor. It was painful, but sufficient to cause the chair to break apart, freeing me. I grabbed another chair and plunged out the window, using the chair to clear a pathway through the glass panes.

A disoriented Don fired a few shots through the window, but they didn't come close. I sneaked around to the side of the house. Donald was staring out the window looking for me. I tossed a few rocks deep into the woods so he'd figure I'd vanished into the trees. I overheard him saying, "I've got him now." Then he made a phone call to a friend of his. This friend was persuaded to bring his hound dogs to track me down. I had maybe ten or twenty minutes to plot my strategy.

I made a path through the forest to a stream that I remember crossing while driving Donald's truck. I urinated at a few places upstream. Then I doubled back the way I came, running as fast as I could. I arrived at the house undetected. I grabbed the eaves of the back porch and performed a pullover onto the roof of the house. I crept up to the apex of the roof and felt a brisk breeze fanning my hair. About that time, another pickup rolled in carrying two bloodhounds in the bed. They tromped around to the back yard where Donald used my wallet to school the dogs on my scent. Don handed his pistol to Maggie stating, "If he comes back here you shoot him." Then Don's friend handed him a shotgun and they scampered off into the woods with Maggie shaking her head in disgust.

I jumped off the roof and sneaked into the house through the front door. When Maggie entered the back door, I grabbed the gun, wrapped her in my arm, and cupped my hand over her mouth. I explained to her that I meant her no harm as she peered at me with frightened eyes. I removed my hand slowly, hoping she would not scream, and she didn't. I figured the dogs would lead Donald and his pal to the stream and they would continue along the banks, looking for the place where I entered or exited. I judged it to be an hour before dark. It was likely they would give up the search by then.

I told Maggie I needed to bathe and change clothes, since I was all grubby and bloody. I explained that she would have to come with me, so she wouldn't grab the gun or try to escape. I wasn't yet sure if I could trust her, but she was pleased to oblige. We both disrobed and she turned on the water in the shower as I locked the bathroom door. I left the gun in the sink and we both entered the shower stall. I soaped myself down, gazing at Maggie's gorgeous body. I mentioned, "I hope you don't take this the wrong way, but I think you are a very beautiful woman, Maggie." She replied, "I think you are a very handsome man, mister whoever you are. You must really work out a lot." I told her my first name. She queried, "Well, Kelly, what do we do now?"

A brief moment of silence elapsed, and suddenly we fell into each other's arms. We embraced and kissed for quite a while. I gradually became sexually aroused. We toweled each other off and made a beeline for her bedroom. After making love, I told her that she was the best I'd ever had. The fact was, I hadn't had any for who knows how long, and I never remember it being better. She informed me that I was the best she'd ever had, though I was only her third, adding that she was very turned on by my muscular body.

I asked her, "What could you possibly see in Donald?" "Isn't he married with children?" She sighed, "Yes, he is. I don't care about him, and he's a lousy lover. Luckily for me, he can't ever get it up anymore, he's so drunk all the time. I put up with him because he helped me after my husband died."

Apparently, her husband was drafted into the Army, went to Vietnam and died there, leaving her eight months pregnant. Donald helped her get back on her feet with a good job; of course, he expected sex in return. Eventually she saved enough for a down payment on her little cottage. When her daughter started going to grade school, Donald became scarce. But time had sped along; her only child had recently eloped and Maggie was alone again. Donald started becoming a regular, as if she still owed him something.

"Why don't you remarry?" I inquired, "You can easily get another man, much better than that low-life. He's no good for you. Anyway, he'll never leave his wife and kids." "I guess the perfect man just hasn't happened by," she explained.

I continued, "I bet he's going to blame you when he discovers I was here. He'll especially be furious when he returns to find his truck gone, along with his motorcycle." "I don't care," she said, "In fact I'm glad. But I wish you didn't have to go. Promise me you'll come back and visit me again someday," Maggie whined. "I promise, baby," I whispered, as I kissed her goodbye. What she didn't realize is that I was planning on returning as soon as possible.

I drove to Atlanta that night. The next morning, I had a new wheel put on Donald's Harley. I informed the garage owner that Don would pay double for the repair bill in order to get his truck back. Then I returned to that lazy town buzzing on Don's ride, only this time I was accompanied by two federal marshals. Donald was arrested immediately and taken to the county lockup. We quickly managed to hunt down his buddies and convince them to testify against Donald so they could avoid criminal prosecution.

A preliminary hearing was scheduled in which Donald would be formally charged with kidnapping, robbery, extortion, assault with a deadly weapon, reckless driving, and a few misdemeanors. I convinced the judge and Donald's lawyer to agree to a meeting of the minds. I told them I would appeal to the Feds to drop all charges if Donald would plead guilty to assault and battery. (I was sure the government would comply because they didn't want to blow my cover any more than I did).

Donald had to agree to give me the Harley and $1000, and pay Maggie another $5000 for pain, suffering, and damages. Donald's insurance would have to replace the rental vehicle that I was driving, which no doubt would result in his insurance being cancelled. Another stipulation was that he had to join Alcoholics Anonymous. Furthermore, he would spend six years on probation, two of those years with a nine o'clock curfew, meaning he would not be allowed out of his home after dark. Periodic urinalysis tests would ensure that he remained sober.

Donald remarked, "I guess I can handle everything except having to part with my Harley, it's my pride and joy." That was the best part of the deal. A 1948 Pan Head in prime condition was a real collector's item; it was the first year they made that model. I always wanted a vintage hog, and this one was built the same year I was born. The judge informed Donald, "I suppose you'd rather spend the next ten years in a federal penitentiary." Donald looked at his lawyer who nodded in affirmation. Donald whimpered, "Oh, all right."

I shook the judge's hand, the lawyer's hand, and then I offered my hand to Donald. He grabbed it, trying to squeeze hard, surprised to discover that I was stronger. "Who the hell are you?" he asked. "Someone you don't want to mess with," was my reply. I left him with a puzzled look on his face and an aching hand.

Maggie was pleased as punch to see me. She told me I had been correct about everything. Donald got mad and tried to assault her, until she ran and grabbed his semi-automatic that I left in the bathroom sink. She said she chased him out of her house, firing several shots at his feet, telling him to go back to his wife who he didn't deserve. Apparently, he pranced and danced off her property like a scared jackrabbit. I busted out laughing. I sure would like to have witnessed that.

I explained to Maggie about Donald's arrest, the plea bargain, his sentence, and everything. She was bubbling with joy, so glad that Donald was out of her life for good. He would have to start being a responsible father and husband for once in his life. I invited her to go along with me to visit my sister. I said she could ride with me on the back of my new Harley. She was thrilled.

"You must be some kind of angel!" she exclaimed. I countered, "I don't know about that, but I will submit that the Lord definitely works in mysterious ways." She followed up by inquiring, "Will you settle for being my knight in shining armor?" I responded using a British accent, "Yes, my lady, and would you care to take a seat on my iron steed?" She climbed aboard, and I fired up the bike. She firmly grasped my waist and we rode off into the sunset.

<hr>

## REFLECTIONS AT DAWN

### (1976)

Who would be the ones to outlast the others but you and I?

Their destiny makes me wonder how we managed to survive.

But I do not wish to remember this den of foolishness;

Fortunate are we, for our night is not wasted like the rest.

So, the only thing that we can retain from this time is now.

Daylight is coming, and what should we make of this early hour?

I think it appropriate that we spend the dawn together.

Since this place has lost its meaning, let us find somewhere better.

# PLAYING FOR KEEPS

## (1987)

He was famous, but nobody would ever recognize him. Because when he was out in the world, he was a different person than when he was performing: different in appearance, personality, and demeanor. He had learned years before that privacy was a valuable commodity, and the only way to maintain it was to travel incognito.

He wore his dark blonde hair tied back in a ponytail and sported four days growth of black and gray whiskers on his face. He wore faded blue jeans and a matching jacket that covered a T-Shirt with the logo of a hard-rock band called *The Bumz*. It's not exactly ironic that he resembled one of the "bums" that adorned his shirt. But he portrayed the country hic and a man of humble roots, who rambled from town to town. A closer look would reveal that he wasn't exactly poor, with his designer granny glasses, his 18-karat gold chain with crucifix, and his black leather orthopedic sneakers. You could say he resembled a well-dressed hobo.

He was perusing the artwork when she approached him: a slender Asian lady with ebony, shoulder-length hair. He couldn't help ogling her. She was the most exquisite creature he'd ever laid eyes upon, perfectly proportioned for his taste, with smooth ivory skin, crimson lips, and chocolate eyes. He stopped his thoughts quickly before succumbing to lust.

"Forgive me for staring," he exclaimed, "but I find you to be more captivating than the paintings!" "The gallery will be closing in fifteen minutes, sir," she uttered. He examined her nametag, announcing, "Miss Ching, allow me to introduce myself, my name is Stanley Brooks." He offered his hand and she grasped the end of his fingers and quickly let go. "Nice to meet you," she mumbled.

"And what do you think of Dali?" he asked, relating, "Surrealism is my favorite genre of art. I used to paint a little myself, you know." "Pardon me, sir," she pleaded, "But I must notify the other patrons that we are closing." He observed her slink away before refocusing his attention on the exhibit. After a short while, he reached the last partition in the museum, having completed the full circle of display rooms. There she stood in the foyer, escorting people to the door. Undaunted by her coldness he inquired, "Would you be my guest for dinner tonight?"

She hesitated, as if she had to think twice about her answer. She was attracted to Stanley but very leery of his forwardness. "I'm sorry," was all she said. "I'm not the rough and dusky guy I appear to be," he informed. "Back where I come from this is considered formal attire," he chuckled. "If you'd prefer, maybe I can meet you somewhere, or have a taxi pick you up and drop you off," he affirmed. "I'm afraid not, Mr. Brooks," was her final word. "Well, it was a pleasure making your acquaintance," he proclaimed with a salute, a wide smile on his face. "Have a nice evening and have a nice life," he blared as he skipped down the stairs to the sidewalk.

She watched him saunter away, wondering if and when she would ever find Mr. Right. As she leaned against the jamb a voice came from behind, "Good night, Miss Ching, I'll see you next week." "Oh goodnight, Mr. Daniels," she replied, stepping down to the walkway. Daniels bounded over the stairs while security guards locked the door behind him. He climbed aboard a van that was idling in front of the museum and it sped away. Miss Ching rounded the corner and hastened across the avenue to a small parking lot. While she loved her job, she hated the location. She especially loathed the solo trek, night after night, just as it was getting dark. Oftentimes she would ask the security guard to escort her but she didn't want to impose upon him every night.

Meanwhile, Stan was cattycorner from the museum where he stood inside a phone booth, impatiently waiting for the dispatcher of a taxicab company who had placed him on hold. He noticed Miss Ching as she hurried along the asphalt. He became troubled when four shady characters rapidly began to close in on her just as she reached her car. One of them grabbed the young Asian beauty from behind. She emitted half of a muffled scream before he gagged her mouth, dragging her towards an alley.

Stan immediately dropped the phone and sprinted toward the scene of the crime. He heard some commotion behind a dumpster where he found one man trying to force a kiss upon his prisoner and three others watching and cheering. Stan quickly surveyed the situation. Four against one, each one of them armed, two with knives, one with a cutoff baseball bat, the other with a heavy chain. "We can do this the easy way or the hard way," chided the aggressor. "But if you want it the hard way, I'll have to cut up your pretty face."

"Leave her alone," Stan demanded. All four gang members spun around abruptly, with the leader placing Miss Ching in a headlock and holding a knife to her neck. "You're making a big mistake," said the ringleader, his hand now clutching the lady's throat. "You took the words right out of my mouth," replied Stan, "In fact, you're looking at ten to twenty years in the slammer." "He's got a death wish," snickered one of the rookies. "That's a fact," agreed the leader, "I think we should send him to hell." "You've just upped the ante to life without parole," Stan conveyed. "Let me take him," growled a rookie holding a stiletto. "He's all yours," was the obvious answer.

Stan tried to think back to hand-to-hand combat training during his stint in the infantry, but he drew a blank. After all, it had been almost twenty years. Fortunately for Stan, he was still as quick and agile as ever, a little heavier perhaps but in good shape, and strong. Further, he had a substantially faster mind than his opponents. The young gangster waved his knife back and forth, alternating hands occasionally to make it look as if he was handy with the blade. Stan could tell he was a novice, simply by the way he held the knife and how his body posture lacked balance.

The kid took a few swipes with the knife and Stan backed up, feigning like he was falling. The kid lunged, not realizing that Stan was positioned for that maneuver with his weight supported on his back foot against the dumpster. Stan lurched forward and caught the young man's wrist with his forearm, entwining their arms together. Grabbing the assailant's collarbone, he forced the arm backwards, causing the kid to stoop downward. Stan kneed him solidly in the middle of the chest, once, twice, collapsing his right lung; Stan struck him a third and fourth time cracking one of the guy's ribs. Then, jerking the arm upward, he straightened the kid onto his feet, catching the assailant's blade with his free hand.

Stan backed up to the dumpster, holding the creep's locked wrist with one hand and a knife to his Adam's apple with the other. "How's about a trade?" Stan posed, "The girl for your pal." "Waste him," replied the leader. The other two hoodlums slowly advanced. Stan used the pivot to thrust forward his captive. Then Stan swung the kid around using the twisted arm, correspondingly karate kicking the hood holding the bat in his stomach. The other kid's shoulder came out of its socket when he was rolled across the blacktop causing the guy with the chain to trip over him.

As bat man moved in for a swing, Stan hurled the knife with all his might using a technique he'd learned years before. The knife made one-half rotation traveling speedily through the air and lodging under the attacker's right armpit. The brute wobbled back and forth, appearing nauseous, as if he would vomit. Stan placed a side kick atop the butt of the knife, driving it deep into the guy's flesh, simultaneously wrenching the bat from his hand as he collapsed to the ground. Miss Ching managed to squeak "Look out!" Stan dropped to a kneeling position on the ground with bowed head, the bat raised vertically above him. Chain man had taken a big swing which struck the bat squarely, the chain wrapping firmly around the wood. Stan grabbed the club at both ends and began a tug-of-war with his opponent. Stan allowed him to pull back causing him to lock his leading knee; then Stan jumped into the air and landed a gravity kick right into the hood's shin. The hood let go of the chain and fell to the pavement, holding his knee and screaming, "The son-of-a-bitch broke my <bleep> leg." Next, Stan slammed the bat on knife boy's ankle as he attempted a flimsy kick towards Stan's crotch. When chain man reached for the chain, Stan stomped on his hand, cracking a bone in his forefinger. Meanwhile, a wounded, bleeding batboy had managed to remove the blade from his side. Stan confiscated it, wiped it on the guy's pants, retracted the blade, and placed it in his jacket pocket. Stan held the bat in one hand and the chain in the other. After looking them over, he hurled the bat into the dumpster with his left hand, and grasped both ends of the chain in his right hand.

"You're next, butthead," Stan explained as he stared the leader in the eye, swinging the chain in a circular motion. "Come any closer and I'll cut her," the thug replied, placing his blade closer to her jugular. Stan disputed, "If you hurt as much as a single hair on her head, I'm going to pound you into dust and chop you into pieces. Your own mother won't recognize what's left of you." Stan continued, "But if you let her go right now, I'll let you walk." Stan inched ever closer to his rival, keeping his right foot planted behind him and his left side exposed to the perpetrator.

Suddenly, the man shoved his captive into Stan. She fell across Stan's breast, throwing her arms around his neck, while Stan caught her with his left arm. The bully dashed around Stan's rear. With the quickness of a Ninja, Stan swung the end of chain behind himself, snagging the hood around the heel as he attempted flight. The hoodlum went crashing to the curb, partially breaking his fall with the left hand. His right knee made a loud smack as it struck the pavement. Stan muttered, "Excuse me Miss Ching," while he repositioned her firmly on her feet. Then he proceeded to place a strategic and forceful punt, his right foot landing emphatically on the hood's behind. "Drop the knife," Stan commanded as he spun the chain, encircling his hand. The hoodlum made a final assault by throwing the knife in the direction of Stan's face, which Stan blocked with the chain-wrapped hand. "You said you were going to let me go," groaned the leader. Stan picked up the switchblade refolded it and placed it into his pocket. Then he slung the chain into the dumpster, declaring, "No, I said I'd let you walk; my guess is you can still do that."

Stan and Miss Ching looked over the scene with wonderment. Four strapping young lads lay prostrate on the ground. One had a nasty stab wound; another had a fractured ankle, a broken rib, and a dislocated shoulder; the third had a shattered tibia and a broken finger on his mashed hand; and their leader wailed over a badly sprained wrist, a crushed kneecap, and a bleeding rectum. Stan lectured, waving his forefinger, "I suggest you seek medical attention, especially for that guy with the chest wound. I also recommend that you get a life, maybe an education while you're at it. There's no future on the street, except for an early grave."

The four gangsters collected one another and staggered down the alley in pairs. Stan made a turnabout and slid up to Miss Ching. "Are you all right, little lady'?" Stan queried, as he placed his hands gently on her shoulders. She leapt into his arms, trembling and clutching him tightly. Stan held her head and stroked her hair, whispering, "Shh. You're safe now." After several seconds Stan softly panted, "We've got to get out of here right now."

He guided the genteel lady towards the lot, where they ambled hand-in-hand to her car. The keys were still dangling from the door lock, and her purse was beside the left front tire. Stan picked up her purse and handed it to her; then he opened the car door. "Are you going to be okay?" he asked. She froze there shuddering and speechless. "Would you like me to drive you home?" he asked. She shook her head up and down, peeking up at him with timid eyes. Stan escorted her to the passenger side of the car, opened the door and helped her in. He buckled her seatbelt, closed the door and maneuvered into the driver's seat. Stan turned the ignition key and heard the hum of the engine. He suggested, "After you are safely inside your home, you can call me a cab. Will that be all right with you?" She nodded. He did a U-turn back to the main drag and asked, "Where to?" "Arlington," she murmured. Stan followed, "I'll get us to Arlington and then you can direct me from there, okay?" She stammered, still shaken from the ordeal.

A moment of silence elapsed and Stan spoke, "So do you have a first name, Miss Ching?" A half-smile appeared on her face, "It's Sumiko." "What a pretty name for such a pretty face," noted Stan. "My friends call me Sue," she added. "Well, Sue," continued Stan, "I think you ought to be more careful. That's not exactly what I'd call a classy neighborhood. How come the guards don't walk you to your car?" "

You are the bravest person I have ever met," Sue expounded after another momentary pause. She quickly implored "How can I ever repay you?" Stan responded, "You don't owe me anything, sweetheart. I'm just grateful you were not harmed. I think you should give credit to a higher power. You probably witnessed a miracle. The Almighty must have sent a few angels to help out."

"I'm sorry I was so mean to you at the museum," she whimpered. "Aw forget it," Stan assured, "I understand completely. It's wise to keep your distance from strangers. I suppose I don't exactly seem an upstanding guy, as grubby as I look." "I know you are an honorable man," she argued, "And I don't think you look grubby at all, in fact, you are very handsome." "Well, thanks, little darling, and you are exceptionally gorgeous," Stan replied as he glanced back at her eyes.

Her countenance returned to its original luster when she warmly smiled at Stan. He was taken by the twinkling in her eyes and the radiance of her smile. "Are you sure there's nothing I can do for you?" questioned Sumiko, with a wishful tone in her voice. "Well," replied Stan, "I've got a powerful hunger and the dinner invitation is still open." "I'd love to have dinner with you," she pledged, "But let me treat." "Nothing doing," Stan countered, "I asked you first, so you will be my guest." "If you insist," she giggled. "I understand there's some great seafood restaurants in this city," Stan posed, "I trust you like seafood." "I love seafood," she declared, "And I know an excellent place not far from here." "Point the way," Stan rejoined.

"Wow!" exclaimed Sue, "Do you realize this is the first real date I've been on in over a year?" "Really?" inquired Stan, "Why's that?" Sue explained, "The last couple of guys I dated were constantly trying to push me into bed. They wouldn't keep their paws off of me. All they could think of was sex. I wasn't about to have sex with them. They never hinted that they wanted to get married, although the last guy said he loved me. Yeah, he loved me all right, and who knows how many other women. My best friend, her name is Barbara, she saw him downtown one afternoon with his arm around a prostitute. We were supposed to be going out that night but I stood him up. I haven't been on a date since. I cannot trust men, except for you maybe."

Stanley proclaimed, "I haven't been on a date for over a year myself." "I find that hard to believe," offered Sue. "It's true," Stan continued, "Ever since my wife got plowed by a drunk driver September before last, I haven't really found anyone who interests me; well until now. I've just been trying to keep busy and get over it." "That's terrible," cried Sue, continuing, "Do you have any kids?" Stan answered, "Yeah, one son, he's been staying with my brother and his wife; they have children his age so he goes to their school now. I think it's helped him get over the loss of his mom. I miss him a lot though. I haven't seen him for almost three months but I call him just about every other day. He's a junior in High School and has lots of girlfriends to keep him occupied." "You don't look old enough to have a son in high school," Sue asserted. "Well I appreciate that," replied Stan, "I hope you don't mind being seen with an old fogy like me." Sue interjected, "I'm attracted to what's inside a person, Stanley, and I can see you have a kind heart." "Flattery will get you everywhere," Stan chortled as he made a left turn in accordance with Sue's curving arm.

"Let's talk about you for a while, honey-pie," declared Stan, "I want to know everything about you." "Huh, well that's a switch," Sue concluded, "I've finally met a man who is interested in me and not himself or my body." Stan laughed. Sue continued, "Well, I was born in the town of Hiratsuka on the island of Honshu Japan. My parents cashed in all their savings and sent my older brother and me off to America to study and find good jobs. They decided that we would have better opportunities here in the states than we would back home. That was six years ago. How I miss them. I'm saving up my money to visit them during Christmas vacation; I want to share the true story of Jesus's birth with them. My friend Barbara taught me about the Bible and now I go with her to a Baptist church. Anyway, I attended Georgetown University and finished my bachelors in Art Education, and then I attained my Masters in Art History. My brother is an engineer with a local defense contractor. I guess you could say we're successful because we both have decent occupations. We became United States citizens last year. I didn't really want to at first, but my brother needed his citizenship for the job and I let him talk me into it."

Stanley interrupted, "Well, for being in this country six years, you sure have an excellent command of the language, and you barely even have an accent. Heck, some of my friends don't speak English as good as you." "I have worked hard to be fluent and to speak without an accent," informed Sue, aiming Stan towards an attractive eating establishment. Stan angled the car into a parking space and shifted into park. Sue placed her hand on top of his. A rush of emotion shot through his arm into his heart. Darkness of night already had settled in, but he could see her eyes glowing; like the moon reflecting off a mountain lake, Stan thought. "Shall we?" grinned Stan, breaking the silence. "Let's!" was her reply. Stan exited the door, slipped off his coat and dropped it on the driver's seat. "I still have those switchblades in there," he said, "I don't figure I'll be needing them anytime soon." He sauntered around to the other side of the car and opened the door. He held out his hand and she clasped it firmly as he pulled her to her feet. He dropped the car keys into her purse and secured the door.

Stan offered his arm and she hooked her arm around his, while they slowly began to proceed toward the entrance. Simultaneously, both stopped, faced each other, and embraced. Then Stan, holding Sue's face softly in his palms, made a request, "May I kiss you, Sumiko?" "Yes, you may," she sighed, as their lips met. They caressed one another's lips for several seconds and then their tongues met. They tickled the tips of their tongues for a minute and then nestled into each other's arms, their tongues penetrating deeply into the mouth of the other. This ultimate kiss lasted for over five minutes until they quietly broke for a breather. Gazing into her eyes, Stan declared, "That was the most delightful kiss I have ever experienced." "It was fantastic," she agreed. "I'm not used to having my dessert before the main course," Stan declared as he led her to the door.

At Stan's request, the waiter showed them to a table with a view of the marina. Stan placed a fin in the waiter's hand, then he held the chair for Sue to sit. "What do you recommend," asked

Stan as he studied the menu. "Everything is good," Sue said, "But I always order the Tokyo shrimp." "Sounds great to me," Stan remarked prior to placing an order for two glasses of white zinfandel. The waiter returned with some wine and salad.

"I presume you're not from around here, Stan" Sue deduced. "I'm originally from the deep south," he replied, "But now I live in Colorado." "What brings you to DC?" she inquired. "Oh, well, I'm just ah, working at the show tomorrow night," Stan averred, pointing to his T-Shirt. "This is their last stop on a forty-two-city tour," he added. "No kidding," she chirped, "Wow, I just love *The Bumz*, they're my favorite rock group; I've got two of their CDs." She continued, "Barbara and I were planning on going to the concert, but it sold out. She waited five hours in line, just to be turned away when she was only like five people from the ticket booth."

"Maybe I can get you in," Stan informed, "I'm pretty good friends with the road manager. He may have some extra tickets; would you like me to call him?" "Absolutely," she shouted, loud enough for others in the eatery to glare.

"Be right back," Stan affirmed as he strode towards the pay phones. He returned minutes later informing, "I left a message at the hotel for him to call me." About that time the waiter was serving dinner. Seconds later Stan blurted, "This is scrumptious." "But not as tasty as your kiss," he whispered. "If you're a good boy, I may let you steal another later," she chimed. "Ooh, yes, please," was his reply.

The waiter came to the table with a portable phone relating, "I have a call for Stan, is that you sir?" "Yes it is my good man, thank you very much," Stan replied, handing the waiter a ten spot. "Yo," Stan said into the phone. Sue perked up in her chair as she attended to Stan's conversation. "Yeah, yeah, two if you've got 'em. Okay, great. Hey you're the best. Cool; later." Stan pushed the off button and set the phone down. "You're in, and so is your friend Barbara," he conveyed. Sue cheered, "Really, that's wonderful. I'd better call her." Stan handed her the portable phone and she began dialing. "I'll go wash up; be back in a flash," Stan informed.

Upon Stan's return, Sue was delighted. "Barbara is simply thrilled that we're going to the concert. What's more, she can't believe I'm having dinner with a man. I can't believe it either. This is like a dream." "Well, don't wake up because I'm enjoying it just as much as you," Stan remarked. The waiter offered pastries and pies but the romantic couple had other plans for dessert. Stan dropped a hundred-dollar bill on the table and the happy pair meandered through the jungle of tables and out the door.

"Let's go down to the Potomac and stroll along the river walk," she suggested. "Sound's great," was his reply. They spent an hour by the river, kissing, hugging, and enjoying the company and the serenity. It started getting chilly so Stan suggested they depart. Just then Sue stopped, and with a serious look on her face declared, "I think I'm falling in love with you, Stanley. I have never felt like this before. How can this be happening? You have captured my heart and I'm afraid that you'll be leaving for good." "I feel the same way, Sumiko," Stan replied. He continued, "And I'm not sure I can leave, if it's without you." They clinched again, resulting in another lengthy smooch.

Stan drove Sue to his hotel, which also was in Arlington. The two were silent the entire way. He parked the car outside the lobby and assured, "I'll only be a minute, dear." He returned quickly, climbed into the idling car, and sped towards Sue's apartment not many miles away. Again, they scarcely spoke, unsure as to what to expect next. Stan walked her to the door; she invited him inside. They collapsed on her living room couch, melting into each other's arms, unable to resist touching and caressing their partner from head to toe. Sue grabbed Stan's hand and led him into the bedroom. They rapidly disrobed, for the passion of their love could no longer be suppressed.

After making love, Sue declared, "You are my first lover." "Oh my God," Stan gasped, "If I'd known beforehand, I would not have allowed this to continue," he added. "I wanted you to be the first," she claimed, "Because I need something to remember you by after you're gone." She started to sob. Stanley pulled her closer to him, inquiring, "Who says I'm taking off?" "Won't you be returning to Colorado after the concert?" she whined. "Not necessarily," he replied. "This is the last stop on the tour for a spell. Unless you're with me, I ain't going anywhere." Sitting there looking at each other, Stan broke the silence, "I want you in my life. I know this is kind of short notice but, will you to marry me?"

"Are you serious?" she inquired. "Oh yeah," he replied convincingly, "I am." "I would love to marry you," was her immediate decision. "I'll make you the best wife in the whole wide world. I will give you as many babies you want. I would do anything for you," she divulged. "Are you absolutely sure you want to live with me forever?" Stan queried, continuing, "You really don't know very much about me. I could be a pauper or I could be a prince." "I believe you are a good person, you know God, and you love me," she replied concluding, "That's all I need for now." They made love again, and then fell asleep in each other's arms.

It was well past sunup when Sue roused Stan. Stan dressed, combed his golden locks, and searched for Sue, finding her in the kitchen where an inviting breakfast of bacon, eggs, toast with jam, juice, and coffee awaited him. "All right!" exclaimed Stan, "She can cook too." Sue snorted loudly, sitting down to join him. Stan took an envelope from his back pocket and opened it, laying the contents on the dinner table. "Here are your tickets," he said, "You gals are in the fifth row, left of center." He further instructed, "These are backstage passes. You'll need to wait until the coliseum clears, and then go to the far-right side of the stage. There's a small staircase in the back leading up to a door. Knock on the door until someone answers and present these passes. They will direct you from there. Make sure nobody watches you or follows you." "Wow, you mean we're going to meet the band?" Sue crooned. "Yeah, uh, the band's manager said it was okay with him," Stan slurred.

After the late but tasty breakfast, Stan informed Sue that he had to return to the hotel and start getting everything together. She dropped him off at the lobby, kissed him goodbye and said, "See you tonight, my love." "You know it, gorgeous," he responded and then trotted away.

Sue was in stitches waiting for the evening to come. She spent all afternoon primping and pruning, to make sure she looked her best. Barbara came to Sue's apartment at six o'clock, bringing some hamburgers for them to eat. Sue informed her, "You're not going to believe this, but Stan spent the night with me." Barbara was astounded, yelling, "No kidding, really?" "He wants to marry me," Sue added, "And I told him yes." "This is awfully sudden," complained Barbara. Sue described everything that happened from the moment they met. Barbara pleaded, "You barely even know this guy." "He's probably some backstage hand that picks up girls all the time," Barbara reasoned. Sue reacted, "You don't understand, Barbara. He's not like anyone I've ever met. He loves me deeply in his heart. He's my knight in shining armor. I just can't explain it." "I hope you know what you're doing," was all Barbara could say.

They made it to the auditorium with time to spare. Soon a group called *The Weeds* came on stage; they were followed by *Nobody's Business*. While the warm-up bands were sensational, Sue and Barbara feverously awaited the featured act. The crowd came unglued when *The Bumz* sashayed out. The screams from the crowd were deafening. Soon the shrieks from bedazzled fans became obscured by the thundering of amplifiers and the pounding of drums.

After eight musical presentations there was a break in the action. Sue began to marvel aloud, "No it couldn't be," she cried. "What did you say?" asked Barbara. "Oh nothing," replied Sue, standing there looking confused. She had been analyzing his every move while he played lead guitar and sang backing vocals. He resembled Stan somewhat in his voice and stature, but the hair was different: longer, straighter, and platinum-colored. Plus, he wasn't wearing glasses, his complexion was fairer, his face looked smooth as silk, and he appeared much younger, but still…

Right then another vocalist who played bass guitar announced, "Well folks, we have some good news and some bad news." The audience cheered. "The good news is our own Bobby

Chance will not be breaking young ladies' hearts anymore. The bad news is this: the world's most eligible bachelor is tying the knot." The crowd seemed to explode as they stomped, applauded, and screeched. After the roar quieted down, Bobby Chance chimed in, pointing a guitar pick in the general vicinity of the front rows saying, "This song is for you, Susie Q."

Then she knew. It was Stan all right. She was engaged to one of the most popular artists in the rock music scene. How clever he had been hiding his identity. Sumiko was overwhelmed, excited, bewildered, elated. Everyone was looking around, wondering who had captured the heart of the great Bobby Chance. Sue didn't know what to think, but she knew it was true, it was real, and she wasn't dreaming. Besides, Stan had revealed their engagement to the whole world, and he had dedicated this song to her.

Barbara peered at Sue with an inquisitive stare. Sue leaned over and spoke clearly into Barbara's ear, "That's him!" Barbara peered again with an even more flabbergasted look on her face. "It's you!" Barbara sighed. She watched Sumiko's infatuated eyes as they locked intently upon her fiancé. Now there was a woman in love, thought Barbara who was overjoyed for her friend. Sue's heart was pounding, her excitement emanating in all directions. Each word caressed her ears as Stan sang the lyrics to his recent hit single, entitled *1001*. The refrain lifted her spirit as he serenaded her, "I've met a thousand girls before, and finally love one."

---

## HOURGLASS

(1974)

like grains of sand
in an hourglass
my past
gently
falls
into the
future of
my life as the
grains slowly build
a mountain of dreams.

# THE BEST OF COMPANY
## (1996)

Dad was furious when I joined the Marines. What did he expect? He taught me how to fish, hunt, stalk, and shoot. I guess he always wanted a son but got me instead, a real tomboy. When he wasn't abroad, we did everything together. Mom couldn't take the pressure of wondering if Dad was going to return, but he always did. She drank herself into oblivion, dying of heart failure two weeks after my graduation from basic training. Who would figure that Dad would die a year later from a stupid little germ? I mean, he spends most of his adult life engaged in dangerous covert operations about the globe, and then he up and dies from bacterial meningitis contracted from a Turkish bath house.

After getting my degree in Forensic Science and reaching the rank of Lieutenant in the military police, I joined the Company just like my old man. My second life started then. I had no parents, I was a single working woman, and being a cop was getting monotonous; it was time for a change. The only thing I knew was law enforcement, but I had greater expectations. That's why I signed up; plus, they promoted me. The challenge of facing death was a real turn-on, and I felt like I was serving my country in a significant way. There were no actual wars to fight, just our own secret battles.

I learned a lot in those five short years, and I fell in love. I'd never loved a man before, not truly. Of course, there was my high school sweetheart Lucius. I thought I loved him at times, but never as much as he loved me. I gave him my virginity but never my heart. He flipped his lid, probably from all the drugs he consumed. He's comfortable now in his own little perplexing world.

I met Jason on a makeshift drop zone not far from the Tigris River. His team had secured the area awaiting our arrival from the air. I'd heard his name before; he had quite a reputation with the Company. I never dreamed he'd be good-looking, especially since he wasn't much younger than my old man.

We maneuvered all the way to Baghdad, where we managed to free the hostages, assassinate the Prime Minister and members of his cabinet, and make it back to Wiesbaden in time for church. We didn't lose any of our meager force of fourteen; of course, we owe a lot to the Kurdish insurgents that helped us fend off aggressors. The former president of Iraq was reinstated, the Kurds got their homeland, the Mid-East economy soon stabilized, and the price of gasoline dropped fifteen cents in the states. I've never seen an operation go that smoothly. Jason and General Pinelli planned the whole escapade. What a couple of military geniuses! How privileged I have been. I learned from the best of the best: Dad, Jason, and the General.

Jason probably would have made general officer, if he hadn't been blackballed for killing one of his own men during a search and destroy mission in Cambodia. It's so unfair; the fool would have given away their position. The guy freaked during an ambush set up near a Khmer Rouge encampment. Only one American soldier was lost on that mission, from a knife wound inflicted by Jason, himself. The General backed Jason all the way, but those idiots at the Pentagon always think they know everything. Jason was allowed to stay with the Company but was told he would never reach the rank of Colonel. That's why everyone referred to Jason as "The Major." He was the major of all Majors. But Tong and I changed his nickname to "The Z Monster."

It was after Project Babylon. We were getting loaded in downtown Frankfurt. After downing about ten pitchers of dark German beer, Tong made a joke about how Jason puts his enemies dead asleep, using his unique style. You see, Jason was given an authentic blowgun complete with two darts as a gift by Amazonian Indians. He was helping the government of Brazil drive away a criminal operation specializing in poaching, drug running, and smuggling. The natives were appreciative because the syndicate also trafficked indigenous slaves and artifacts. Jason got along better with the Indians than local law enforcement. They taught Jason how to use the blowgun, but he improved upon the design, as usual. The Company learned how to synthesize venom found on rare blue tree frogs. Jason usually brought along an ample supply of poison darts; he made short order of any outposts or sentries. He would fire one tiny projectile into the victim using a gas-operated four-shooter equipped with a silencer. The target would swat at himself as if stung by a wasp or something. The victim would keel over within seconds, never knowing what hit him, and never to awaken.

Jason and I hit it off immediately. He had known my father because the two conducted quite a few missions together. He witnessed Dad's cremation; all I got were the ashes. We drank the entire crowd under the table that night. Jason was impressed. He'd never seen a woman put away beer like I did. I'll never let on that I puked my guts out three times just so I could keep up with the guys. We joked, laughed, and sang songs with the Germans until daylight. The grand finale was Jason's strip tease down to his skivvies while dancing on a table. What a riot! Jason and I started partying together on a regular basis after that and we became the best of friends.

I suppose my crush on him was immediate, but I was too proud to reveal it. Besides, I was overly cautious because of that black-white thing, what with him being Caucasian and all. It's so silly those idiotic racial stereotypes imposed by society. He never noticed what color I was; He's color blind with regards to skin. He influenced me to think the same way. His only prejudice has been against those who would use race, creed, or religion as a dodge, or a con, or for a handout. He treats people with respect who respect others, regardless of ethnicity, gender, or social status. I have considerable admiration for him; he would make a great role model for every American. I thank God for Jason every day.

It was sad when we parted ways, but I couldn't show him how devastated I was. I'd never told him I loved him, and he never assumed it. And why should he? He knew how much I loved my job. I missed Jason so much after he resigned. He often spoke of quitting but I never took him seriously. He wanted to spend more time with his boy, who was now a man. Jason's ex abandoned him and the boy for some jock, so Adam was raised by Jason and his mom back in Texas. Jason hadn't seen either of them in over two years and wasn't about to let that continue indefinitely.

I volunteered for every mission, trying to get Jason out of my mind. It didn't work. I'd thought I could live without him; man, was I mistaken. I wanted to be near him. Oh, I knew he'd write, and I figured he'd probably visit the headquarters in Langley from time to time, but that would never have been enough. My heart burned for him all those years but I never let on. Without him I was miserable, and I allowed that to affect my performance, to the extent I blamed myself for being captured by the Chinese.

It's a miracle I'm even alive, and I wouldn't be if not for Jason. He saved my life in the greatest escape of all time. Jason masterminded the whole affair. I didn't think I'd ever see him again. I just knew I was about to die. I prayed to God to take me swiftly so I wouldn't have to bear the pain of losing Jason forever. It was far more excruciating than the bullet wounds in my gut. I knew I was going to be tortured, and once they were through with me, assassinated; but that didn't bother me as much as the emptiness inside. I wasn't worried about ratting on the Company; I was worried that Jason would never know what happened to me.

I would replay his departure over and again in my mind. The night before he left there was a huge going away party. Everyone was spruced-up in their uniforms or other formal attire. Jason looked so dashing in his old Army class A's. He had all those ribbons and medals, as many as the General. Jason said I looked swell in dress blues, even though I didn't have many medals. We exchanged Airborne wings and had a toast to everlasting friendship. As usual, we were the last two to leave the ballroom. We continued the party in the day room at the barracks.

I showed him the homemade birthday card Lucius had sent to me from the asylum. Jason was surprised that a schizophrenic could be so creative and articulate. But the poem Lucius wrote to say hello had little impact compared to the words Jason wrote to say goodbye. Just before leaving, Jason handed me an envelope and said, "Remember when we were in Germany and we had our picture taken at the bar? Well, I had it reproduced and enlarged, one for you and one for me." Then he kissed me hard on the lips for the first time ever and said, "Take care." I opened the envelope; there was some writing on the back of the photograph. I read the inscription as Jason hurried down the stairs to catch a helicopter that was waiting on the tarmac.

He wrote, "This is the way I'll always remember you, that night in Frankfurt. We sure have had some fantastic times. I am honored and proud to have you in my outfit, and it has been a pleasure to serve with you. You have come a long way. I wish you the best of luck in the future, I know you will do fine. But be careful, and don't stay too long if you want to beat the odds. Farewell, Warrior Lady. Always, the Z Man."

I looked out the window with tears in my eyes and watched him as he saluted the crowd that had gathered by the helicopter. Then he boarded and the chopper lifted off. I stared as the aircraft got smaller and smaller, disappearing into the pale blue sky. I didn't notice that the General was tugging at my arm, explaining, "Everyone is waiting in the briefing room." Our next mission was already cooking on the front burner.

I accepted numerous dangerous assignments that year. It was as if I was flirting with the Grim Reaper himself. My latest mission was supposed to be one of the easiest I'd had in quite some time. It turned out to be the worst. We were going to retrieve a defecting Chinese diplomat who was holed up at the U.S. Embassy in Beijing. Unfortunately, the scheme was thwarted thanks to some blabbermouth moles in the State Department operating contrary to the wishes of the President. The Secretary wanted to force the Company under their jurisdiction so they could steal our funds. They thought, by making us look incompetent they could demonstrate how we required their guidance and control. At least that's what the General figured, and when was he ever wrong?

There arose a shootout while we were attempting to enter the limousine. The dignitary was killed, along with our leader, Navy Seal Commander Stapleton. The rest of the squad was apprehended; everyone was severely wounded or dead. Survivors were brought to a hospital, miles from the capital, where our bodies were partially mended. We were restrained in separate recovery rooms and interrogated three to four times a day. I had plenty of time to think, and my only thoughts were of Jason.

Word got back to the General that our mission was a catastrophe. He didn't know yet that an embassy official had tipped off the Chinese government. Billy eliminated the busybody as he was being escorted to safety by the Chinese police. That's when all hell broke loose. A hail of gunfire cut us down like it was a shooting gallery. We never had a chance.

General Pinelli sent word to Jason, imploring him to help plan our liberation. The General knew that the only way to find out who was behind the fiasco was to bring us back alive. Jason didn't hesitate; he was packed and on a plane to Virginia within the hour. When he discovered that I was among the victims, he asked to be reinstated for one more assignment because he wanted to lead the effort. The General agreed wholeheartedly. Intelligence sources identified the compound where we were being held. Reconnaissance photographs revealed every edifice, the perimeter, emplacements and installations.

It was like a concentration camp, surrounded by chain-link fences and concertina wire, and extremely well-guarded. Each building in the facility was protected with masonry walls and steel doors. It didn't appear anyone would be able impregnate it unnoticed, much less break anybody out.

What an ingenious plan Jason concocted. Everything was organized to the smallest detail. The Company spared no expense. We later testified before the House of Congress. It sure made me feel important. A few big heads were rolled in the Pentagon and in the President's cabinet, including the Secretary of State who was sentenced to ten years. But I'm getting ahead of myself.

This is the way it went down. One midnight in August, Jason, Tong, and Ling jumped out of a stealth jet bomber at 20,000 feet. During the freefall, they used bat wings to guide them towards the installation. Illumination of the compound and its inhabitants was enhanced thanks to night vision goggles. They opened below 1000 feet, just barely enough time for their chutes to inflate. They guided their landing to a secluded area inside the fences where a helicopter pad was located. As usual, Jason took out several guards using his poison darts, two while airborne and two more as the assault force worked their way toward the infirmary. Tong and Ling disposed of a few sentries the old-fashioned way.

My three favorite marauders donned their protective masks. Tong and Ling climbed to the top of the two main buildings. They used small acetylene torches to bore a hole in ventilation shafts used to control the environment within the interior. It was summertime, and the airflow was slow but continuous. They inserted a hose attached to a canister containing a new chemical nerve gas that would cause the muscles to arrest for several hours. The enemy was totally incapacitated within minutes, not to mention me and my fellow prisoners. The blowtorches were

PROSE AND POETRY

then used to cut through the lock on the door at the back of the infirmary. Jason ensured that all the souls inside were out of commission as they searched room to room. They found us. Unfortunately, Billy was too far gone; he had severe trauma to the head and was comatose. He was being kept alive using a respirator. Jason had to leave Billy behind. He removed life support and allowed Billy to die naturally and mercifully. This troubled Jason deeply, much more than the previous silencing of a comrade. Tong and Ling collected numerous documents and assorted medical supplies, including IVs, drugs, medical charts, and so forth. Meanwhile, the Z Monster was performing his routine on the sentinels manning the main gate.

Jason backed an ambulance to the front door. Raymond and I already had been placed on gurneys near the entrance where we were loaded into the ambulance. Timing was essential because a strike on the compound was scheduled just forty minutes from the initial high altitude, low opening jump. A submarine hiding in the Bering Sea launched three Tomahawk Cruise Missiles with multiple warheads. The team had several minutes head start before the entire compound was obliterated from the face of the earth.

It was assumed the Chinese would suspect the Company had destroyed the place so prisoners wouldn't be able to talk. It was hoped they would not discover too quickly that two captives were missing from the debris. Ling drove the ambulance to a garage in the city, which had been used by underground freedom fighters. This pro-democracy contingent had prepared a small clinic complete with physician and diagnostic equipment.

I awoke about noontime with a powerful headache. I looked around and realized I was somewhere else. On a bed next to me was Ray; he was lying there, hands perched behind his head and a huge grin on his face. I asked, "Where are we?" He replied, "We've escaped. Unfortunately, Billy didn't make it." "How is that possible?" I queried. Ray remarked, "Name one person who could pull it off." My heart jumped for joy; I immediately knew, but I didn't say. Right then, a doctor walked in and asked me how I was feeling. I told him I felt great (I had forgotten about the ferocious headache), but he gave me a painkiller anyway.

A couple of hours later, Jason entered the room looking half-asleep. He gave Ray a firm handshake and then stood beside my bed. He grasped my two hands in his, and said, "Hey Baby, what's happening?" I exclaimed, "Boy are you a sight for sore eyes! I prayed for a miracle, and here you are." He looked deeply into my eyes, as if his eyes were smiling at me. I held out my arms and he hugged me; I was putty in those arms.

The doctor explained how we would be recuperating for several days before the next phase of the operation. I asked him what the damage was. He said I had part of one lung removed, I was minus a kidney, and I had bone damage in my left leg that would require reconstructive surgery. A few additional minor bullet wounds had mostly healed. I raised the top of my gown; the skin below my breasts looked like a road map. I was embarrassed. The doctor informed me I could have some of the disfigurement repaired with plastic surgery.

Late one night we were transported to a fishing boat along a remote region of the shoreline. Hours later we rendezvoused with the submarine that had totaled the enemy installation. The accommodations in the sub were rather cramped but comfortable. I was feeling well enough to sit in a chair, and soon started walking a few steps at a time. Jason never left my side; he helped me regain my strength. We embarked upon Pearl Harbor after a few days. The General was there to welcome us. Two full days were spent discussing with the General and his staff the events that had transpired, then another day briefing government bigwigs.

A private wing of the hospital had been reserved for us. Jason slept in the bed next to mine; he was my private nursemaid. Finally, after about a week or so, I conjured up the nerve and asked Jason to kiss me like before. He beamed and obliged. After about a ten-minute kiss, we stood there holding each other and gazing at one another. I told him, "Do you have any idea how much I love you?" He responded, "You mean we don't have to pretend anymore?"

We flew to the East Coast the next morning, getting rather sauced while riding first class on a commercial airliner. We testified before a whole slew of personalities and politicians. Later, a ceremony was arranged where we all received decorations for valor and service to our country. The Vice President pinned us. Jason was given an honorary promotion to Lieutenant Colonel as a parting gift, which was sizeable given the increase in his retirement pay. I was promoted to Commander. However, my career as a government-backed mercenary was finished due to my injuries, and I received a medical discharge with full benefits.

The General decided he'd had enough as well. The Base threw a gigantic retirement celebration. Everyone was decked out in formal attire, except Jason and me; we wore holey jeans and raggedy T-shirts. We already had retired our uniforms at that point. The General was not offended, but others were. Screw them! Jason and I danced a few dances, despite the fact that I was still limping. I'd never felt so alive. When Jason proposed to me, it was the perfect end to a perfect evening.

Now we live on an eighty-acre spread in New Mexico. Adam is still in college so we see him during holidays. Yesterday I discovered that I no longer can bear children. Jason consoled me with the assurance that if I wanted to raise children we could adopt. We're having so much fun and there's still plenty of time. I feel so richly blessed.

# WHEN WILL YOU LEARN?

### (1970)

If I can't see, then I can feel.
If we do not listen, are we being real?
It seldom occurs when thinking of you
That wanting was getting and living was too.

I lived in a shadow, but saw not the dark.
We played in the meadow. Did we leave our mark?

The changes I learned of I found out too late.
Remember you can love, which may be your fate.
But only above can you forget your hate.

So please partake of words in your head.
You know you can't fake, because life isn't dead.
And girl, for our sake, keep the things that I said;
You're often awake when you're lying in bed.

# THE MISSOURI KID

### (2001)

Papa was a sharecropper. He worked like a slave in the cornfields alongside the blacks. My fondest memories are jawing with Papa on the front porch. He was a great man. I always wanted to be like him. I wonder if I'd have made him proud now that I'm famous.

From the earliest age I was fascinated with life west of the Mississippi. I must've read the account of the battle at the Alamo a hundred times from newspaper clippings Papa kept regarding the war for Texas independence. Then, before we knew it, the War Between the States was upon us. Papa went away to fight with the Union army because he felt slavery was morally wrong.

I tried to pull my weight around the farm, but I reckon I was daydreaming most of the time. Uncle Joel did the lion's share of the work. He was an amazing fellow. Folks said he was feeble-minded, but he was quite a talented person in my mind. He knew everything about farming, and whatever he touched grew. He was one heck of a whittler, too. He carved for me a six-shooter out of pinewood and fashioned a holster from real leather. I pretended I was a gunfighter while playing with Leroy, a Negro boy from a neighboring farm. I practiced my quick draw for hours every day. Mama didn't like it, but she tolerated it just the same.

Papa returned a broken man. He'd contracted the coughing disease while a prisoner of war in Andersonville. Papa toiled hard as ever until he owned our farm outright. Try as he did, he just couldn't keep up with the pace he'd set for himself. The consumption finally killed him, but not before he taught me to shoot a Winchester rifle and a Colt revolver.

Uncle Joel kept the farm in operation, until one night he went to bed and never woke up again. Mama had to sell out and we moved to Sedalia. Auntie Faye let us live with her. She was the widow of a former aide to the governor and reasonably well-to-do. Mama was an accomplished seamstress and helped support the family. After a spell it was only Mama, Faye, and my little brother Alex. Sister Carrie had run off and married some dude in Saint Louis, while I was in Jefferson City studying law. My interests gradually changed to journalism, however. I wanted to head west and report on Indian wars and interview Kit Carson. Unfortunately, I learned soon afterwards that the great trailblazer already had passed on.

I never finished college. The urge to roam overcame my interest in scholastics. I sold my belongings and departed in the spring of 1874. All I had was my horse, pack, bedroll, the six-shooter Papa bought me, Papa's deer rifle, and about seventy dollars in silver. I also carried plenty of paper and pencils so I could record every detail of my journey. I worked odd jobs along the way to gain eating money, and I won a few extra dollars competing in shooting contests.

My experience in Abilene Kansas was especially memorable. I had a week's worth of trail dust on me, and I was parched from the sun. I flopped my carcass on a barstool using my overcoat as a cushion. The bartender served me a cool beer and a shot of whiskey. He could tell I was a stranger and asked where I was from. I said I was born in Missouri. I downed the whiskey and sipped on the beer, making small talk with the bartender. Suddenly he stood straight up and grunted, "Here comes trouble."

A husky and dusky bushwhacker entered the tavern with two lowlife characters following behind. I paid little attention to them, until the big guy approached me. He pointed out, "You're new around here, ain't you?" "What of it?" I groaned. He replied, "Well, it happens to be a custom around here that newcomers buy the first round." "Your custom, not mine," I informed. Then he became belligerent trying to feign friendship. "Tell you what," he said, "You buy a round, and then I'll buy a round." I finished my beer and arose from the stool. "Sorry, but I was just leaving," I announced. "Not so fast!" he exclaimed, grabbing at my arm. I jerked my arm away giving him a cross look. I could tell he was bucking for a fight. I studied his movement. He took a swing with his fist, but I backed away, fully prepared for it. He charged at me, burying his head in my stomach and backing me up against the bar. I punched him in the groin then shoved him back with my boot heel.

He backed off several paces, pulled his coat around his gun, and told me I was about to die. I focused my gaze on his gun hand while the patrons in the bar slowly moved to the corners of the establishment. As everyone expected, he went for his gun. All I remember was the sound of two guns discharging in rapid succession, followed by the clatter of a mirror falling to the ground in pieces behind me. A moment elapsed before reality set in and I regained my senses. The varmint lay in a pile on the floor. I felt queasy in the stomach, but forced the beer back down as I holstered my revolver. I watched when one of his sidekicks flipped him over on his back. There was a hole in his chest surrounded by blood where his heart used to be.

A sheriff came rushing to the scene with his six-shooter drawn. He looked at me with steely eyes and demanded that I unbuckle my gun belt. The bartender pleaded my case, relating that the dead man went for his gun first. That story was corroborated by a well-dressed gentleman wearing a derby hat. Apparently, he was the local judge. He explained the situation and ordered the sheriff to complete a full report including the observations of the bartender, himself, and a few other witnesses. He mentioned that he would sign the document to make it official, declaring there would be no need to hold me for trial.

The sheriff concluded the episode warning me, "I better not see your face when the sun comes up." No matter, because I was planning to bust the dust anyway. As I flung the doors open, I overheard people talking about "how fast the kid was" and how "Connors had barely cleared leather." Already my legacy was developing and beginning to spread.

I traveled half the night, finished off the rest of my beef jerky, and bedded down in a washed-out riverbed. Despite the fact that I'd killed a man, I slept rather soundly; until I jumped out of my sleep from a frightening dream. The sun was blazing in the sky, but rain clouds were looming on the horizon. I rode hard for several weeks, bouncing from town to town, not staying long enough to make acquaintances. Summer was waning by the time I found the heart of Texas.

I was trotting through the scrub oak, half a day's ride from San Antonio, when I was ambushed by three Mexican bandits. They ordered me off my pony, claiming all they wanted were my mount and my weapons. I figured them to take everything, including my life. I turned my horse before dismounting, shielding myself from one of the banditos. I pretended to unbuckle my gun belt, but instead, drew and fired. As one vaquero bit the dirt, another took a shot. His horse reared backwards and he slipped off, dropping head first onto the ground. He rolled over to take aim, but I had him dead to rights, plugging him twice. He immediately became motionless. The third highwayman high-tailed it down the ridge. I grabbed my rifle and got a bead on him; then I aimed lower and shot his mount out from under him.

I hopped on my steed and chased the last bandit down. It was then I noticed a distinct pain in my thigh. I had been grazed by a bullet but I wasn't badly wounded. I cautiously approached, finding the rascal squirming in the mud with a broken leg. I confiscated his gun and rounded up two horses. I draped two dead Mexicans over one horse and tied the live one onto the saddle of the other.

I breezed into town just before sundown and located a constable who happened to be organizing a posse. He was surprised to see I had managed to bring in three desperados. They were members of a gang of raiders that were wanted dead or alive for murder, rape, robbery, and rustling. I was equally surprised to learn how the three were worth a total of $750 in reward money. I got to keep their guns too, which I later traded for additional supplies at the General Store. Their horses and saddles were sold to cover official debts and expenses. The lawman asked me if I was a bounty hunter. I assured him that I was just passing through. He gave me some papers to sign. I didn't want to give my real name so I signed Uncle Joel's name, figuring nobody would be able to trace me through my mother's deceased brother. I also lied about my hometown, naming Independence as my birthplace.

I had a long hot bath, a steak dinner, several shots of whiskey, and then spent the night with a harlot in the hotel. It was the first bed I'd slept in since leaving Missouri. The next morning, I visited what was left of the Alamo. I stood in awe as I envisioned the thirteen-day siege and the fall of so many brave patriots. I stayed another night in town, heading out the next morning at the crack of dawn. It was getting towards nightfall when a group of Texas Rangers caught up with me. They persuaded me to join them in rounding up outlaws. Word had already reached the ears of the rangers who were short-handed. It seemed a worthy cause and a steady stream of income

I worked with the Rangers one full year earning a meager salary. They taught me to track and to snipe. The Rangers were a great bunch of hombres, and we had a lot of laughs. Our outfit hunted down some forty-five desperados in twelve months. During that time, I made a couple of fine friends, Hector and Vance; I learned to trust them with my life. The three of us brought in more fugitives than you can shake a stick at, half of them alive. Hector and Vance were the only ones in the unit to learn my real name. It was while I rode with the Texas Rangers that I earned the nickname, The Missouri Kid.

In late autumn of '76 I moseyed into El Paso. I was new in town, but my reputation preceded me. I spent a week enjoying the sights of El Paso and its Mexican neighbor across the Rio Grande, Juarez City. There I met a young Mexican senorita by the name of Cecilia. I spoke practically no Spanish, and her English was limited, but together we kindled a little fire that grew every day into a rage of passion. Her parents learned about my exploits and prohibited her from seeing me, but she sneaked out all the same in order for us to be together.

Unfortunately, too many people pegged me a killer. On Thanksgiving Day, I was about to enjoy a delicious meal at the inn where I lodged, when some crazed gunslinger challenged me to a duel. I refused, but it was apparent that he was determined to fight, to the extent that he threatened harm to Cecilia and her family. I faced him at high noon, with forty paces between us. I was quite nervous. This was the only time I'd ever met a man in the street for the sole purpose of seeing who had the faster gun.

I watched him like a hawk without blinking an eye. The second he made his move, I drew. Time stood still. My arm hooked and my wrist jerked forward as my hand grasped the hickory handle of my Colt .45. I thrust the gun outward once it cleared the holster, while simultaneously pulling back the hammer with the palm of my left hand. Once I'd raised the revolver to shoulder level, I let the hammer free. The immediate recoil from the discharge of the bullet made the barrel jump upward. All this seemed to take hours, yet it was over in less than one second.

I steadied my gun for another shot, but there was no target. I lowered the weapon and my head dropped. Lying flat on his back and spread eagle in the dirt was a young man about my age, with a gaping hole in his belly. Blood formed in a puddle beneath his back. I could see his eyes bulging out as I stepped forward to examine his corpse. You could see the expression of disbelief frozen on his face. It was terrifying. Once again, I got a seasick sensation in my gut. I'd lost my appetite for dinner; indeed, I'd lost my appetite for gunfighting. I was given an hour to get out of town, again. I hadn't the time to bid farewell to my girl. It was the most depressing day of my life. I lost my dignity, my self-respect, my reputation, and my first true love.

I cogitated about going back home but I had come too far. Besides, I was leery of the kind of reaction I might get there. I hadn't even taken time to write to my mother. By now, however, she probably knew all about me. I kept moving westward to Columbus, but received a lousy reception there, so I put Tucson in my sights. I hoped that I could outrun myself, but I learned that word of mouth traveled faster than the Pony Express. The citizens of Tucson weren't too happy to see me either. Everywhere I went people frowned on me, despite the fact that I had killed only a half-dozen men, each in self-defense or under the authority of the law (notwithstanding those who died at the hands of fellow rangers in my company). I wasn't the despicable murderer that people made me out to be; at least that's the way I judged it.

Fortunately, the governor wasn't against me. In fact, he offered me a job as a peace officer to enforce the law in a vast untamed territory. I was one of five who were sworn in as Deputy U.S. Marshall. For three long years I patrolled the Gila River all the way to the Sonoran Desert, searching for criminals and renegade Indians. It made me age before my time, however. I was sandblasted, windblown, and sunburned. My skin was like wrinkled leather, and my hair like loose straw. I seemed a codger, though I hadn't yet turned thirty.

I left the employ of the Arizona territory bound for California, having received commendations for bravery and dedication to duty, and leaving a few more bodies to bury. With aspirations of escaping my past, I trimmed my hair, shaved my beard, and bought me some city slicker attire. I wandered up the Pacific coast, searching for a job as a newsman. I finally found my niche as a reporter for the Sacramento Herald.

It's ironic how events transpire in one short life. I set out to report on the Wild West with the vision of meeting great men and writing their stories. As it turned out, I ended up penning my own autobiography, which for many was every bit as engaging. Back East there was a flourishing market for short novels and unofficial biographies, telling tales of desperate outlaws, courageous freedom fighters, and hardship survivors. I compiled my notes and wrote a factual history of myself, using a pseudonym. I obtained a publisher, and my book was distributed around the country and in England. I earned a handsome commission telling of my experiences and close scrapes while a drifter. I later married, had three children, and lived my life in obscurity. I corresponded by mail with my mother, sister, and brother, but I never laid eyes on them again.

# COUNTERTERRORIST

(2004)

I first met Dr. Lockhart prior to boarding a 737 leaving Baltimore for Atlanta. It was a gloomy, overcast day in autumn. I was on my way to Advanced Individual Training (AIT) in biochemical warfare at Fort McClellan. I had spent a short week on leave to visit my parents after finishing Basic Combat Training. I hadn't been in the Army three months so I was quite the novice. Dr. Lockhart was also on his way to Alabama, to assist with some research being conducted by a reputable defense contractor in Huntsville. During our conversation he began reflecting on his initial military experiences from the late sixties: Basic and AIT in infantry at Ft. Polk, then to Ft. Benning for Airborne Training, followed by Ranger Training which took him through Okefenokee Swamp during the hottest days of summer. Funny, he didn't look that hardcore, with his spectacles and graying beard; but everyone knows how looks can be deceiving. Under his 42-long tailored suit was a well-conditioned body and mind.

I will never forget that day, as I expect may be the sentiment of the entire USA. Somehow, five Arabian terrorists from an Islamic jihad faction were able to smuggle plastic daggers and box-cutters aboard our jetliner. They used these utensils to hijack the aircraft and gain access to the cockpit. We were flying over Richmond when they made their move. Three terrorists ordered passengers and crew to the rear of the aircraft while two others took the controls. I was already sitting at the rear of the plane; Dr. Lockhart was about six rows from the front of coach section. As two hijackers herded people towards the back, another grabbed a pretty stewardess and dragged her to first class to ravage her. I overheard him speaking in Arabic, declaring how he was going to get one more piece before he dies. I learned to speak the language as a child growing up in Lebanon. I was the son of Christian parents who had immigrated to the United States after the suicide bombing of the American Embassy in Beirut back in 1983.

Dr. Lockhart already had assessed the situation. He'd fashioned a weapon using a sharpened drawing pencil embedded into an art gum eraser as a handle. He was pretending to be a bumbling klutz to conceal the weapon, as terrorist one summoned him to join the rest of us in the tail section. Terrorist two was facing the rear of the ship directing traffic; he didn't notice what was going on up front. Lockhart plunged the makeshift spear into the bastard's neck, guiding it up the thorax and into the brain, where it likely lodged in the medulla. The terrorist managed to get in a lick with his box-cutter, cutting into Dr. Lockhart's side. Lockhart grabbed the man's arm with one hand and his neck with the other, driving him across the aisle into a window seat. He wrapped a seatbelt around the guy's neck, fastened and tightened it. Lockhart removed the blade from the hijacker's hand and cut ligaments in his wrists so he couldn't free himself and would bleed out. The commotion from the passengers and the noise of the aircraft masked the gagging of Lockhart's victim. He wiped his hands on the guy's turban, then donned his suitcoat to hide a bleeding wound. It seemed like forever, but the entire episode took maybe a minute.

Dr. Lockhart was slinking towards the back of the plane when terrorist number two turned to call for his missing accomplice. Terrorist two began making his way forward shoving Lockhart aside. Lockhart hopped on a seat and lunged through the air grabbing the guy around the neck, piggy-back style. The terrorist attempted to shake free, jabbing his plastic knife into Lockhart's thigh. Before he could repeat that move, Lockhart had used the box-cutter to slit the guy's throat from ear to ear. They both stumbled to the floor while one badly severed jugular spewed blood across the carpet. The hijacker reached for the knife but Lockhart stabbed him through the hand with the box-cutter, the razor blade breaking off in the small bones of his upper wrist. It wasn't long before terrorist number two remained motionless. Lockhart picked up the pig-sticker and struggled to his feet. He removed his necktie and tightened it around his wounded leg, using a handkerchief as a bandage. He ripped the sleeve off his coat and used it as a bandage, securing the wound in his side by tying his shirttails together.

A few passengers began to chastise Lockhart. One dumbass griped, "What are you trying to do, get us all killed?" Lockhart calmly replied, but loud enough for others to hear, "If we do not get control of this plane immediately, everyone aboard will die along with countless others." The copilot pointed out, "They turned the plane around and now are on a northerly course." "My guess is they've targeted Washington," Lockhart added. Then he started towards the cockpit, saying, "You people can just sit there if you want, but I'm going to try and prevent that SCB from raping our stewardess."

Lockhart dragged the body of terrorist two to the emergency exit and tossed the remains of his coat over the corpse's face. Then he opened an overhead bin and grabbed somebody's tote bag. Once arriving at the first-class curtain, he crept forward on all fours hoping not to alert terrorist three, who was entranced in a private show watching intently while his victim reluctantly undressed. Terrorist three chuckled saying in broken English, "I'm going to enjoy this," as he opened his fly and revealed an erection. "You wish," countered Lockhart, shoving the carry-on bag into his face and reaching for his right arm which wielded a box-cutter. They were entangled and struggling when terrorist three sliced across Lockhart's left forearm. Then Lockhart pulled the dagger from between his teeth and impaled the guy in the groin and deep into his colon. The evil brute slumped back against the bench. Lockhart drove the blade deeper with the kick of his heel; then jumped atop his head, and with both knees used the tote bag to muffle the guy's screams. Soon the man stopped breathing. Lockhart arose, removed a blanket from the cabinet, and wrapped the stewardess who was shivering and shaking, naked to the world. Lockhart gathered her clothes and escorted her to the lavatory. He softly and affectionately told her to lock the door, dress, and remain there until he called; and not to be alarmed if there was some violent turbulence. Then he tore the left sleeve off his dress shirt and wrapped the wound on his forearm.

Meanwhile, five of us had volunteered to help Lockhart continue the fight. We knew we had to enter the cockpit with as little resistance as possible. Lockhart asked if anyone spoke Arabic. I raised my hand. "Great!" he exclaimed. He told me I was to go to the cockpit door, knock, and say in Arabic, "Open the door, quickly." Another volunteer, who said he was an ex-Marine, would be at the ready to accost whomever opened the door and jerk his butt into the hallway. He and I would disable terrorist four while two middle-aged men, husky, tattooed and rowdy looking, were to rush the cockpit. Their mission was to subdue terrorist five who was piloting the aircraft; our copilot would take the helm in the process. Lockhart was going to lie with his back on the floor and shove the door open with his foot the second it became ajar. "I sure hope this works," the copilot sighed. It did.

After terrorist four cracked the door Lockhart rammed it open, bracing it with his extended foot. We dragged terrorist four into the aisle and beat him unconscious. Once terrorist five had appraised the situation, he forced the plane into a nosedive. The plane rapidly dropped to almost forty degrees making it difficult to remove terrorist five from the Captain's chair. The copilot practically flew into his control station due to the sudden decrease in altitude, and immediately commenced to pull the nose upward. Lockhart joined the frenzy in the cockpit helping to wrestle terrorist five to the floor. The hijacker continued to put up a fight until Lockhart placed two solid kicks into his groin; you could almost hear his nuts crack after the second kick. The two men proceeded to pummel terrorist five mercilessly, until he lost the will and the means to fight back. Lockhart found our Captain slumped in the corner of the cockpit suffering from a chest wound. He was bleeding profusely and barely alive. Lockhart kneeled beside him, placed a pillow over the wound, encased his torso with a blanket, and folded the Captain's arms around it, consoling him and assuring him he was going to make it. Lockhart, bleeding from several deep wounds of his own, staggered back to find two living terrorists slumped on the floor, dazed and humiliated. He ordered us to hogtie the two using men's neckties and ladies' stockings, securing firmly their hands and feet. We hauled them to the front of coach, where rows one and two faced each other, and strapped each terrorist face down between the rows using seatbelts. We wrapped one belt behind the back and the other between the legs. I sat on the right side of the aisle to guard one prisoner, and our Marine friend did so at the left.

Amidst the turmoil and the screaming passengers, we hardly noticed how the copilot had managed to right the plane only seconds before it would have crashed and burned, and scarcely miles from the capitol. He immediately contacted flight control and apprised them of the situation. We were cleared for an emergency landing at Dulles Airport. Lockhart summoned the stewardess from the lavatory; she emerged dressed, shaken, and in partial shock. He led her to a first-class seat, buckled and tightened her seatbelt, and took the seat across from her. In twenty minutes, we were safely on the ground and taxiing to a remote area where ambulances, airport security, a fire engine, and countless law enforcement personnel awaited.

Once the plane had touched down, everyone began to cheer and shout. Lockhart arose from his seat to thank the five who assisted him. When the rest of the passengers saw him standing tall, the applause became deafening. Everyone wanted to know his name. Lockhart mumbled to the team, "Just call me Shane." I was probably the only one on the plane who could connect his real name to the face.

Two FBI agents were the first to board. One of them began barking orders and Lockhart told him to shut up and "call a medical team stat" to assist the Captain. The agent with the big mouth pulled out his gun and pointed it at Lockhart. Lockhart slugged him, knocking him to his knees. The two husky guys restrained the agent when he hopped to his feet, telling him if it wasn't for "Shane" we wouldn't be here. Just then, an official looking man in a three-piece suit stepped aboard and asked what was going on. Lockhart explained that we had a wounded Captain requiring immediate medical attention, and that three terrorists were dead with two others in custody. Big mouth wanted to have Lockhart arrested, but the main guy told him to back off and take charge of the prisoners.

Paramedics gently carried the Captain to a gurney and shuttled him off to the Emergency Room. Lockhart, still dripping with blood, exclaimed, "I'm next," so they helped him out of the aircraft and into an ambulance. After things settled down and everyone had disembarked, the five of us who had aided Lockhart exited the plane: Johnny Stevenson the copilot, Dave North the ex-Marine, the two husky guys Rollie and Garth, and finally me holding up the rear. We boarded a shuttle that took us to a terminal gate which had been sealed off for security purposes. We were heroes. Reporters were all over us. They wanted to know who Lockhart was and requested personal interviews with several passengers and the crew. Out of respect for Lockhart, I didn't reveal his name. Most people were so confused they couldn't even remember his assigned seat. The reason I remember such details is because we had boarded the plane together.

As soon as the FBI were through with us, Dave and I rented a car and searched the local hospitals for Lockhart. We asked around and got nowhere. We were leaving a hospital in Northern Virginia when I spotted him smoking a cigarette around the corner from the Emergency entrance. He was bandaged up and waiting for a lift. He implored that we keep it quiet about who he was and where he was going. Soon, a limousine stopped at the curb, Lockhart eased in, and it sped away. A gigantic media frenzy ensued lasting the entire week. Somehow, through all of it, Lockhart was able to remain anonymous. Clearly, he was not interested in glory or recognition. In fact, the American people were so enmeshed in the fantasy of the unknown hero, it seemed better they couldn't attach a face or a name. It was kind of like the Tomb of the Unknown Soldier, an example of the ultimate sacrifice for freedom, ascribed to anyone who serves their country fearlessly, courageously, and anonymously.

The President of the United States declared war on terrorism and a coalition of allied forces began policing the Middle East. Any nation and any person that supported or harbored terrorists or that plotted or perpetrated acts of terrorism were labeled enemy combatants. The terrorists were forced to hide in holes. They were prevented from blatant acts of destruction and large-scale murder, being limited to smaller and softer objectives. I was given an Army commendation, then went on my merry way to continue military training. Two years later I was practically an expert in chemical weapons, explosives, and demolition. I volunteered and was accepted to receive Airborne and Ranger training. I guess I wanted to follow in Lockhart's footsteps, so to speak. It was after the USA invaded Iraq that I would encounter Lockhart once again.

I was deployed to Baghdad as an attachment to a ranger battalion. The Iraqi dictator had been deposed and democracy was being installed. Iraq was a nation of men and women who were tired of tyranny, exploitation, and intimidation, to include a large contingency of disconcerted youth who grew up without knowing anything but terror and war. The old school was on its way out, but still there remained fundamentalists who were not interested in freedom and despised western values. There also were many who simply wanted the western alliance to fail purely out of envy and disdain. Their sole purpose in life was to fuel the chaos and perpetrate disorder. Insurgents from Iran and Syria as well as local terrorists were a constant deterrent to the security and growth of the new democracy, and nobody seemed to know how to stop them.

Enter Lockhart. Here was a guy who had served with distinction in Vietnam, earning three Purple Hearts and two Bronze Stars during two tours. He was given a field-grade commission from Buck Sergeant to Second Lieutenant for guiding a Long Range Reconnaissance Patrol into Cambodia to free four Marine POWs being held by the notorious Pol Pot. During his ten years in the Army, he attained the rank of Captain, became a Military Intelligence Officer, and completed a Bachelor Degree in Criminal Justice. Upon leaving the Army, he worked a stint for the FBI in counterespionage while he continued his education, obtaining a Masters in Military History, and onto a Doctorate in Psychology, publishing his dissertation on the psychopathology of terrorism.

He worked for ten more years as a Defense Industry Consultant with military contractors and the U.S. government on some very technical and highly classified projects. Here was a middle-aged guy who did not appear extremely big, strong, or rugged, but seemingly meek and mild, though extremely bright. Through his quick thinking and cunning, he had single-handedly defeated three well-trained hijackers in a span of about five minutes, earning him the President's Medal of Freedom (which was never publicized). When the State Department looked for answers on how to solve the problems of aggression and terrorism in Iraq, who better to call than counterterrorist extraordinaire, Dr. Carlton Lockhart?

Lockhart had been given complete authority and limitless resources to thwart the terrorists and stabilize Iraq. Although Major General Wieland was our commanding officer, everyone knew it was Lockhart who was calling the shots. I was delighted to be selected for the task force. Apparently, Lockhart had been reviewing the service records of a great number of military and civilian personnel deployed in Iraq. He was especially interested in people with unique skills, and I spoke Arabic fluently. He obviously recognized who I was, because he welcomed me with a handshake, addressing me by name when I reported for duty.

Lockhart's methods were ingenious, albeit unorthodox. His opening statement was inspiring, insightful, and succinct. "The best way to fight terrorism," he maintained, "is with terrorism." He continued, "Terrorists know nothing but fear and torment. They want others who enjoy peace and prosperity, something they lack, to have a taste of their warped worldview. They are hateful, jealous, and wicked. They use religion as an excuse but are no more religious than the devil himself. They use Islam as a ruse to trick the ignorant into believing that suicide is an honorable death, rewarded by a heavenly oasis of earthly delights. But like FDR once said, 'There is nothing to fear but fear itself.' You see, this is precisely what makes them tick. Although they are hell-bent on spreading fear, they themselves are quite unequipped to handle torture and terror. While it makes them feel strong and courageous to intimidate others, in a confrontation they run like the cowards they are. Most are afraid to fight a stronger enemy, but instead pick on the weak, unprotected, and vulnerable. Since they hide their faces in fear, we must bring a greater fear upon them. Their philosophy is that scaring people to death can be a means to an end; likewise, they can be influenced when the roles are reversed."

Lockhart and Wieland meticulously mapped out a strategy of counterterrorism-terrorism. Step one was to establish a contingency among the Iraqi underground which consisted of citizens, military, and law enforcement personnel who were conscientious about restoring order, wanted to realize the freedoms that had thus far been repressed, but as yet had been hesitant to act. Lockhart hoped to identify and organize these people, while at the same time spread propaganda asserting the existing strength, growth, and organization of a new, homegrown Iraqi counterinsurgency effort. Our successes would be ascribed to the local revolutionaries, enabling us to remain undetected. Meanwhile, more recruits were to follow while national interest in the underground rapidly expanded. We were empowering the citizenry to eventually take over the charter, while keeping our involvement forever secret. After all, nobody was aware of our presence, except those in the highest echelons of the allied operation, and we wanted to keep it that way.

My first mission was as hair-raising as it was educational. Intelligence sources had identified a number of prominent people who were backing and equipping the terrorists in order to maintain power and control. They also identified some spinoff terror groups out of Iran whose mission was nothing more than creating more instability. Iraq's imaginary underground had purportedly released messages that were picked up by certain intel agencies and leaked to the media, informing that clandestine gatherings were being arranged. Many of those deemed hostile to democracy were encouraged to believe they were being targeted by the movement. The ruse was, leaks in high places revealed where and when these secret meetings were to be held. Lockhart anticipated the enemy's next move, to send assassins and insurrectionists to the supposed rendezvouses. Thus, the assemblages, held in three major cities, would be comprised chiefly of people desiring to fragment if not annihilate the Iraqi revolutionaries. My role, and that of a few colleagues, was to pose as informant-combatants, infiltrate organizations, and persuade certain antagonists (who we were surveilling surreptitiously) that their bosses were the adversaries. Hopefully, they would think their superiors had deliberately led them into a trap to protect their secret association with the underground. It was like rehearsing for a Shakespearean play the way Lockhart scripted it and we enacted it.

Once the stage was set, we initiated a crossfire making it appear the subversives were engaging the terrorists, while it became mostly terrorists battling assassins and insurgents. During the fiasco, I feigned being wounded, using goat blood to enhance the effect, as I fought alongside a known troublemaker named Hamed Abbas. In my dying breath I told Hamed that we had been betrayed by the same man: Hasid Aldouri. I covered Hamed's escape, gaining his trust and his promise that he would eliminate Aldouri for being a traitor by helping to democratize Iraq. About thirty-five bad guys died in the engagement in which I participated. Another six who were wounded were taken captive. Our modus operandi was to incapacitate the wounded (often with chloroform), photograph their bloody and broken bodies, report them as deceased to hype the media, and then take them prisoner.

A week later, we heard that Hasid Aldouri had been assassinated in a gun battle which took the lives of Hamed Abbas and several of Aldouri's henchmen. It was ingenious how Lockhart manipulated different enemy factions into distrusting and destroying one another. It also was amazing the amount of information acquired from prisoners before executing them. They were afraid of being tortured so they sang like canaries, resulting in the demise of more of their leadership.

My next assignment was equally adventurous. We staged an attack that took out a U.S. Army transport convoy using rocket-propelled grenade (RPG) launchers. We had placed several deceased prisoners dressed as American soldiers in the vehicles. They were blown up and burned to a crisp so nobody was the wiser. A fellow Iraqi freedom fighter named Raed and I rallied a riotous group of revelers around the flaming trucks. We accosted a motorist, ran him off, then used his vehicle as a podium to offer anti-American chants and pro-Sharia accolades. Little did the crowd know that I had previously loaded this vehicle with explosives to be detonated on command via remote control. Gradually, an increasing number of AK-47 and RPG wielding protestors joined the fray. As the mob grew in size and hostility, Raed and I slipped through. I activated the bomb from a safe haven, and it toppled two square blocks, mowing down over a hundred anti-America and anti-Israel protesters in the process. Raed and I returned to the carnage to aid some of the wounded, pretending to be their rescuers. We carried a few to the location of their choice. After dressing their wounds and hugging and kissing all the inhabitants at the shelter, we praised Allah and departed. Later that night the sites were taken out by rocket fire from an American-made Apache helicopter purchased by the interim Iraqi government but flown by an experienced operative. Several similar bombings had been simultaneously staged around the country. Although innocent civilians expired as a result, the collateral losses were minimal. How appropriate it seemed, to use car bombs and suicide slayers to take out terrorists for a change.

As Lockhart anticipated, our successes were instrumental in rallying support of the citizenry for the allied effort to create a Muslim democracy. Many were enlisting in the Iraqi military and police forces; others were organizing themselves and initiating their own retaliation against insurgents who embedded themselves with civilians for use as human shields. Indigenous strike forces were being formed and trained, and some of their elite troops began working for us. Hotlines were setup across the country enabling trusted informants to call at any hour of the day to report on terrorist activities, movements, weapons caches, and hideouts. Follow-up on such intelligence often meant an unpleasant surprise in the form of a firebomb or booby-trap for unsuspecting menaces. Remotely piloted aircraft equipped with cameras and munitions were used for reconnaissance, targeting, and engaging. It was easy to see who the enemy was: they were the ones shooting at these unmanned aerial vehicles (UAV). To their dismay, the UAV shot back, and with lethal accuracy. In another creative tactic we posed as reporters and cameramen. Terrorists loved getting media attention, except when the camera shooting them was a disguised Uzi machine gun with a forty-round magazine.

After three months of collaboration, the U.S. and Iraqi governments established joint ownership and management of prisons and concentration camps. Henceforth, the capturing, interrogating, and incarcerating of invaders and terrorists became a consolidated effort. On one occasion, hostiles kidnapped three British contractors who were helping to rebuild bridges and expressways. Anarchists threatened to behead their captives unless twenty-three prison inmates, identified by name, were released. To express their sincerity, they beheaded one of the hostages and released a videotape of the carnage. In response, the named inmates were beheaded by the Iraqi interim government on the steps of a Baghdad courthouse. This was coupled with a warning to the kidnappers that twenty-three more would be executed in like manner if the two remaining Brits were not released within twenty-four hours. Not surprisingly, they were found alive the next day.

While a number of the terrorist factions were dissolving, others attempted to combine forces. They eventually established a stronghold in Najaf. The enemy contingent was led by a Shiite cleric surnamed al-Bakr. He established his headquarters at a principle Shia mosque, which was situated in the center of town. Broken terrorist groups flocked to Najaf as a last-ditch effort to reconsolidate, but many never made it there alive. Meanwhile, a vast majority of the civilian population had fled the city. It would have been easy just to level the place, but that would cause the loss of some of the greatest archaeological history known to mankind, not to mention the religious shrine where the enemy had retreated and its associated relics. There was no diplomatic way of handling it, so the commanders brought in Lockhart and company to strategize.

Najaf was surrounded by allied militias: American, Iraqi, British, Italian, and Kurdish military men fighting as one. For a solid week, roaming vehicles equipped with loudspeakers broadcast a warning to all the inhabitants of Najaf that persons caught in the streets would be in danger of losing their lives, especially if they bore arms. The media echoed this warning in their daily news reports. Those wishing to surrender or flee were given explicit instructions on how they could depart peacefully. Many took the offer; some were arrested. Holdouts were trapped

Gradually, combined forces were able to create a stranglehold on the city, which became smaller in radius after each passing day. Snipers were situated in strategic positions, with sufficient security and concealment to operate 24/7. Numerous skirmishes ensued, but the terrorists were outnumbered, outgunned, and out-soldiered. They were ineffective in urban combat operations because their hit-and-run tactics had been rendered useless. Two sniper teams with support crews were emplaced in a large building about two-hundred meters from the mosque. Highly sophisticated surveillance equipment was brought in. This included microwave eavesdropping devices, miscellaneous sensors, and directional homing and imaging devices. The architectural layout of the mosque and surrounding installations were examined in a number of different ways. There were windows in the mosque through which infrared could be employed to illuminate inhabitants inside. A discernable pattern of behavior was determined, including the congregation of individuals for daily prayers, and a nightly meeting of the leadership in an upstairs assembly room. It appeared there was a facilitator at those meetings who stood on a slightly elevated stage against the western wall. The portly stature of the individual and the recordings of voice traffic clearly indicated al-Bakr. Wieland gave the order and two expert machine-gunners blasted a burst of fifty-caliber bullets across the square. Tracer rounds screamed through windows and walls splattering al-Bakr from floor to ceiling. Those attempting to come to his aid met the same fate by sharpshooters.

Fortunately, the damage to the mosque was negligible and repairable. Unfortunately, the remaining terrorists set numerous fires in retaliation. This set off a cache of munitions, and in a few hours the sacred shrine was demolished, along with numerous hosties inside. Lockhart observed, "They have committed an unpardonable sin in Islam." Those who were able to escape the inferno were cut down like a weed whacker. The siege was over, but at the devastating loss of a beautiful and historic landmark. The insensitivity and downright cowardice of the terrorists was appalling to people of all faiths. In fact, reasonable and devout Muslims around the world, whether Shia or Sunni, began speaking out against fundamentalist extremism in general and jihadism in particular. Islamic adherents were incensed that the holy Koran was being defiled and used as a tool to promote evil, and to justify killing whomever some cleric deemed an infidel. They were particularly outraged that people purporting to be devout Muslims would destroy a revered mosque out of pure meanness. Middle East governments began rounding up known terrorists and expelling mutineers by the dozens. Numerous additional criminals were tried, convicted, and executed. Others remaining at large were disorganized, lacking resources and financial support. Their efforts resulted in self-destruction due to inadequate planning, poor training, loss of dignity, and utter foolishness. The war on terrorism was being won, and the credit—well a select few knew one person that deserved a lion's share.

⧓⧓⧓⧓⧓⧓⧓⧓⧓⧓⧓⧓⧓⧓⧓⧓⧓⧓⧓⧓⧓⧓⧓

## CRACKED

(2018)

You must slay the dragon and get on the wagon,
Or it will keep draggin' you down.
So take another drag on it, you know you're gonna gag on it;
You'll grow into a hag, which is certainly a drag.

At first it seems erratic, becoming automatic.
You'll act like a fanatic, a failure and a fool.
You'd best not let it beat you, it surely will defeat you.
Allow me now to teach you the hallowed Golden Rule.

Treat yourself and others like sisters and brothers;
Stay focused on love or you'll burn.
Give yourself a break because your life is what's at stake (or was).
Listen carefully and learn or soon you'll lose your turn.

When you decide to fake it, you're likely not to make it.
If that's the road you take, you'll be swallowed by the snake.
Let the Spirit guide you and win the war inside you.
In God you should confide or already you have died.

⧓⧓⧓⧓⧓⧓⧓⧓⧓⧓⧓⧓⧓⧓⧓⧓⧓⧓⧓⧓⧓⧓⧓

## SNIPE HUNT

(2006)

I remember being a youth of twelve and a relatively new recruit in the Boy Scouts. Tenderfoot was an understatement; I was about as green as they come. As part of an initiation to my first Jamboree, I was guest of honor at a snipe hunt. For those of you who are ignorant of this tradition, let me school you. I was basically left in the middle of the boondocks on a dried-up riverbed, sometime after midnight, holding a burlap bag and a stick. The senior boys were going to scare a snipe (a long-billed wading bird) out of the underbrush into my direction. My mission was to capture it. After about half an hour I realized that I'd been duped. Sulking back to the campfire, I endured the ridicule and laughter of being made a fool.

Fortunately, I gained some notoriety the next day by outscoring everyone in my troop at the rifle range. In fact, I received a patch and a certificate designating me a marksman with a .22 rifle. I was recognized at the closing ceremony the final night. The rest is, as it goes, history. I became quite the sharpshooter and won a number of trophies during my short-lived adolescence. And yes, I did enact a few snipe hunts by the time I became patrol leader and a Life scout.

When the lottery numbers for the draft were released, I realized I would be inducted into the Army on my 19th birthday. I jumped the gun, so to speak, and enlisted. My older brother had just terminated service as a Special Forces medic. Not to be outclassed, I volunteered for Jump School after basic and advanced training. Needless to say, I scored expert with every infantry weapon whenever it was time to requalify. As an E4 I was assigned to be the radio man for the unit sniper squad; I quickly made buck sergeant within two years of active duty service. Next, I was attached to a special operations force where I was promoted to sniper team leader. Soon the Vietnam War officially ended, although we were still conducting operations (unofficially) in Vietnam, Laos, and Cambodia. After six years, having achieved the rank of Staff Sergeant, I left the military; they offered me a bonus and promotion to reenlist but I turned them down. Instead, I joined an elite group of mercenaries consisting of combat specialists: fighting men from the British, Italian, Israeli, Vietnamese, and American armed forces.

I made more money in two years than the entire six years I was in the Army. I had amassed forty some-odd confirmed kills by the time I turned twenty-seven. Unfortunately, I possessed no marketable skills other than reconnaissance, orienteering, camouflage, and shooting. Having been a gun for hire, I had a questionable reputation with the military, there was a price on my head with certain foreign governments, and I was being hounded by a crime family for employment. I decided it was time to change my ways, settle down, raise a family, and find a real job. Still, I made better money participating in shooting competitions and exhibitions than my regular job working in security. Thus, my skill didn't fade, it only got better.

Now, if you'd please allow me to fast-forward twenty-five years. At the age of fifty-two I had two grown-up kids with college degrees who were living on the west coast, an ex-wife who was married to my used-to-be best friend, and a mangy old dog that was on his last leg. Mind you, I wasn't hurting financially, I was just bored. My social life was absent without leave and I had retired from security work. That's about the time I received a visitor from the NSA.

It seems they wanted help with a problem but they needed someone to solve their problem without themselves getting involved, at least not legitimately. Usually when they needed something done underhandedly, they would hire outsiders so as to not be implicated if the truth came to light. I informed the gentleman I was retired, but he assured me everyone had their price. He was right, and I fully understood the ramifications. Before relating my latest escapade, some background information is necessary.

In case you haven't noticed, there exists a major dilemma in this country as to how to fight the war on terrorism. In theory, one would prefer to take the battle to the foe so that it doesn't land on native soil; but the bleeding hearts linger who are opposed to conflict even if it could mean saving their skins from an unexpected attack in their own backyard. The nation was divided: invade distant shores and bring fire and brimstone upon the perpetrators versus try to deal with them through diplomacy and peaceful negotiations. But the general public doesn't know squat about tactics and doctrine; they cannot understand that neither of these options represent an ultimate strategy. You can't blast them off the planet, because the instigators hide in homes so there would be too much collateral damage. You can't collaborate with the scallywags because they're hell-bent on annihilating you and everything you stand for. The only real ways of defeating them are to interrupt, divert, and confiscate their cash flows; confuse and deceive them with timely and convincing counterintelligence; plan organized insurgencies that create discord between governments and citizens; provide resources and funding to support rebellions; and covertly take out their leadership.

That's where I came in. Yeah, maybe my experience was outdated, and maybe I wasn't up-to-speed on the latest technology, and maybe I wasn't in tip-top physical condition, but the fundamentals hadn't changed one iota. Anyway, the next thing I knew I was at a beach house along the Virginia coast with a bunch of high-level operatives, a handful of well-decorated military brass, and a few influential politicians. We spent the weekend brainstorming on how to accomplish the above-mentioned objectives; of course, my part was to eliminate wanted terrorists without raising a foreign policy stink.

Everyone suspected that the number two guy, maybe others, were hiding in the mountains bordering Afghanistan and Pakistan. Nobody was exactly sure where, but there were possibilities. Given the remoteness of the region, and the fact these conniving individuals often dictated their evil schemes from remote areas, it stood to reason there would be meetings, couriers, transmissions, or movements which could potentially disclose their whereabouts. I mean, with the giant strides in surveillance capability and sensor technology, actionable intelligence, information gathering, sharing and correlation, and the imbedding of insurgency combatants like me, I figured the allies had to be getting closer to their prize. And I was right, to some degree.

Officials had been monitoring for quite some time a particular mountain range just inside the Pakistani border. Satellite images, high altitude fly-bys, and ground spotters had picked up some variations in the terrain and some apparent infrared signatures migrating in and around the entrances to a particular cave system. Although the enemy had many installations in caverns and tunnels, one location seemed significant to the analysts. The plan was to drop a sniper into the area for a few days and see if any targets of opportunity presented themselves. Guess who they commissioned to do this?

What the heck, I thought, it seemed a worthy cause. And the money wasn't bad either: ten thousand bucks a day, plus a quarter million each for any top ten kills. Of course, the bounty on their heads was way more than that. But the clandestine nature of the mission, and the fact that it wasn't approved or appropriated, meant that there was a limited budget. The problem, I reasoned, would be how to confirm the elimination of those being hunted.

Professionals had most of the snags worked out, but I added my two cents worth to make it agreeable to me. I would drop into the darkness at nine hundred feet over some treacherous territory with two hundred pounds of equipment. I would have to lug all that stuff over rugged and steep terrain approximately five clicks to a vantage point that enabled observing the mouth of the cave, all without being detected. I explained that we would have to cram most of the gear into an enlarged wicky bag, which I could release on a fifteen-foot rope before landing. I talked them into getting a guinea pig about my size to practice the jump a few times before I was convinced it could work. Meanwhile, I received much needed training, practice, and exercise; and I was becoming married to my weapon, maneuvering in terrain and under conditions that mirrored the mission.

Top-of-the-line in military paraphernalia was at my disposal, including some stuff that was authorized only with a top-secret clearance. First there was the cannon: a souped-up, lightweight, semi-automatic, fifty-caliber rifle with two reversible ten-round magazines. This baby was gorgeous: perfect for sniping people up to two kilometers, with its 3000 feet-per-second muzzle velocity, 750-grain armor piercing ammunition, and attached ten-power starlight/daylight scope bore-sighted to 1.5 kilometers. Altogether, it only weighed thirty pounds (not counting ammo).

PROSE AND POETRY

Man, with this you could sight-in on a victim and count the pimples on his face, while under a new moon at dark-thirty. Oh, I almost forgot, there was a silencer/flash suppression attachment resembling an old-timey milk bottle, which would muffle the report to nothing more than a mild crack, undetectable at full range without a sensor pointing at your line-of-sight.

I was provided a night vision device that exuded an ultraviolet wave to illuminate the landscape. It was the latest and greatest, imperceptible by an adversary unless they just happened to have a spectrometer calibrated to that precise frequency. Yeah, right; in their dreams. The attachment was equipped with a built-in digital rangefinder and compass. Oh, and get this: it had an integrated camera unit that enabled zoom photography up to three slides per second, with a memory card that could hold 650 three-second scans.

Another cool machine was the hand-held computer tablet, complete with topographic overlays, grids and landmarks, and a global positioning system enabling the calculation of current coordinates as well as projected coordinates given inputs of range and azimuth. Thus, I could navigate from point A to point B in the dark; I could plot the most concealed, direct, and unobtrusive approach to a designated site, and the apparatus would guide me there. Plus, I had real-time data on range, azimuth, and elevation interfaced to the weapon's sighting device. All the while, the folks in the rear could trace my every move. I was impressed with the strides that had been made in military equipment.

I also had an assortment of weaponry and supplies (in addition to the standard infantry issue): six programmable landmines disguised as big rocks, which were sensitive to movement (vibration waves); a few incendiary grenades and smoke grenades; a .45 caliber pistol with night sights and two 15-round magazines; a satellite cell phone with hot keys that could rapid-dial the support team or the shot-callers back home; a digital atomic wristwatch; camouflage netting; a lightweight lead-alloy, insulated blanket that masked infrared radiation; replacement batteries and parts; and rations and water for four days.

I slid out of a chopper on a windy and cloudy October night with a wind chill factor equal to freezing. The night vision viewer allowed me to maneuver the parachute to a wind-blown, sun-scorched draw, where I arrived with a thud. The place reminded me of my first snipe hunt some forty years before. It took me six hours to trudge my way to a ravine situated between two rocky bluffs and in defilade to the ridge. The blind provided LOS to the objective which was 2000 feet below my position, probably 1500 meters as the crow flies. I set up my campsite using the parachute to fashion a bed; I suspended camouflage over some scraggly trees and pointed rocks, and affixed it firmly to the ground with tent stakes and stones. I positioned the tripod at the crest of the blind and attached the rifle, with the muffled barrel barely peeking out the edge of the netting. Then I waited until dawn before catching an hour of shuteye.

I would maintain vigilance four continuous hours and then snooze for one. There was no activity for two days and fatigue was getting the better of me, not to mention claustrophobia as my area of operations was the size of the cockpit in a small airplane. It looked like the mission would be a bust, having expended over forty-eight grueling hours in the cold. I was fast asleep when a sensor alarm went off in my headset just after midnight. I spotted a helicopter ten miles to the south, heading in my direction. First, I surmised it was coming for me, until I noticed five guys in the valley preparing a landing zone. One went back into the cave and quickly returned, escorting another. I examined this person closely, reading every feature on his face: bushy gray beard, bottle glasses, mole under the left eye, buck teeth, proper height and weight. Yep, it was the number two man all right, getting ready to take a ride to who knows where.

I managed to get a snapshot of his facade while he wandered over to a clump of stones and sat down, head bowed and hands folded as if meditating. I checked the wind: there was a brisk breeze coming down the ridge from my six, but not enough to markedly affect the trajectory of the shot. Accounting for gravity, I quickly lined up the mark in the crosshairs, took a deep breath, and squeezed off a round. It smacked the dude squarely between the shoulders, piercing his flak jacket and blowing a hole the size of a grapefruit in his back, then ripping out his trachea and larynx upon exit. He lunged forward from the impact and plopped face down into the dirt, arms limp and legs bent. After a couple of seconds, he keeled over to his side, blood gushing from his mangled neck. He never knew what hit him.

It was minutes before anyone noticed. Then some dude began jumping up and down with his arms swinging all over the place. Another came and they each grabbed an armpit and dragged the guy's carcass back to the hideout. I got another snapshot of the corpse, so I'd have a before and an after. Two other guys were snuffing flares emplaced to indicate where to land; then one fired a flare into the air to wave off the bird. I observed the flight of the copter for a few minutes until it disappeared behind the distant hills; the tablet revealed approximate destination.

Knowing there would be a search party coming to welcome me, I broke camp and vamoosed out of there; but not before emplacing three mines and setting the timers for one hour. Either they would explode when invaders stepped into my nest and triggered them, or they would explode anyway in sixty minutes. I slipped out the back way and across the saddle, carrying a knapsack containing my munitions, vittles, and accessories. The rifle was strapped to my back, and the blanket tucked into my jacket. I had to carefully shimmy down to the base of the ridge as the incline was very steep, until I'd made it to level ground. Then I covered myself with the blanket and began to double-time across the stony wash using the handheld to guide me towards the last position of the chopper.

I heard explosions off in the distance and I guessed it was my campsite going up in smoke, probably along with a few overanxious stormtroopers since only fifty minutes had passed. I kept hoofing it up the rise and into the mountain, following a trail that I plotted as I went, a route that maximized the use of terrain masking and maneuverability. The fun part came when I got to the cliffs which I would have to scale in order to get a glimpse of the other side. I climbed diligently, ensuring both hands and feet found a hold; it took over an hour but I managed to reach the summit. As luck would have it, the chopper was perched about three clicks away, on a plateau that protruded from the foot of a spur. Just below it appeared to be an entrance to another burrow.

I was briefed how the enemy would operate from mountain caverns that had escape tunnels, some that proceeded for miles. Such ingenuity had thwarted previous efforts to round up fleeing combatants. It seemed an engineering feat that would have taken years, but then again, I guess they had plenty of time on their hands. It dawned on me that this might be a prime opportunity, as it appeared the chopper was awaiting other passengers. I hurried down a six-percent grade, covering a kilometer in fifteen minutes. I amazed myself being able to maintain my balance and endurance, seeing how I was probably too old to be romping around in a hostile environment such as this. I skidded to a halt and immediately emplaced my weapon on a boulder (I had ditched the tripod at the previous site). I didn't have time to get closer and I was at the edge of the maximum effective range of my weapon.

People already were beginning to migrate towards the chopper. Leading the pack was a tall lanky dude, with emaciated and cratered face, hook nose, pursed lips, silver left-upper incisor, long and narrow brown beard with matching turban. What do you know, it was bandito numero uno. I snapped his portrait then manned the weapon, tracking him to the bay door of the Soviet-made helicopter. As he was being lifted to the threshold, I quickly checked range, Kentucky windage, gravity. Once he had stooped inside the bird I sighted and fired. It seemed an eternity, the couple of seconds it took the round to fly to the target. The bullet pierced the back of his head, rupturing his medulla and carving off a few vertebrae. The egress of the bullet removed his lower jaw and tongue; it entered the breast of the person in front of him along with flesh from his leader's face.

Wavering like a reed in the breeze, he slipped backward, his knees sliding down the rim and his front teeth striking the deck of the chopper. He bounced, dropped, and slumped into a clump in the dust. Someone flipped him over and tried to lift him by the back; his neck was so badly broken that the head tilted at a ninety-degree angle. I photographed the scene with delight, knowing that this undertaking would be a smashing success (especially if I made it back alive). Anyway, some of his comrades shuffled him away while others began to pile into the helo. I reckoned they were on a search and destroy undertaking with yours truly as their motive.

Resuming my fix on the aircraft, I aimed the reticle to establish a pathway through the door and into the cockpit. The chopper began to rise from the ground, hovering for an instant. I fired a shot, lucky as it may have been; for it flew past the ear of a rifleman standing in the door and into the seat of the pilot, penetrating his kidney, out the stomach, probably shattering his arm too. The pilot was hurled into the control stick, which caused the aircraft's tail to abruptly ascend. The main rotor blades struck the granite spine of the spur and flipped the chopper onto its side, splattering rocks and shrapnel into bystanders. Suddenly the bird burst into flames exploding in a giant fireball. It was a spectacle worth photographing.

I emplaced two mines. Then I dumped all my nonessential gear, including the knapsack, water, blanket, helmet, silencer, supplies, entrenching tool, and poncho into a heap in a small crevice along my exit route; I popped two incendiary grenades and dropped them in. Then I skedaddled up the ridge, cognizant that whoever was left in command would send more stormtroopers. The mines went off about the time I reached the precipice; my pursuers were gaining on me. Daylight was coming but it was so dark. The descent tested me more than anything I'd ever done. Midway to the base of the cliff I emplaced the last mine, hoping to knock a few more off the side of the mountain. As soon as my feet touched solid ground, I phoned the rescue team and requested a lift, stating the keyword denoting coordinates of the riverbed where it all started. I was informed that help would arrive in two hours via coded response. I assumed I could make it by then if I really hustled.

Fortunately, I was traveling light and with adrenaline racing through my veins. I went bouncing down the wash like a jackrabbit, my knees knocking, my ankles burning, and my heart pounding like it was under arrest. Needless to say, I made it to the rendezvous point only minutes after my ride. They lowered a rope ladder and pulled me away from danger, while I ascended to safety. As we were departing the area, the mountain became lit-up like a gigantic strand of detonation cord. They must have blasted the entire tunnel system because it looked like an earthquake under the creeping rays of the rising sun. Who knows what secrets would forever be buried under tons of earth? I knew the corpses of those two bosses never would be uncovered.

We made it back to Kabul for breakfast. As yet, my green-suited associates had no idea what had just transpired. It wasn't long before rumors started to spread around the compound; soldiers were celebrating everywhere, patting me on the back, buying me drinks, shaking my hand, and offering congratulations. By lunchtime I was on a C-130 to Wiesbaden. I slept the whole trip, waking with my joints aching, muscles cramping, head throbbing and the aircraft touching down.

News programs were popping up around the globe with various renditions, most having very little knowledge of the facts. The administration played dumb, crediting Pakistani militia for offing the two primary players in the terrorist network. I didn't care because I was well-paid; besides, it's a lot less of a hassle being an unsung hero. While the jihadists tried to deny it, a few pictures surreptitiously found their way onto the Internet, displaying to the world the grisly remains, leaving no doubt. Surely there would be replacements standing in line. I had mixed feelings about the ordeal. Yes, they deserved to die. But in their eyes, I was the terrorist. And I vowed it would be my last snipe hunt.

---

# OLD MEMORIES DIE YOUNG

## (1995)

My interest in Psychology began in high school. That's when I became fascinated with such things as dreams, clairvoyance, and the unconscious mind. I received my Ph.D. in Clinical Psychology when I was only twenty-three years old, publishing my dissertation in a major medical journal on clinical hypnosis to facilitate treatment of anxiety and depression. Upon graduation, I immediately began working at the State Center for Disturbed Youth, a two-hundred bed facility; over a hundred kids from the ages of twelve to nineteen called the institution home each year, with another hundred or so passing through. Needless to say, most of the beds were occupied every month.

In the first year I was exposed to just about every psychopathology you can imagine. We housed victims of sexual, physical, even ritual abuse; most were grossly neglected and traumatized; many were runaways; there were gang members and others with a criminal record. I worked sixty to eighty hours a week trying to make a difference in the lives of each patient.

Clearly, I was not aware of my limitations; I became fatigued and developed my own depressive moods. This is largely because the clinician seldom knows how a kid turns out. Will they become a responsible adult or do they even make it that far? I had a classic case of what those in helping professions call "burnout". Anyway, I gave my thirty-day notice. I figured I would be more suited for academia. But after a few months to think about it, I returned to the Center and asked for my job back. They were taking interviews to replace me; I applied interviewed and got the job retaining my salary. I wanted to help these defenseless children regardless of the cost to me.

I was especially concerned about the welfare of a teenage girl named Heather. She was special, talented, smart but totally disconnected; the technical term is dissociation. She was repressing something horrible and was unable to let it out or let it go. She had just turned sixteen when she arrived, right before I came on board. She completed her high school diploma in one year yet she acted stupid and crazy, seemingly on purpose. She had a rare case of hysterical, retrograde amnesia. And although the vast majority of patients eventually recover essential lost memories, she hadn't. Further, hypnosis was ineffective in helping her unlock her past. I was determined to help her open up the closets of her mind and release whatever demons were hiding there. Heather was nearing eighteen when I returned and began working with her again.

She had become worse after I left; she couldn't remember who she was half the time. I knew who she was; we all knew more about Heather than she knew herself. The Center obtained her history from an aunt on her mother's side who lived in Cleveland. Heather's mother had become pregnant in high school and dropped out. She married a man twice her age for stability and security purposes. Heather and her stepfather never got along, but she was very close to her mother and her aunt. And here she couldn't even remember their names.

Heather had been convicted of murdering her parents. She had no recollection of them or the alleged incident. I reconstructed her entire life for her and she still refused to accept the facts as they were presented to her. That's what made me suspect we did not have enough of the facts, or what we thought we knew wasn't factual. Funny thing though; while she claimed not to remember anyone or anything, she always kept a photograph of her mother by her bed.

In January, the Center had a small party to celebrate Heather's birthday. About ten staff members and ten patients were present. How pretty she was, in a brand-new ensemble the senior staff pitched in to buy for her. I was struck by her attractiveness, actually she was quite stunning with hazel eyes that matched her outfit and semi-long auburn hair that matched her shoes. She did not hide the fact that she was attracted to me, but I always was able to maintain a professional outlook; at times this required considerable restraint on my part.

For example, I was starting a hypnotic induction with her, and she hopped to her feet, pulled up her top, and shook her boobs in my face. Then she plopped down on my lap and kissed me on the lips. I lifted her to her feet, pulled her shirt back down, and told her, "You know there is a time and a place for everything; and this is neither the time nor the place." She often played ignorant, but she was well aware of the established morals of civilized society; she merely ignored them at her convenience.

Three months passed and I was getting nowhere with her. All she wanted to do was talk about sex, make jokes, or complain about the accommodations and the staff. I wish I had paid more attention to her complaints, however; I might have been able to prevent another traumatic experience in her life. Yet, in retrospect, the event would prove to be the break I needed to untangle the web that existed in her unconscious.

Heather griped often about a certain staff member whom she accused of sexual harassment. There was no proof; it was her word against his, and everyone knew what a con artist she was. However, I too had great disdain for this particular person. He was too arrogant, bossy, aggressive, and heartless to be working in a therapeutic setting. He was the head of security. He ran the place like a concentration camp, and many of his subordinates behaved like thugs. However, he had more seniority than I and that kept him employed. Though I had more authority than he, my requests for his termination were never seriously entertained by the board.

Winter passed and Spring was in the air. With Springtime came blossoming flowers, and budding girls. Heather was an extremely sensual woman, and quite the tease. While she invited people to ogle at her, to her it was just a show. She was actually very inauthentic with regards to her sexuality. With others there was just the flirting, but with me it always involved touching. During our last session prior to Holy Week she exclaimed, "How in the world am I ever going to fall in love, get married, have babies, or experience any of the things normal girls my age experience if I have to stay locked up in this prison?"

She had a point. She was destined to stay in institutions indefinitely, unless she could demonstrate to society that she was not a threat to herself or to others. Her future looked pretty bleak. Soon, we would reassess her case. She likely would be moved to another facility until she turned twenty-one. Then she would go to a residential shelter for who knows how long. This scenario was upsetting even to a psychotherapist.

I went to the chapel at the Center on Easter Sunday; a Methodist preacher presided over the service. Heather attended, wearing a beautiful yellow and white gown and white gloves that her aunt had sent last Christmas. She looked magnificent. Apparently, I'm not the only one who thought so. There was an ice cream social after church for most of the residents. I complimented Heather on her appearance and she blushed. It was a rare moment when her true emotions were genuinely expressed.

I arrived at work Monday morning and the institution was in an uproar. So many things happened the night of Easter Sunday it's difficult to know where to begin. Someone had attacked Heather, attempting to rape her. In addition, one of the adolescent boys had been murdered. There were no suspects for either crime, only I had a hunch they were connected.

The detective who was assigned the case asked Director Collinsworth for an assistant who knew the dispositions and pathologies of the patients. I was selected to be that assistant. Our old friend Charlie, head of security, tagged along. Each resident was interviewed one by one to identify any potential witnesses or suspects. The interviews took a week to complete. Naturally, nobody knew anything.

Detective Larkin insisted we interview the staff, asserting that we shouldn't assume anyone's innocence. I agreed; Charlie disagreed. Larkin questioned staff members who were at the facility that night including Charlie. I had discreetly mentioned to the detective that Charlie was acting awfully nervous of late; further pointing out that he had several complaints against him including sexual harassment. After his interview, Charlie was excluded from further participation in the investigation, much to his dismay. So, Charlie proceeded to commence his own so-called investigation.

Detective Larkin and I fixated our attention on eight witnesses, four were staff members and four were patients. Each person was called back for a second interview. Two clients had acted suspiciously when they were asked if they had heard or seen anything. One absolutely refused to talk, as if holding something back. Another appeared afraid to speak, and feigned a delusional episode. A third client was the best friend of the murder victim and had the most to say about the events that transpired that fateful night. The fourth client was Heather herself. Two of the staff members were security guards who were supposed to be on duty during the period in question. Another staff member was the night nurse, and the other was Charlie. Although Charlie was off duty that night, he lived within the confines of the facility and was therefore, present. Everyone else had an acceptable alibi.

The murder victim, named Cory, was a pyromaniac who had accidentally killed his brother after starting their bedroom on fire. He was only thirteen years old and had been with us about a year. He had become close to another thirteen-year-old who witnessed the death of his mother when she was caught in the crossfire during a foiled drug deal. The two boys were practically inseparable. They were playing cards together in the television room when Cory had gone to the kitchen for some lemonade. He never returned.

About the same time, Heather was assaulted in the laundry facility where she was washing her bed sheets and pajamas after a menstrual accident. It was easy to put two and two together. Cory probably heard Heather cry for help and went to check it out. He interrupted a rape in progress and was silenced by the perpetrator. His body was found behind the auditorium; he had been strangled to death. Being the feisty little guy that he was, it was likely that a strong arm would be necessary to subdue the boy.

That nobody had heard anything was puzzling. The two security guards on duty were allegedly playing pool in the recreation hall with Charlie. Conveniently, nobody else was in the rec room at the time since it was closed on Sunday nights by 7:00 p.m. On duty personnel were not allowed to use the facility except to take short breaks, or to supervise when several patients were congregated there. The guards maintained they were there for fifteen minutes. Charlie claimed he was briefing them on security issues. It all sounded like a crock of you-know-what to Larkin.

But what case did Larkin have? There was no physical evidence except the bruises on Heather's arms, legs, and face, and on Cory's neck. It was obvious from medical examination, whoever attempted to rape Heather never completed the act. As before, she had total amnesia of the entire episode. I feared for her life. At my insistence she was given a private room in the infirmary and a nurse was assigned to keep an eye on her.

Larkin focused on two witnesses. The first was a fifteen-year-old boy diagnosed with a conduct disorder who was progressing towards full blown sociopath. He admitted to knowing something but informed that hell would freeze over before he had anything to say. The second was a seventeen-year-old girl who was obviously shaken by the incident; she appeared to have been coerced to remain silent.

Despite the flimsy circumstantial evidence, Larkin convinced the District Attorney to have a grand jury assembled. Charlie was the primary suspect, and by going to trial Larkin was hoping to smoke out any potential accomplices or witnesses. I was in attendance at the trial, and I convinced Heather to accompany me. I was hoping she would remember something but she just sat there as if being entertained by a TV mystery. The first day of the hearing produced absolutely nothing.

That night I decided to hypnotize Heather, hoping she might remember something, anything about the night she was assaulted. With any luck, since the experience was still fresh, she hadn't the time to bury it deeply. She was always an excellent subject because of her ability to dissociate. She was able to relax completely, and she was able to reach a deep state of trance, but she was unable to regress in time. Except this session was different. I took her step by step through the events leading up to the physical assault. Then I asked her to remember the assailant up against her. She cried, "No Daddy, please!" She immediately came out of the trance, sprang from her chair, and bolted out the door.

I had to think. There was something very disturbing about what she had said. I wondered if the assault had triggered an earlier experience involving her stepfather. I wondered if the memories were somehow linked, or possibly stored in the same location in her subconscious. Regardless, once again she had expressed herself spontaneously and there was no disputing it.

The next morning, I phoned Detective Larkin about the hypnotherapy session with Heather the previous night. He was intrigued but assured that the information was irrelevant as well as being inadmissible in court, which was soon to be in session at ten o'clock sharp. Heather and I arrived at the courthouse about five minutes late. Charlie was on the stand trying to convince the jury he had nothing to do with the murder of Cory or the assault on Heather.

We were sitting in the audience, listening to Charlie's sob story, when he was asked about previous harassment complaints levied by Heather. He denied it. Suddenly Heather arose from her seat shouting, "You lying son-of-a-bitch." Everyone gasped and stared at Heather. She sat back down beside me and whispered, "I remember everything." "Everything?" I queried. "Absolutely everything," she answered. I motioned to the D.A. as I approached the table. I whispered to him that now would be a good time for a recess to examine some new evidence. He agreed, and the judge complied.

Apparently, something Charlie said on the witness stand jogged Heather's memory. He testified, "I don't have the slightest interest in Heather, sexually or otherwise." Heather knew it was untrue from several previous encounters, especially after he tried to rape her. She couldn't hold back anymore. She insisted she would be willing to testify that Charlie was the one who assaulted her. The D.A. asserted that her testimony would probably carry little weight with the jury considering her mental condition. Had she come forward earlier, things might have been different. We had to come up with another strategy.

Larkin had a brainstorm. He concluded, "If we lean on the two guards, they might provide the state evidence, especially if they think they might be charged with accessory to murder." The D.A. agreed it was worth a chance. I was allowed to observe from the one-way window as Larkin and the prosecutor interrogated the guards individually. Knowing that Heather was ready to testify, both guards agreed to plead guilty to aiding and abetting in order to avoid charges of accessory to murder and sexual assault. It meant the difference between eighteen months and fifteen years in prison if convicted.

The next day the guards were called as rebuttal witnesses, and they spilled their guts on the stand. Both testified that they held lookout as Charlie accosted Heather in the laundry room. When Cory happened by, they apprehended him and held him for Charlie. Again, they stood guard when Charlie forced the boy to a secluded area to "counsel" him. They had no idea that Charlie would take the boy's life. They feared for their own lives, worried about the consequences if they ever were to betray Charlie.

The jury bought the story and indicted Charlie for aggravated sexual assault and second-degree murder. Other witnesses came forward at that time. The girl who had been threatened by the guards was ready to testify, since the guards had testified themselves. She'd heard a scream and noticed the two guards standing outside the laundry room. The kid who said he would never talk changed his mind, no doubt for the attention. He was watching from the window of his room when he noticed Charlie dragging a struggling boy by the neck. The case was open and shut.

Things normalized at the Center in a few months. Charlie pled and got twenty years. The entire security section had to be overhauled. Heather began a rapid return to complete mental health. Uncovering the memory of that frightful Easter enabled Heather to recover the memory of the night her parents died. She relived each moment in her mind. It was a grueling but necessary journey for her.

Her stepfather raped Heather one night when her mother was playing bridge with her girlfriends. The following week on bridge night he attempted to repeat the crime. Only this night, the bridge party had been cancelled due to illness. Heather's mother returned early to find her husband in the process of molesting her daughter. The stepfather continued, not realizing that Heather's mother had come in from the garage and was standing in the kitchen. She grabbed a kitchen knife, rushed to the living room, and stabbed him in the back as he was ravaging Heather. He immediately got up, pulled the knife out of his back and chased her back into the kitchen, where he impaled his wife in the stomach. Meanwhile, Heather had grabbed another knife, and with both hands ran it deep into her stepfather's back. The blade found his heart and he died instantly. Then Heather pulled the knife out of her mother's stomach and tossed it aside. She held her mother's head in her arms in total shock. The ruckus was heard by a neighbor and reported to the police, who found Heather in that same spot. Since Heather never recalled the incident, and since her bloody fingerprints were on both knives, she was found guilty of murder though motive was never established.

I had her case reevaluated by the governor's office and they agreed that the facts fit her story. Heather was immediately granted a new trial and promptly acquitted of the murders. A week before her nineteenth birthday was her assessment hearing at the State Center. I pleaded her case. I convinced the board that there was no reason to keep Heather in the system any longer. She was delighted when she heard she was going to be set free. She agreed to go to college, where she would be given a grant and offered a room at the dormitory. She would still receive regular checkups and medication management services. Heather decided she wanted to study law and possibly become a judge.

Heather was packed and ready to go on her birthday. A combination birthday and sendoff party was held that afternoon. Heather was so happy; all of her emotions were sincere, positive, and spontaneous. It disbanded at quitting time, after which I took her out for a night on the town. She was wearing the same dress that she'd worn to chapel one fateful Easter Sunday. We went to a very expensive restaurant for dinner; the waiter brought some complimentary wine with our dinner. Heather asked if it was okay and I allowed her the one glass. It was the first time that she'd tasted alcohol of any kind. We danced for a few hours and then she asked if we could visit the beach, which always was a priority if she ever became free. I answered, "Why not?"

I parked by the boardwalk and we doffed our shoes and stockings. We walked hand-in-hand along the shoreline in the soft, wet, and firm sand. The moon had just arisen in the eastern sky; its reflection glistened on the water. We stopped, facing the ocean. The golden moonlight sparkled on each wave crest, creating tracks from the horizon to our feet. Heather sighed, "Isn't it beautiful?" I looked into her moonlit eyes, and responded, "Most definitely. And you are quite beautiful too, I might add."

After a brief moment of silence, I kissed her. I knew she didn't have much experience, but I never would have known it from her kiss. She was so passionate and her kiss so stimulating that my heart skipped a beat. I could tell she was moved as well when she remarked, "I guess we just had to wait for the right time and the right place." I suggested, "We have all the time in the world now. Is there another place I can take you?" "I'd go anywhere with you, anytime, every day," she replied. After a brief pause she continued, "I have an idea! Why don't we go to your place?"

About six months later the state of Florida passed a regulation prohibiting licensed mental health professionals from having relations with former clients or patients. By then, Heather and I were happily married and expecting a child. I was still working at the center and Heather was in college. I can't say I disagreed with the new law, but neither did I feel in violation of it. Besides, it was not retroactive. Oh well, live and learn the people say; it happens every day to everyone. But there is a purpose behind everything. And for that we must be grateful.

## NO TIME

### (2015)

I've been stacking up the miles though no two are alike;
Well, except to the bike they are mostly the same.
I've been counting the trials and subtracting the blame.
But it all evens out—that's the name of the game.

On the freeway of life, it's a mile a minute;
I'm in it to win it, whether fortune or fame.
Amidst hardships and strife, but to none I have claim;
For it all evens out—that's the name of the game.

The mileage takes its toll on my body and soul;
Not to mention the tires and electrical wires.
I choose my direction, my rising and falling.
God grants me election, and shows me my calling.

I've been piling on years and I'm getting neck deep.
But before I can sleep there are miles yet to go;
Past the tears and the fears, through the rain and the snow.
Until it is over, there is still room to grow.

I've a journey ahead, when I'm raised from the dead.
No roadmaps in the sky, but lots of space to fly.
No time limitations, but innumerable destinations.

# THE MERMAID

## (1998)

I accepted the temporary position of Senior Marine Biologist for one practical reason: I needed to get away for a while. The increase in my salary was a minor consideration. My social life was monotonous, my love life had been nonexistent, and I was growing increasingly impatient with the hectic pace of life in the city. An extended trip aboard a mini-cruiser was just the therapy I needed.

The personnel assembled for the adventure comprised extremely professional and knowledgeable oceanographers and marine scientists. The only exception was the pugnacious Project Manager, who had very little knowledge of science, much less personnel management. He was terribly arrogant and egoistic. His primary goal in life was to become famous, and enjoy the fortune, power, and riches associated with his anticipated glory. I will refrain from providing names; I'm sure most of the crew would prefer it that way.

Our six-month excursion was to seek out new life forms. The PM had financial backing to investigate a story appearing in several tabloid periodicals. Apparently, sea monsters had been reported on occasion by ship officers from Japan and the Philippines. We were commissioned to establish if there was any validity to these tales.

Our voyage brought us to some remote islands in the South Pacific. Much of this particular island group was not on any official maps. The land masses had been rapidly evolving as a result of continuous tectonic activity beneath the sea. We spent six weeks exploring the islands by dispatching reconnaissance patrols on each of three skiffs. We catalogued a few invertebrates, mollusks, and ferns. The first day of the seventh week I spotted a cove where there was an abundance of fresh water flora and fauna. The area was fed by a number of underground springs that were heated to temperatures exceeding one hundred degrees Fahrenheit via volcanism. Low tide revealed a series of subsurface and aboveground caves. The entire scene was as fascinating to me as it was puzzling. In accordance with my recommendation, we focused our attention there. A base camp was erected in an elevated area along the shore.

This locality had several unique species that thrived in both fresh and salt water. Our studies kept us quite busy. After a few months we started sighting creatures resembling large sea serpents. Constant vigilance was maintained in hopes of getting more than just a glimpse. Unfortunately, these creatures never came within 150 meters, and they never surfaced long enough to obtain a clear view or snapshot. They were likely fearful of human beings, and rightfully so. We examined them on occasion from afar using binoculars.

I was able to ascertain a few basic facts. They were fresh water creatures that thrived in warm water. Apparently, they made their homes in the caverns beneath the sea. They had to surface to breathe, yet they remained in the water all the time. They were amphibian in nature, seemingly caught in a metamorphosis that was never completed. One thing was certain: this species was unlike any I had ever studied.

During the sixth month of our seclusion from civilization, I became somewhat of a recluse. I camped alone, about a kilometer from the main installation. I guess I needed time to contemplate, and to compile my notes. I was in the process of bathing myself in a gigantic heated pool when I was startled by the sound of a splash behind me. I turned around to see a beautiful water woman emerge from the ripples. This was a novel experience! I had never believed in mermaids; I'd never even fantasized about them. It was a scientific impossibility, I thought.

Her hair was long and rainbow-colored. Her eyes were sea green, her skin pink, and her lips, violet. She had small fleshy breasts, but no nipples, navel, or pubic region. Her hands were humanoid, but webbed, with no fingernails. As I stood there flabbergasted, she made a back dive into deeper water. I noticed a yellow-green dorsal fin that spanned the length of her back, reaching to her posterior, which revealed a partial buttock joined to a dolphin-like tail also yellow-green in color.

She resurfaced about thirty meters away where she floated stationary on her tummy and peered back at me, her head resting on folded arms. I wanted to speak but I was dumfounded. We gazed at one another for an hour before she submerged. I stood there, awestruck, unaware of my nakedness. It was as if I was Adam and this place was Eden; I wasn't yet sure if she was Eve or the serpent.

I remained by the pool for several days, although I had long since run out of rations. I was collecting clams near the shoreline for a meal when she appeared again, keeping her distance as before. I held my hands out inviting her to come closer, and she did. She stopped about ten feet away; then looked into my eyes with a searching stare that caused time to stand still. Somehow, she knew that I was hungry so she brought a fish, and we had lunch.

She visited me four times during the next two days. I was amazed at her ability to communicate telepathically a profound sense of caring. I never verbalized anything; it would have been meaningless, anyway. Finally, on the evening of the third day we made physical contact. As our fingers touched, I felt an electrical charge that spread throughout my body, stimulating my very spirit. I was aroused, not sexually, but nevertheless, emotionally. Suddenly, she darted away.

Approaching along the coast was a search party that had been sent to liberate me. I dressed myself and returned with them on the skiff. I assembled everyone and related my close encounter. After informing them of my findings and sharing my notes, they were astonished. They thought I'd lost my marbles but were intrigued nonetheless. I wanted to stay behind, but the Captain insisted that we did not have sufficient rations or supplies. The PM assured that additional funding would be forthcoming, given this extraordinary discovery.

The group encouraged me to spend my last day at the secluded pool. They wanted me to get a photograph. I didn't need to be persuaded, because I had fallen for the lovely nymph and I very much wanted to be near her. I anxiously waited for her to come, which she did, reluctantly. She sensed my burning desire for her and responded with subtle enthusiasm.

Finally, we embraced. Again, I had no accurate sense of time. As I held her soft and slick body next to mine, I could feel an intense love emanating from her heart. The feeling was stimulating and mesmerizing. I was becoming sexually aroused, when she was scared away.

Several of my cohorts had attempted to hide in the dunes with photography equipment and fishing nets, eager to capture her one way or the other. I was indignant. I hurried ashore and confiscated everything, hurling the lot into a deep crevice from which molten lava regularly spewed.

The Director began chastising me and threatened me, but I stopped him cold with my retort. It was time he learned to reorganize his priorities. We had a chance to reveal to this fascinating specimen that humans could be trusting and compassionate, but the surprise party managed to convince her that the opposite was true. The PM became violent. He grabbed at my throat, but I twisted his arm backward. He pleaded for mercy, suggesting that I had nothing left to prove. For once in his life, he was correct.

The skiff left for base camp. I gathered my belongings and slowly followed along the beach. The mermaid maiden called to me without making a sound. I turned to see her sad eyes return my tearful glance. Our eyes were locked for several minutes before she disappeared one last time into the blue depths. I stood there awhile, hoping she would reappear, knowing that she would not. I contemplated the possibility of being seduced into joining her in her world forever.

The return cruise was arduous. Nobody could agree on what, if anything, they had witnessed. The PM was a constant nuisance, especially after I informed him that I would not be renewing my contract. He was unwilling to believe me when I told him that another expedition would prove fruitless. Human vanity and deceit had destroyed any opportunity to continue interacting with this fascinating species. Besides, there was a spontaneous evolution occurring that likely would change all the creatures we encountered.

The crew was divided when we disembarked. Most of them were appalled at my apparent self-righteousness. The ones I truly considered comrades silently applauded the integrity and sincerity of my decision. They too had realized the actual purpose of our mission, the meaning of life itself. The unbelievers would eventually waste the better part of their formidable years pursuing a fantasy that would never be realized, much less proven.

Later, I wondered if the experience was absolutely genuine. I mean, a mermaid lady—who would believe it? Perhaps I had been touched by an angel. Regardless, I knew I would never be the same. I had a renewed sense of hope and peace, and her constant memory always made me glad.

## A SURFACE LOVE

(1976)

A surface love is all we own;
It doesn't seep into the heart.
How deep we've come is still unknown;
'Twere better off to be alone
Than strive for love yet stay apart.

You say you love, but do you know?
Then show me that your love is real;
For love, if true, would overflow.
To be sincere, your love must grow,
For me to feel the way you feel.

And if it's fate that you'll be mine,
Our minds together, one would make.
Would this be so then now it's time
That you would show me just one sign,
Before I've lost the love you'll take.

# CROSSROADS

(2000)

This is a story about love and hope, about growth and responsibility. It is also a story about purpose and commitment, desire and accomplishment. The impetus is a critical period of life, when children are expected to behave as adults: a transition point of no return.

In early August, 117 teenagers between the ages of sixteen and eighteen converged on a quaint little village in the Blue Ridge Mountains of Virginia called Camp Woody. There they would exercise their talents to meet the demands of a changing world, while developing the interpersonal skills necessary to deal with people on a professional level. The retreat provided a unique experience to prepare young adults for competing in the world of business and commerce. Parents wishing to enroll their kids had to sign up a year in advance and pay a non-refundable fee; the waiting list was quite extensive due to the popularity and success of the program.

The teens loaded onto busses that picked them up at designated locations from the surrounding region. Each teen was allowed two medium pieces of luggage and one carry-on bag for the ten-day ordeal. They were permitted to bring $100 in spending money for entertainment, crafts, and snacks. The money, kept in an envelope bearing the individual's name, was turned over to the business office immediately upon arrival onsite, and could be withdrawn in $10 increments. This virtually eliminated any occurrences of theft. Anyone committing an act of violence, vandalism, or breaking the cardinal rules would be expelled immediately; any damages to the facilities incurred charges to the parents or legal guardians.

The busses meandered up a winding dirt road to a clearing at the foot of a large mountain ridge. There were several tributaries intersecting the outer boundaries of the site, which was carved out of the dense forests that encircled it. Several buildings were arranged in a horseshoe configuration. The administration building was in the middle, with the business office on one side and a small infirmary on the other complete with a live-in attending nurse and an on-call second year intern from a nearby medical school. North of the admin building was the auditorium, which included a stage and assorted musical instruments to be reserved for use by students. Toward the south was the mess hall and kitchen. Next to the mess hall was a large recreation center, equipped with a trading post, arcade, board games, pool tables, snack machines, jukebox, restrooms, and lounge areas inside and outside. Next to the auditorium were an indoor swimming pool, equipment room, boys' and girls' bathhouses, and locker area. On the

PROSE AND POETRY

outskirts of the horseshoe were ten dormitories, five on either side. The girls' dorms faced the boys' dorms across a combination football-soccer field, and three concrete tennis courts. Within each dorm were six bunkbeds and one double bed; thus, the dorms housed up to twelve students and one counselor. Attached to the rear of the admin building were apartments for the senior staff.

Friday evening teenagers began to disembark, crowding at the parking area located between the road and the compound. Everything appeared disorganized at first, but it was all part of the grand design. The kids interacted while they awaited their baggage and subsequent orientation and tour. Relationships began to evolve and cliques were already being formed as the students selected the barracks that would be their home for the coming days. They dumped their gear on their bunks before consuming the evening meal that was served promptly at 6:30. After dinner was a mandatory assembly in the auditorium, which featured an introduction to the program, a presentation of the rules, and distribution of materials including an activity schedule. Short, compulsory classes were held each day in which the students would be educated in such topics as job searching, business ethics, budgeting, parenting skills, communications skills, and self-discipline.

Numerous competitive events were part of the program including sports, brain games, the arts, and academics. Attendees were encouraged to participate in assorted activities and events, particularly the various competitions being offered. Blue, red, and yellow ribbons were incentives for participation in the competitions. Little silver charms depicting the events were attached to the ribbons. The teens were allowed to compete in as many as six events.

Lights out was at ten and reveille was six-thirty. Admittance to the barracks was prohibited between eight a.m. and eight p.m., unless accompanied by an adult with a key. Breakfast was at seven sharp and lunch was noon to one. The requirements for promptness were imposed for all meals, events, and classes: show up on time or miss out; parents would receive attendance and deportment reports so students usually did what they were told. While the place appeared to the kids like a concentration camp at first, they quickly became accustomed to the regimen and began enjoying themselves.

The first full day, Saturday, was mostly free time. Kids got acquainted, they signed up for activities, use of equipment, and competitions; and they relaxed. They played volleyball, touch football and tennis, and went hiking and swimming. They conversed, joked, and argued. Late that afternoon there were a dozen boys playing football together when the first altercation occurred. A big teen shoved a smaller teen to the ground after he'd caught a pass for a considerable gain. Immediately a face-off occurred. A counselor observing the incident paused to see how the young men would handle it.

A recent graduate named Benny leapt to his feet and confronted the other, larger boy. His nickname was Hoss, who had finished his junior year during which he played varsity defensive guard. "The rules say no rough play, and you pushed me down on purpose," accused Benny. "It was an accident; I couldn't stop," lied Hoss. "Accident my ass," interjected Benny's high school chum Robbie. "Game's over," concluded Benny as he tossed the football at Hoss's feet and marched off the field, with the rest of his interim partisans close behind. "You're just a bunch of wusses," shouted Hoss, who stood there with two other fellows who had yet to abandon the game. One of the guys, a senior named Brent, was the quarterback of Hoss's high school team and had been eagerly anticipating scholarship offers from reputable universities. The other fellow, named Perry, was the kicker at a high school from a neighboring town that had defeated Brent's team in the regional final by scoring a field goal in the closing seconds.

Just then, Benny made an about face and returned to the field. "Who you calling wusses," he countered adding, "I'm not afraid of you." Brent butted in, "It's 'cause you're quitting since you know we're better players than you." "Real big words for a varsity quarterback, but I bet I can catch better than you," remarked Benny. "Five bucks says you can't," was Brent's retort. "Fine, then," said Benny, "We'll throw passes at each other starting at 40 yards, then 30, 20, 10, and 5; the one who drops the most passes loses." "Agreed," Brent stated as they shook hands. "The pass has to be catchable, though," added Robbie.

They faced one another, Brent standing under the sole goalpost and Benny on the thirty-yard line. At first glance, it didn't appear to be a fair match. Brent stood well over six-feet and weighed about two hundred pounds. Benny was a mere five-ten and maybe one-fifty. Brent tossed the first pass, deliberately aiming it high above Benny's head. Benny sprang into the air and grabbed the pigskin with both hands to Brent's amazement. Benny's pass was lobbed high so as to make a wide arc to the ground. Brent bobbled the toss, but managed to haul it in. Brent moved forward ten yards for his next throw, which he purposely aimed at Benny's feet. Benny dropped to his knees and caught it right in the breadbasket, again to the surprise of his opponent. Benny's pass was not as challenging and was easily controlled by Brent. Benny moved forward for Brent's next effort, which he threw towards Benny's left side with high velocity. Benny had to take several quick steps before nabbing the ball in his armpit. Next, Benny tossed a spiraling lateral with amazing speed, which floated above Brent's head. Again, Brent had a little trouble handling it but did not let it drop.

Now they were ten yards apart. Brent aimed a dart towards Benny's crotch, cutting loose with a tight spiral, expecting it would knock Benny down. Benny caught it securely, bending his right leg to help cushion the blow of the incoming missile. A look of frustration came over Brent, who couldn't believe that Benny was able to control his best bullet. Then Benny, who had been holding back, gave Brent a little of his own medicine. In his own right, Benny was a fairly accomplished passer, unbeknownst to Brent. Benny steered a bullet with all his might, which bounced off Brent's chest and through his fingertips, falling to the ground. At this point, Brent was fuming, knowing that Benny had the advantage. As they faced off at five yards, Brent looked intense for he desperately wanted to hurt Benny. He fired the football at Benny's face. Benny hopped back, extended his right hand into the air, and blocked the pass into the sky; then he ran under the ball and snagged it before it touched the grass.

A crowd of spectators cheered with delight. Then they stared at Brent wondering what he would do. Clearly embarrassed but not wanting to lose face, Brent reached into his pocket, located a five-dollar bill, wadded it up and threw it at Benny. One of the observers named Francis who sported radically thick glasses ran forward, picked up the bill, straightened it out, and handed it to Benny. "Thanks," replied Benny. By this time, a small gathering had congregated on the field, while Brent and Hoss slithered away. Perry congratulated Benny, introducing himself with a handshake. "Have you ever played varsity?" asked Perry. "The football coach cut me 'cause he thought I was too small," explained Benny continuing, "So I tried out for tennis instead, but I quit the team 'cause the tennis coach was a major butthole." I kind of wanted to letter in something but it wasn't to be." "You've got a good pair of hands and an arm to boot." Perry informed. "Punting was my forte; that was the position I started at," added Benny. "I guess we'll both be fighting for the grand prize in the punt, pass, and kick competition," Perry determined. "I guess so," Benny agreed. Then Benny shouted, "Come on everybody," waving his trophy to the small group still remaining, "The sodas are on me!"

Benny was already developing quite a following. There were his schoolmates Robbie, Robbie's girlfriend Sheila, and their mutual friend Antonio who had flunked one year for ditching too much. Perry joined the group, as well as Francis. Francis had made friends with another boy everyone called Brain because on the bus he boasted of his straight-A status ever since the third grade. There were also other girls, Thelma, who had already begun to develop a crush on Antonio, and her chubby little friend, Betsy. One distinct characteristic of this assemblage was that they were all very intelligent and talented individuals.

After supper, the group temporarily disbanded, reconvening at the recreation center around the jukebox. By nine, the teens were worn out and adjourned to their respective dorms to unwind before curfew. Sunday morning began with a generic church service advocating reverence to God, duty to country, and resolve for brotherly love. Following the service was an ice-cream social in the picnic area. Music was provided via a portable stereo AM/FM cassette player belonging to the site coordinator who had brought several popular tapes. The congregation engaged in dancing, singing, socializing, grilled hamburgers and hotdogs, homemade ice cream, fruit punch, the works. The festivities went on for hours. By three o'clock, Benny and Robbie became weary of the noise, and escaped to the tennis courts to loosen up. Robbie and Sheila already were signed up for the mixed-doubles tournament, but Benny had yet to find a partner.

As Benny and Robbie returned volleys, they noticed two young ladies two courts down playing rather vigorously. The boys were intrigued, so they ceased play and watched the girls in action. After about fifteen minutes, the ladies took a break. Benny approached exclaiming, "I'm impressed. You chicks are great!" The four introduced each other. Benny was quite attracted to a girl named Linda. She had curly blonde hair that bounced around her shoulders, and she had striking blue eyes. She had a well-proportioned, curvaceous and athletic frame. Her companion named Helen was muscular and tall, but nevertheless, feminine. Helen suggested, "You fellas want to double up?" "Sure," their counterparts replied in unison.

Benny joined Linda on one side of the court and the play began. The four finished two full sets, with each team winning one set by a margin of 6-4. It was a very invigorating match to say the least. As the four stood there, gulping water and discussing the facilities, Robbie's girlfriend Sheila approached; she was clearly upset that her partner was playing with another. As Robbie was smoothing things out with Sheila, Helen slipped away. About that time Perry and Antonio were arriving. Antonio announced, "I'm ready for an ice cool beer, Benny." "A cold brew would really go down good right now, Tony, let's do it," was Benny's reply. "Where are you going to find any beer?" Linda inquired. "Follow us," Tony responded.

The six of them trekked down to a stream where Tony had stashed a six-pack of beer he'd managed to sneak into camp in his suitcase. He'd placed the beer in the water to keep it cool the night before. Tony passed a can of beer around to all and they simultaneously popped the tops. Tony had also smuggled a pack of cigarettes, so the guys lit up a smoke as they sipped their beers. Suddenly, they were startled by Francis, who had crept up from behind exclaiming, "You're busted!" "I always thought you looked like a narc," joked Robbie. Everyone began calling him Narc after that.

Linda drank half of her beer before handing it over to Narc to finish. After about an hour they gathered the cans, crushed them, and wrapped them in a dirty towel for disposal, then returned for supper. As they were strolling along, Benny asked Linda if she had a tennis partner. She informed that she did not so the two agreed to sign up, becoming the final eligible mixed-doubles team. They made it back just in time for dinner, being the last to be served. That night a nature film was shown in the auditorium, and most everyone attended but it was not mandatory.

Tournament events began Monday morning with foot races, swimming heats, and tennis matches. Although Linda and Benny hadn't much practice together, they managed to defeat their opponents in a hard-fought match lasting an hour-and-a-half. Robbie and Sheila also advanced, as did Helen and her partner, Jamie. That afternoon began the academic decathlon, the one event having the largest number of competitors. Not surprisingly, Narc and Brain were the one's everyone believed they had to beat. Competition resumed on Tuesday. Robbie and Sheila were eliminated in the second round of tennis by none other than Helen and Jamie. Linda and Benny handily defeated their opponents. By Wednesday, competition was beginning to get fierce in every category. Linda and Benny squeaked by their adversaries and moved onto the semifinals.

The gang was unwinding that evening outside the rec hall, while the jukebox blared and several couples danced. Just before chow time, Brent and Hoss approached the table where Benny and Linda were chatting. Brent rudely interrupted, saying, "Let's dance Linda," as he reached for her hand. "Get lost," she replied. "Come now," said Brent, proclaiming, "You shouldn't be seen with these nerds." Benny interjected, "If you get your head out of the clouds, you'll realize there's some really cool people down here on earth." Hoss tugged at Linda's arm saying, "Let's go." Linda replied, "No," as she jerked away. Hoss reached for her arm again and Linda pleaded loudly, "Leave me alone." About that time Benny rose to his feet, posing, "What about the word *no* do you not understand?" "Stay out of this," said Hoss, "or I'll have to rearrange your face." Linda stood up, saying, "It's OK, Benny, I don't want any trouble."

Benny commanded Linda, "Linda, you sit down this instant, uh please." Dazed, she complied prompting Hoss to become enraged. Hoss rounded the table snarling, "You've been asking for this." He took a swing at Benny but Benny nonchalantly backed away as the arcing fist pulled Hoss off balance. Hoss charged at Benny like a crazed bull; quickly Benny slid a chair between them resembling a twirling matador. Hoss wrestled with the chair a few steps before stumbling over it and skinning his elbow on the walkway. At this point, several spectators began laughing. Hoss was red with rage. He snatched the chair and chucked it over a rail, breaking a window in the facility. He moved in on Benny bracketing him like a linebacker. Benny took a few swift steps sideways, then backwards. Anticipating Hoss's next move, Benny placed a running roll block in front of the massive oaf, who subsequently tripped as he lunged forward striking his cheek on one of the tables. The table and attached umbrella shade collapsed and fell upon him while he tumbled to the cement. The spectators were roaring.

Three counselors came rushing to the scene; one apprehended Benny, and the other two subdued Hoss. The supervisor announced, "The penalty for fighting is expulsion, so both of you can pack your bags immediately while we call your parents to come get you." They began to escort the boys to the barracks when Linda ran up to the supervisor who was escorting Benny and poked him in the back with her forefinger. "Just a doggone minute!" she screamed. "Benny didn't do anything; he never even threw a punch. It was that tub of lard over there who started everything." She continued, "You have no right to accuse people when you don't even know the facts. You think you can just jump to conclusions. You didn't even bother to ask anybody what they saw, and there must be at least ten eye witnesses standing right here."

Several others chimed in, "Yeah that's right." "Who do you think you are, the judge and the jury?" Linda continued, "This isn't fair and we're going to tell our parents; this is a bunch of BS. They give you a little power and then you take advantage." Again, the crowd chimed in, "Yeah, we're gonna tell." "This is an outrage!" "You'll be sorry." Finally, the parade halted, and the supervisor announced, "This is mutiny." He continued, "Doesn't anyone here believe in law and order?" Benny looked him squarely in the eye and explained, "Law and order without justice is tyranny, Sir!"

There was a brief period of silence. "Okay," the counselor said, "You tell me what you saw," he demanded waving his hand at Linda. She proceeded to describe the entire episode and those present corroborated her testimony. Hoss intervened, "That's a lie. He hit me in the face with a chair. Tell, him Brent." The counselors looked at Brent who hesitated before stating, "I only just caught the end of it; I really didn't see what happened." "All right," the counselor said pointing his finger respectively at Narc, Linda, and Betsy, "You, you, and you, be in my office immediately after supper. I want detailed statements about what you witnessed in case this guy's parents try to sue us or something." "No problemo," declared Narc. The supervisor turned to Benny and chided him, "I'm going to let you off this time, but if you get into any more trouble, you are history." "Don't worry," Benny assured.

The crowd disbanded. Robbie changed the subject, announcing, "I'm famished." "You all go ahead," said Benny, "We'll catch up in a minute." Benny led Linda to their table, while the rest of the group departed for the mess hall. Benny flopped down and scooted his chair to face Linda.

He grasped her hands in his and explained, "That's the neatest thing any girl has ever done for me, Linda, sticking up for me like you did. I just wanted you to know how great that made me feel." Linda declared, "What you did, defending me from that monster, and taking charge of the situation and all... Well that's the bravest and most decent thing any guy has ever done for me, and I want you to know how much I appreciate you too." A moment passed as they gazed into one another's eyes, until they slowly leaned forward, touched their lips together, and kissed.

"I could really fall for you," confessed Benny. Linda blushed. A moment of silence elapsed; then Benny stood up and suggested, "Let's get in line before we miss dinner." He held Linda's hand as she arose from her chair, interlacing her arm in his. They began walking toward the mess hall when Benny stated, "I bet you'd make a great defense lawyer, the way you made those counselors back down." "Hmm," was her response. They took a few steps, then at once abruptly halted, spontaneously faced the other, passionately kissed, then embraced. After a minute or so, they quickly looked up to see if anyone was watching, then hastened toward the mess hall holding each other closely. Linda reminded Benny, "We can't be caught disobeying the rules or they'll kick you out, so let's just hold hands for right now and everyone will think we're completely innocent." "That's another thing I like about you, Linda," declared Benny, "You're always thinking. You've got a sharp mind. I bet you have an IQ of one-forty or something," he concluded. "Hey, you're pretty bright yourself, Benny," she argued. "You're definitely almost as intelligent as I am," she snickered. Benny rejoined, "Just think, if we ever were to have children together, they'd probably be freaking geniuses." "Imagine that!" Linda exclaimed as they took their place at the end of the chow line.

They had just dropped their trays on the table where the gang was seated when Brent approached. "Mind if I sit down," he uttered as he plopped onto the empty chair across from Linda. "It's a free country," sneered Narc who was sitting in the chair beside him. "You're lucky Hoss didn't tear you to pieces, Benny boy," remarked Brent. "Brawn is no substitute for speed," Benny responded continuing, "You ought to know that as well as anyone." "Yeah, but even the quickest backs can get stopped behind the line of scrimmage," countered Brent. "Only if the tackle beats some lineman who's slower than he is," was Benny's counterargument. Brent continued, "If Hoss ever got his hands on you, you'd never forget it." Perry interjected, "I gotta hand it to you man, it took balls to stand up to Hoss like you did."

Linda glanced back at Benny with a twinkle in her eye. "Just what the hell do you see in this dud?" questioned Brent as he leered over at Linda. Brent continued, "You could've had me and instead you'd rather hang out with this loser." Benny peered inquisitively over at Linda who related, "Can you believe I actually dated this goon twice last year?" Then Linda looked at Brent and informed, "You think you're God's gift to women, but it's all a figment of your imagination." "What's he got that I ain't got?" Brent whined. Linda replied, "He's got tact and versatility." She continued, "And you want to know what you've got that he doesn't?" "Arrogance, self-centeredness, and an inflated ego," she charged, answering her own question. Benny interrupted, "The only person you'll ever find, Brent, is someone like you, completely self-absorbed; and you'll discover that neither one of you can satisfy the other because all you care about is yourselves. You'll have nothing you can share because you don't know how to give, only to take." "There you go preaching again," declared Brent. "I know what I'm doing, and I don't need any advice from you," he barked stomping away. Linda shouted back at Brent, "Someday you're going to fall from your high horse and it'll hurt more than you know."

After sundown a motion picture was shown in the auditorium. Benny and Linda, Robbie and Sheila, Tony and Thelma, and Jamie and Helen were among the couples siting in the back so they could steal a smooch every so often. Numerous couples had paired off over the past several days as planned. Thursday morning came quickly. Benny and Robbie barely missed breakfast and had to dine on junk food from the snack bar. Shortly afterwards were the two semifinal matches in which Linda and Benny, and Helen and Jamie advanced to the final round. That afternoon a contest in academic trivia was held for the five finalists. As expected, Brain took first place, followed by Narc; third went to a girl named Danielle. Awards ceremonies were held that evening for the academic decathlon, educational board games, the swimming events, and the track and field events. This was followed by performances in the areas of art, music, drama, and poetry. During that segment, Betsy sang a beautiful ballad and seemed a cinch to win first prize in the talent contest.

On Friday morning were the tennis finals. There was scarcely enough room around center court for the spectators. Benny and Linda fought hard but were defeated in three sets and had to settle for second place. Linda disappeared after the tournament. Benny searched until he located her in the auditorium sitting at the piano. She explained that she was rehearsing for her performance that night in which she would play her favorite classical piece in the talent show. Benny informed that he would be reciting a poem he had written. They were both anxious to catch one another's performance. Before departing the auditorium, Benny announced, "I feel like I'm ready to give you my heart, dear Linda." "Really?" she replied, with a slight nervousness in her voice. "Take your time and think it over, and let me know if you can handle that," he requested.

Following lunch were the finals of the punt, pass, and kick contest. In this meet, the competitors were graded on how well they performed all three tasks. Rankings from the three events would be combined to produce a total score. Brent had been bragging the entire week about how he intended to blow away the competition. Benny had warned him about being overconfident but was summarily ignored. Brent was the first to proceed. He tossed the ball 59 yards but was off the mark by three and achieved a total score of 56 from the best of three passes. Benny earned a respectable rank of fourth, after one forty-five-yard toss landed right on the line. Perry managed a longer toss but it was way off the mark placing him in fifth. The punting competition that followed was a clear upset. Benny launched a boot of fifty-six yards, barely edging out Perry by the length of a ball. Brent came in at fourth, making Benny and Brent tied for the lead after two events.

The field goal kicking event was last. When the distance was increased to forty-five yards, all but three competitors had been eliminated: namely, Brent, Benny, and Perry. Brent failed in all three of his attempts, missing two to the right, and then clipping the left upright on his final shot. As Benny lined up for his turn, Perry took Brent aside and posed, "I bet you five bucks he makes it." Brent replied, "You're on," reasoning that Benny didn't stand a chance since he barely cleared the crossbar at the previous distance. Brent was also convinced that he was better than anybody else, and there was no way he could possibly lose to Benny in football. Benny charged at the ball and struck it firmly but the ball dropped short of the goalpost. On his second attempt, he was once again, short. Brent grinned, self-assured that he had a win in the bag. But on his final attempt, Benny smacked the ball solidly and it sailed right into the crossbar, rotated upward, and toppled to the other side.

Brent couldn't believe it. He was devastated as Perry gave Benny a "high-five." Benny asked Perry, "What's your longest field goal ever?" Perry replied, "I kicked a fifty-one-yarder at the regional final." Benny suggested, "Place the ball at fifty-two yards and blast that baby through the uprights." Perry did as Benny suggested. Benny looked over at Brent and whispered, "Five bucks says he makes it on the first try." Brent, figuring he could offset the bet he just lost decided, "Sure, why not?" Perry punched the pigskin clean through the middle, with a yard to spare. The completion of the football competition resulted in Benny taking the blue ribbon with a combined rank of seven. Brent and Perry tied for second with equal scores of eight. Brent was depressed; he couldn't face the victor and sulked off the field. Second place was unacceptable. He finally mustered the gumption to approach his opponents while they enjoyed refreshment at their favorite table on the patio.

Handing Benny and Perry each five dollars, Brent uttered, "You guys got lucky. I know I can make that forty-five-yarder; I should've won." Benny explained, "You tried too hard; you acted in desperation. Consider Perry. He nailed that fifty-two-yarder because he was relaxed and composed. You know, you'll probably get a scholarship at a good college. But if you want to play first string, you need to calm down, don't be so anxious. Be deliberate not desperate; be poised not panicky; and most of all, relax and you'll be surprised what you can do." "Sounds like good advice," agreed Perry. "This dude is always lecturing me," complained Brent, "and I'm getting sick and tired of it." "Just constructive criticism," Benny explained, "Take it or leave it, it's free."

The awards ceremony for tennis and football was at eight p.m. Then came the last segment of the talent show. Linda knocked them dead with her rendition of Rachmaninoff's Prelude in G Minor. The last to appear on stage was Benny with a poem he'd written while at camp. He began, "*Love Song* by Benjamin Clayton Blakely." These were the first two stanzas.

This poem is written just for you
Miss golden curls with eyes of blue.
Your wit and charm have seized my heart.
Your style itself is a form of art.

You always keep me in suspense,
But then you come to my defense.
And when you softly speak my name
It sets my passion full aflame.

As he continued to recite there was a great hush over the audience. Linda was overcome with emotion, almost ready to burst into tears. His words pierced her heart like arrows flying from Cupid's bow. She smiled at Benny from the front row, her entire countenance glowing with the radiance of her affection. When Benny left the stage and took his seat next to her, she didn't have to speak a word, because he knew by the look in her eyes that she too was ready to give her heart in exchange for his. The judges unanimously chose Linda to receive the first-place ribbon, followed by Betsy for her lovely song. Benny received the yellow ribbon for his moving tribute to the girl he loved.

Saturday was their last full day in this serene and scenic environment. Like the first Saturday, the time was unstructured. Everyone shared their feelings of accomplishment and comradeship, as well as their misguided apprehensions about how boring the retreat was expected to be. Even Linda, who originally became rebellious for being forced by her parents to participate in such a "childish thing as summer camp," knew she would never be the same now that it was nearing an end.

Everybody was changed by the experience, but perhaps none more than Brent. During dinner, he approached Benny and asked permission to sit, awaiting Narc's approval this time before doing so. Then with calmness and sincerity, Brent informed the group, "I thought about what you said, Ben, and decided that you're right. I've been trying too hard to stay above everyone else, and as they say, it's lonely at the top. I picked people to be my friends who would support me on my pedestal. But I see now that the higher you raise yourself, the more difficult it is to live up to everyone's expectations, including your own. If you pretend to be superior long enough, you're bound to be disappointed sooner or later, especially when you discover you're not. I realize that my talent and ability is a gift, not something I achieved totally on my own or that I necessarily deserved." "Well halleluiah!" exclaimed Narc. Then Benny and Brent shook hands and butted shoulders, making their peace.

Saturday night there was a dance outside the recreation hall. Everyone attended; students and staff alike. The party lasted until two a.m. People were allowed to sleep late the next day with breakfast being served between nine and ten. The kids were packed and the busses loaded by noon. Sack lunches were provided for the lengthy bus ride. However, the trip going back home was not as monotonous as the one coming to camp. Spirits were high, lasting friendships had been established, and love was in the air. Pleasant memories were etched into the minds of 116 youngsters who would return to their worlds having matured a great deal over a period of only ten days.

Epilogue:

Benny and Linda went on to become professionals, Benny a professor of philosophy and Linda an attorney. They were married in college and had a son and a daughter. Robbie and Sheila broke up a year later, when both left to attend different universities. Robbie majored in engineering and Sheila became a registered nurse. Tony and Thelma dated a few times but could not sustain their relationship as they lived in different cities. Tony opened his own hardware business and Thelma became an interior decorator. Narc and Brain both attended the same pre-med program. Narc eventually became a pharmacist and Brain became a brain surgeon. Brent went on to play professional football as a backup quarterback, but soon succumbed to a shoulder injury that ruined his career. He later married, obtained a master degree, and became a youth counselor. Perry also played pro football, being ranked the number one kicker in the NFL during his fourth season. He married his childhood sweetheart and had six kids. Hoss dropped out of college when the conference suspended him for steroid use. He was killed shortly afterwards in a tragic one-car accident while driving intoxicated. Helen became a professional tennis player winning two grand slam titles in consecutive years on the women's circuit. Jamie was her manager and coach and they eventually married. Betsy followed her dream and became the lead singer in a musical combo that produced three gold albums and four top forty hits. Danielle studied business management, becoming a successful real estate broker.

# MIRROR TO THE SOUL

(2017)

Growing up on a farm in the Midwest was a bittersweet mix of hard work versus great fun, of beautiful country versus acres of wheat, of quality family time versus being alone for extended periods of time. Everyone had errands and responsibilities that kept them busy, ten to twelve hours a day sometimes; for the girls that included chores, duties, and studies, with a half day thrown in on Sunday to enjoy a family meal, followed by an hour of devotional study, prayer, and self-examination. After the harvest, however, there was a month of rest, relaxation, and recreation during which the twins frolicked in the woodlands, skinny-dipped in the lake, and caught tadpoles in the creek.

Still, the young lasses would not have traded that life for anything. They had two loving parents, and they shared a room with their best friend. They were so much alike, Esther and Ruth, both named for biblical characters from the Old Testament. Identical twins in almost every respect, separated in age by a mere four minutes. Only Mama and Papa could tell them apart, mostly from the single mole that Ruth had on her left ear lobe. They traded clothes, dolls, laughs, and looks, as well as tears for seventeen-plus years. It was the week after Independence Day when life took an awful turn, as day laborers carted Papa back from the fields one fateful afternoon. He had pushed himself so hard, and the heat was scorching; the midday sun baked his brain and he stroked out. He was dead on arrival when they brought him into the house; the doctor hadn't even shown up yet to make the declaration. But the womenfolk knew.

Mama couldn't hold it together. Besides, it would never be the same, not for her anyway. So, she sold the farm to the conglomerate for a reasonable price and moved the girls back east to be near her sister Auntie Irene and Uncle Herbert. The family vacationed there about every other year, being the only kin left. Both sets of grandparents had passed on and Papa was an only child. While the girls weren't that close to their cousins, both mischievous rascals, it was moot since the boys were attending college out of state. Esther and Ruth were left to take care of Mama, who was rapidly fading from her husband's untimely death. They graduated from high school and attended the commencement, which was sheer formality as they didn't know anybody in their senior class. There was scant celebration, since Mama had become addicted to painkillers; she took them for her back pain and her emotional pain. She was groggy and staggering one day and tripped on the tile, falling and breaking her hip. The operation was a success, but the additional anesthesia and morphine turned her into a zombie. The eve before her discharge from the hospital she just stopped breathing, her brain so sedated that she forgot to inhale. Another funeral ensued, dragging with it another traumatic setback for the twins.

A substantial nest egg was bequeathed to the lovely ladies, who sold the house and moved into a country cottage upstate. Putting their heads together about what to do next, the two decided to maneuver into the antique business, as they fancied the fine artistry and durability of things built when their parents were kids. They bought catalogs and magazines, checked out books from the library, spoke with experts in the field, and obtained a first-rate education on buying, dealing, refurbishing, and displaying odd and uncommon artifacts and furniture, preferably over fifty years old. They furnished their home with such items, much of which was left to them by their parents, and redecorated the place in a very special way. Their favorite part was the extensive collection of dolls they had acquired, which became their area of specialization. They added an office which extended into the entry way of the house, and built a prefabricated warehouse alongside, all of which rested on three acres of land surrounded by trees. In time, they had amassed the necessary merchandise, had the proper licenses and permits, and opened an antique shop right there on the property.

In the meantime, they became engrossed in the industry, attending showings, auctions, seminars, estate sales, and such; networking with others, making friends and meeting competitors in the process. All was going quite well, for their enterprise was a smashing success. In a few years the debutantes, now in their mid-twenties, were the talk of the town. They were the most eligible and desirable bachelorettes in the entire county in all probability, not to mention the most charming, exquisite, intelligent, and comely.

As chance would have it, they both met gentlemen with whom there was mutual attraction. Certainly, they had their pick of the litter so to speak, as there was no shortage of suitors trying to woo them. Ruth had met a trader who grew up in Georgia named Hunter; he'd swept her off her feet with his country charm. Esther had met a young man from New Jersey by the name of Monroe, who happened by their store one day; he was a local merchant that frequented the same gatherings that she did. The love grew and so did mutual friendships. Needless to say, the four of them spent quite a lot of time together during the following year; they had cookouts, went to parties, traveled, and worked hand in hand. In fact, both women became engaged on their twenty-fifth birthday, during which the guys threw a bash at the community center for friends and fellow businesspersons to celebrate the occasion, and during which the sisters were each presented with a diamond studded engagement ring before the entire assembly. They brainstormed having a double wedding, and scheduled one for the first of June, or approximately four months hence.

During one outing, the couples diverged at the crossroads, on a mission to explore separate prospective bazaars. Each returned with an interesting find. Ruth had found an old vanity style dresser with drawers intact; it was weathered and somewhat dilapidated, perhaps two centuries old. Likewise, Esther had found a mirror, from about the same period and of the same genre or style. Interestingly, the two pieces seemed to match, insofar as the mirror was a perfect addition to the vanity and vice-versa. Each item seemed to be missing the other and melded like they were meant to match. No doubt, they were; for together they formed a mystical and powerful union whereby an unnatural paranormal entity was subsequently conjured, unbeknownst to anyone.

Preparations for the upcoming wedding were arduous and time consuming. The men were left to fend for themselves. Monroe spent most of his time working, keeping busy and occupied to avoid a case of the nerves. Hunter spent a great deal of his time drinking whiskey in local bars to calm his anxiety; it came to a point where he was consuming massive quantities on a daily basis. He was blasted one afternoon, and came to the cottage looking for his fiancé, for no other purpose than to ravage her like a mad dog. Only nobody was home, so he broke into the warehouse and reclined on a sofa, nodding off. Esther arrived in early evening before the others, with an ornate end table she had discovered. She found it curious that the warehouse door was ajar, as she entered to store the piece she had bought. Hunter was aroused at her entering and snuck up behind her, mistaking her for her sister. As he smothered her with yearning, Esther resisted, fighting him off and protesting vehemently. Still, he advanced, despite her insistence that she was not Ruth and was betrothed to Monroe, and that he was totally out of line. Ignoring her pleas, he raped her on the sofa as she continued to scream and claw at him, but he pinned her arms with his elbows and cupped her mouth with his hands.

Once he had finished, feeling proud, powerful, and satisfied, he sat at the foot of the sofa. He looked at her gorgeous body, her luscious lips, and her beautiful green eyes which were wide open. And then it dawned on him that she wasn't blinking and she wasn't moving; try as he did, he could not revive her. It was then he realized that it wasn't Ruth, because there was no mole on her ear. He also knew he was a rapist and murderer. He lit out of there like the polecat he was and drove three hours, well after dark. You can imagine the horror when Ruth arrived. She had returned empty handed when she noticed the warehouse door was open and the light was on. Figuring her sister to be there since her car was parked and the house was dark, she hastened to the warehouse. There she found her sister's half-naked dead body in rigor mortis. She fell to her knees and cried, totally in shock. Eventually, Monroe happened by and quickly appraised the situation. He too fell to his knees, but gathering his senses called the authorities.

Holding Ruth in his arms they both stumbled to the house and sobbed together in the parlor. The sheriff and forensics team worked all night, gathering evidence and searching for clues. Monroe, though distraught and broken, finally got hold of Hunter the next day to tell him the bad news. Hunter explained that he had been two hundred miles away at an auction; he feigned being shocked and broken-hearted. Monroe was too stupefied to notice the somewhat callous and short voice on the other line.

The citizenry was stunned throughout the region as well as statewide. It was another funeral for Ruth, having now buried her entire family. Monroe was curious why Hunter didn't make it to the funeral; so were the detectives investigating the crime who were present at the funeral looking for clues. They sought to question Hunter for there were no other leads or suspects; none of the neighboring cabins or farmhouses had produced any witnesses. There was forensic evidence of the rape and suffocation, as well as the blood type of the perpetrator determined from a sperm sample and raw flesh underneath Esther's fingernails. That was all they had to go on. Eventually, Hunter showed his ugly face, and though he had the same blood type it was a very common one; he produced what seemed a solid alibi giving the names of drinking buddies in a nearby county who would vouch that he was there the night of the crime. Though the timeline did not exactly line up, there was insufficient proof to charge him. But Ruth and Monroe never ceased to suspect him; and though Hunter vowed to quit drinking, the wedding was called off indefinitely. Unfortunately, Hunter was still on the hunt for his former fiancé, and though she had already returned his ring he began to stalk her.

Ruth tried to keep busy running the office and transforming the decrepit vanity; she stripped the antique of stain and varnish, sanded it smooth, stained it with cherry, and varnished it with spar. Meanwhile, Monroe maintained a vigil to keep Hunter away. He helped repair the mirror by polishing it and restoring the wooden frame with filler and the same antique finish as the vanity. After a week the piece looked magnificent; too special to be placed on sale, and elegant enough to decorate the parlor where all invited guests could admire it. The two stared at the matching set in awe, when suddenly an image appeared in the mirror. It was not the two of them, it was Esther (or so they thought) wearing the dress she was murdered in. She reached forward her hand and Monroe reached out his to touch hers. Immediately, a portal was opened and Monroe was allowed to step through. Only he was not able to return. The mirror turned dark while Ruth was standing there alone, frightened out of her wits.

Monroe was seemingly trapped in-between two underworlds. There the face resembling his lost beloved turned into a hideous enchantress who sneered at him. That is how she welcomed him into her world of lost souls. She must be the queen of the undead, Monroe surmised, traipsing about the halls of darkness. He begged the witch to let him return while she commenced to persuade him to stay, tempting him with the idea that she could easily become Esther for him in every way and for all eternity. Without a reply he slumped away, all the more determined to escape. She mentioned in passing that the only way he could return would be to find a replacement. Monroe figured that, if he was to touch the hand of another outside the mirror, they could exchange places.

Monroe monitored the necromancer and the portico, hoping to get a glimpse of Ruth; not to coax her in but to pass a message. As fate would have it, Ruth would not leave the mirror; she had been camping out in the parlor, exiting only to heed nature's calling for food and hygiene. It was exactly one week from the time Monroe disappeared when he reappeared in the mirror, and Ruth was alerted and arose from the settee. She saw him reaching forward with a written note; he warned her not to enter but only to take the note from his hand and it would explain everything. The letter ordered her to follow instructions and execute the plan at exactly midnight next Saturday, as that was the only minute of the week that entry would be possible.

Ruth found Hunter at his usual hideout; a tavern located mid-city. She explained to him how she missed him, and that she would consider taking him back if he remained clean and sober for one week. He jumped at the chance of getting into her pants and accepted. When Saturday arrived, he picked her up at eight for some dinner and small talk at his favorite restaurant. She would tease him for three hours until finally charming him into submission. He drove her to the cottage arriving at 11:40 p.m. She had him perch his behind on the settee while she went to the kitchen to prepare coffee and dessert.

Meanwhile, Monroe had convinced the seductress he was enamored with the idea of having Esther back forever, and they started spending a lot of time together, virtually twenty-four hours a day. Acting ignorant of the time and place, Monroe held her hand and guided her alongside the gateway at the stroke of midnight. Ruth had positioned Hunter at the mirror, allowing him to admire the handiwork and beauty of the antique that she and Monroe recently renovated; he still had not lost his interest in great antiques. He became mesmerized when Esther appeared in the mirror; he was confused, thinking it was Ruth's reflection. He called out Esther's name and the witch in disguise answered his summon, hoping to capture another soul for her collection. As she reached forward, he touched her hand so she guided him to the border of the threshold. Monroe had been standing to the side and was not visible in the mirror; he grasped Hunter's left wrist and jerked him forward. Simultaneously, Monroe slipped through to the other side, the two trading places. For a brief moment, Hunter looked back from the beyond, pushing against the doorway but unable to breach it. Glancing back at Esther he encountered the dreadful enchantress in all her ugliness. Although the evil sorceress was displeased that she had been tricked, she quickly moved in on her new victim when the image faded out.

Monroe and Ruth embraced, and sighed, and kissed. Having each lost their most cherished companion, they too found a much-treasured replacement. And the wedding went on as scheduled: Saturday, June 1, 1957. Hundreds were in attendance to congratulate the happy team, who staved off their losses, temptations, and possessions to become one in flesh and mind, as well as one in spirit and love with the God of the universe to guide their union.

Weeks later, at the start of the witching hour on Saturday night, they lit a bonfire previously prepared for the memories, the items, and the sins associated with the hurt and destruction that had become their life, and almost their fate. Among the items were the vanity-mirror set and stained sofa; the rest was trash, debris, branches, and papers from a cleanup of the warehouse and the yard. They huddled together on a log and watched it burn all night, until the only thing left were ashes and dust. At dawn, when the fire pit had grown cold, all the remains were raked together and shoveled into a wheelbarrow, driven to a sump at the perimeter of the property, dumped into a prepared grave and buried six feet under.

Sunday was the Lord's Day, and they worshipped at the local church, thanking God for deliverance from the pit and from the attractions of a corrupt material world. The grateful couple lauded his wisdom, mercy, and blessings; especially for giving them another chance and another soulmate. Arriving home again, they plopped upon the settee and embraced, discussing the providence of God and the justness of his verdict. They concluded that nobody can escape the wrath of God; and that nobody can enter into his presence without forgiveness and reconciliation. Suffice it to say, they lived happily ever after. Hunter, well he was dead to the world, already condemned to an eternity of torment. And nobody really seemed to miss him, speak his name, or remember who he was.

# FIRE, WATER, AIR, EARTH

## (1972)

It has been my desire to advance as a fire,
And endow warmth and brightness on sorrowful souls.
For they wouldn't remember more powerful embers
Than those which would shine from the heart of my coals.

I've aspired to be the magnificent sea,
Where a drop in the ocean could never be found.
I would wash away tears that have multiplied fears
From faces of those who might be heaven bound.

I have longed to be near to the wide atmosphere,
And be filling the lungs of the sick and oppressed.
If they breathed in my air it would show how I care,
And would change their misfortunes to spiritual rest.

It was once my demand to be part of the land;
As the earth, I could bear every burden in mind.
My best friend, he awaits. He shares all of these traits.
I admire my Lord Jesus who saved humankind.

# THE PACT

## (1975)

Judd Lohman was a man who was never satisfied. He always wanted more than life had to offer, and he would do anything to get ahead. He often behaved dishonestly when trying to make an impression on the boss.

For instance, one day after work he took credit for securing a major contract with a client corporation. The boss was very pleased. Although Judd had lent a hand in finalizing and signing the agreement, it was his aide who had slaved for weeks to ensure a satisfactory compromise, not to mention authoring and disseminating the document. Nevertheless, Judd had a higher position with the company, and he felt it was his turn to sit back and gain recognition.

His home life wasn't exactly what one would call pleasant. He did nothing of importance around the house; he forced his wife and son to accomplish all chores, repairs and housework. He spent very little time with his family. The only time he paid any attention to them was for the sake of argument or reprimand. Instead, he wasted all his free time drinking beer and watching television. He did, at least, get his own beer from the refrigerator.

Judd was far from a model parent. His only interference in raising his son was for disciplinary action, during which time he usually beat the boy unmercifully. Judd was not an understanding husband and father, nor did he fear God. The concept of God was ridiculous to Judd. In fact, the only thing Judd believed in was padding his ego.

One day at the office, during the ten o'clock coffee break, the conversation progressed to religion. One of the secretaries happened to mention her hope that God would see her through the day. Judd intervened, saying she would never receive any help from God, because God didn't exist. This prompted a discussion about God, the devil, and the existence of eternal life. Judd decided it was all nonsense and left the room to drink his coffee alone.

That night, Judd had a dream in which Jesus Christ and Lucifer both appeared. In this dream, Judd kissed the Lord on the cheek, said goodbye, and shook the hand of Lucifer. The following day, the dream was heavy on Judd's conscience. He could recall every detail, for it seemed so realistic, as if the three of them actually had been in the same location together. He eventually dismissed the dream, believing it was simply his imagination, maybe some mental trap associated with the coffee break incident. Judd reaffirmed his position that such beings do not exist in the world.

However, that night Judd had a similar dream, only this time Lucifer was alone, prepared to make a deal with Judd. If he would agree to turn his soul over to Hell, Judd would be allowed any wish. The next morning Judd awoke with the dream still fresh in his mind. He began to wonder what he would wish for if he actually could make a pact with the devil. He neither considered the value of his soul nor its importance to human life.

Judd thought he had the better part of the deal. After all, he considered his soul to be a small price to pay for such an opportunity, given that Judd couldn't prove he even had a soul. Judd concluded he would like to live for one thousand years. He was convinced there was no life after death, and he figured that would be long enough to enjoy life without getting too bored. This way, nobody could take his life from him and he could dictate the terms of his death.

Once again on the third night, Judd had the final installment of the dream. The vision was more realistic than ever before, and Judd was initially scared to death. But the fallen angel was persuasive. Judd agreed to sell his soul to the devil for a millennium of life. He tossed and turned in his sleep due to over-anxiousness. He awoke and looked at his sleeping wife. He quietly got out of bed and went to the kitchen. He opened the refrigerator and pulled out a beer and some cold cuts. He made a snack and sat at the table to eat.

Halfway through his snack, Judd noticed a glowing image stirring all around the kitchen. He figured it was just a mirage from his late-night sleepiness and ignored it. The more he ate, the more awake he became, and the clearer the image became. It was distinct, resembling the impression of Lucifer from his dreams, now sitting right across the table from him. Completely coherent, Judd realized this was not a hallucination.

Suddenly, as the clock in the adjoining room struck midnight, the apparition spoke to him, inquiring if Judd remembered the deal. Judd answered affirmatively, requesting assurance that what was happening was real. Lucifer handed Judd a contract, which if signed, would be a valid and binding agreement between the two of them. It was the shortest contract Judd had ever read; quite a fancy document, he thought, like an unrolled scroll with a single sentence. Lucifer slit Judd's wrist with his fingernail, dipped a feather pen to sop up a few drops of blood, and handed the pen to Judd. He signed his name in blood, and shook hands with the devil just like in the first dream. Lucifer vanished with the contract, cackling like a grackle. Judd finished his beer and returned to bed, entirely satisfied with his decision. Hence, the sequence of events unveiled in Judd's dreams were destined to become his reality.

The next morning Judd was somewhat skeptical of the events the previous night. He didn't believe he was going to live a thousand years, but on the way to work he was to become a bit more convinced. Judd was driving down the highway when a car began to pass a diesel truck on the opposite side of traffic. He had no time to dodge the oncoming vehicle and they collided head on. Luckily, Judd was thrown from his car into a grassy field, but the other driver was not so fortunate.

Judd was unhurt while the other driver was crushed beyond recognition. The police and ambulance arrived and Judd informed everyone he was fine and explained the incident. They were amazed that Judd had escaped without injury, since the two cars were demolished and inseparable.

That afternoon, Judd arrived for work and explained the mishap to his boss and his fellow employees. They were shocked and surprised. The boss told Judd to take the day off, but Judd told him not to worry and continued about his business.

When Judd returned home, he described the accident to his wife and son. They were particularly hurt to see how glad Judd was about it, not realizing his motive. Judd celebrated all night, getting extremely intoxicated. By three in the morning he was barely able to make it to bed and fell asleep immediately. The devil reappeared in his dreams, reassuring Judd that he meant business. Judd was never again to doubt this promise or try to make void their agreement.

Judd overslept that morning and called the boss at noon to say he was too ill to go to work. It wasn't a complete lie because Judd had a ferocious hangover, but that didn't prevent him from continuing to drink all day long to slough it off. Before long, Judd was in the same predicament as the night before. He refused to go to work again giving the same excuse.

Week after week, Judd's irresponsibility increased. He continued to avoid work and to drink, until he was spending most of his paycheck on liquor. His wife pleaded with him but he disregarded her wishes as always. Finally, the boss confronted Judd in a private conference concerning his apparent lack of interest at work and his continued absences. The boss informed Judd that he needed help; perhaps he was traumatized by the accident. Judd scoffed at him. His boss told him if the irresponsibility continued Judd would suffer the consequences. Judd screamed, "You can't fire me because I quit."

Judd punched his boss in the eye, telling him what he could do with his lousy job. Judd stormed out of the room, cursing all the other employees, knocking down shelves and furniture, and strewing paperwork all over the office. He hurried home and told his wife he had resigned.

His wife, totally frustrated with Judd by this time, threated to leave him if he didn't stop the drinking and the abuse. Judd's temper exploded and he slugged his wife, who dropped to the floor senseless. He stomped out of the house and went to the nearest bar to get wasted.

Judd sat alone at a table, drinking away his problems, and contemplating his future. He decided it was a good idea quitting his job. After all, he didn't want to spend a millennium doing the same old thing. He wanted to find his fortune the quick and easy way, without working for it. He had sweated and slaved all his adult life and was ready for a change.

Judd began to consider crime as a profession. He had an advantage over others, he reasoned; he should have no trouble stealing, mugging, or burglarizing. He felt he couldn't be defeated, because with Lucifer on his side he was invincible.

After considering the alternatives, Judd became convinced of his calling; for a practice run he decided to rob the cash register at the bar. He broke a bottle over the bartender's head, who was busy watching a ballgame on the television. The bartender fell backwards in his chair, unconscious. Judd opened the register and cleaned it out. He returned home and counted his profits. It was the easiest $185 he ever made, almost a whole week's pay. Judd's wife demanded to know where the money had come from. Judd told her it was none of her business and to get lost.

Judd's wife read about the robbery in the daily newspaper the next morning. After reading the description of the assailant, she put two and two together and concluded that her husband was guilty of the crime. She accused Judd openly, but he denied everything. His wife told him she was filing for divorce. Judd said he didn't care and added that it was an excellent idea.

Judd ignored the divorce proceedings and spent his time drinking and robbing to support his habit. Naturally, the divorce was granted and Judd was ordered to forfeit the house and most of their savings. Judd gathered what few things were allowed him through the settlement and moved out. By then, Judd's ex-wife and son had overcome any sorrow or loss; their future lives would advance, much happier than ever before. She sold the house and left the city, to start a new life in her hometown with her son and their loved ones.

Judd was satisfied, even though he owned nothing and had no wealth. He took the remainder of his cash and rented a room in a tenement house, where he drank himself into a stupor. By midnight, Judd became sad because he was broke, so he decided to conduct another robbery.

He went to a liquor store down the street. He told the clerk to empty the cash register. The clerk replied that Judd was drunk and to go home and sober up. Judd clobbered the clerk and

PROSE AND POETRY

proceeded to open the register himself. The clerk snatched a hidden revolver and pointed it at Judd. Judd shoved the man to the floor. The clerk fired the gun, point blank, into Judd's chest. Judd kicked the clerk into a coma, finished emptying the register, grabbed a few bottles of booze, and hurried back to his room. This time he brought home $253, so he had a special celebration.

Judd spent the next few weeks in solitude, leaving only to replenish his liquor supply. Eventually, he exhausted his funds, presenting him with only one recourse, to hold up another liquor store. He splurged and robbed two liquor stores and a gun store that day. Henceforth, he started carrying a semiautomatic pistol wherever he went. It was easier to get the cash by just pointing his loaded gun.

One morning, Judd picked up the newspaper from his neighbor's doorstep. The headlines told of several robberies and two killings. The cover story explained how it was the same maniac who committed these crimes. Further, the suspect had been shot on several occasions, and didn't appear to be affected. It was assumed he wore a bulletproof vest and was armed and dangerous. Judd thought the article was funny and snickered; he considered the news to be praise. He liked being the most wanted man in town.

Judd remained a recluse and an alcoholic, only to wallow in his hate which was developing rapidly. After a while, Judd got bored again. He strolled outside, across the street, and wandered into a "greasy-spoon". He ordered a sandwich and a beer. A man accidentally brushed Judd as he passed by. Judd told the man to apologize. This prompted the man to take a swing at Judd, landing a fist against Judd's cheek. In a matter of minutes, Judd had beaten the man to death.

The police arrived and Judd pleaded self-defense. The proprietor corroborated that the other man threw the first punch, adding that Judd got carried away. Then, one of the officers recognized Judd as a possible murder suspect. The officer informed Judd that he would have to accompany them to the station for questioning. This is not what Judd had in mind, so he ran outside, firing his gun at the police. The officers pursued Judd; they both raised their pistols and fired. They were surprised to see Judd continuing down the street, after taking a number of bullets in the back and head. It was as if he had never been touched.

News of the incident traveled fast. Judd's portrait was on the front page of all the newspapers and plastered on the TV. After that, Judd could walk the street and people would run from him, fearing for their lives. It was easier than ever for Judd to steal now. All he had to do was enter an establishment and demand whatever he wanted. Soon, Judd became a rich man. He had more money than he knew what to do with. He didn't desire a mansion or a limousine; all he cared about was his alcohol, cigarettes, and other vices.

Judd sank deeper into his self-made pit of sin. He never bathed, and he would urinate and defecate on the floor. His room began to stink, and it was crawling with roaches, rats, and all manner of vermin. Judd considered these creatures to be his pets. He allowed them to thrive on his unsanitary living conditions. Eventually, the entire tenement house became deserted save for Judd and his pets. Nobody would pass his home, but rather avoided it by blocks or even miles.

For years, Judd lived happily among his diseases and filth. He drank daily from his vast supply of liquor, never seeing the light of day. One day, Judd peered out of an upper-story window. He noticed a high concrete wall had been erected around the tenement house.

Judd became angry. In his rage, he scaled the barrier and roamed around the streets. People ran for safety as soon as they saw him. Judd caught up with one of them, who vomited after seeing Judd's ghastly appearance. Judd strangled the poor individual to death. He stalked the town, killing every living thing in sight; shooting his pistol, yelling profanities, and raising hell. He continued this pastime until dark. Then he went into the nearest liquor store and drank until he passed out.

Judd awoke the next afternoon and decided to go downtown for some more entertainment. When he arrived on the streets, he discovered the entire town had abandoned him. For the first time in his life, Judd felt sorry, even lonely. He considered leaving town to pursue the deserters, but he didn't want to leave his pets, his booze, or his hate behind. He confiscated a sledge hammer from a hardware store, broke a hole in the wall, and returned to his private hotel.

Judd's meanness continued to build inside him, to the extent he became angry with his pets. To teach them a lesson, he began eating them, roaches, scorpions, and rats alike. It was the first meal he had eaten since he could remember. After the banquet, the effects of the alcohol were counteracted and Judd became partially sober for the first time in, well as long as he could remember.

Judd despised being sober, and he became all the more violent. He started throwing furniture, punching holes in walls, and destroying everything within reach. However, this was still not enough of a release. He was so frustrated he began tearing at his own body. He took hold of his cheek with a fierce pinch and ripped a chunk of flesh from his face, tossing it to the rats. The raw tissue of his torn jaw burned in the air. He looked into a dusty mirror at the ugly gash on his despicable countenance.

Judd became all the more enraged. He decided to seek out some people to kill, rape, and molest. He was so agitated and in such a hurry to inflict pain on others, that he sprang out a fifth-floor window. He bounced on the ground and rolled up to the concrete barricade.

He tried to get up but he stumbled back to the ground. He discovered at that moment that he had broken both legs and his right collar in the fall. He didn't understand how this could happen. He never understood having a capacity for inflicting injury upon himself. He knew he could crush others without being harmed by them; but, while others could not hurt him, he now learned he could hurt himself. Judd crawled back to his apartment building like a worm squirming along the ground.

There was no way he could escape very far from the barrier, or even climb the stairs to his room without considerable misery. He set his broken legs as best he could; he wished he had a doctor but hated that he needed anybody. For once in his life he realized there would be nobody. Judd was so sad he began to cry. It was a pitiful sight, even to see such a contemptible person as Judd in such a loathsome situation. He wondered what it would be like, being stuck with himself in this environment for the remainder of his time. He found a few bottles of booze left behind by other tenants and drank himself into oblivion.

He awoke one day with his feet completely enveloped in gangrene. After overcoming the initial shock, he creeped up to the next apartment and located another liquor supply. He chewed off the top of a bottle and returned to his normal diet. He was finally serene again, drinking away his troubles and lounging amongst his creatures. This continued for a lifetime, until his liquor supply had been exhausted.

Judd was no longer enamored with his situation because he couldn't get stoned. He became scared, contemplating a future that would never change for the next nine centuries. The days dragged along as his hatred became overwhelming; he was boiling with meanness and madness. He retaliated against the only loved ones in his life: his pets. He resumed squashing his pals, eating them, throwing them against the walls, and so forth. This behavior continued day after day. Consequently, his only true family was forced to abandon him as well.

Now Judd was entirely alone, with nothing to eat or drink, no friends or family, nothing but himself and a painful, broken and decaying body. He realized he would have the dreadful misfortune of spending the rest of the millennium in a prison of his own device, completely alone, absolutely sober, and in intense agony.

Judd was shocked, having faced the veracity of Satan and the consequences of evil He would regret his encounter with the devil the remainder of his life. Unfortunately, Judd would never consider repentance, nor would he seek God or pray to him. He did, however, learn the value of his soul; but it was way too late, he surmised.

Judd broke down and cried himself to sleep like an infant. Night after night he would have a dream in which Lucifer appeared as a serpent, pointing and shrieking. This dream was to reoccur every time Judd slept. In the beginning, Judd thought he was going to have it made. but all he found was disaster and desolation in his own private hell.

# SONGBOOK

| Song Title (Listed Alphabetically) | Originated | First Copyright |
|---|---|---|
| 1. 1001 | 1972 | 1981 |
| 2. Angel Heart | 2001 | 2004 |
| 3. Another Day, Another Life (For Jeff) | 1991 | 1995 |
| 4. Apocalypse (The Fall of Babylon) | 1992 | 1995 |
| 5. Armor of God | 2010 | 2019 |
| 6. Bad Girl | 1990 | 1995 |
| 7. Ballad of a Rambler | 1968 | 2001 |
| 8. Ballad of Sycamore Smith | 1970 | 2001 |
| 9. Black Beauty | 1981 | 1995 |
| 10. C'est la Vie, Baby | 2018 | 2019 |
| 11. Christ the King | 1992 | 1995 |
| 12. City Blues | 1973 | 2001 |
| 13. Crown of Life | 2001 | 2001 |
| 14. Down the Road | 1979 | 1981 |
| 15. Dreamchaser | 2005 | 2019 |
| 16. Easter's Song | 1980 | 1981 |
| 17. Escape | 1983 | 1995 |
| 18. For God So Loved the World | 2004 | 2004 |
| 19. Freestyle Boogie | 1974 | 1995 |
| 20. Genesis | 1993 | 1995 |
| 21. Giving it All | 1992 | 1995 |
| 22. Inside of Me | 1978 | 1981 |
| 23. I Saw You | 1974 | 1981 |
| 24. Jail Quail | 1989 | 1995 |
| 25. Jewel | 2004 | 2004 |
| 26. Lady of the Shadows | 2008 | 2019 |
| 27. Lost and Sleeping | 1973 | 1981 |
| 28. Love of Yesterday | 1976 | 1981 |
| 29. Love Vs. Time | 1979 | 1981 |
| 30. Memorial Day | 2018 | 2019 |
| 31. Never the Same | 1991 | 1995 |
| 32. New Sun | 1984 | 1995 |
| 33. Psalm 151 | 2004 | 2004 |
| 34. Rise and Fall of Rock and Roll | 1981 | 1981 |
| 35. Seasons | 1995 | 2001 |
| 36. Second Coming | 1979 | 1981 |
| 37. S.O.M.F. | 1979 | 1981 |
| 38. Spying Game | 2004 | 2004 |
| 39. Stoned to Death | 2001 | 2001 |
| 40. Street Rap | 1994 | 2001 |
| 41. Take Time | 1997 | 2001 |
| 42. Tease Queen Boogie | 1978 | 1981 |
| 43. Together 'til the End | 1977 | 1981 |
| 44. Tough Love | 1999 | 2001 |
| 45. Ugly Girls Have Got It Made | 1981 | 1981 |
| 46. Victoria | 1971 | 2001 |
| 47. We're the CIA | 1996 | 2001 |
| 48. Winning | 2018 | 2019 |
| 49. Woman at Seventeen | 1980 | 1981 |
| 50. Yes | 2015 | 2019 |

# 1001

Written and arranged by Andy Barber, 1972
First copyright © 1981 (PAu 321-648)

G. C G G. F... G. C G G. G... C

VERSE 1

(C)                              A
And the lovely lady said to me,
(A)           B*b*     F
"Honey what's it going to be?"
(F)       B*b*   F F      G
"I love you faithfully; I'm your perfection."

C G G. F... C G G. F... C

 (C)                                  A
And I said, "My dear, don't waste your time."
(A)          B*b*     F
"Maybe I could love today."
(F)       B*b*   F   F      G
"I can't love anyway; ask me tomorrow."

G. C G G. F... G. C G G. F...

CHORUS 1

      C                 F    C
I've never walked on greener grass
      C          B*b*
But I always saw the sun.
      C         F  C    C      B*b*
I've met a thousand girls before, but never loved a one.

D... B*b*. F. D... B*b*. F. D... B*b*. F. C. G. B*b*. F...

VERSE 2
And she walked with me and held my hand.
Said, "Honey don't refuse,"
"Somehow I cannot lose when it's just beginning."

Then she put her arms around my neck,
Kissed me and held me near,
And said, "Forever dear, I'll make you happy."

CHORUS 2
I've never walked on greener grass,
But I always saw the sun.
I met a thousand girls before, and finally love one.

D... B*b*. F. D... B*b*. F. D... B*b*. F. C. G. B*b*. F. C. G...

C#. G#... E. B... G. D... A. E...

# ANGEL HEART

Written 2001and arranged 2004 by Andy Barber
First copyright © 2004 (PAu2 914-571)

VERSE 1

    A          D
This song is written just for you
      E         A
Miss golden curls with eyes of blue.
    A          D
Your wit and charm have seized my heart;
     E       A
Your style itself is a form of art.

CHORUS 1

     F        G   A
You like to keep me in suspense,
     F        G   A
But always come to my defense.
     F        G    A
And when you softly speak my name
    F       C  G A
It sets my passion full aflame.

VERSE 2

Angelic face that smiles so sweet,
You're always humble, calm, discreet;
And thoughtful, graceful, loyal, kind;
I'm richly blessed because you're mine.

CHORUS 2

True love that I could never earn.
What can I give you in return?
Except my life, my trust, my days;
My gratitude, my love, my praise.

REPEAT VERSE 1 AND CHORUS 2

EPILOGUE
     C       D     A
I've never met a girl like you,
       C            G   A
Whose love is pure, whose heart is true.
     C       D   A
I'd love to have you for my bride,
     C      G    A
To live forever by my side.

# ANOTHER DAY, ANOTHER LIFE (For Jeff)

Written and arranged by Andy Barber, 1991
First copyright © 1995 (PAu 1-986-264)

VERSE 1

```
Bm      D         A         E
```
Nobody smiles, nobody laughs, nobody sings.
```
Bm         D          A          E
```
The vain and vile will see the wrath that evil brings.
```
Bm           A       Bm          G
```
Here yesterday, gone today; either way you're going to pay.
```
 A      E       F#... F#. D.
```
But there's another day.

VERSE 2

My brother roamed, my brother played, my brother died.
We never phoned, we never prayed, we never cried.
Despite my hopes and fears, I'm holding back the tears,
To face another day.

CHORUS 1

```
      A                   G
```
If you listen, you'll see what this song is about.
```
         F                    E
```
If you want to be free, then you've got to reach out.
```
      A                   G
```
If you open your mind and you open your heart
```
     F#          E   Em7
```
You'll find another part.

VERSE 3

Your brother love, your neighbor love, love God above.
Each other find that peace of mind that conquers time.
Don't say good-bye, I'll tell you why:
You can fly, or tie, or die,
But you'll meet another day.

CHORUS 2

Life is for free; it can be forever.
But listen to me, don't ever say never.
If you open your heart and you open your mind
You'll find another start.

# APOCALYPSE (The Fall of Babylon)

Written and arranged by Andy Barber, 1992
First copyright © 1995 (PAu 1-986-264)

PROLOGUE

    A                F#
The white horse brings peace, but soon it will cease.
The red horse brings war that lurks at the door.
The black horse, with scales, means big money fails.
The pale horse begins; the death rider grins.

VERSE 1

    Dm              G
They grasped to the shield but raised not the sword;
    Dm           G
They promised so much, but gave not their word.
 Dm            G
Speaking of peace, while in the back room,
 Dm           G
Plotting grand deeds of evil and doom.

CHORUS 1

    A               C  B  C   D
The nations were gathered about the great whore,
    A          B  CB   A G
And those that refused her were ravaged by war.
    A           B CB  C   D
The warmonger stripped them of even their pride,
    A        B  C  B  A G    C  D   C  B  A
With nowhere to run and nowhere to hide, they fought and they died.
    C  B   A   G       D  C Bm A
The angels they cried, and God even sighed.

VERSE 2

Increasing the tax to pay for their greed; ignoring the fact this would not succeed.
Prosperity was the word that they spoke; economies only caved and went broke.

CHORUS 2

Huge earthquakes collapsed the earth with great might.
Vast darkness transformed the day into night.
The great tribulation was ripe with God's wrath,
Destroying one-third of all things in its path.

INTERLUDE 1

D... E F G. D... E F. D C.  D... F E D G. D... E F.. C.

    D            F E  F  G
The old grim reaper started his raid,
    D          E    F   D    C
A murderous rogue with a double-edged blade.
    D         E    F  E D G   D
A whole one-quarter would die by his hand,
    D        E     F  E  D C
By famine, disease, and the beasts of the land.
 F   G   F   E   D    E   F   E   D   C    F  G Fm Em D
They took their last stand, were conquered and ran—the failure of man.

REPEAT VERSE AND CHORUS (chords only)

INTERLUDE 2
The beast overwhelmed them, with magic and wit.
Some monsters were freed from the bottomless pit.
The wretched one's mark brought Babylon down.
Throughout the earth the great fall would resound.

D... F E C G. D... E F. D C. (repeat and fade out)

# ARMOR OF GOD

Written 2010 and arranged 2018 by Andy Barber
First copyright © 2019 (Anthology)

E... F#... E... F#...    E . . . . . F# . . .


CHORUS 1

   F#...                         E                A...                           B...
If you sense Christ is knocking, please open the door for a fine suit of armor that's free.
   F#...            E...               A...             B...
It is time to prepare for a terrible war, fighting enemies you cannot see.
     A...             B...              G...          A...          B...
For the Lord will deliver them into your hand; when the battle is over it's you that will stand.


VERSE 1

 Bm...                   F#   A...                    E...
First, put on the helmet of salvation; it controls your thoughts and shelters your brain.
It can thwart the vain imagination, preventing your mind from going insane.


VERSE 2

Righteousness creates a mighty breastplate, protecting your heart from evil deeds.
Invested in God you get the best gift: love, the guarantee to meet your needs


VERSE 3

Firmly wrap the belt of truth around you; it unveils a multitude of lies.
In the light, true wisdom will astound you.  Disbelief results in your demise.


VERSE 4

Shod your feet with good news and contentment; ever walk in peace and serve the Lord.
Don't give in to envy or resentment; just forgive and feel your soul restored.
                             F#
For the blood of Jesus was outpoured.


E... F#... E... F#...   E . . . . . F# . . .

CHORUS 2

```
        F#...          E              A...                B...
You can hear Jesus calling to settle the score, with a fine suit of armor that's free.
        F#...          E...           A...                B...
You're about to engage in a spiritual war, against enemies you cannot see.
        A...           B...              G...          A...          B...
But the Lord will deliver them into your hand; when the battle is over it's you that will stand.
```

VERSE 5

Shield of faith, your ultimate protection; it deflects the fiery darts of Hell.
Faith makes clear your path and your direction, guarding when temptation casts its spell.

VERSE 6

Arm yourself with God's sword of the Spirit. His Word penetrates one's very soul.
You must have a willingness to hear it; otherwise, for you the bell will toll.

INTERLUDE

```
   G...                            A...
When Christ comes in judgment, heads will roll.
     G                      A
For the saved, His kingdom will unfold;
       G...                    A...
They will walk on streets of solid gold.
```

G... A... B... B... E . . . . . F# . . .

CHORUS 3

```
        F#...          E...           A...                B...
You will see your Messiah for life evermore, in your fine suit of armor that's free.
        F#...          E...           A...                B...
With the armor of God, you will win every war facing enemies you cannot see.
        A...           B...              G...          A ..          B...
And the Lord will deliver them into your hand; when the battle is over it's you that will stand;
        B...              C#...
On your way into the Promised Land!
```

E... F#... E... F#...(fade out)

# BAD GIRL

Written and arranged by Andy Barber, 1990
First copyright © 1995 (PAu 1-986-264)

```
 E    B    D       A        E    B      D       A
Bad girls around the world. They learn young and have their fun.
         E    B       D      A
They're not all bad once you get to know them.
         E      B       D      A
They know what to do, you don't have to show them.

F#      E    A       B     F#      E    A      E
I met one and I followed her there. She was sixteen and sweet and mean.
      F#         E A B   F#                     A     E
Like a knight escorting his lady fair, discovering those things you've never seen.

C#... E F#. C#... E B...  F#. C#... E B...

   C#        B   E    F#    C#          B. E. B...
She led me down old lovers' lane; a backseat love affair.
         C#           B    E     F#    C#        E B. C#...
Like a smooth aged whiskey with the kick of a mule; I had my share.

E. B... D A... E. B... D A... E. B... D A... E. B... D A...

   F#      E    A    B       F#      E    A E
Was I in love, or was I in pain? Was it all for real or was I insane?
      F#         E    A    B         F#              A    E .. F#
Did we love in jest? Did we love in vain? And the time we shared, was it loss or gain?

 E    B         D    A   E    B       D    A
Bad girls, they've seen better days. You can tell by their distant gaze.
     E    B    D        A     E    B       D       A
They don't always do like they should, but the one I loved, she was awfully good.

   B       A    D    E     B        A D A
She carried inside such a heavy load; a depressing scene.
   B         A    D     E     B         D      A F#
A sordid upbringing forced her out on the road, until I found this teenage queen.

     E         D  G    A     E          D  G    D
Her troubled heart and her battered soul let the truth hide away while fear took its toll.
 E         D  G   A     E              G    D B
Giving me love was her only goal; but I lost my grasp when she lost control.

   D         E  B D. A... E  B      D       A
They called her, "Bad girl."     A sad girl with a tormented mind.
            E  B D. A... E  B      D    A B
But she was my girl.      Society lost, as did all mankind.

C#... B E. F#... C#... B E. B... C#... B E. F#... C#... E. B... G#...

F#. C#... E. B... F#. C#... E. B... F#. C#... E. B... F#. C#... E. B...

D. A... A. B...
```

# BALLAD OF A RAMBLER

Written 1968 and arranged 1996 by Andy Barber
First copyright © 2001 (PAu 2-613-596)

D... C... G A C D... D... C... G A C D...
D... F... B*b* F C D... D... F... Em D C D...

VERSE 1
     A           G
Girl, my love for you will always be true,
    F       C      D
For love is the greatest of powers.
     A          G
I'll make an endeavor to love you forever,
      F      C      D
Since our kind of love never sours.
    C              D
So say you won't cry, 'cause I'm that kind of guy
        C    B    G    A7
Who can never remain in one place;
      C           D
Understand if you can, I'm a traveling man;
    F      Em    C    D
So please wipe the tears from your face.

VERSE 2
Oh, don't ask around for the place I'll be found,
Because that can't be answered by me.
To know where I've trod, you'll have to ask God,
For no-one will know except He.
I'll find me a chart that will show every part
Of this nation and every state in it.
When I point to the ground, that's where I'll be bound,
And I'll leave for that place in a minute.

CHOURUS (repeat chorus again after guitar solo)
    F       Em    D
For I want to be free from all reality.
    C       G      D
If it runs down, I'll just rewind it.
      F           Em  D
And the world I will see will be all fantasy,
    F    C   G C    D...
But if you really love me, you'll find it.

(D) C... G A C D... D... C... G A C D...
D... F... B*b* F C D... D... F... Em D C D...

# BALLAD OF SYCAMORE SMITH

Written 1970 and arranged 1979 by Andy Barber
First copyright © 2001 (PAu 2-613-596)

B... G... A. A. A. A.  B... G... A. A. A. A.    E... C... D. D. D. D.  E... C... A... G...

   B            G
This is a story that tells of the glory,
  A A       A A
Of a man named Sycamore Smith.
     B             G
He was liked very well, and his friends will all tell
  A A      A A
That he didn't care who he was with.
      E             C
Well, he talked to the trees and he listened to the bees,
  D D      D D
And he loved all the wildlife outside.
    E           C
Voted best guy around, any place to be found;
  D D      D D
He lives on even though he has died.

B... G... A. A. A. A.  B... G... E... D... B... G... A. A. A. A.

    E             C
I remember one day, the beginning of May,
  D D      D D
He said to me something to heed.
       E          C
He said, "Man when I die and go up to the sky,
   A             G         B... G... A. A. A. A.  B... A... F... G...
I'll be glad I could live here indeed."

    A             F
"So be gracious and give for as long as you live;
  G G      G G
Seek guidance from heaven above."
    A         F
"Don't worry or hurry; don't lie or deny;
    D            C        A... F... G. G. G. G.  A... G... Eb... F
And remember, the answer is love."   ...
    G         Eb
Now, I'll say it to you, that it ain't nothing new,
  F F       F F
And I'll tell you the way he told me.
    G         Eb
"If you want to survive, just be glad you're alive;
    C             Bb       D... Bb... F... G...
And accept death like it had to be."

# BLACK BEAUTY

Written and arranged by Andy Barber, 1981
First copyright © 1995 (PAu 1-986-264)

VERSE 1

    A          B            A          B
In the hotel lobby (I tried not to stare), a Jamaican lady with coal black hair;
    G              A      F#
Her skin so smooth, her complexion so fair.
    A          B            A           B
I smiled at her and she winked at me, but we both knew true love could never be;
    G          A
Never respected by society.

Bm. G. A. E…    Bm. G. A. E…    Bm. G. A… E… F#…

VERSE 2

I could tell she was born from a royal line, with the style and class of a vintage wine.
I discovered her room was right across from mine.

CHORUS 1

  Bm         G          A     E
I said, "Pretty baby won't you let me in?"
       Bm     G        A       E
"I could be your lover; I could be your friend."
    Bm         G           A        E… F#…
She said, "I know, honey, but you'll never win."

A B… A B… A B… A. B. A. B.       A D… B… A D… B… G… A… F#…

VERSE 3

We drank champagne and laughed all night. We didn't believe in love at first sight,
But we kissed in the dark, it was black on white.
A wonderful evening of passion and grace; faded blue denim on satin and lace,
A compliment to the human race.

CHORUS 2

She said, "Pretty baby, why don't you begin,"
As her sexy smile met my foolish grin?
Ooh, black beauty, was it really a sin?

CHORUS 3

I said, "Pretty baby, take me there again."
She loved me despite the color of my skin.
Hey, black beauty, did it have to end?

VERSE 4

    A          B           A          B
I'm unable to think, I'm unable to feel. I'd never encountered a love so real.

G                  A    B. A. D… B… A. D… B…    G… A… B… A. D. Bm…
Love that wasn't just sex appeal.

# C'EST LA VIE, BABY (Eleven Come Seven)

Written and arranged by Andy Barber, 2018
First copyright © 2019 (Anthology)

```
   D...                        A.     D.
The second I thought there wasn't ample room,
   C.     G.      A...
I'm popping out of the womb.
```

And ever since that fateful day of my birth,
I would try to prove my worth.

It wasn't enough to know the Golden Rule,
They required I go to school.

Though every day I'd pretend to be tough,
I was never old enough.

Since I could not afford to swindle and rob,
I went looking for a job.

They said I didn't have sufficient knowledge,
So I attended college.

Although I knew relationships were scary,
I consented to marry.

As soon as she tried to take it all by force,
I happened next to divorce.

If I would have scrimped and saved my whole life through,
My bills would now be past due.

To do it over I should make revision,
Not another decision.

# CHRIST THE KING

Written and arranged by Andy Barber, 1992
First copyright © 1995 (PAu 1-986-264)

VERSE 1

```
(E)          G    E  A      G    E
```
When is there time to think? At threshold, on the brink!
It terminates in a blink. Where is the missing link?

VERSE 2

I searched inside my mind; was nothing there to find.
Loose ends I had to bind; undelivered and unsigned.    (E)

CHORUS
```
   A          A
```
Now it unfolds; it's out of control!
```
     G          D
```
It's taking its toll, mind, body, and soul!
```
     E      G  E   D  E   G      E    D
```
My Savior, redeemer of mankind, direct me for I am blind.
```
      E      G    F#      D
```
I've witnessed truth, glory, and grace,
```
   E          G          A
```
Love and peace; I never could replace.

VERSE 3

Killing, lying, and greed: fruits of the evil seed.
For this Christ had to bleed; please let Him take the lead.

REPEAT CHORUS

VERSE 4

We'll meet Him face to face! To see Him, to embrace!
Let us the human race, offer our thanks and praise.

REPEAT CHORUS

# CITY BLUES

Written 1973 and arranged 1976 by Andy Barber
First copyright © 2001 (PAu 2-613-596)

A… D. A. G. C G C D. A.  A… D. A. G. C G C D. A.
B… D… A… B. B.  B… D… A… B. B. B.

VERSE 1

   A                                 D         A

I was looking for my answers, but the question wasn't known;
     G                 C      G C    D          A

While the simpletons were saying that their minds were never blown.
   A                            D        A

Then the money was all given to the businessmen as loans;
     G           C   G   C D     A

But the boss said that he'd have to change the subject.

When the general was livid over foreign pressure plays,
He told his staff to wait 'til he remembered what to say;
But I couldn't wait that long because the night had made the day;
And they said the town was closed to all the public.

CHORUS

     B                            D

Well the city blues have got me and I've got no place to turn;
   A                           B    B

So I'll sit inside the bathroom 'til the court has been adjourned;
 B                           D

While folks are outside laughing 'cause there's nothing left to learn.
    A                           B    B

But they're all afraid of dying 'cause they think they're gonna burn.

VERSE 2

I asked why time was made a factor if it wasn't real;
But they scorned me and they stoned me, and they made a big ordeal;
But even God, when He was down, decided He would kneel.
When they said "look up" His answer was "you'll find it".

The senators swam deep in mud when they thought things were hot;
They eased their minds by saying they'd recall what they forgot.
While their ship was slowly sinking, they convinced me it was not;
And the president got trashed before he signed it.

REPEAT CHORUS

INTERLUDE (chords only)

G. D. A… G# G. D. D C A…     G. D. A.. G# G… D… B… B.. (A#)

# CITY BLUES (Continued)

VERSE 3
I was walking down the street and saw a little girl molested,
So I took her to a cop to say that surely they had jested;
But the cop pulled out his gun and said that we were both arrested;
And he snuck her in the alley to assault her.

When "hello" sounds louder than "goodbye" the woods will be behind us;
But there's always someone lurking there who leaps up to remind us.
And politicians tell the world they know that they will find us;
But today I will not lay upon the altar.

REPEAT CHORUS

INTERLUDE (chords and lead only)

EXCURSION
A... A.. B*b* B... B.. B*b* A... A.. G#
G... C. G. F. B*b* F B*b* C. G.   G... C. G. F. B*b* F B*b* C. G.
D A.. C G.. D A.. C G..   D A.. C G.. D A.. C G..

INTERLUDE
     G             D            A
So I might as well forget it, 'cause I've smoked my only pipe;
 G#    G        D         D  C      A
For we'll fall into the grinder when they think we're turning ripe.
G#  G            D          A
And some people still are saying that they don't think they're the type,
G#      G            D         B
Then they close their eyes and hear the hurdy-gurdy.

INTERLUDE
Is my freedom so important that I mustn't bend the rules?
Should I find a place to live where I may walk among the fools?
Should I build the house of Congress without using fascist tools?
Should I let my mind explode before I'm thirty?

A... D. A. G. C G C D. A.   A... D. A. G. C G C D. A.

REPEAT CHORUS

E B.. D A..   E B.. D A...   (repeat and fade out)

# CROWN OF LIFE

Written and arranged by Andy Barber, 2001
First copyright © 2001 (PAu 2-613-596)

G.. F# E...  G.. F# E... (repeated with lead)

VERSE 1
```
      F#..           C#  B.       A.
In the Garden of Eden were Adam and Eve,
        F#..              C#    B.   A.
But they fell from God's grace and they had to leave.
      F#..        C#   B...
They passed onto us their original sin,
        G...              A...                G... D B E.......
And it's bound to continue 'til I don't know when.
```

VERSE 2
But we've been set free by the blood of the Lamb.
You'd better believe or you're going to be damned.
Keep watch for His coming. Play it safe; play it straight.
On the day He returns it will be too late.

G... D B E.......  F. C

CHORUS
```
 D...         A...
Jesus, I will wait for you,
 C...              G    C   A.
Hoping that you'll come back soon.
  D...           A...
Strengthen me, I pray dear Lord,
      C.......              D.......
Whereas I cling unto your Word.
      C...              D.......
Whereas I cling unto your Word.
```

C... A... C... A... C... A... B.......

G.. F# E...  G.. F# E... (repeated with lead)

VERSE 3
Being saved through faith just because of God's grace,
I'll strive to persevere until I win this race.
Overcoming my trials, tribulations, and strife,
And attaining first prize of a Crown of Life.

G... D B E....... F. C

REPEAT CHORUS

C... A... C... A... C... A... B.......          G.. F# E...  G.. F# E... (repeated with lead)

# DOWN THE ROAD

Written and arranged by Andy Barber, 1979
First copyright © 1981 (PAu 321-648)

VERSE 1
```
F#   (F#)              C#       E              B
My Daddy left home when I was twelve; didn't leave a darn thing on the shelf.
F#           C#       E                  B
My Ma became a prostitute; after a while she didn't give a hoot.
```

F#. C#. E. B. F#... D

CHORUS 1
```
(D)          A               B  A
I was born to head on down the road;
   D         E           B  A
Sleep without a coat in the freezing cold.
D            A           B
Ain't nobody gonna tell me what to do.
   A   D             E           B  A
'Cause I've been through a lot more hell than you.
```

F#. C#. E. B. F#. C#. E. B.

VERSE 2
Fought my way through the Civil War; must've killed twenty men or more.
I was sixteen by the end of the strife; all I had left was my gun and my life.

CHORUS 2 ("It was time to head back down the road;")

C. G. D. A. G C. G. A... G F. C. D. A. G F. C. D... E... (D)

CHORUS 2 (Repeat)

VERSE 3
I got hitched when I was twenty-one to a red-haired lady who carried my son
They both died while she was giving birth; I done lost everything I ever had on this earth.

VERSE 4
Sitting on a stool at the end of the bar. I've traveled all over but I never got far.
Everything I loved is long since gone. Guess I'll have another shot and be moving on.

CHORUS 3 ("So now it's one more for the road;")

POSTLUDE
```
(D)       A       B     A    D
So now it's time to hit the road.
It's time to head back down the road.
I'm heading back on down the road.
I was born to head on down the road.          D... A...B...B. A. D... A... B...
```

# DREAMCHASER

Written and arranged by Andy Barber, 2005
First copyright © 2019 (Anthology)

VERSE 1

```
  B                           G           A.DA  EE  EB
I once loved a woman she was all that I had;
     B                              G           A.DA  EE  EE
She made me feel so good she made me feel so bad.
     B                         G           A... DAB.
She loved me then she left me without saying goodbye;
     B                    G        A... EAB.
And never gave a reason, no not even a lie.
```

CHORUS

```
   A            F#
Dreamchaser, that's me.
   A              B    A  B
When I fall asleep that's where you'll be.
   A            F#
Dreamchaser, come home.
     A              E        B
It's been a nightmare dreaming all alone.
```

VERSE 2

```
 B                          G
Since she ran away I've tried to track her down;
   A      D A      E       B
I'll be forever lost until the day she's found.
     B                    G
I'm playing for keeps; she's playing hard to get.
     A          D A      E       E
I'm chasing down a dream I haven't caught it yet.
 B        G          A  A  D  A  B
Dream baby, I haven't got a clue; dream lover that's true.
 B              G           A... EAB.
Let me remind you, I'm just one step behind you.
```

REPEAT CHORUS

VERSE (chords and lead guitar)

REPEAT CHORUS

# EASTER'S SONG

Written and arranged by Andy Barber, 1980
First copyright © 1981 (PAu 321-648)

A... C D. A... C D G. A... C D G. A... C D G. A... E. G D. A...

A. G. D. A E. A. G. D. A E.

A. G C. G. A. A. G C. G. A. A. G C G. A. A. G C. G. A.

```
A          G        D      A     E
```
Anytime was perfect once, it only lasted for a while.
```
A          G D      A          E
```
Being alive was easy once, but suddenly it's not my style.
```
 A       G    C G A (A)        G C G A
```
Searching for some peace. Needing some release.

A. G C. G. A. A. G C. G. A. A. G C G. A. A. G C. C... G... C.

```
     A        G C   G    A          G C   G
```
The sky was clear, it echoed blue; like untold dreams, as yet untrue.
```
     A        G C G E... A    B      G    A  F. G.
```
The broken, dusty avenue distracted me from feeling you.
```
     A           G C G        A            G C  G
```
The pathway narrowed at midnight black. I wandered from the beaten track.
```
     A           G C  G  E...A    B    G      A    F. G.
```
I wrestled there with frozen death; I wondered who restored my breath.

A... G C G. A... G C G. A... G C G.

```
  D       A     E       B   C  G..G..                A G C.  C A.
```
Vague impressions, phantoms, ghosts? Shadows from the Lord of Hosts!

.... A. G C. G. A. A. G C. G. A. A. G C... C. G... C.

```
     A        G   C G    A            G C  G
```
The agony wore stripes of red, but still some followed what He said.
```
     A        G   C G  E...   A    B    G      A  F. G.
```
A fugitive from worlds unknown? They wondered who removed the stone.

A... G C G. A... G C G. A... G C G.

D A. E B. C G...

```
  A          G    C G A (A)        G C   G A
```
Searching for some peace? Needing some release?

A... C D. A... C D G. A... C D G. A... C D G. A... E. G D A...

# ESCAPE

Written and arranged by Andy Barber, 1983
First copyright © 1995 (PAu 1-986-264)

VERSE 1
```
   D        F    Em     D
Escape the eternal void within;
D        F      Em       D
Open your heart and mind to begin.
   D        F        Em        D
Abandon all foolishness, sorrow, and pride.
   D        F      Em        D
Release your faith, let it be your guide,
```

CHORUS
```
     F     G       G# G    F
And soar through enchanted bliss!
F       G     F   D
Ecstasy awaits your kiss!
```

VERSE 2
The body is a cell in which we exist.
Virgin love unveiled! Can you resist?
Faith, hope, and charity beneath the mask;
To set them free, you need but ask.

REPEAT CHORUS

INTERLUDE
```
   G            A   Bb
Admit to yourself you're lost;
   F        Eb     F      D
Glory and greed aren't worth the cost.
      A            B C
In your God and yourself believe,
      A        G    F
And the power you will receive.
```

VERSE 3
I leave you now in your innocent youth,
The gifts of righteousness, wisdom, and truth.
Learn from these, and teach your neighbor.
Strength be yours throughout your labor.

F… G. G# G F…  F… G F D…

D… F. G. D…  D… F. G. D…

F… D…  F… D…  F… D…  F. G. D…

# FOR GOD SO LOVED THE WORLD

Written and arranged by Andy Barber, 2004
First copyright © 2004 (PAu2 914-571)

CHORUS  [C… D. A C… D. A…]

```
    C                        D        A
For God so loved the world He gave His only Son.
    C           D     A
Hosanna to the giving Lord!
        C                      D        A
That who so would believe could eternal life receive.
    C         D     A
Hosanna to the living Word!
```

A G E… A G E…

VERSE 1

```
    A        (A) G   C     G
Death and Hell have been defeated;
        A          G F     G
The Law has been fulfilled, yeah.
     A             G  C     G
At God's right hand the Lord is seated
  A          G   F B♭ F  G C G
Just as God had willed, brother.
```

A. D A.  A. D A…

REPEAT CHORUS

VERSE 2

Christ, the first fruits of the resurrection,
Our faithful cornerstone. Oh,
His Spirit sanctifies us to perfection,
In route to our heavenly home, sister.

REPEAT CHORUS (chords with lead)

EPILOGUE

```
B……. D A B……. D A
G……. D A B……. D A
B……. D A G……. C G
A……. D A B.. E B. E B…
```

# FREESTYLE BOOGIE

Written and arranged by Andy Barber, 1974
First copyright © 1995 (PAu 1-986-264)

VERSE 1

```
        A                    C        G        A    C G
When I woke up this morning, the sun was just beginning to shine.
(G)  A                    C        G        A    C G
So I walked out the door, took a deep breath, and man I felt fine.
(G)    A                   C        G        A    C G
You know I didn't have nothin', no I didn't have nothin' to do;
(G)  A              C        G        A    C G
And I felt so alive, well you know that I felt brand new.
  A                C    G        A    AAA
I just have this boogie, deep down in my bones;
(A)    C              G        A    C G
There ain't nobody nowhere who makes me feel alone.
```

VERSE 2

Well I once had a girl and we got it on all the time.
Oh, we never had money, we never had a single dime.
We just followed the road, and it didn't matter where we went.
We didn't have no worries, no bills to pay, not even the rent.
We only had our boogie; we boogied every day.
When the boogie is blooming, you mustn't let it wither away.
So boogie! Just boogie baby!

D C G A   D C G A   D C G A

VERSE 3

You know I know a lot of people who will lend me a smile when I'm down.
You keep a smile on your face and you never even see a frown.
I've got a lot of friends that boogie, and they feel all right;
And if you give me your hand, girl, you know we're gonna boogie all night.

D C G A   D C G A   D C G A

VERSE 4

I've had good times and bad, but I'm gonna tell you what is true:
If you've got a good boogie, you're never gonna ever be blue.
So just boogie down; I do whenever I can!
God gave me this life, and I'm gonna live it like a man.

G… A   G… A   G… A   G…A

# GENESIS

Written and arranged by Andy Barber, 1993
First copyright © 1995 (PAu 1-986-264)

VERSE 1

```
D                                    C
In the beginning, when the cosmos was born,
 D                      F
God's creations were taking form.
  D                    C        F       D   C   D
When God said, "Let there be light," there began day and night.
```

F. D... C. D...   F. D... C. D...   F. D... C. D...

CHORUS 1

```
     F    A  F   A   G#          G    C
The vapors and elements found their own place:
  F    A    F   A  G#      G    C
Earth, wind, water, fire, all by His grace.
       F     A   F   A    G#       G    C
The seasons were formed and the earth bore fruit;
     F    D      C       D
Animals thrived and plants took root.
      F      D      C        D
And so it was to be; and it was all so free.
      F   C     D
And God said it was good.
```

CHORUS 2

God shaped a man, and from him a mate;
Letting us master the world and our fate.
And humans lived, but then we died;
We grew, and loved, and laughed, and cried.
Though in His love we did not abide.
And God knew that we couldn't hide.

VERSE 2

Then God planted His own seed.
And through this great, eternal deed,
In Christ every living soul was blessed. Through faith in Him we pass the test.

CHORUS 3

Christ saves us from death; restores us with His breath.
He forgives us still when we do His will:
To love each other and become fulfilled.
Life can be a burden; life can be a thrill.

# GIVING IT ALL

Written and arranged by Andy Barber, 1992
First copyright © 1995 (PAu 1-986-264)

CHORUS
```
(D)      A        D    A      D        A    D    E
```
I'm giving everything to Jesus, giving Him it all; I'm giving everything to the Lord.
```
     G          A        D        G       D    A      D
```
Every night and day He sees us. He protects us and He frees us; so I'm giving it all to the Lord.

VERSE 1
```
     G          A              D           G
```
God gave to us His Word, that through faith we could afford
```
     D        G      A
```
To be spared from His mighty sword.
```
     G          A          D           G
```
Let us heed the sacred birth, and the death that saved the earth!
```
     D        G        D        G
```
Let us sing with joy and mirth, "Now my life has good and worth,"
```
        D      A        D
```
"Since I'm giving it all to the Lord".

CHORUS
I'm giving everything to Jesus, giving Him it all; I'm giving everything to the Lord.
Every night and day He sees us. He protects us and He frees us; now let's give it all to the Lord.

VERSE 2
I was lost but now I'm found, so when judgment comes around,
I'll be glad I'm heaven bound.
Let us sing with the chorus, "I know He won't ignore us."
"He paid the ransom for us; from death He will restore us,"
"And, I'm giving it all to the Lord."

CHORUS
I'm giving everything to Jesus, giving Him it all; I'm giving everything to the Lord.
Every night and day He sees us. He protects us and He frees us; yes I'm giving it all to the Lord.

VERSE 3
Well your faith and hope will grow, and the love inside will show.
You'll defeat the evil foe.
From your heart remove all greed. Help your fellow man in need.
Be fruitful, sow God's seed; you will reap above indeed,
If you've given it all to the Lord.

CHORUS
We're giving everything to Jesus, giving Him it all; we're giving everything to the Lord.
Every night and day He sees us. He protects us and He frees us—Giving it all to the Lord.

POSTLUDE
```
(D)      A        D    A...D        A      D    A...D
```
I'm giving everything to Jesus.      I'm giving everything to Jesus.          (repeat or fade)

ANTHOLOGY                                     128

# INSIDE OF ME

Written and arranged by Andy Barber, 1978
First copyright © 1981 (PAu 321-648)

VERSE 1

```
F              C              F    C
When I was just a boy my folks went west.
F            C          D            G       E7      F   C F C
Searching for that homestead until they found the land they thought was best.
      F          C      G    F   C
We struggled hard to make the land provide.
      F          C              D              G      E7     F   C F
For ten long years I plowed the soil and worked the fields right by my daddy's side.
```

CHORUS 1

```
     D                A        C          G
Then along came a pack of renegades, looking for some fun.
     D           A        C        D
They raped my ma and shot my pa, so I began to run.
     F              C       G    E     F   C
They caught me and they beat me, until I couldn't see;
     D         G    E7    F    C F C
And I couldn't bear the loss inside of me.
```

VERSE 2

I came to with my head spinning round.
I looked across the land we'd built, said a prayer, and burned it to the ground.
A ruthless gang of outlaws took me in.
They taught me how to rustle, how to hold-up banks, they taught me how to sin.

CHORUS 2

One day we robbed a city bank, my friends got shot that day;
I grabbed the cash and ran outside to make my getaway.
I slipped into a chapel and I got down on my knees,
Hoping for some good inside of me.

VERSE 3

The preacher found me praying to the Lord.
He volunteered to hide my hide, told me I'd be safe and gave his word.
The preacher's lovely daughter brought me food.
I'd never seen a girl so pure, and she had never seen a man so crude.
I told her father love had changed my life.
I promised I'd return the stolen loot if she'd consent to be my wife.

CHORUS 3

I took the stolen money to the sheriff without fail;
Instead of being grateful, he just threw me into jail.
I looked outside and saw a noose was hanging from a tree;
And I thought about the love inside of me.

VERSE 4

Late that night my girl brought me a gun;
She told me that the only chance I had to stay alive was to run.
I made the sheriff come unlock the door.
I knocked him out and gagged his mouth, tied his hands, and left him on the floor.

CHORUS 4

I grabbed my hat and gun belt and ran into the street,
And there a horse was waiting beside my love, so sweet.
I kissed her hard and rode away as she waved back at me;
And I dreamed about the love that set me free.

F. C. F... A D...

# I SAW YOU

Written and arranged by Andy Barber, 1974
First copyright © 1981 (PAu 321-648)

VERSE 1

```
D          G          A
I saw you just as I was leaving,
   C        G          D
Strolling so carefree to look so aware.
D          G          A
I saw your body, so deceiving;
   C                   G          D
Seeing your eyes was all my heart could bear.
```

G. A… G. A… G… D…

VERSE 2

They looked into mine so completely,
Piercing my eyelids, attacking my mind.
Expressing interest so discretely;
Feeling emotion but wondering what kind.

VERSE 3

I thought about it, kept on going;
Glad to see beauty for once in the day.
I turned to look again, not knowing
You had turned also to look back my way.

VERSE 4

Between our lives the doors were closing,
(It seems they knew they were open too long).
Your image, still my mind imposing,
Until my thoughts had digressed to this song.

C. A… C. A… C. G. D… C. G. D… C. D. G…

# JAIL QUAIL

Written and arranged by Andy Barber, 1989
First copyright © 1995 (PAu 1-986-264)

VERSE 1

```
      A         C     A      G
There is a young lady in my neighborhood,
      A           C     G       A
She's just a sophomore, but she sure looks good.
      A         C     A      G
She feeds my dogs when I'm on the road,
   A          C     G      A
Cleans and takes care of my humble abode.
      A          C     A    G
I'm not that bright, but it's plain to see,
      A         C     G      A  A... C G A.
That little honey has a crush on me.
```

CHORUS 1

```
   G              D
The other day I was kicking back;
 C    A   A  C   G    G
She barges in; hops on my lap, and says,
D        C        A
"I need an experienced male!" I tell her,
C                  D    A
"Ain't lookin' for a stretch in jail."
   C              F     G
"Pretty soon you'll be ready to sail,"
   A    A      C   G    A
"So be a good girl and hit the trail."
```

VERSE 2

She says, "Someday I'm gonna make you mine." I tell her,
"Take it easy, you've got plenty of time."
"All the boys will be waiting in line,"
"But as for me, well I've passed my prime."

CHORUS 2

How could I be such an ignorant fool?
She's craved by all the guys at her school.
She calls me on the telephone.
She can't stand to see me alone.
She chills me down to the bone.

# JAIL QUAIL (Continued)

INTERLUDE

<pre>
     G            A
I'd like to take her into my arms;
   C            D
Have a taste of her many charms.
A                     G
I want her so much that I could scream;
   D          E
But it's only when I dream.
</pre>

A. C G A... A. C A G. A...

VERSE 3

Compared to her, I'm just too old.
Still, nature takes its toll.
At least I've got my soul,
And good old rock-and-roll.

CHORUS 3

A young girl's heart in a woman's frame,
Playing this adolescent game.
Who knows, maybe I'm to blame?
I think she'd like to share my name.
She thrills me all the same.

C G A... A. B C. B A G. A...

# JEWEL

Written and arranged by Andy Barber, 2004
First copyright © 2004 (PAu2 914-571)

VERSES 1 & 2  [A… B… A… B…]
   A           B
My first impression: What a cutie!
A            B
Emerald eyes that sparkled bright.
   A        B
I'd never seen such grace and beauty,
   A        B
Gliding like a bird in flight.

Her ruby smile was so inviting;
Her voice, a soothing melody.
The memory was so exciting,
Setting my emotions free.

CHORUS 1
A…               B. F…     F…
   I felt a strong sensation, the source of inspiration.
A…                 B. F…    F…
   Then lingered my frustration, a little aggravation.
A…        B. F…
   A simple ideation, became determination…
Am            G               E
How in the world am I ever going to make her mine?
   A      F#m         G         A
If we could be together, it would be… simply divine!

VERSE 3
Last night I saw her in a vision,
Dancing across a sapphire sky.
I promised God, "I'll find religion,
But never let the music die."

CHORUS 2
I had a predilection for the perfect love connection;
And after close inspection with adequate reflection,
She was the best selection, approaching pure perfection.
How in the world am I ever going to make her mine?
If she would be my true love, I would be her valentine.

BRIDGE
      A            C          A             C
For the topaz gleam of a golden key that opens wide a faithful heart,
    A          C          A               C… G… A…
I've searched in vain relentlessly. I'm hoping for a brand-new start… (hold)

# LADY OF THE SHADOWS

Written and arranged by Andy Barber, 2008
First copyright © 2019 (Anthology)

Am... C... D... F...

VERSE 1

    Am...             C...                  D...                F...
At twilight in the greenwood grove, adorned in white silk flowing,
A mystery girl with hollow eyes, but radiant and glowing;
She strolled as if a sailing ship across a polished mirror,
Elusive like an autumn gale; I wanted to be near her.
 Am...               F. G.  Am...  A..
Lady of the shadows, I love you.

INTERLUDE

    G...          D...                C...            F. G.
My spirit heard a whispering cry that spoke of grief and sorrow.
    G...          D...              C...       F. G.
She roamed as free but yet confined; no past and no tomorrow.
Am...             F. G.  Am...  A..
Lady of the shadows, I love you.

A.        G...      D.     E E7.. A.
You could still this restless soul, and
You could fill my empty bowl, and
You could spill your heart of gold on me. (A…)

You could thrill like dreams untold, but
If you will I'll lose control, so
You must kill your awesome hold on me. (A…)

VERSE 2

    Am...             C...             D...          F...
She disappeared like phantoms do, into a shroud of darkness;
    Am...             C...             D...           F...
And broke our secret rendezvous, to leave me lost and heartless.
Am...             F. G.  Am...
Lady of the shadows, I love you.
Am...             F. G.  Am...
Lady of the shadows, I love you.
Am...             F. G.  A...
Lady of the shadows, I love you.

# LOST AND SLEEPING

Written and arranged by Andy Barber, 1973
First copyright © 1981 (PAu 321-648)

VERSE 1
```
    E                       G   A
I never met a woman who could hold me down;
    A           G     E
It seems I'm always on my own.
      E                         G      A
I've always had my freedom, but it's taught me well,
      A         G   E
That I never want to be alone.
```

VERSE 2
With the sun right behind me and the sky above,
I'm searching just to find the truth.
But every time I leave, I come back home to you,
It reminds me that I've lost my youth.

CHORUS
```
  E           G  A       E
You know I've been lost, I've been sleeping,
        G       D     E
I've been living in a deep blue dream;
(E)     G     A     G    E
And you know I'm going to find me,
        G           D   E
I may never see your face again.
```

VERSE 3
My life keeps me living and my soul shines bright,
But my heart is sometimes hard as stone.
How much that I can love you girl, I just can't say;
My destiny is still unknown.

CHORUS ("Because I've been lost, I've been sleeping…")

VERSE 4
I've met a lot of women who are full of love,
But they never seem to understand.
I may leave them in the darkness, though I do mean well;
Seems it never happens like I planned.

CHORUS ("I said I've been lost, I've been sleeping…")

# LOVE OF YESTERDAY

Written and arranged by Andy Barber, 1976
First copyright © 1981 (PAu 321-648)

VERSE 1  [C. D. Em...]

```
   C     D    Em        C. D. Em.
I can't depend on aspirations;
      C       D     Em         C. D. Em.
Love leaves no trace across your eyes.
     C     D      Em       C. D. Em.
I'll waste no time with recitations;
       C      D       Em        C. D. Em.
Words won't divert your promised lies.
     C     D    Em        C. D. Em.
So suddenly your love departing?
   C     D    Em       C. D. Em.
I was convinced I understood.
    C      D    Em       C. D. Em.
No answers I expect regarding
        C       D        Em         C. D. E
What fooled my conscience guessing good.
```

CHORUS

```
   D     G    D     E
Flashing to my past forgotten,
D        G      D  E
Other lovers passed that way.
   D     G       D     E
Searching made me forfeit their love
       E        G D G... D. Em...
For your love of yesterday.
```

VERSE 2  [C. D. Em...]


I stand beside my window watching
The life inside me walk away.
My heart your love was deeply touching,
'Til you removed the touch today.
Suppressed emotion in me sleeping,
Was recently allowed to live.
And just for you my heart was keeping
More love than I thought I could give.

REPEAT CHORUS

# LOVE OF YESTERDAY (Continued)

INTERLUDE

```
  D   G      C     F
Reminiscing time together—
  D        G   C   F
First time that I felt alive.
    D        G        C   F
Though you're gone, I'm glad I loved you;
    D    G     C    F... F. C G... G. D Em...
Now I must try to survive.
```

INTERLUDE (chords and lead only).

VERSE 3  [C. D. Em...]

My chance to show that much affection,
I never had before we met.
Poor heart that it must face rejection;
Abiding for time to forget.
My future fate, all time revealing:
Another love occurs, I pray.
Would I be able to show feeling?
Express such love as yesterday?  (ends on "day" in E major)

# LOVE VS. TIME

Written and arranged by Andy Barber, 1979
First copyright © 1981 (PAu 321-648)

```
E        D    A    B
Love—Is such a lovely thing.
         D        A      E
    It makes you want to sing,
         D    A  B
    Until you lose it.
```

Time—So hard to understand,
    But always in demand
    When you don't have it.

You— You taught me how to feel;
    You showed me love was real,
    And time, eternal.

Now—The time we had is gone;
    The love still lingers on.
    My life continues.

Once—I thought that I knew,
    But all my strength was you;
    And yours was life.

Oh — Now I know!
    The end is always fixed.
    Time and love don't mix.

    D. A.  B...
    Oh, why? (repeat and fade out)

# NEVER THE SAME

Written and arranged by Andy Barber, 1991
First copyright © 1995 (PAu 1-986-264)

D E. G. A... D... E...

VERSE 1

(D) E    G    A    D      E     D E    G   A    D      E
What about you? Never the same? What about us? Never the same?
(D) E    G    A     D      E     D E    G     A
What about love? Never the same? What about sex?
  D      A     D      E     G     A     D      E
Both of us came! Never the same! Lively or lame? Savage or tame?

VERSE 2
What about love? Never the same? What about faith? Never the same?
What about hope? Never the same? What about truth?
Virtue or shame? Honor or blame? Never the same! Favor or flame!

CHORUS
   D              A      E
What do you see, hear, want, or need?
     D      G     A
You know you'd better take aim!
      D            A       E
You'd better take care and you'd better take heed!
    D    A     B
Because this isn't a game!

VERSE 3
What about peace? Never the same? What about love? Never the same?
What about joy? Never the same? What about life?
Never the same? Failure and fame? You've got a name! You've got a claim!

CHORUS
What do you see, hear, want, or need?
You know you'd better take aim!
You'd better take care and you'd better take heed!
Because it's never the same!

D E. G. A... D... E... D E. G. A... D... E...
D E. G. A... D... E... D E. G. A...
D. A... D. E... D. A... D... E... D. A... D. E...

# NEW SUN

Written and arranged by Andy Barber, 1984
First copyright © 1995 (PAu 1-986-264)

VERSE 1
```
  G     A     E     A    G     A E A
My life was swiftly passing as you caught my eye.
     G     A   E     A  G A  E A
You gazed at me so helplessly, I froze in time.
     G   A   E    A   G   A E A
For centuries we slept among the amber hills.
     G    A     E    A   G   A    E A
We didn't know it was a show, but we still got our thrills.
```

VERSE 2
Suddenly a storm arose and we got wet.
I guess I knew you better before we met.
Everything was changing; you were lost and I was found.
I left my gifts behind, there was no time to look around.

CHORUS 1
```
G D     E D  D        E G E  G
I spoke so freely, "You've got to realize,"
(G)  A      E       D      A        E
"Our days have broken, and it's time a new sun was on the rise."
```

E G E G E G A G E A G A E A

VERSE 3
Everybody just jogs in place.
That's what they mean by the human race.
But you once drove me on a rainbow ride
To the house of confusion and his lunatic bride.

VERSE 4
I had to choose to either leave your dream
Or sacrifice my self-esteem.

CHORUS 2
```
G D  E  G       E D E G
It wasn't easy. No, it wasn't nice.
(G)  A  E        D A      E
But I see it coming, there's a new sun on the rise.
```

E G E G E G A G E A G A E A

REPEAT CHORUS 2 (use chords in Chorus 1)

E G E G E G A G E

# PSALM 151

Written and arranged by Andy Barber, 2004
First copyright © 2004 (PAu2 914-571)

VERSE 1

  Am             D          Am  D
A desert breeze rolls across the land;
     Am            D          Am  D
The western sun sinks beneath the sand.
 G       F        G       A
Peacefully submitting to God's command;
      G            F       G      Am   D  Am  D
Like a symphony that is following His right hand.

VERSE 2
Celestial orbs traverse the night sky;
Radiant beams speak the glory on high.
But the greatest light is invisible to the eye;
Reminding me that my spirit will never die.

CHORUS 1
A... B C... B A... B C... B A... B C... B A... B C...
    Alleluia        Alleluia

CHORUS 2
D... C D. Em ..
D.. C D. E...

VERSE 3
Imagination is the last frontier.
Perception doesn't always show us what's here.
The mystery is something we must not fear;
For life is real and the truth is crystal clear.

REPEAT CHORUS 1

CHORUS 2
    D          C  D      Em
In heaven and earth a song we raise;
    D         C   D     Em
Let every living soul bring praise!
D... C D. Em ..
D.. C D. E... E...

BRIDGE
  Am         D
I know that I will always be free.
I'll live with the Lord for eternity.
Nobody can take that away from me.  Am... D.....    D... E

# RISE AND FALL OF ROCK AND ROLL

Written and arranged by Andy Barber, 1981
First copyright © 1981 (PAu 321-648)

```
B... G. A. E...  C. D.  B... G. A. E...  C. D.
B... G. A. E...  C. D.  B... G. A. E...  G. D.
E... D A D  E... D A D  E... D A D  G. A. E...
```

CHORUS
```
     B   C   G     E              G D     B   C   G     E              G D
```
The rise and fall of rock and roll.     The rise and fall of rock and roll.

VERSE 1
```
     E                        D A D
```
We really loved those rhythm and blues,
```
   E                          D A D
```
Down at the hop, in our blue suede shoes.
```
   E                      D
```
Nowadays, if you want to dance,
```
         G              A       E
```
Wear knee-high boots and skin-tight pants.

REPEAT CHORUS

VERSE 2
Music these days has just one beat;
No more boogie to move your feet.
The clubs are packed with disco ducks;
And everyone knows that disco sucks.

INTERLUDE
```
  A     B        G     E    A     B     G        E
```
Hit the sixties like a flood from above. Reached its peak in the summer of love.
```
   A       B     G    E      G           D
```
Woodstock was the final show.  Since then, rock's been dying slow.

```
E. G. D. E...  E. G. D. E...  E. G...  D. A...  C. G. F#...  F# G. E...
```

REPEAT CHORUS (chords only)

VERSE 3
Born from jazz, pop, folk, and soul;
Progressed to acid, heavy metal, funk.
Next it's called disco, wave, and punk;
Looks like rock has taken its toll.

INTERLUDE
Remember the twist, frug, and bunny hop? The bossanova, alligator, boogaloo, bop?
The mashed potatoes, locomotion, and skate? Swingers today just learn too late.

REPEAT CHORUS

# SEASONS

Written by Andy Barber, 1995; arranged by Andy Barber, 2001
First copyright © 2001 (PAu 2-613-596)

G... B... A... A... G... G... E... E... (repeat)

VERSE 1
  A... A.  A.  G#.     G...   G.
Summer; started out as a bummer.
G.    G#.       A...    A.
All of a sudden, I'd meet her;
  A.    G#.      G... G...
Never saw anything sweeter. I was in love.

CHORUS 1 (chords only)
A... E... C G. A A... A... E... C G. C. G.. C G. A    A... G... E... A... G... E...

VERSE 2
Autumn; I would be hitting rock bottom.
Expecting the blues and I got them;
Down in the dumps where I caught them, when she said goodbye.

CHORUS 2
   A        E     C G     A
Took her for granted; next she had flown.
A      E       C G     C     G  C G. A.
Anytime, anywhere, anybody can be all alone.

A... G... G... E... E...

VERSE 3
Winter; returned every letter I sent her.
Nothing that mattered could please her.
Guess she was only a teaser. I felt the fool

CHORUS 3
I am nobody. I have no name.
Summer, Autumn, Winter, Spring: It's all the same.

VERSE 4
Spring rain; thought it was going to bring pain.
All of the girls looked so sexy.
Knew it was going to vex me. Then she came home.

CHORUS 4 (chords and lead)

A... G... G... E... E...      G... B... A... A... G... G... E... E...

# SECOND COMING

Written and arranged by Andy Barber, 1979
First copyright © 1981 (PAu 321-648)

VERSE 1
```
  G#        F#        G#          B
Listen to me everyone, I'm called upon to say,
  G#          F#        G#        F# "
A warning sent from heaven is delivered here today."
  G#          F#        G#          B
"Beware of certain strangers who say that they're the way,"
  G#          F#          G#        F#
"For servants come from darkness to lead many souls astray."
```

CHORUS 1
```
    G#          E        A      B  F#
So prepare for the Messiah, don't be fooled by clever hands;
    G#          E        A    B  F#  C#...
For the Judgment Day will burst upon our persecuted lands.
```

VERSE 2
Beware of these false prophets with their miracles and tricks;
They're led by Hell and Satan who these charlatans he picks.
Sodom and Gomorrah will become the style of life;
With suffering and slavery, the peak of human strife.

CHORUS 2
The earthquakes, floods, and famines, and the pestilence and war,
Will be a sign to everyone His coming lay in store.

C#... B... A. G#. F#... G#. F#. F#. G#. G#. F#. F#. G#.

INTERLUDE
```
    G#          F#          F#            G#   G#... F#. F#... C#.
The sun will lose its radiance while darkness fills the world.
    G#              F#    F#... G#.   G#... F#. F#... G#.
The stars will fall behind the gloom.
    G#              F#      F#            G#
And fate—eternal life, not doom, to those who hold the pearl.
```

REPEAT VERSE 1 AND CHORUS 1

C#... B. C#... B. C#... B. B. B*b*. G#.

# S. O. M. F.

Written and arranged by Andy Barber, 1979
First copyright © 1981 (PAu 321-648)

VERSE 1

```
 E G E   A G E G    E    A G
Fui a la cantina, sediento por cerveza.
E    G E    A G   A G G E D E
Adentro la fichera vino bailando en la mesa.
```

VERSE 2

```
   E  G E  A G E  G    E A  G D
La chica era bonita, con cuerpo muy hermoso.
   E G E   A G   A G  G E D E
Me enamore de ella, y no soy mentiroso.
```

CHORUS

```
Y le dije,
   A      B G E   G         D E
"Sientese en mi cara, es un lugar confortable."
     A       B G E   G   G    E
"Si quieres dormir conmigo, te tratare amable."
```

VERSE 3

```
   E  G E    A G D E   G  E   A G
Despues de seis cervezas, cuando yo estaba boracho,
   E  G E  A G    A G G E D E
La chica me dijo bajito, "Te quiero mucho, macho."
```

REPEAT CHORUS

# SPYING GAME

Written and arranged by Andy Barber, 2004
First copyright © 2004 (PAu2 914-571)

VERSES 1 & 2

```
D.D.        D   E   F
I'm a spy, you're a spy.
D   D       D     E    F
It's eye for eye; it's do or die.
  C...   C...   C  F  E  C...  C   C   F    E  C D. D. D. CDCD...
But, I'm gonna get to you if it's the last thing that I do.
  C   C   C  F  E  C   C   C  F  E   C  D. D. EF.  EDCA. D...
And it's plain to see that you aim to get me too.
```

He's a spy and she's a spy.
Is he the right guy? Should I give her a try?
Will he make me cry? Will she tell me goodbye?
Is it all a big lie? Do we ever know why?

CHORUS 1

```
      C           F   C    D. D. D. C D C D...
Are you a hawk or are you a dove? Are you in or out of love?
      C                F    C    D. D. D. CDCD...  D. EF.  EDCA. D...
It's the spying game; it's a crying shame!
```

VERSE 2 (repeat chords with lead guitar)

VERSE 3 (second part only)

Did you peek behind a book as you tried to sneak a look?
And your very first clue: they were spying on you.

CHORUS 2

It's a game of cat and mouse. It's a lot like playing house.
It's the spying game. It's a crying shame!

INTERLUDE

```
 G  G    F   C   D  E  F  E D C A  D
Get along, get a life; find a husband find a wife.
         G            F    C    D.D.D.CDCD...
It's the spying game; it's a crying shame!
```

REPEAT VERSE 1 (first line only then fade out)

# STONED TO DEATH

Written and arranged by Andy Barber, 2001
First copyright © 2001 (PAu 2-613-596)

A... E. A.  A... E. A.

VERSE 1

  A.        D.        C.     A.
Last night I crashed a weekend bash.
A.      D.    C.      A.
All the people there were smashed.
       A.       D.      G.     C.
Yeah, they were gassed, and I mean trashed,
    A.    D.     G.     A.
Lest otherwise, they out had passed.

CHORUS

     D...           G...
What really chaps me to the bone,
  A...           E. A.    A... E. A.
Is why must everyone get stoned?

VERSE 2

If he ain't loaded he's totally juiced.
I wish she would her tongue unloose.
Who goosed the moose on her caboose?
Who can sing the blues when it's all bad news?

REPEAT CHORUS

VERSE 3

So now it's time to take my leave,
And from their fate I find reprieve.
The only way they'll ever be free
Is to spend more time in reality.

REPEAT CHORUS

# STREET RAP

Written by Andy Barber, 1994; arranged by Andy Barber, 2001
First copyright © 2001 (PAu 2-613-596)

A. A. A. G.   A. A. A. G. (chords and lead)

VERSE 1

  A                           G
Don't do the crime if you can't do the time.
Don't spend your prime with the scum and the slime.
Don't hang with gangs. Don't score with whores.
Don't strut with sluts. Don't swipe with hypes.
Don't sniff with a stiff. Don't smoke 'til you choke.
If they invite you to go you should just say no!

A. A. A. A.

CHORUS 1

  A...            D...         C.         B.      A...
Look at the market on the street, nothing but pieces of meat;
  A...            D...         C.  B.    A...
They're out turning tricks just to cop another fix.
  E...            C...    D...         C. A.
They're already addicted, some are even afflicted.
E...              C...           D...      D.  C.  A.
Once their mind goes ballistic, they become a statistic.

A. A. A. G.   A. A. A. G.   A. A. A. A.

VERSE 2

Met this dude on the street, he was not too discreet.
He was hanging with thugs; tried to sell me some drugs.
"Have some smack or some blow," but I just said, "no".
"I don't want to get hooked, or arrested and booked."
"I don't want a disease or to go through DTs,"
"Or much worse, end up dead! Plus, I ain't got the bread."

A.A.A.A.

INTERLUDE

B*b*... C... A. A. A. A. B*b*... C. B*b*. A. A. A. G. A. A. A. G.

VERSE 3

There's this chick at my school, she's a vamp and a fool.
Once, she gave me the hex, tried to lure me to sex.
She was feeling real frisky, but I said, "It's too risky."
"Since you're kind of a sleaze, you may have a disease."
"You could get knocked up; I could get locked up."
"You entice me, that's so, but I've got to say no."

A. A. A. A.

CHORUS 2

You can drink 'til you stink and you're drunk as a skunk.
You can screw 'til you're blue and you're sore as a whore.
Go get high 'til you fly and you're high as a kite,
But you're not having fun, and your friends: there are none.

A. A. A. G.  A. A. A. G. (chords and lead)

CHORUS 3

You can clean the needle before the injection.
You can wear a condom for extra protection.
You take all these precautions 'til you feel content,
But that doesn't protect you one hundred percent.

A. A. A. G.  A. A. A. G.  (fade out)

# TAKE TIME

(written and arranged by Andrew V. Barber, 1997
First copyright © 2001 (PAu 2-613-596)

VERSE 1
```
  A       G      D       A
```
Take time for living, take time to be free;
```
  A        E         G          D
```
Take time for caring. Won't you take time for me?
```
  A       G      D      A
```
Take time for helping another in need.
```
  D       G      D      A    D
```
Take time to bury your pride and your greed.

VERSE 2
Take time to listen and take time to think;
When it's time to take action, don't take time to blink.
Time can be bought and time can be sold;
But time ain't for wasting, it's more precious than gold.

CHORUS 1
```
      E       G      G        D
```
Don't get there too early, but don't you be late;
```
     G       D       A        D
```
If you use your time wisely, your reward will be great.
```
  B       D      D     A
```
Take time to cherish your time for today;
```
  D      A      E       A
```
Take time to worship, and take time to pray.
```
  G      D      D      A
```
Take time to study the words of the Lord,
```
   G        D      A     D
```
It is time that's well-spent; time you can afford.

VERSE 3
A time to be born and a time just to die;
A time to be laughing, a time just to cry.
A time to sow and a time to reap,
A time to work and a time to sleep.

CHORUS 2
A time to embrace and a time to refrain;
A time to feel good and a time to feel pain.
A time to fight and a time to make peace;
Forever with hope for the time hate will cease.
There's a time for all seasons, and all time is prime.
There is no time to fear, there is love for all time!

# TEASE QUEEN BOOGIE

Written and arranged by Andy Barber, 1978
First copyright © 1981 (PAu 321-648)

B. E D B. A. C A D C... G. B*b* G. C. G...
B. E D B. A. C A D C A G... B*b* G. C... G...
A... D A...  A... D A... (B)

VERSE 1

   B (B F# G# D7 B)
I watched her just the other day walkin' to class,
  B
Strolling down the hallway just shakin' her ass.
    A (A E F# E C7 A)
My buddies told me, "Hey man, don't go that route."
       A
"She flirts with all the fellows, but she never puts out."

VERSE 2

Later that night after the football game,
I saw her sack the quarterback; what a shame!
I tried to approach her at the victory dance,
But there was such a crowd, I didn't even get a glance, at

CHORUS

    B            A
The campus queen, the local tease.
  G                      C     G
Before you ask her out, you gotta get on your knees.
        B       A
She's the typical flirt, in a mini-skirt.
  G                   C       G
Before you get a kiss, you gotta say "pretty please"
   A  (B)
To Tease Queen.

VERSE 3

The teacher made me stay after history class,
Saying, "Boy you'd better study, or you ain't gonna pass."
I said, "It ain't my fault, so cut me some slack."
"I can't concentrate unless you move her to the back."

VERSE 4

I saw her after school and said, "You sure look fine!"
"You're the best lookin' thing this side of the Rhine."
Since I had her interest, I took a chance,
Said, "Meet me tonight at the homecoming dance."

REPEAT CHORUS

VERSE 5

She watched me on stage playin' in the band.
She brought me a drink from the refreshment stand.
She told me that my music made her feel alive.
We met when it was over for a moonlight drive.

REPEAT CHORUS

EPILOGUE

          C                    D        G      A
She's the tease queen baby, you know she's got everything.
You're a tease queen honey, you know you've got everything.
You're my tease queen darlin', I know you've got everything.

C... D. G. A...

# TOGETHER 'TIL THE END

Written and arranged by Andy Barber, 1977
First copyright © 1981 (PAu 321-648)

VERSE 1

```
  A    G   E  GEA   A              E  GA
```
I left my home and family just as my dawn was breaking.
The restlessness inside my heart told me that love was waking.
I tried to get every girl I met, within the making;
I guess it seemed to meet my dreams, but I was mistaken.

CHORUS 1

```
     F   G  Am   G    F   G      Am
```
And then I met a certain girl, who taught me how to love.
Together we were always free, and blessed by God above.
Recalling all the other loves, the ones I'd treated wrong;
```
          F   G   A   G   F          A
```
Showed me that I must keep this girl; then suddenly, she was gone!

INTERLUDE 1

```
  A         B  E  B     G   C  G  CGA
```
So I became the heart of stone, the miser, and the fool.
I tried to shatter young girls' hopes, and break the golden rule.
I gathered all the pretty maids within my reach.
I'd choose them just to use them, like a leach.

G C G B   E. A. C G E G  E. A. G. A.

VERSE 2

Well I was happy for a while; I swam in all my glory.
But I got bored and left alone, to read a sad love story.
Some chicks I thought looked pretty hot, but they were all just faking;
Because I knew as my love grew that I would be forsaken.

CHORUS 2

I tried to show my face again; I tried to change my way.
But all my dates were one-night-stands; my women wouldn't stay.
My reputation held me back from every heart I tried.
The pressure caused anxiety from love I'd kept inside.

# TOGETHER 'TIL THE END (Continued)

INTERLUDE 2

As years passed by eventually, a true love was forbidden.
Sure, I knew lots of women then, but now my love was hidden.
My mind regressed to other stress I'd known when I was younger.
As I recalled those loves so sweet, my heart resumed its hunger.

CHORUS 3

One day when I was strolling down a lonesome avenue.
I spotted a familiar face, she recognized me too.
It seems that she was just like me, her love was in the wind.
Now once again we're hand-in-hand, together 'til the end.

F. G. Am. G… F. G. Am.  (repeat with lead)
F… A…

# TOUGH LOVE

Written and arranged by Andy Barber, 1999
First copyright © 2001 (PAu 2-613-596)

B... G... D... A... (repeat) B7......

VERSE 1

```
  B7                    B7                G      D       B7...
The angel there, shining in the garden, speaking of heaven's delight.
B7               G     D        B7...
I was scared; her brightness shattered the night.
B7                           G         D     B7...
She declared, "You have vision but you have no sight."
B7                  G D       B
I became aware, and realized she was right.
```

CHORUS 1

```
(B)   F#      A       E (DED) B
Tough love, surrounding you like a moat.
(B)    F#   A      E (DED) B
Tough love, not being able to vote.
(B)     F#   A      E (DED) B
Tough love, barely keeping afloat.
(B)    F#   A         E7...
Tough love, better get back on the boat.
```

INTERLUDE 1

```
D     A     B       F#...
I was heading down the wrong path,
  D     A        B...
Darkness followed my way.
  D       A          B      F#...
A razor's edge distance from the brink of God's wrath;
    G  (AG)          A
But then I was lifted, another would pay.
```

B... G... D... A...

VERSE 2

I dreamt she glowed like a shimmering rainbow, warning me one other time.
For there below: a lake of fire sublime.
Didn't want to go, but I was living a crime.
Heard a trumpet blow, and then I heard a voice chime...

# TOUGH LOVE (Continued)

CHORUS 2

Tough love, cramming it right down your throat.
Tough love, giving up your mantle and coat.
Tough love, dividing the sheep from the goats.
Tough love, one slip and that's all she wrote.

INTERLUDE 2

Take off the black mask or it'll go to your face.
I'm not going to tell you again.
You've got to make a choice just like the whole human race.
You can gain the world and still not win.

B… G… D… A…

C D… G A… B7……

POSTLUDE

C   D          G      A         B7…
All contracts with death and hell will be null and void.
All memory of evil will be utterly destroyed.

C D… G A… B7……

# UGLY GIRLS HAVE GOT IT MADE

Written and arranged by Andy Barber, 1981
First copyright © 1981 (PAu 321-648)

CHORUS [AAAB]

F#   D      A     B   A B
Ugly girls have got it made;
   F#   E   D   A       E   B
Goofing off and lying in the shade.
F#   E   D   A   B
Any man is an even trade,
A B     F#    E D    A       E
If they're looking bad and they act low grade.

VERSE 1

Bm           D    A
There she is sitting in the sand,
   Bm      F#    A
A smoke and a beer in her hand.
Bm        D    A
From L. A. up to New York
     Bsus2      F#   D
The pretty girls are all at work.

REPEAT CHORUS

VERSE 2
It's no hassle getting laid, just say so and there ain't no doubt.
Ugly girls have got it made, while foxes wait to be asked out.

VERSE 3
She never cheats on her main guy, but if she ever catches him,
She'll punch her old man in the eye, and tear his lover limb from limb.

REPEAT CHORUS

VERSE 4
If I marry in my life (now that the facts are weighed),
I'm going to pick me an ugly wife, 'cause ugly girls have got it made!

EPILOGUE [ABBB]

A  B B B  A B B B    A  B B B   A  B B B       A  B B B
Ugly girls, Plain Janes.  Acne Alice,  Cross-eyed Carol,  Buckteeth Bertha…
   A       B
Love them all!

# VICTORIA

Written by Andy Barber, 1971; arranged by Andy Barber, 1978
First copyright © 2001 (PAu 2-613-596)

VERSE 1

```
Dm                        Cm
I wait for you behind a line of monarchs,
     Dm                         A
Who watch to see a crumbling heart of stone.
     Dm                          F
You climbed the Andes looking for your shadow.
     C                        G
And now you're going to leave me all alone?
     Dm                      Em
But who are you, the peasants never offer?
  Dm                           A
Where do you stand when everybody's gone?
  Dm                      F
I laugh until I cry because I know you.
        C                     G
Tomorrow all the dogs will sing my song.
```

CHORUS

```
  D                              F#
Now what's become of you? Well, you haven't got a clue.
     G                         E
I've looked inside my pockets, you're not there.
  D                          F#
Precious time has blown away, and it withers every day;
  G                         E
Convince yourself it's my fault, I don't care.
```

Dm. Am. Em. Bm. Dm. Am. B… Am…

VERSE 2

```
Every time I see you, winds are blowing;
The skies are always cloudy when you're here.
I guess I'll never know why you're so stupid.
The love of me is all you'll ever fear.
The flies they congregate outside your window.
The drunkard serenades you until dawn.
I've gathered all my broken ukuleles;
I've stacked them up in piles upon your lawn.
```

# VICTORIA (Continued)

INTERLUDE (Verse and Chorus: chords and lead)

VERSE 3

The vultures they await upon your bedstead.
The roaches they parade across the floor.
I've summoned thirteen slaves that will employ you,
Knowing that you're closed behind their door.
The grave that you will live in has been ordered.
The 82nd Airborne guards the gate.
Eleven nomad preachers chant the prelude;
So should I walk with them, or should I wait?

REPEAT CHORUS

VERSE 4

Don't tell me how it feels to be deserted.
My time has come and gone, it's plain to see.
But yours is just beginning, for forever.
The things you want to be you'll never be.
I haven't time to listen to your story.
There's too much to be done to bear your grief.
You're drowning in your tears without your glory.
You're dead to all the world, it's my belief.

REPEAT CHORUS (chords only with lead guitar)

# WE'RE THE CIA

Written and arranged by Andy Barber, 1996
First copyright © 2001 (PAu 2-613-596)

VERSE 1

```
  E   F#G   E   D   E
```
We're the CIA and we're coming today,
```
  D      B A B    E
```
Follow, lead, or get out of the way.
```
  D           B A  B  E
```
Heed what we say or you will have to pay,
```
         G    D E D E
```
Going to scare the you out of hell.

VERSE 2

We're not underground; we're easily found.
You'll know by the sound of the hammer we pound.
Better keep us around, or we'll dust off your town;
You'll scream, cry, holler, and yell.

CHORUS 1

```
  D             A G A   E
```
Christians in action will receive satisfaction.
```
   D        A G   A      E
```
If you are too busy then swim in your misery.
```
   D          A  G  A   E
```
The end is beginning, and still you are sinning!

G. F#. E D E...

VERSE (chords and lead)

CHORUS 2

Christians in action, just like General Jackson,
Will rout you completely, and not too discretely.
But Hades is hotter than the valley of slaughter.

INTERLUDE 1

```
  E F#  G   G   F# E  D  E      B
```
We are black, brown, yellow, red, tan, and white.
```
  B   Bb A     G A B    E
```
Look! Our eyes are shining very bright!
```
  E  F#  G     F#  E D E    B
```
You can glow as the light, or fade as the night;
```
  B   A   G       A B   E
```
Take your sword and fight, or take flight!

# WE'RE THE CIA (Continued)

INTERLUDE 1 (Continued)

```
        D      A G     D A G    E
Either rise into heaven, or stay in the grave.
    D        A  G  A    E
It's only your soul you can save.
    D          A  G  D  A   G  E
Freedom is just for the strong and the brave;
    D     G   F# E  D E
Fear only treats you like a slave.
```

INTERLUDE 2 (first half with vocals)

No sorrows, worries, woes, troubles, or cares;
No pain, no problems, no scares.
There are no more spares, no time for repairs;
Don't dare to be caught unawares!

INTERLUDE 2 (second half with chords)

CHORUS 3

Christians in action are rolling with traction;
If you don't take cover, we'll run you right over.
It's a mere fact of death, versus life-giving breath.

# WINNING

Written and arranged by Andy Barber, 2018
First copyright © 2019 (Anthology)

G… F#… E…

VERSE 1 (intro followed by chords)

     E..   D  B  A.      G  A  G   E.
I'm cruising like an eagle down the highway.
I'm thinking that it's time for me to fly away.
I'm hoping that adventure's coming my way.
G… D … E…….     G… D … E…….

CHORUS 1 [E..]

   D…        E…    D… E…
Experience, distraction;
  D    A ..        E…  E…
Taking notice, time and action.
  D        E…      D… E…
Timing, risk and consequence,
  D    A  G  G……   A  G    F#    F#…….   G… F#...   E     E…….
Providing ample evidence; to put it off would make no sense, but never act from false pretense.

G… F#… E…  G… F#… E…  G… F#… E…

VERSE 2 (Intro chords and lead)

I dreamt it, then I saw her in the distance.
I asked her, "May I pretty please have this dance?"
Surprisingly, she offered no resistance.

CHORUS 2 [E..]

Achievement is a drummer drumming,
Singer singing, guitarist strumming.
Facing off and then outgunning;
Struggling and overcoming; tears, blood, pain, then numbing: on the edge but not succumbing.

G... F#... E...   G... F#... E...   G... F#... E...

VERSE 3 (intro chords and lead)

Minds joined together to barter and trade;
Meeting the challenge prepared, unafraid.
Desire mixed with effort, though not without aid.
Success despite obstacles—game well-played.   (pause)

E...   D... E.       E...   D... E.       E...   D... E.       E...   D... E.

# WOMAN AT SEVENTEEN

Written and arranged by Andy Barber, 1980
First copyright © 1981 (PAu 321-648)

VERSE 1

```
 A                     D   G
Who's the girl that's on my mind?
(G)          C   G
Oh, Lord, she's only seventeen!
 A               D
Looks as if I'm in a bind,
   G                   C   G
For she's the best thing I've ever seen.
 A               D   G
I tell myself she's not my kind;
(G)        C   G
Too young, if you know what I mean.
 A                     D   G
But after that I've just got to say
           C  G   A
I want to see her anyway.
```

INTERLUDE

```
 G    Eb   Bb      C
Come on darling, take my hand,
   G    Eb      Bb
The night is cool and clear.
     G     Eb    Bb       C
The waves are crashing on the shore;
   G    Eb    Bb  Bb  F  G
But honey, have no fear—It's all right.
     A                    B
We stopped at a cove and she said to me,
  C  G    D     A
"My heart is beating fast."
  A               B
I said, "Baby just take it slow;"
C  G     D    A
"I want this night to last."
```

B. E B... A. D A. B. E B... A. D A D B. E B... A. D A

CHORUS 1

```
 G    F#  E    G              A
Now I feel so strange. I don't know what to do.
 G        F#   E  G
I just want to be with you.
```

VERSE 2

I sit alone and I face the sun,
Wondering if she's the one.

REPEAT INTERLUDE (chords and lead)

CHORUS 2

I thought she was just a girl.
She showed me what she could be.
She stepped into my world as a woman.

A… D. G. C G…  A… D. G. C G. A

# YES

Written and arranged by Andy Barber, 2015
First copyright © 2019 (Anthology)

Dm7... C... G7...

VERSE 1

Dm7..     C.              G.     A7..
I always thought that I would be with you,
         Dm7.       C..   G7..
Until I found you with another man.
Dm7..         C.       G.  A7..
You turned my heart into the color blue;
            Dm7.   C..      G7..
My mind was struggling trying to understand.

CHORUS

 F..         G..            C.       Dm...
You always said you would believe in me,
     F..       G..          A...
Convincing me I could believe in you.
 F..      G.         C...
But now I'm finished with believing...

VERSE 2

Anyone who says to me their love is true;
I'm never going to trust those words again.
I've no intention seeking someone new,
You're better off just being a friend.

B*b*...   C...  F...  G7...   B*b*...   G#..  E*b*7.  F7...
B*b*...   C...  F...  G7...   B*b*...   F..  C7.  G...

VERSE 3

One day she called me on the telephone,
Telling me she'd made a mistake.
I asked her, "Kindly would you leave me alone?"
"I'm not about to risk another heartbreak."

CHORUS

She said, "I have so much more I can give,"
Persuading me that I should give in.
But I didn't feel much like forgiving...

VERSE 4

Anyone betraying sacred trust is cruel.
Beware because it may not last.
Everyone that plays with love becomes a fool.
Be careful not to charge in too fast.

B*b*...    C...  F...   G7...     B*b*...    G#..  E*b*7.  F7...

B*b*...               G#..   E*b*7.  F7...
Is there any reason for believing?
Is there any purpose to forgiving?

B*b*...    C...  F...   G7...     B*b*...    F..  C7.  G...
B*b*...    F..   C7.  G...
Is love ever absolutely pure?
Am I ever absolutely sure?

B*b*...    G#..  Eb7.  F7...    B*b*...    G#..  Eb7.  F7...

# THE FREELANCERS

A short novel and screenplay
By Andrew V. Barber

Note: The original novel was written between 1976-1978, and submitted for publication under the title *Diary of a Gangster* but never published (revised: 1993, 2019).

# PHASE ONE

Dear Diary, pleased to meet you. My name is Barry. The year, well it's not important. The day, I'm not even sure what day it is. I'm sitting on the floor in a prison cell, stubby pencil and note pad in hand. I'm starting this journal because I'm going to have a lot of time on my hands. It's certain I'll be railroaded like the others. Manuel and Teresa both got fifteen years. I wish I'd died in the shootout instead of Jack. On the other hand, he deserved to die; but Skip did not deserve to die. I vaguely recall the name Barabbas from Sunday School; however, in my story I was the scapegoat and allowed to survive. Now, having lost my blood brother and my girlfriend, I'd sooner have died. Although, my future wasn't more or less bright than those who perished. Who deserves to live or die anyway? I'd prefer it not be up to me. But heck, what kind of life is jail? Better still, I could use Ard's luck; granted, it was rarely luck in his case. I learned a lot from him. His analytical skills were unmatched in my book; he could apprise a situation before it developed. I could use some of Ard's smarts too, especially if I am to survive in the joint.

Let me tell you about Ard. He's the smartest guy I've ever met. He used to crack me up with his philosophy and the way he'd make sentences rhyme when he spoke. There was almost a melody to his speech. He told me that my thinking had wisdom sometimes, but it was Ard who brought out my deeper understanding of things. He would sit very meditatively sometimes, like a yogi you might say. You couldn't attract his attention when he was concentrating, and you shouldn't try. He was very observant, seldom distracted, constantly mindful, assessing the matter in seconds. He had no problem sizing me up, and most everybody else.

His last words to me were, "What if you've smoked your last pipe?" My reply was, "Fork it?" He answered, "Well said." What I'd said didn't make sense to me, but he thought it meant something. Maybe he knew we were about to be captured.

I wonder where Ard is now; probably Canada, maybe Mexico. He often spoke of leaving the country if things got too hot. Talk about hot. If they caught him now, they probably wouldn't consider taking him alive. Of course, knowing Ard, he wouldn't be caught dead being caught.

I sure am going to miss Ard, and Teresa, and especially my best buddy Skip. Possibly he's the most fortunate of us all, going down fighting and now wearing a halo. At least he doesn't have to spend the best years of his life in jail or on the run. Ard will be running for a long time, that would be my guess. Of course, he probably won't stop robbing the rich and giving to the poor; he's too good at it to fully settle down. I reckon you could call him a modern-day Robin Hood, with considerably more flair I might add.

I suppose I'll never get to kiss Teresa again, or hold her in my arms. To think, I would have married her; that's a first. She acted like she loved me sometimes, but when I brought up the subject she snickered. "Me married," she exclaimed, "I'd fool around too much!"

I remember the night we met, when it all started. Teresa was a waitress at a bar and grill. Skip and I were having a friendly drink when Ard and Manny barged in. They held-up the whole stinking joint, taking Skip and me for two hundred smackers.

We were going back to toil in the oilfields when I spotted Manny's Cadillac at a diner outside of Stanton. We burst inside and affronted Ard and Manny who were having breakfast. Manny looked up in surprise, eggs dangling from his Fu Manchu mustache. Ard acted like he was awaiting us, poured some coffee, and motioned for us to take a seat. I was surprised to see Teresa pull up a chair and join us at the table. I didn't know she was Manny's little sister until Ard introduced everyone. Ard offered Skip and me a thousand each to throw in with them I can't believe we gave up a good job to enlist, but we did. I daresay it was Ard's audacity and charisma.

We lived high-on-the-hog for the next few weeks. It was one continuous party. When we ran out of cash, Skip sold his SS-396 and we screwed off for another week. By that time, we'd wandered into Kansas and the dough was thinning out. It was time to pull another heist, but where?

Early one morning, we were cruising down a country road when Ard told Manny to slow to a stop. Ard was monitoring migrant workers toiling in a large field. Suddenly, he dropped the binoculars, hopped out of the car, double-timed it up a private drive, and accosted a man who was beating a Negro laborer with a stick. Ard took the stick from the man and chucked it into the field. Then Ard shoved him into his farmhouse while Manny parked the Caddy; we followed Ard's lead and barged in. The farmer's wife was startled half to death; she was sitting in the front room in a rocking chair reading a tabloid. Ard grabbed the daily newspaper from a coffee table, rolled it up, and started rapping the man on the head and face.

Ard (pushing the farmer onto the couch): You should never treat a fellow human being like a mangy dog! Tell me, how does it feel living on the backs of the poor, you, ignorant cur?

Farmer: I'm not getting a full ten hours of work from that peon.

Ard: And what are you paying him besides pea-nuts? And I bet your cut's a clean six figures.

Ard (to gang): Search the house, this guy's a louse.

We started ransacking the place while Ard stood there with his fists on his hips, clutching the newspaper in his right hand.

Ard (shaking the newspaper at the farmer's wife): Toss together some food for us please.

The farmer's wife gave Ard a big smile and winked at him, as she rose from the rocker and duck-walked into the kitchen. A few minutes passed and the woman returned with a tray full of vittles.

Ard (to farmer's wife): I feel sorry for you, madam, because your husband is a scoundrel. My guess is that you are too good for the likes that mongrel.

The woman sighed as she flopped on the couch with her husband. Manny returned from the bedroom holding a manila envelope filled with money.

Manny (waving envelope upward): Hey vato, you gotta see what I found under the mattress!

The rest of the gang rallied to see what Manny uncovered.

Ard (opening the envelope): Looks to be eight grand in it. I guess we'll have to demand it. I'm sure you folks can understand it.

The farmer stood up to protest when Ard wagged his finger back and forth, Skip elbowing him back into his seat.

Ard (to Teresa): Grab the food; the dude is crude, rude, and screwed.

Teresa picked up the tray from the dining room table and we followed Ard outside. Ard gave about a third of the money to the poor pilgrim who was still kneeling on the ground, humiliated.

Ard: Take this money.

Migrant (looking in amazement): I never seed that many dollas afore!

Ard (lifting the man to his feet): Return to where you came from and go in peace.

The feeble laborer took off in a hurry; it was kind of funny watching him wobble in high gear. The gang piled into the car which immediately sped away.

Barry: That old lady had the hots for you, Ard.

Manny (chuckling): By the looks of her old man, I bet she hadn't had any in years.

Skip (holding a chicken drumstick): This food is great.

Manny (still chuckling): She has to be a good cook, given that fat geezer she's with. And I bet she'd really cook in bed, too; andale, andale! (That's Spanish for get a move on, by the way.)

Everyone laughed except Teresa.

Teresa (looking out the window): I wonder why those country folks don't believe in banks.

Ard (scanning the farmer's newspaper): Manny, take the next junction to Liberal.

We were in Liberal about six hours later. Ard directed Manny toward the center of town.

Ard (pointing at the City Hall building): Park the Caddy in that no-parking zone.

Skip: What's up?

Ard: We're about to have a little parlay with the mayor. Manny, get the crowbar out of the trunk; Barry grab the blue toolbox; Skip, bring your shotgun.

The gang pranced up the cement stairs and casually entered City Hall. A pretty-as-a-petunia receptionist was sitting at a desk near the front door. She was a natural blonde, well-developed, wearing a tight beige sweater and a baby blue skirt that matched her magical eyes.

Ard (to receptionist): I must speak to the mayor.

Receptionist (glancing towards closed double-doors): He can't see anybody right now.

Ard (peering at the closed doors): It wasn't a request.

Ard (to Teresa): Bring the girl. Let's meet the squirrel.

Ard tried the doors; they were locked. He karate kicked them open and they slammed into the wall. We rushed in at once. Six men were sitting around the room; five of them arose from their seats. Ard ordered them to be seated.

Ard (loudly, to a man sitting behind a large desk): Sadly, here sits bad news Bradley.

The man became visibly nervous.

Ard (throwing a folded newspaper into the mayor's face, the one he'd lifted from the farmer's table): You've been skimming off the top; you're just a crooked cop. How dare you embezzle from the people you're supposed to be representing and protecting! I can see right through you; this isn't anything new; guys like you belong in the zoo. Misappropriation of funds, contract overruns; pilfering off of everyone; how utterly despicable, son.

Bradley (brushing the paper aside): Don't believe everything you read.

Ard (sweeping his hand with fore-finger extended): I want all you bozos to empty your pockets immediately. That's right, pull them pants pockets out so I can see and dump the stuff from your suit jackets.

Ard (to Teresa) Collect their valuables using the mayor's hat. (to Manny) Empty the desk. (to Barry) Search the office. (to Skip) Keep that sawed-off trained on these rascals.

A rather large man arose and started to say something. Skip butt-whipped him across the mouth with his shotgun. The man fell back into his chair, holding his mouth and groaning.

Ard (addressing the man): If I want your opinion, I'll ask for it.

Manny cleared the desk with one fell swoop of his arm. Then he pried open each desk drawer using the crowbar, since the mayor refused to unlock it. Manny dumped out the contents, scattering everything across the top of the desk, and pitching the drawers into a heap by the lampstand.

Barry (pulling books off the shelves and onto the floor): There's a wall safe behind this bookcase.

Ard (grabbing the tool box): That's my department.

Manny: I found a strong box in the bottom drawer.

Ard (pulling a power drill from the tool box): Open it.

Manny slammed the crowbar over the top of the box a few times until it popped opened. Ard began drilling holes into the safe as Manny sifted through the contents of the box.

Manny: Hey, these papers look important.

Ard (opening the safe): Bring them to me.

Ard (looking at the papers): These are labor and building contracts. Put those back into the box. We caught us a fox.

Ard (looking into the safe): Hmm. This little black book looks interesting. Oh ho! Names of contractors and moneys allocated. I wonder how many of these transactions are genuine.

Ard pulled another strong box from the safe.

Ard (handing the box to Manny): Open this.

Manny slammed the crowbar over the box until it opened.

Ard (looking into the box): Yesiree. Must be fifty-thou there. Personal operating expenses of the beloved mayor, who'd better start saying his prayers.

Ard (to Bradley): Looks like your term as mayor has expired. In other words, you're about to be fired. Like, you should have retired, but now the entire town will know what a rat they hired.

Ard (to gang): Let's get outa here.

Receptionist: Can I go with you?

Ard: Of course.

The gang marched out the building and filed into the car. Ard placed several thousand dollars into his coat pocket. Then he told Manny to parade around town honking the horn. As the people of the burgh started coming out of their homes and offices, Ard commenced to scattering money everywhere we went. Crowds gathered, listened, and jumped for joy.

Ard (screaming out the open windows): This is money your mayor and his staff stole from you and your city!

Ard (to Manny): Stop right here.

Ard got out of the car and handed a bent-up box containing the contracts and black book to a man coming out of the local newspaper office.

Ard (emphatically): Make sure the appropriate people examine these documents.

Ard got back into the car and Manny stepped on the gas.

Ard (to girl): What's your name, sweetie?

Girl: Laura.

Ard: Which is louder, your hello or your goodbye?

Laura: Hello, I guess.

Ard (putting his arm around Laura): Good. I can hear your train leaving for destiny.

Laura (blushing and snuggling up to Ard): You can?

Manny: She's fallen head over heels already.

We traveled all night until we were well into the Dakotas; there we laid low for a day or two. Eventually we stopped at a country store for groceries and such. A national newspaper had our story on the front page. The mayor of Liberal was being held without bail for illegal dealings, unauthorized expenditures and overruns, hiring ghost employees and businesses, laundering money, and using taxpayer dollars for personal purchases. Two other rogues were implicated. We were celebrities. The townspeople indicated they wanted to reward us, unaware how they already had. It was at the country store where we encountered Jack.

Manny (pointing): Look!

We saw a man running with a stolen box of whiskey, trying to elude two foot-patrolmen.

Ard: Give him a lift.

Manny screeched to a halt and slammed the gearshift into reverse. The dude dove into the backseat across our laps cradling the booze. This guy was a real cretin, but for some reason Ard liked him; maybe Ard appreciated the guy's taste in liquor. We sure got messed up that night on some fine, aged bourbon. That was the first night I made love to Teresa.

After a week of hanging out in the boondocks, and just loving, eating and drinking, Ard told everyone, "It's time the mockingbird flew off to mock other lands," and we were in Indiana by daybreak.

After a few weeks in the boonies, Ard sent Jack and Skip into the nearest town for supplies. Unfortunately, they never returned. The next day, Ard sent Manny and me into town to search for our missing comrades. We hoofed several miles and found the Cadillac at a warehouse parking lot. I noticed a television at the store announcing the arrest of an escaped murderer. Apparently, the sheriff had recognized Jack as a convicted felon wanted by the FBI; Skip was arrested for being with him. Fortunately, they had not discovered the car which was parked two blocks down the street; Manny hot-wired it and we drove back to the hideout.

Ard decided we had to bust them out of the slammer. Ard always looked after his soldiers, like a hen guarding her chicks. He dug through a box in the trunk and located his detective disguise. How he managed to bluff his way into the hoosegow is beyond me. I still can't believe he got the prisoners released to his custody posing as a federal marshal. Manny whizzed the car around to pick them up at the gate. Then, two officials started firing their revolvers at us. Manny mashed his foot on the accelerator and peeled rubber. We managed to outrun any pursuit. Little did anyone know that Skip had taken a bullet in the back. When we stopped, we discovered Skip had expired; he had bled out from internal and external bleeding long before we reached Louisiana. We buried him deep in the woods near an abandoned sawmill. Ard gave the eulogy and quoted some scripture from the Bible.

Ard: Skip made a decision to sacrifice himself so that we could be free. Get the message?

Barry (anxiously): Skip shouldn't have died that way. Why didn't he say something? We could've gotten him to a doctor. It wasn't his time to die.

Ard (calmly): Why make time a factor? Can you prove that time is separate from reality? Or is life just a mere fantasy?

Laura: What does that mean?

Ard: Today is not what yesterday thought tomorrow would be.

Laura: Can the past no longer be the past?

Ard: Only in the future.

Laura (to Barry): Maybe, when you've had time to forget, you can remember what you forgot.

Ard: You're learning toots.

We hunkered down at the old sawmill. We were sitting around our tiny campfire when two floodlights broke the darkness and a voice sounded from a bullhorn.

Policeman: You are surrounded, give yourselves up.

Jack (standing): You'll never take us alive coppers!

Jack fired both barrels of Skip's shotgun into the black of night. Before we knew it, all hell had broken loose. Jack was chopped up immediately by a barrage of bullets. Teresa and I dove under the car; Manny jolted around the back of the mill. Somehow in the confusion, Ard and Laura managed to maneuver to a police car. It's a miracle they escaped, but I'm glad they did. I overheard the jailer saying the squad car they'd hijacked was found by the freight yards. They're long gone by now.

Well, Diary, I guess I'll sign off for now. I'll let you know how the sentencing goes; it should all be over by the end of the week.

## PHASE TWO

Guess what, Diary, I'm in Mexico. Sorry for not getting back to you sooner. I thought I was up the creek without a paddle, and here I'm on the run again. I'm also on the FBI's most wanted list. Personally, I don't think I'm that notorious.

It was really something to behold. I was sitting there in court, listening to all the testimony, knowing that the deck was stacked against me. I got to see some of those people we'd harassed. I could tell they hated my guts but I didn't care. I knew I was about to be sent up the river.

I was standing before the judge, prepared for the inevitable judgment, feeling sick to my stomach. I glanced back at Teresa; she had tears in her eyes. Just as the judge began to speak, I heard a gunshot; the light fixture behind me exploded simultaneously. I spun my head around to see Ard standing at the rear doors. On either side of him was a soldier in combat fatigues holding an automatic rifle.

Everyone in the courtroom fell to the floor. Ard waltzed down the center isle and handed me a .45 caliber pistol. We tramped to the rear of the courtroom where we linked up with Manuel and Teresa, who were handcuffed together. Ard snagged the prosecutor along the way as the rest of us stormed out the door. The two riflemen carefully watched for movement like a couple of guerrillas.

Outside the courthouse was a collection of people standing around including reporters and cameramen. One of the riflemen sprayed about five rounds over the tops of their heads. All the people dropped to the ground and covered up. A path opened for us to pass through, where a car was waiting with the engine running. Ard took his .45 and fired it again toward the dirt.

separating the handcuffs between Manny and Teresa. Manny took the wheel of the car and we zoomed down the road, while Ard gave Manny directions.

Ten minutes later we were at an airstrip where a helicopter was waiting. We boarded the chopper after Manny jerked the pilot out of his seat. Ard released the "suit" and we lifted off. I certainly didn't know Manny could fly a helicopter. As we ascended, an army of law enforcement officers came rushing onto the tarmac. They began shooting at us and the helo took a few hits. Fortunately, nobody was hurt and the aircraft wasn't seriously damaged. A few hours later we landed somewhere in Mexico along the Gulf Coast.

A Mexican man was waiting there with a boat. Boy, Ard sure could plan things. We left the chopper and boarded the boat, sailing farther south until we reached a secluded lagoon. Ard gave the Mex a hundred-dollar bill. We disembarked, and the Mex took off in his boat. We stood around in a circle looking at each other when Ard burst out laughing. All of us joined in.

Barry: Who are the newcomers?

Ard introduced us. One guy was tall and thin, but muscular. His name was Bob. The other guy was short and stocky, with a wide jaw and forehead. They called him Sarge. It figures; he looked like a drill sergeant.

Ard: These guys fought with me in Vietnam.

Barry (to Ard): I didn't know you were a veteran.

Sarge: We're all veterans. Are you a veteran?

Barry: Nope. I was drafted, but they labeled me 4-F, whatever that means.

Ard motioned for everyone to follow him into the jungle.

Ard: Let's move out.

Sarge: We ran covert operations in Vietnam and Cambodia. Manny was our chopper pilot. Bob was our demolitions expert. My specialty is weapons. I'm a gunrunner. I sell military arms on the black market. I stole these from the Army.

Barry: The military always has been a reliable source for arms.

We hiked for about twenty minutes until we came to a clearing. There was Laura sitting on a pile of hiking and camping gear holding a pistol. When she saw us coming, she dropped the gun and ran to greet Ard, embracing him. She had been there for countless hours and was visibly shaken. Bob grabbed a pair of bolt cutters and snapped the bracelets off of Teresa and Manny, then flipped the irons into the underbrush. I changed clothes and donned hiking boots along with my fellow felons. Ard broke out several bottles of bubbly from an ice chest. We celebrated until nightfall. Then we stashed our trash, packed up the rest, and resumed trudging southward.

I was kind of inebriated on the champagne; it made me dizzy in combination with the physical exertion. I felt sorry for the women, because they had to tote their share of the load, and they looked bushed. These army guys really knew their stuff, trekking through a tropical forest in the dark with only Ard's compass, machetes, and flashlights.

At the crack of dawn, we arrived at a cave near a lake buried in the wilds. I wondered how Ard could've known about this place. He showed me where it was on the map but the map didn't even show the lake. Everybody slept in the cave the rest of the day, taking turns at guard duty while it rained off and on. I awoke just before sundown, quite rested but a little stiff.

Barry (walking out of the cave): Is there anything here to eat?

Bob (kicking a box toward Barry): Here, have some C-rations.

Barry (taking the box): I guess that'll have to do, seeing how I'm about starved to death.

Ard was sitting a few yards from a small campfire drawing figures in the moist dirt alongside the shoreline.

Barry (approaching Ard): What's going on?

Ard: I'm ciphering.

Barry: What the heck are those diagrams?

Ard: Probabilities and statistics; linear regression.

Barry: What the?

Bob: Maybe he's calculating our chances of pulling off the job.

Barry: He must be a genius. Is there anything he can't do?

Bob (mumbling with a mouthful of crackers): Not that I know of.

Teresa (joining them): I'm hungry.

Barry (handing Teresa a cardboard box): Have a box of C's. Look, there's even a little pack of smokes for after dinner.

Laura joined us, dropping on Ard's lap.

Teresa (tossing a can and a plastic spoon into the fire): These rations taste rancid.

Barry (grabbing Teresa's hand and raising her to her feet): Let's take a walk, Terry.

Teresa and I wandered off into the trees. We came to a small inlet with a pebbly beach, when Teresa slapped my butt. I clutched hers in return.

Barry (with his arm around Teresa): I saw you crying in the courtroom.

Teresa: I had something in my eye.

Barry (stopping): Why won't you admit that you really care?

Teresa (cocking her head and looking into Barry's eyes affectionately): I really care.

I cupped my hands around her face. She looked enchanting. Her long umber hair was flowing in the breeze and her big bronze eyes were twinkling in the moonlight.

Teresa (turning towards the lake): Isn't this place romantic. It's so beautiful here.

Barry (rotating Teresa back towards him): I like this view better.

We kissed so hard I thought my mouth was going to bleed. I caressed her body from top to bottom. Every part of her flesh was softer than the part before. She moaned as we sank into each other's arms and rolled over a bed of smooth stones. I'd never felt so much in love. We made it for a couple of hours until we were spent, and slept for a couple more by the banks of the lake. We were startled by a gunshot, followed by a scream. We dusted each other off and rushed back to the campsite.

Barry: What's all the commotion about?

Laura (whimpering): Sarge encountered a pig and shot the poor thing.

Sarge: It's called a peccary.

Manny: Javelina, menso.

Ard: Barry, Terry, gather some dry wood. Bob, set up a skewer. Sarge, field-strip the sow. Let's have us a barbeque.

Sarge: I've a couple bottles of Vodka stashed; been saving 'em for a special occasion.

Barry: Fantastic; this is obviously a reason to celebrate.

Ard: You should've been celebrating every day of your past, because any one could be the last.

We had a great feast and got plastered. I'll take roast pork over C-rations any day. After supper I proposed to Teresa. Believe it or not, she accepted. I told the gang the news; Ard declared we could get married at a nearby hamlet. He said it was time to vacate anyway. It was sad leaving our secluded paradise. I'd never felt so free in my entire life, the way I felt at that lake in the middle of the Mexican jungle.

We tramped all day until we arrived at a quaint Mexican village. Manny, who spoke perfect Spanish, told the townspeople about our wedding plans. Before nightfall, the entire town turned out to congratulate us. We drank tequila and danced in the dusty streets. Then this obese fellow invited us to his hacienda. I guess he was a chief or something. When he laughed, his teeth protruded out. He looked so funny it made you want to laugh with him. He reminded me of a Mexican Santa Claus. He married us for a small fee.

Ard managed to persuade him, with a modest bribe, to provide transportation to Vera Cruz. The next morning, we crammed into the back of a beat-up truck. As we drove off, all the villagers ran behind us waving goodbye, or hello, I couldn't tell which.

The road to Vera Cruz was something else; I've heard of bad roads before but this was ridiculous. By the time we got to our destination my back and my butt were killing me. We stayed at a rundown hotel. The mattress was lumpy but the sheets were clean; we were allowed to take a hot shower and eat a hot meal.

Laura: These tacos are delicious.

Barry: It's always been my experience that you can't beat Mexican food when it's cooked by real Mexicans.

Ard: We're leaving in the morning.

Manny: What's happening, jefe?

Ard: We don't have enough money to make it to South America; we need to rob the Bank of Merida.

Sarge: Sounds good to me, Captain.

The trip to Merida was long and smelly, thanks to that gas-burning bus we rode. Everyone got sick from the carbon monoxide. Ard told us to get some rest while he took care of a few details. The hotel we stayed at was a carbon copy of the last one, but it beat sleeping on the ground or in a jail cell.

The next day, Manny rented some Mexican's personal car for twenty bucks. He sounded his arrival with a long blast on the horn and we climbed in. Arriving at the bank, Manny parked around back; then we walked through the front door to make a withdrawal. As we entered the bank, Bob and Sarge pulled out their handguns and waved them in the air. Immediately, all patrons and employees of the bank had their hands in the air. Ard decided that we would rob only safety deposit boxes knowing full well we would find drug money in them. He wanted to steal from people he considered more reprehensible than us, I imagine. Ard guarded the employees, holding a pistol on the bank's manager. I popped open several boxes with the crowbar while Sarge opened several more shooting them with his gun.

We grabbed legal tender and jewelry until Ard announced he had what he needed. Then we high-tailed it out the back door, where we left the loaner car and marched down to the harbor

There we boarded a boat loaded with cans of gas and supplies. By then, a swarm of federales had formed at the docks. We shoved off during an exchange of gunfire. The Mex on the boat got paranoid and dove off the stern. That was a stupid thing to do, because the feds weren't very civil to him when he reached the dock.

Two boatloads of officials were in hot pursuit. Manny sure could maneuver that boat. We were zigzagging left and right, between inlets and across canals. Manny took us over a sandbar and into a cove guarded by two overhanging trees. We slid under one tree while a police boat slammed into it. This blocked the passage, forcing the other boat to veer, jumping onto dry land. We were home free.

We ran out of gas somewhere around Nicaragua. As we began unloading the boat, we found a teenage stowaway. How she got aboard was a mystery to us all, but we were stuck with her.

Manny (to girl): Como se llama?

The scared girl bowed, looked up at us through half-closed eyelids, but said nothing. She was about sixteen or seventeen, very pretty, with dark complexion. Sarge started getting fresh with her.

Sarge (putting his arm around the girl): I'll look after her.

Barry (to Sarge): Hands off, you letch.

Sarge (growling): You want to fight me so see who gets to bust her cherry?

The girl escaped Sarge's grasp and ran up to me. Teresa pulled her away, twisting her wrist.

Teresa: Este hombre es mio!

Barry: I guess that cooled her heels.

The girl ran into Bob's arms.

Ard: Well, Bob, it seems you're elected. Now, let's get going before we're detected.

We hoofed it for a couple of weeks through thick forests, swamps, rivers, you name it. At last we reached a small village in Costa Rica. I suggested we dump the girl there but she refused to leave us. We ended up adopting her. Everyone started calling her Virginia, since she never gave her real name and we figured her for a virgin.

Ard bought a motorboat, and we continued down the coast. We bivouacked adjacent to a palm beach surrounded by thick foliage. It was there I experienced the worst night of my life. Teresa and I were awakened once again by the retort of firearms.

Manny (frantically): It's a bandito ambush! Sarge must have fallen asleep during his watch.

Sarge: I'm hit.

Ard: Everyone scatter.

Bob (grabbing a pistol): I'm going after them.

Barry (grabbing a pistol): I'm right behind you.

Bob and I pursued the bandits into the black of night deep into the jungle, firing our guns. We returned to the campsite after half an hour.

Barry (gasping): We nailed two of them.

Bob: Two others escaped.

Teresa was lying on the ground, Manny cradling her head in his arms. Laura and the young girl were crying uncontrollably in the tent.

Barry: Oh my God, what happened?

Manny (whimpering): She caught one in the chest; I think it pierced her heart. She's gone, man.

Barry (breaking down): No! It cannot be!

Manny placed her head in my arms and I held her tightly until daybreak. I think that's the only time I've ever cried, outside of when I was a baby. We buried Terry and Sarge. Manny said a prayer in English and in Spanish. After that, nobody uttered a word all day; we just plodded farther south. The excitement of our adventures had left me. I wanted to commit suicide. Finally, Ard spoke to me privately. He said this in closing.

Ard: Somewhere, in another dimension of space and time, your Teresa is watching and waiting.

It didn't make me feel any better. I didn't say a peep for a week. Virginia tried to comfort me. One evening she unbuttoned her blouse offering herself, but I wasn't going for it. Besides, I think Bob was beginning to fall for her. We laid low while Ard went to a nearby town. He returned with an outdated Panama City newspaper detailing our exploits in Merida.

Ard: During idle times, experience suffers.

Bob: Ard, you should've lived during the times of Ben Franklin and those guys.

Barry: Where the Sam Hell are we going, Ard?

Ard (handing the open newspaper to Barry): Haven't you heard about the revolution?

Barry: Yeah, isn't there some revolt going on in Argentina or Brazil, or somewhere?

Manny: It's in Uruguay, baboso.

Ard: Well, it's going to be our revolution. It's already Manny's revolution.

Barry: How so?

Manny: I was born in Uruguay. My grandfather was a member of the ruling council, until they murdered him.

Barry: Aren't you aiming a bit too high? I mean, how can we take over a country? Seems to me we'd need an army to do that.

Ard: Precisely. I want you all to think about strategy while Manny and I are away.

Laura: Now where are you going?

Ard: We need to spend a little cash, but we'll be back in a flash. Bob, you're in charge. Laura, you and Barry should keep each other company; he could use a pretty face around him. Barry, I want you to look after Laura while I'm gone.

Barry (looking puzzled): Sure thing, Ard.

Ard: Any more questions? Adios then.

Dear Diary, since Ard's been gone I've gotten to know Laura a lot better. She's a real religious person. I told her I was born and raised in Texas by religious parents, but their faith never seemed to wear off on me. I wondered how she ever got mixed up with us. We're not exactly righteous vigilantes, although I guess Ard and Manny are spiritual. Teresa always crossed herself under special circumstances. Laura's really happy being with Ard and the gang; she says it's the best thing that ever happened to her. I guess I have to agree; it's the best thing, and also the worst.

Last night I had this strange dream. I was soaring above the clouds like a disembodied spirit, when suddenly a thunderstorm arose. I began stumbling and falling, but managed to forge onward. Finally, the storm subsided and there was blue sky all around me, although I was still in a fog. An angel appeared decked-out in bright white and approached me. Her face reminded me of Laura. I was about to touch her when she disappeared. I guess I'm getting a little too close to Ard's girl. I wish he'd hurry up and get back.

Well, Diary, another month has passed. Sorry once again, it's been hectic; I'll get you up to date. Ard finally returned with a good-sized boat loaded with new supplies. We spent several days breezing down the coast. We arrived in Brazil where Ard sold the boat. Near the docks was a garage holding a military 2½ ton truck loaded with more supplies and weapons. Manny fired up the engine after about a dozen tries and we were on our way.

The gang is traveling to Uruguay, where the country is in chaos after the overthrow of their government from a military coup. Numerous officials have been assassinated, including Manny's grandfather. A ruthless general has taken charge. I'm not sure what Ard's plan is, but it's going to be a dangerous assignment. Apparently, Ard has been planning this mission for a long time.

Everything he does has a purpose and a plan. The best thing about being a member of this company: we party before and after each of our errands.

Barry (sitting in the front seat between Ard and Manny): When were you going to fill *me* in, Ard?

Ard: Glad you asked. Several independent forces have taken turns trying to recover the Capital of Uruguay from the mutineers, but to no avail. That's because they aren't organized.

Barry: So, we're gonna find us some rowdy revolutionaries in search of guidance and lead them to the promised land?

Ard: Indubitably.

Manny: Ard is the most capable military leader you will ever find. He is also an expert in guerilla warfare and insurgency tactics.

Ard: Manny and Bob are perfectly competent military tacticians as well.

Barry: Where do I fit in?

Ard: You're a fine leader and a good thinker but you have yet to realize your potential. This is the best training you're going to get in order to hone those skills. Further, your knowledge of terrain and map reading will be valuable. Besides, you've already assumed the role of scribe, have you not?

Barry: Wow, I guess I do have responsibilities.

The daily routine was C-rations or K-rations: breakfast, lunch, and dinner. I was rapidly tiring of them, feeling constipated constantly. We rode day and night, taking brief occasional rest stops. In due course we reached the border of Uruguay. We had ridden along some back roads for an hour or two when Ard spotted a man in the side mirror. The man was sneaking across the road well behind us, toting a duffel bag. Ard told Manny to make a quick U-turn. Ard flew out after him and chased the man down. He brought the guy back to the truck at gunpoint.

Ard: Bob, check the bag. Manny, assure him we're friends.

Manny (to man): No preocupes. Estamos amigos.

Bob: It's medical supplies and two rifles.

Ard (to man): Do you speak English?

Man: Poquito.

Ard (slowly): We have come to restore your government. What is your name?

Man: Chacho.

Ard: I know you are not alone. Where are the others?

Chacho: Why should I trust you?

Ard (looking intently into the man's eyes): You have no choice. We will be successful with or without your help. If you want to join us, fine. If not, you will be sorry. (Pausing) Now, get into the truck.

Chacho reluctantly showed us to a secluded campsite among some hills and between two cliffs. The place was heavily guarded throughout the canyon, and lookouts on top.

Ard: Tell the guards we need to speak to the leader.

Manny (to guard): Necesitamos hablar con su jefe.

The guards guided the truck at gunpoint to a large tent. An aged man came out. He was wearing a dusty blue jacket with gold stripes on his slacks and sleeves. He had a scar on his face along with a scraggly two-week beard. He walked with a slight limp. He spoke fluent English.

Man: What are you people doing here?

Ard: We've come to help you.

Man: Are you loco? How can you be of help to us?

Ard: You'll see. Who are these people?

Man: They are refugees. We are loyal to our country yet we are outcasts. We hate those dogs who would bring our country to its knees, including you outsiders.

Ard dug into his pack and pulled out the notebook he always kept with his personal belongings. He showed some newspaper clippings to the officer.

Ard: Have you seen this before?

Man (snorting): You are these renegades? You came a long way to escape the authorities. You are welcome here.

Ard introduced the gang to the leaders of the rebel group. Their leader introduced three of his top brass, and then himself.

Man: I am Capitán Pérez. You may call me Capitán or you can call me Señor Pérez. General Gonzalez and his dogs tried to kill me when I refused to go along with their treachery. I escaped with a rifle ball in my leg. I have been recovering here with these loyalists. One day, I will get my revenge.

Ard: You can count on it.

Capitán (turning to Manny): Señor Sanchez, are you related by any chance to Lorenzo Sanchez?

Manny: He was my abuelito.

Capitán: Lorenzo was a very good friend of mine. He spoke of you and your sister often. He said he raised you two. Your parents were preparing a new life for you in the United States. It was a shame they never made it.

Manny: I am here to avenge my grandfather's death.

Capitán: Viva la Revolución!

Well Diary, the Capitán called all his followers together, telling them we had joined them in their cause. The people let out a giant roar. A jubilee ensued. During the festivities, I became familiar with a woman named Rosa; her eyes reminded me of Teresa. Between my limited Spanish and her limited English, we managed to communicate. Her husband was killed during the overthrow; he was another military man who refused to throw in with them. He was tortured before her very eyes.

Rosa has a younger sister named Rita. Manny and Rita appear to be hitting it off pretty famously. Rosa and Rita are both very attractive ladies.

Everybody calls members of the criminal military regime "perros". That means "dogs" in Spanish. I think the term is appropriate. Tomorrow we will begin battle drills. It's going to be like boot camp. I'm actually looking forward to it.

## PHASE THREE

We were up before the sun; there was some fruit and bread to eat. The first order of business was census and subdivision. There were eleven women, ten children, and thirty-three men, not counting the gang. Four squads were formed; I led one, Bob led one, Manny led one, and Chacho led one. Rita supervised a medical detachment of women; she proved to be a very capable nurse. Childcare and schooling were provided for kids under twelve directed by Rita's sister Rosa; boys over thirteen were perfectly able to assist in logistics support. Three spies were sent to investigate known enemy installations and encampments; two of them were no older than fifteen but they knew the area and would not arouse suspicion.

All able-bodied adults participated in basic and advanced training. Combat drills were tedious and tiring, but fun. I learned a lot of Spanish in the meantime. I came to hate the perros as much as the exiles did, even though I had yet to encounter a single one. I felt a purpose in this mission. In fact, all of Ard's escapades seemed to have an element of mercy and another of justice. It was going to be a giant service to the Uruguayan people if we could eliminate this evil regime.

I spent every night with Rosa. She helped me forget Teresa on occasion, but I must admit I mostly thought of Terry when I made love to Rosa; I expect she was thinking of her heroic husband who refused to cow-tow to traitors. We slipped away one day to escape the hoard. After roaming for a half-mile or so, we stopped to rest under a shade tree. We were in a passionate embrace when I heard a vehicle approaching. I gave the "shh" sign to Rosa, then crept up to the crest of the ridge. Below were a couple of perros standing by a jeep on a dirt path, relieving themselves. I surmised they were patrolling for our hidden base.

Immediately I felt a surge of bravery, creeping down the hill and tiptoeing behind the jeep. Then I lunged, belting the first guy over the head with my pistol butt as he was preparing to zip his fly. The other guy was trying to button his pants when he turned around to stare into the barrel of my .45. He immediately dropped his drawers and raised his hands. I slammed him down into his pool of piss. I made my famous wolf whistle signaling for Rosa to come quickly. I tied the guys up with rope and rifle straps found in the jeep while she covered them with the gun.

Together, we pitched them into the back of the jeep; I drove to the hideout while she continued to hold the gun on them. Ard was proud of us capturing the patrol. Manny and the Capitán interrogated the prisoners who spilled their guts; that is, after minimal torture coupled with threatening gestures in the vicinity of their genitals. We obtained information on troop positions and strength, and the location of weapons and ammo to include some enemy tanks nearby. I couldn't figure out why the prisoners talked; they must have known their situation was flaky regardless of what they said.

Ard and the Capitán were very pleased. Ard knew we had to hit the tank position pronto, because they were getting too close. He wasted no time organizing an assault force. We moved out all four squads. Bob and Chacho led their squads to reconnoiter the objective, which was about eight kilometers away. They returned knowing the position of outposts, headquarters, and troops. There were two enemy tanks and an estimated seventy-five foot-soldiers. We proceeded toward the enemy encampment.

Bob and Chacho eliminated two guard emplacements while the rest of us maneuvered into position. My stomach was in my throat; I'd never done this before. This was war, the real thing! A single shot signaled us to rush their perimeter from four directions. We caught the enemy totally by surprise while they slept, showering the camp with automatic weapons fire, grenades, and pistol shots. In minutes, we had annihilated half their force. The remainder of the battle was dedicated to close combat. It didn't take long for us to subdue them.

Manny and Chacho marched the prisoners that could walk back to camp for inspection and interrogation. Bob and I put the mortally wounded out of their misery. We returned to our hidden post before the crack of dawn, tired and bloody. I got two hours of shuteye before we assembled.

Bob: The spoils of battle are two tanks, two jeeps, and a truck, not to mention arms, ammunition, and grenades.

Manny: The enemy body count was fifty-five.

Chacho: We lost fourteen; three others are in bad shape.

Barry: Darn!

Bob: Due to inexperience, I'm afraid some of our casualties were caused by friendly fire.

Manny: Of the twenty-one perros that surrendered eight are wounded. We couldn't get any additional information from the prisoners. Most of them don't know jack, and don't want to know.

Chacho: Several of them seem anxious to join our forces.

Barry: What are you going to do with the rest of them?

Capitán: They will be put to death without delay. To prove their worthiness, the others will be allowed to execute their compadres.

Around midday, two Uruguayan spies returned with information.

Ard: Give me the abridged version, Manny.

Manny: An entire battalion is coming. I guess the perros heard about their defeat last night.

Barry: How many is a battalion?

Bob: About five-hundred.

Everyone was scared, except Ard and the Capitán. I think I was starting to become religious. I even whispered a little prayer. We spent the next twenty-four hours in six-hour shifts, digging trenches, setting up barricades, emplacing booby traps, with little rest. Just after dusk, a third spy named Enrique returned with a mob of people. He'd recruited them from a nearby town. Our numbers were almost doubled thanks to the brilliant work of the spies. The odds were reduced to a mere five-to-one. The new arrivals had a modest underground operation which included some hotshot snipers. Ard deployed sniper squads to stall the perro advance.

Everyone was issued a weapon, including women and children. I doubt if anybody got any sleep that night. We were expecting an attack in the morning and we got one. We exchanged gunfire until late-afternoon; there was silence the rest of the day. The Capitán appointed guards allowing some of us to sleep. I slept like a log, despite the fear. My ears were still ringing when I awoke again to the sound of gunfire. Frequently waking up to gunshots can make a person crazy, I reasoned. It made me feel a tad patriotic when thinking of the horrors our veterans had to face.

Again, there was a long shooting exchange. Suddenly, a platoon of perros conducted an assault. We cut them down like it was a shooting gallery. Our tanks bombarded their rear positions trapping the second wave in a crossfire. Before I knew it, nightfall was setting in and we had held them twice. The fortified position in the cliffs gave us the high ground which was an advantage, but our resources were diminishing.

Capitán: In my judgment, they will have reinforcements on the way.

Bob: We won't hold out if their reinforcements arrive in force.

Ard: We have to attack immediately. Bob, take a team and recon the enemy position.

They returned two hours later.

Bob: We were unable to get close enough to get a fair estimate of their strength, but I'd say about three hundred. However, I discovered a possible avenue of attack. It's a dry riverbed that passes their perimeter to the east.

Ard: It's a calculated risk, but we must take the offensive. The riverbed is their only known vulnerability, so that is where we will amass.

Bob and Manny gathered fifty fit and experienced men to initiate the assault. I packed as many hand grenades I could carry. We low-crawled in single file up the riverbed for about a hundred meters. It was grueling and I was winded. We halted where the riverbed turned, about twenty meters from the enemy line. The first fifty troopers charged, firing away; they paused a quick second to reload while the rest of us rushed and joined the line, spraying the encampment with another torrent of bullets.

I couldn't believe the ineptness of the perros. They fumbled around like chickens with their heads cut off. We overran their camp, losing only sixteen men. It was almost another miracle. I was reminded of the Battle of San Jacinto where Houston defeated Santa Ana with an inferior force to gain Texas independence. Over two-hundred of the perros were dead or wounded, and another twenty-six captured by the time we were finished. The spoils included vehicles, radios, maps, ammunition, and a couple of fifty-caliber machineguns.

The clamor of victory resounded as we returned to camp. We had defeated the perros and captured a comandante. The Capitán convinced him to radio a message to his superiors, saying that it was we who had been defeated and there was no need to send reinforcements. Then, the comandante was promptly interrogated and executed along with eighteen others. Seven of the perros joined us. I was impressed with the Capitán's policy concerning prisoners. POWs were a burden we couldn't bear; once they outlived their usefulness they were eliminated. It sounded rash but logical at the same time. In the meantime, silent loyalists were able to choose life.

Ard: We cannot remain here.

Barry: Where can we go?

Ard (pointing to map): There's this town Ric (Enrique) was telling me about. East of us, right here.

Manny: The town is fortified with machinegun positions.

Ard: I know. We're going to convince them to surrender to our tank power.

Manny: We only have three tank rounds left.

Ard: They don't know that.

Manny (extending his hand): A flush don't beat a full house, vato.

Ard (slapping Manny's outstretched hand): We'll bluff them, vato. We're gonna look like a royal flush.

Our destination was a town, the name of which was too long to remember. I rode with Rosa in a jeep; she drove while I studied relief maps, evaluating the terrain, and tracing our movements. It reminded me of my days as an oiler, when I used to analyze the geology of the oil-rich basins. We were five miles from the outskirts of the city by nightfall. Early in the morning before sunrise Ard organized an assault force ready to be deployed posthaste.

Ard: Ric and Manny will lead with tanks, fifty cals mounted on them. Barry, you follow them in a truck full of riflemen. Bob and Chacho, take your patrols ahead and replace the perro outposts with our own then monitor their radio traffic. Rally into town at your discretion and direction

To begin the battle, tank gunners opened up with the fifty cals as we passed the edge of town. After inching forward for a quarter mile or so, I stopped the truck, which was already getting shot full of holes. I maneuvered into town on foot with the riflemen. I directed my infantry element into alleys and buildings, with two fire teams to infiltrate both sides of the street.

Enrique steered his tank toward the center of town. He aimed the cannon at an ammo stash, the location of which he'd discovered as a result of prior scouting missions. The artillery round landed on target and a loud explosion ripped the building to shreds. The impact shook the entire town. The blast created fireworks better than any I'd seen on the Fourth of July. Come to think of it, this was the fourth of July.

Manny's tank followed up with another strategically placed howitzer blast into the enemy's headquarters. The building burned like an inferno. Some of the ranking brass came rushing out, only to be shot or captured.

Then there was silence. We waited for the perros to make a move. Our tank guns veered left and right, as if to show indecision as to where to place the next devastating blow. Unexpectedly, the perros began to swarm like flies into the streets, with their hands on their heads. The bluff had worked; we'd licked them again with a smaller contingent.

Manny radioed to the rest of our band to advance. Upon entering the town, the procession was met by a crowd of rejoicing civilians. Talk about celebrate; Latino people sure know how to throw a bash. I hadn't eaten good, slept much, or had great loving for days. Rosa and I got to bathe and we snuggled in a king-sized bed. It was fabulous.

During the next several days, our army grew rapidly. Word got out and dissenters from the evil regime came to join us. The spirit to fight kept our morale high. The perros were afraid of us in a big way. Ard figured we'd eventually have to come to them, with the purpose of retaking Montevideo. We worked our way south towards the coast. We continued without serious resistance, setting up our headquarters at a port city not far from the capital.

We had plenty of munitions but were desperately short of artillery rounds. Ard organized four four-man detachments to infiltrate Montevideo and gather intelligence, recruit sympathizers, set booby traps, and locate more tank rounds. Ard accompanied them, against my vehement opposition. I wanted to join, but Ard had placed me in charge of security. During the following week the patrols began to return with supplies, arms, ammo, and more loyalists. The problem, Ard wasn't among them.

Barry: Where's Ard?

Manny: He was apprehended.

Bob: He was caught snooping around the bank while we were swiping 1-0-5 rounds across the street. It was like he wanted to get captured.

Laura (sobbing): Mr. Capitán, what will the perros do with Ard?

Capitán: Hopefully, they will mistake him for a disoriented tourist.

Bob: I doubt if they're that stupid.

Capitán (pointing his finger at Bob): Never underestimate their foolhardiness, it could get you into trouble.

Barry: We've got to rescue him.

Enrique: Manny and I will go.

Barry: I'm going too. It's the least I can do after his springing me back in the states.

It was long after dark when we arrived at the outskirts of the city. We hid the jeep and sneaked further into town. We came across a solitary soldado and beat his ass until he disclosed the location of a certain gringo; then Enrique bashed him over the head. Manny exchanged clothes with him while Enrique dragged the body into an alley and finished him off; I flipped his rifle onto a roof and we continued onward. We saw two guards standing outside a known ammo cache. Manny asked one for a light. As the guard lit Manny's cigarette Ric belted him over the head from behind while I ran the other through with a bayonet. Then we removed their bodies from the street and donned their uniforms. The bloodied uniform was way too small for me, but it was unlikely anyone would notice in the dark.

We reached the enemy HQ building. Guards were all around, two of them stationed at a back door. Manny and Enrique (Ric) posed as their relief. The guards bought the ruse and left. Manny peeked inside where he saw two other guards sitting at a table. I waited outside while he and Enrique pulled another cigarette routine. Six soldiers approached in formation while I was standing there alone. I think they were the actual relief guard. Just then, Ric came outside. Since he was wearing sergeant stripes, he was able to persuade them we were on special duty because of top-secret business going on inside. He ordered them to post themselves in another specially designated location. I let out a sigh of relief.

When they were out of sight, we reentered the building, silently searching each room on the ground floor. I located some basement steps leading down to a door guarded by another soldier wearing corporal stripes. I signaled to Ric. Manny and Ric descended the stairs and began to chew the cud with the guard. Manny asked him for a cigarette. The irritated guard reached into his pocket. Manny kicked him in the stomach and he slumped over; then Manny brought the butt of his weapon down on top of his head. Ric bashed in the locked door.

Inside we found Ard with cigar in hand, blowing smoke rings, his feet propped up on a desk. You could tell he was glad to see us because he inadvertently smiled as he arose from his chair, masking any sign of surprise.

Ard: Took you long enough.

He donned the uniform of the unconscious guard and we made our way back to the street. There we encountered soldiers looking for insurgents masquerading as guards. Ric declared we were searching for three impostors; little did the dummies know there would be four imposters.

We stopped at the ammo dump on the way back to the jeep. Two new guards had taken that station. Manny and Ric reenacted their cigarette routine and disabled them once again. I busted open the door with the barrel of my rifle. The building was loaded to the hilt with munitions. Ard started a fire, Manny and Ric grabbed a few boxes, and we hauled ass. We were about two blocks away when the place blew. The explosion was so great it knocked us to the ground. The commotion created a nice diversion, however, allowing us to depart unnoticed with a passel of tank and machinegun ammo.

We returned just before daybreak. The reception committee included Laura, Rosa, Rita, and Enrique's girl, Concha; the girls had been waiting all night for our return. We each received a huge hug and kiss from our respective girlfriends. It resembled a black-and-white motion picture, a war movie I once saw; at least that's what came to mind. Ard told the women to beat it because we had to discuss schemes. Ric roused the slumbering Capitán who assembled the rest of his commanders including Bob. Let me tell you, in the midst of battle, warriors take every opportunity to catch some zzz's.

Ard: I convinced the perros I couldn't speak a word of Spanish, feigning how I believed this was Brazil.

Capitán (to Bob): See what I mean about underestimating their stupidity!

Bob: No doubt.

Ard: I overheard the perros discussing plans of an air assault. Apparently, they purchased some fighter planes from the Soviets. The planes are supposed to arrive tomorrow.

Capitán: This is exactly what we do not need.

Ard: We've got to destroy those planes.

Capitán (pointing to the map): There's only two airstrips within one-hundred kilometers where they could land: here, but more likely here.

Ard: Let us prepare to strike both targets.

Bob: We acquired five mortars, by the way.

Ard: Good thinking. We'll pulverize them just as the planes are landing. It has to be timed precisely. We want the planes to be on the ground and never take off again. Bob, you've got four hours to train five mortar squads. I'll figure out the calculations of azimuth and elevation for each mortar position.

Ard (waving for Enrique to come to his side): Ric, I will need exact measurements to establish the distances to each airstrip from five optimal mortar positions.

Capitán: An air strike could defeat us (pounding his fist in his hand). We will be successful.

Barry (plopping down on a couch): Looks like another night with no sleep. (Funny how I dozed off anyway for about twenty minutes.)

Ard: We have agreed where we will deploy. Bob, Manny, Chacho, Ric, Barry, you will emplace fixed mortar positions in these locations (pointing to the map). Captain, I need roving jeeps equipped with fifty cals. I want them to make random strikes as a diversion. When the planes are nearing, I will need two of them to act as forward observers in the event we need to adjust fire.

Capitán: We will organize routes through the city where the jeeps can maneuver and attack, within striking distance of the landing zones. I will find the best drivers who know the area well.

Ard: Excellent. That's it, gentlemen. Be ready to move out at 0500 hours.

It only took about thirty minutes to learn how to operate the mortars. I found Rosa fast asleep. She awoke, wondering what was happening. I told her. She made me say a prayer with her. Her faith was wearing off on me; I actually believed we had a good chance. We had beaten the odds too many times for it to be random. I wondered how many more times we could defy the laws of probability. Here now, it was me thinking scientifically; obviously Ard was wearing off on me too. Imagine, being able to think spiritually and scientifically at the same time without conflict? I was learning new things every day from many extraordinary instructors.

I took a catnap before getting my squad ready. We made it to our mortar position well before sunup, concealing ourselves in a junkyard. We waited and waited, all day long, but saw no planes. It was getting dark, and we were hungry and tired.

Out of nowhere, there arose the sound of jet plane engines. I spotted them easily for they displayed running lights; there were three of them. They passed overhead, preparing to land in procession at the longest, westernmost airstrip. We fixed our mortars for that location, which was just within weapon range. The last plane was touching down, one was taxiing, and another parking at the crude terminal when we received the command to fire over the radio. We couldn't tell if we were on target or not. We kept adjusting and firing as directed until we ran out of rockets, per Ard's instructions. Then we returned to the operations center.

One of the roving jeeps already had arrived with good news. The planes and airstrip were completely demolished. Here was a good reason for another wing-ding. But I was too tired to socialize and slept instead. I was awakened about noon by Rosa, with news the perros were coming to greet us. I hurried to headquarters building. Several people were outside preparing Molotov cocktails. I went inside. Everyone else was already there.

Ard: We're expecting tanks from the southwest. Manny and Ric, position the two tanks at each end of main street, here and here; be prepared to fire, retreat, or both. Barry, set up a fifty cal position in the church tower. Bob, you and a fifty cal across the street. Chacho, you emplace a fifty cal right here in this room. Captain, you and I will organize a cocktail party for our guests.

Capitán: I'll drink to that.

Everyone was in position in one hour. Ten perro tanks arrived half an hour later devastating everything in sight. Molotov cocktails were flying everywhere along the main drag, managing to disable only two of their tanks. Manny and Enrique had a point-blank duel with two enemy tanks and out-gunned them both. I was spewing out fifty-caliber shells like it was going out of style. When I ran out of ammo, my whole body was still shaking. The end of the gun barrel was so hot it melted slightly, bending downward.

The town tumbled and groaned under the strain. Suddenly, a tank round hit the hospital Rita had set up two blocks down from headquarters. I rushed to the burning inferno carrying a satchel and five grenades. I entered to find Rosa with her brains splattered all across the floor. Rita was kneeling over her, hands on Rosa's face, screaming hysterically. I couldn't watch. It hit me hard as if Teresa was dying all over again. I had to drag Rita out of the fire; she was in shock.

I jolted down the street tossing grenades this way and that. Just then, two armor rounds hit Enrique's tank in rapid succession. Manny eliminated one tank with a well-placed projectile. I took out the other tank's machine gunner, emptying a twenty-round magazine. I dropped my rifle, jumped aboard the tank, and dropped a live grenade down the gunnery hatch. It exploded as took a dive. I'd seen that maneuver on a television program, surprised that it actually worked.

Another tank was rolling toward me. Before it passed overhead, I'd placed the satchel filled with explosives on the ground and tossed a live grenade inside. I sprinted away as the machine-gunner lined me up in his sights. Just then the entire satchel charge exploded next next to the track, blowing out a sprocket. The tank swerved into a building which crumbled atop it. I looked over to see innumerable foot-soldiers approaching and made a dash for the sideline.

I joined Bob at his position to continue the fight. Six more hours the battle ensued. The whole town echoed as bodies dropped like flies. The place looked like some of the photographs I'd seen of Civil War battlefields. Finally, right after sundown, the perros retreated.

The avenue was paved in gore. We started moving the wounded to headquarters building, the only edifice left reasonably intact. Rita had come to her senses and set up an improvised hospital there. We had a conference outside the hospital.

Ard: Your heroics, Barry, were something to behold.

Manny: In other words, muy loco.

Bob: He's a regular Audie Murphy.

Barry: We lost Rosa and Enrique, not to mention probably five-hundred more.

Ard: They lost a couple of thousand, not to mention their tanks.

Capitán: It was a great victory.

Bob: What's our next move?

Chacho: Their pride is in the dirt; let us kick them while they are down.

Ard: We'll kick them alright, but we'll be ever-so subtle this go-round. Have you heard of psychological warfare? This battle has bought us some valuable time. Let's spread some propaganda, take out known sympathizers, and publicize the ineptness of the perros.

Capitán: We will advertise the fact that the perros are faltering. Each day that goes by will add to their fear.

Barry: Stall tactics, huh?

Chacho: Puedo ver. They will cause themselves to be ashamed and confused.

Capitán: I will send ambassadors throughout the territory. Everyone will see them as the rabid dogs that they are.

Ard: Meanwhile, we'll have time to rebuild our forces and repair some tanks

The response to our victories was overwhelming. Our army grew rapidly. We received dispatches from neighboring countries praising our efforts. Meanwhile, Concha and I became close, out of convenience, as she was grieving Enrique, and I, Rosa. She was kind of chubby, though built like a brick outhouse. She had the largest jugs I'd ever seen, but forget that part.

The time became ripe for us to march on Montevideo. All renegade regiments rendezvoused at Durazno; our combined forces now matched that of the perros. The odds were even. Ard knew we had to invade without further ado. We silently advanced in the dark of night.

The morning was overcast and gloomy; a stormy day for a comparable event. I was confident. I judged if I was supposed to kick the bucket, I would have done so by now. The assault on Montevideo seemed a parade. The tanks led, followed by gun jeeps, followed by trucks and infantry. We stormed into town with the thundering of artillery, machineguns, you name it. This volley was complemented by another downpour of bullets, and another; a recurring storm of firepower.

The perros were fully alert and waiting for the attack, but they had seemingly lost their will to fight. Individual soldiers began surrendering their arms; then entire groups of soldiers followed suit. By midday the battle was over, and the sun began peeking through the clouds sending its penetrating rays in all directions. It was a spectacular sight up above; not so much down below.

Our rebels started rounding up perro officers. A number of perro soldiers attempted escape; nobody tried to stop them. Droves of rejoicing people ran into the streets. There was mass mayhem. A cheering mob surrounded the Capitán's jeep. A wounded perro officer made his way through the mob, aimed a pistol, and shot the Capitán while he was standing proud. The crowd retaliated against the assassin with unrelenting rage.

The beloved Capitán lay on the ground, a pool of blood beneath his head. I knew he was a goner. Too bad because he was a great leader, and he would've made a distinguished president. I figured Capitán Pérez would become a legend in Uruguay's history. This final victory was the only one that would not be celebrated. Although it was a relatively easy win, it was very costly. The Capitán's last words cut to the quick.

Capitán: I have prayed that I would not die until we were victorious against the perros. God has answered my prayer. I am honored to die like Abraham Lincoln. Now it is the duty of you, mis hermanos, to carry on. Manny, your grandfather, Dios se bendiga: he once told me that someday you would return to your homeland. He was right. Uruguay needs you now (shutting his eyes). I'll give him your regards when I see him.

We were in all the newspapers, superstars again. American journalists couldn't decide if we were criminals or heroes. There was no argument among the people of Uruguay. Our names were listed in the New York Times. Even the names of Sarge and Teresa, who were no longer with us. That's when I saw Ard's real name, Alan Royce Denton. I always wondered where he got the name Ard; it stands for his initials. I guess the reason I didn't know his full name was because I never bothered to ask.

Surrounding countries began helping Uruguay in their reconstruction. A temporary ruling party was installed, and Manny was selected to lead them. An official election was scheduled to establish a democratic government. Manny's was the only name on the ticket for the position of President. A great wedding banquet was being prepared for him and his first lady to be, namely Rita. Yes, that's right, Manny and Rita were getting hitched. The celebration was complete with a Mariachi band, champagne fountain, and formal dance. After things simmered down, Ard convened the gang.

Manny: There is still much work to be done.

Ard (to Manny): Our work in Uruguay is finished. Yours is just beginning.

Bob: I'm ready for a change of scenery.

Laura: Me too.

Barry: What's next, Ard?

Ard (passing out some travel pamphlets): Have you ever been on an ocean cruise?

Barry (browsing through a brochure): Can't say that I have.

Ard: How does the Mediterranean sound?

Laura: I've always wanted to see Europe.

Bob: Are we talking business or pleasure?

Ard: A little of both. You people need a vacation, and I need some working capital for our next chore.

Manny: The people of Uruguay would be happy to help.

Ard: Nonsense! It'll be quite awhile before the Uruguayan economy is back in the black.

Manny: I wish I could go with you guys, mis amigos, y mi familia.

Rita: Tus amigos y tu familia estan aqui, mi esposo.

---

# PHASE FOUR

Manny offered an official farewell to the gang, along with a twenty-one-gun salute for our fallen comrades in arms. It was another happy yet sad occasion. Early in the morning we left on the president's plane destined for Rio. Ard gave us fake passports made by a professional forger from Buenos Aires. We traveled incognito for obvious reasons.

We rehearsed our new names and identities en route to Puerto Rico on a hired puddle-jumper. We had one full day to buy expensive, fashionable clothes and any accessories we wanted, before boarding a luxurious ocean liner docked in Miami. Ard had given each of us a bundle of cash; it was exciting blowing all that dough. The night before the voyage we met at the hotel for a last-minute briefing. Ard was waiting at the bar where I joined him.

Barry: Hey bartender, gimme a scotch on the rocks.

Ard: Remember we're to pretend that we are rich and sophisticated.

Barry (chewing on some ice): It ain't easy acting like an aristocrat. I've always considered myself an informal kind of dude.

Ard: Just try to look and act uppity and conceited. Pretend you're the typical ladies-man, heartless and arrogant; flirt with all the women like a sugar daddy from a family of wealthy oil tycoons.

Barry: I don't have any problem with the ladies-man part.

I offered Ard a cigar and we puffed, sipped our drinks, and shot the bull until Laura showed; not far behind were Bob and Virginia (everyone started calling her Vicky after that, figuring that she wasn't a virgin anymore). We had fun showing off and play-acting, with our spruced-up duds, clean-shaven faces (or legs), and new images. We each enjoyed a thick juicy steak dinner. Ard began the meeting with a toast to the President of Uruguay.

Ard: We must not be seen together in public during the cruise. Pretend to be strangers throughout the entire trip. We gradually can become reacquainted after we board the ship. Oh, and keep the do-not-disturb sign on your doors; we do not want housekeeping snooping around.

Bob: You mentioned mixing a little business with pleasure.

Ard: What sort of people go on an ocean cruise?

Barry: A bunch of rich old fogies.

Ard: The operating word is rich. Investigate anyone who spends money extravagantly, who wears expensive jewelry, and who acts carelessly with valuables. Steal anything that isn't nailed down. I can fence it back in Rio. Do not pick on honeymooners, or hard-working middle-class stiffs.

Bob: Where are we supposed to stock the crap we've kyped?

Ard: I'll determine that by the time we have enough to stockpile.

We reassembled while it was still dark to catch a chartered boat to Miami. I boarded the cruiser early, ironically dubbed the *Maid Marian*. While strolling around on deck I met the ship's captain.

Captain: Captain Chuck Burke's the name.

Barry (shaking hands): Sam Carter from Texas. It's a pleasure.

After our little talk, Ard and Laura approached and I broke away.

Ard: We're Jon and Laura Wilson.

Captain Burke: I'm the ship's skipper; Burke's the name. Where are you fine folks from?

Ard: San Diego. I'm an executive for a life insurance firm. We're on our second honeymoon after five years of marriage.

Ard sure was convincing. Later that day I noticed Robert and Virginia Johnston moving into a first-class cabin four doors down from mine.

There was a bon voyage party in the ballroom that night once the ship was at sea. I hung around the bar most of the evening. One codger kept talking to me. He wore a gold watch and sported diamond and ruby rings. After a while he escorted his wife to their cabin but returned shortly thereafter. He got so smashed he was weaving back and forth in his stool, until he fell against me. I managed to pickpocket his watch as I set him straight.

Next, a young lady asked me to dance who had parked herself at a nearby table. She was charming, with long, straight, pitch black hair, steel blue eyes, and a turned-up nose.

Barry: I'm not too hot of a dancer, especially when it comes to rock and roll stuff. The only dance I ever learned was the two-step.

Girl (giggling): That's OK. It's easy (shaking back and forth). Just move with the rhythm of the tune.

She begged me to give it a try. We danced several dances; she taught me a dance called the *Frug*. We blew the breeze a bit, in-between songs. When relating that she was seventeen and had just graduated high school, I thanked her for the dance and resumed my place at the bar. She looked more mature to me, like twenty-one. She continued making eyes at me until her parents arrived, and promptly left the ballroom dragging the teen behind them. I shrugged it off.

I got drunker and braver, so I asked this lady about ten years my senior to dance. She was sitting at a table with an elderly woman. She was as bad at the Frug as I was. But I felt more comfortable with her, even though she was older. She had bleached platinum hair in a shag style, which looked nice on her, but it didn't match her brown eyes. She had a fairly nice body with modest tummy bulge. She was stunning in her long red dress that flowed about her ankles. It was cut just low enough to reveal some appetizing breasts. Her name was Elaine.

After a few dances, Elaine's companion began to complain. Elaine informed that she needed to escort her mother back to their cabin, assuring me she would return once her mom had settled into bed. I offered to help and she was delighted, so we took her carry-on baggage back to their room. [Sorry diary, you can strike that last remark; I think I'm taking this arrogant ladies' man personality too far.] Anyway, we were returning to the party when Elaine stopped at the railing.

Elaine: Isn't it beautiful, the moonlight shimmering on the water?

Barry: Yes, very.

Elaine: I like to listen to the waves splashing.

Barry: So, what's the deal with your mother?

Elaine: I've been her primary caregiver ever since my father passed away.

Barry: It must be very difficult for you.

Elaine: I'm used to it.

Barry: Don't you ever get lonely?

Elaine looked at me with a tear in her eye. I took it as a cue to kiss her. She became overwhelmed with passion. I escorted her to my cabin and we made love. She acted quite guilty after the lovemaking and promptly left. I returned to the party and got ripped even further, contemplating that Elaine's bleached hair did not make her look better than her natural hair color would have.

We were in the middle of the Atlantic when I awoke hours later to chow down. I was enjoying some eggs Benedict when Bob discreetly dropped a note on my table. It was a small map showing two places where we could stash our stolen booty. After breakfast, I familiarized myself with the locations and tossed the map overboard.

I began to scope out some oldsters who were playing shuffleboard. They were completely decked out in jewelry. I recognized two of them as my neighbors on level six. Next, I moseyed down to the billiard room to see if they had a Snooker table; Snooker used to be my favorite pastime. There were six pool tables and one Snooker table; two gentlemen were playing for a dollar a point.

I challenged the winner; he was a fat dude wearing lots of rocks. I was glad I hadn't lost my touch with a pool cue. In a few hours I had taken the guy for 485 bucks. He pulled out a wad of dough worth a couple of grand, peeled off five crisp C-notes, handed them to me, and stomped away. I nonchalantly shadowed him, recording his cabin number.

I was on my way to the main galley when a lady flew out of her cabin and ran right into my arms. She was wrinkled, looking older than she really was. She was wearing a genuine pearl necklace. I said, "Excuse me, ma'am," and went my way. After a snack I roamed over to the crew's quarters to see how the other half lived.

I got acquainted with a sailor from Oklahoma. He showed me the room that he shared with another seaman; there were pinup girls pasted all over the walls. He was a muscular man with a crewcut and long sideburns. He had a tattoo on his left arm that looked like Mae West. His name was Tom. He'd been working on the ship for about two years, after spending six years in the U.S. Navy as a cruiser mechanic. His duty shift came up so I returned to my stateroom. Before I got there, I ran into Elaine who was holding a box lunch for the wrinkled bat (oops, sorry again).

Elaine: I was looking for you. I want to apologize. I really did enjoy last night.

Barry (coldly): Maybe we can do it again sometime.

Elaine (warmly): I'd like that.

Barry: I'm not looking to get close to anyone.

Elaine: I won't ask you for any commitments or obligations. It's just...

Barry: Something the matter?

Elaine (reluctantly): Well, I haven't been with a man since my husband divorced me eight years ago.

Barry: Oh?

Elaine: First Dad died; next our son moved out; then Mom moved in; gradually our marriage fell apart.

Barry: I can understand you being lonely and horny, but I can't see any reason to feel guilty about it.

Elaine: It's my mother. She depends on me. I have to leave now. (Pausing) I hope to see you soon Sam.

Barry: Uh huh.

I was uncomfortable behaving standoffish but was executing the role I was instructed to portray, and beginning to fully adopt the character. Besides, Ard didn't want me getting overly attached to anybody; it could blow our cover. I felt sorry for Elaine, being stuck with her mother and dealing with multiple hardships. I could tell she was a decent, honest, and sensual person.

She had her work cut out for her, playing nursemaid to her possessive mother. She deserved a man worthy of her to break the monotony.

As I began to enter my room, I noticed my neighbors accidentally left their door ajar. I peeked inside and called out. Nobody answered so I went inside. A jewelry box was on the vanity; I proceeded to open it. The contents of the box reminded me of the crown jewels. I pocketed a few expensive items and slinked away. Later that night I took some stuff to one of the drop points located in a lifeboat. I lifted the tarp and ditched the goods. It already was looking like a treasure trove under there; the gang had been busy.

I hopped back down and made my way to the short-order cafe for an early supper. I was enjoying a cigar break outside when the girl who taught me how to dance to rock music approached.

Barry: Aren't you afraid your parents will see you with me?

Girl: They just sat down to eat in the main restaurant; they'll be busy at least another hour.

Barry: I never did get your name.

Girl: Mine's Becky. What's yours, lover?

Barry: I'm Sam, and I ain't your lover.

Becky: Yet.

Barry: Don't you think I'm too old for you. After all, you're just a kid and I'm a grownup.

Becky: I'm old enough to make my own decisions. I'll be eighteen next month and legally a woman. Besides, we're not in the USA now, and I'm sure they don't check for ID or take notes about who people are making it with on this cruise.

Barry: Maybe so, but still…

Becky: Uh oh, here comes my brother. I'll be in the rec room later if you want to meet me there.

Barry: Bye.

I tossed my cigar butt into the sea and strolled to the closest bar for a drink. At a table sat the wrinkled old lady, but she wasn't wearing her pearl necklace. Her husband was joining her so I knew their cabin was empty. I downed my gin-and-tonic and went to their cabin. I tried to pry the lock with my pocketknife, unsuccessfully. I was on my way back towards the bar when I ran across Ard. I told him about the cabin with the necklace. He told me to show him.

When we got there, he looked around to make sure the coast was clear. Then he pulled out a small leather kit that had some tools in it. He chose two and played with the lock. In five seconds, presto, it was open. He departed and I went inside.

The necklace was on the nightstand. I was getting ready to snatch it when I heard someone at the door. I ducked into the bathroom. The old lady entered the bathroom, went to the toilet, combed her hair and left, with me standing just three feet away behind a shower curtain. I snooped around some more and discovered a tin box under the bed; I pulled it out and opened it. Inside was a pile of money in large bills. I grabbed a stack and put the box back under the bed. Then I pocketed the necklace and ambled out the door, wondering why the ignoramuses didn't take advantage of the ship's safe deposit boxes.

I went to another bar after stashing the necklace. Bob was sipping a martini and I joined him. Then Vicky arrived and they went to dinner. A frail woman wearing horn-rimmed glasses was sitting alone at the bar so I scooted over a few stools and introduced myself.

She was wearing a big-ass diamond on her wedding finger and an emerald brooch between her boobs. She had rubbed lipstick around her mouth to make her lips look bigger, but instead it looked idiotic. She talked in a monotone voice. She was the widower of a retired Air Force colonel. I figured her husband must have left her a fortune.

The woman's sister came out of the restroom and sat down between us. She was younger and considerably more attractive. She put a smoke in her mouth and I lit it for her. As she placed the cigarettes in her purse, I noticed she was packing a derringer. The sister was divorced from a banker in New York City. I immediately saw dollar signs times two. I bought the women what they wanted and we talked a bit about their finances, if you get my drift. They excused themselves after two drinks.

I was heading to my room to hose off, when I redirected my path to the arcade to see if Becky was there. I don't know what compelled me to look for her. I was playing pinball when she slithered up behind me and pinched my behind. I could tell she had a crush on me but I was trying to hide my attraction to her. She was too astute to be fooled. She grabbed my hand and pulled me outside.

Barry: Where are we going?

Becky: Let's go dancing.

Barry: Again? I'm already sweating like a pig. I haven't had a shower or changed clothes since yesterday. I can smell my own body odor. Tell you what, I'll meet you later in the ballroom.

Becky: I don't mind your B.O. because you smell like a man to me. Hey, I have an idea. Let me go with you. I promise to behave; I'll just watch TV while you do your thing.

We went to my cabin. She turned on the television and plopped on my bed as I went to the bathroom. I showered, shaved, brushed my teeth, and wrapped a towel around myself. I went to the closet for some fresh clothes. She hopped out of bed and jerked the towel off me.

Becky (hands on her hips): Now that's what I call a real man.

Barry (picking up the towel): I thought you were going to behave.

Becky: You think I've never seen a naked man before?

Barry: How should I know?

Becky began to undress.

Barry: What do you think you're doing?

Becky: What does it look like?

Barry: But, what if…

Becky: Relax, I'm on the pill.

Before I knew it, Becky was completely in the raw. She had a gorgeous body, firm and tight. I was aroused immediately. She swaggered up to me, placed her arms around my neck, and planted a juicy French kiss on my lips. I was nervous; she could tell and recommended that I relax. I finally did and we had some dynamite sex.

After an hour romping in the sack we got dressed and went dancing. I had a great time. I think she was turning me into a rock music fan. Before, I always used to listen to country-western. Her little brother started looking for her around one o'clock.

Becky: Uh, ohh, there's my brother again. I was supposed to check in at one. He'll squeal if he sees me with you.

Barry: I guess you'd better skedaddle.

I returned to my cabin to find Elaine waiting outside. She hinted that she wanted it. I obliged her. I felt like a gigolo, but then again, that's who I was supposed to be. I was beginning to like being a gigolo.

Elaine nodded off; she must have been exhausted. I got out of bed, dressed, and took a smoke break outside. I ended up at the nearest bar. As I began to enter, I stopped cold in my tracks. I noticed the bartender sifting through a man's pockets who was passed out on a table. I hesitated a moment before going inside so he wouldn't know I was wise to him. The bartender told me he was closing the bar. He asked if I would help him with the sloppy drunkard. I said sure.

We helped the guy to his room. I bid goodnight to the bartender, then tracked him. He stashed something in an unlocked fire extinguisher box. I returned to my room; Elaine was gone. I proceeded to polish off the rest of a bottle of primo scotch from my personal supply.

I awoke, showered, dressed, and went for some chow. As I was wolfing down waffles, the morning announcements were broadcast over the intercom.

Announcer: We have received several complaints about missing jewelry. Captain Burke suggests that guests consider using the safe for their priceless valuables. We cannot be responsible for lost or stolen items. We will make every effort to return recovered articles to the rightful owners. Please provide a list of missing items along with their descriptions to the business office. Now for the good news: We will be arriving at Lisbon in one hour.

I saw Ard and Laura disembark in Lisbon. They were strolling the marina when I caught up to them.

Barry: Did you hear the announcement?

Ard: Yeah.

Barry: We aren't the only ones swiping stuff.

Ard: Really?

Barry: I saw one of the bartenders lifting items from a crocked patron. I was following him when I thought I saw him hide something in a fire extinguisher box. I inspected the box this morning; inside was a tin can containing a diamond tie clip with matching cufflinks, a sapphire ring, a gold money clip, and a diamond wristwatch.

Ard: Interesting. Keep an eye on the guy. Report to me what you hear and see.

Barry: You bet.

After taking a look around Lisbon, I returned to the ship for dinner. We shoved off shortly afterwards destined for Algiers. I gulped down dinner and went looking for that thieving bartender. I found him working the billiard and recreation area. Bob was playing eight-ball with the fat guy I'd hustled before. The fat guy won. I challenged the table.

Fat guy: That's all for me fellows, the table is yours.

Barry: Don't you want a rematch?

Fat guy (to Barry): Not now. (to Bob) Watch this shark mister, he's liable to run the table on you.

Barry (to Bob): Where's Vicky?

Bob (chalking a cue stick): She turned in. She had a bout with seasickness earlier. What do you think about the announcement this morning?

Barry (racking the balls): We aren't alone.

Bob (breaking): Oh yeah?

Barry (making a shot): I saw the bartender over yonder pick-pocketing a guy. Later I watched him placing jewelry in a fire extinguisher box.

Bob: Come to think of it, I noticed one of the staff members stuffing a life preserver. I didn't think much about it at the time.

Barry (missing a shot): Ard told me to spy on the bartender and his stash. Maybe you should monitor that staff member and that life preserver.

Bob (sinking the eight-ball on purpose): You're right. I'd better run along.

Barry (louder): Nice game Mr. Johnston.

Bob: The pleasure was all mine Mr. Carter.

A half-snockered guy challenged me to some nine-ball at fifty bucks a game. I took him up on it. He took off his rings before chalking his cue. I let him win a few games; then I hustled him six games in a row. He changed the game to rotation at five bucks a point. I hustled him for another three hundred.

The guy got mad and left in a huff, with his rings still on the table. I picked up the rings and went to play pinball. The guy came back looking for his rings. I pretended to help him look. He left in a fury again. Bob and Ard came into the bar later that night. I was nursing a Manhattan.

Bob: Well Mr. Carter, I see you are still here. Let me introduce you to Jonathan Wilson.

Barry (shaking Ard's hand): Pleased to meet you, Sam Carter's the name. Let me buy you boys a drink.

Ard: Let's take that table in the corner.

Bob: I filled Ard in about our earlier conversation. I also inspected that life preserver. There was some jewelry crammed inside a hollowed-out section.

Barry: We have competition.

Ard: Too bad for the competition. I have a plan. Barry, stay here until closing and get inebriated.

Barry: It's a tough assignment, Ard; but then I'm half-way there already.

Ard: Cut the comedy. I've got a reason.

Barry: I'm listening.

Ard: You'll be the guinea pig while we catch us a weasel.

I had the easy job. I drank profusely until two-thirty. I was so loaded I could barely move. Finally, the bartender announced he was closing. I acted obnoxious. He insisted I get up, helping me to the door. As he was locking the door, I staggered down the deck with my wallet hanging part way out of my pocket. The bartender took the bait and hurried to lend me a hand as I rounded the corner. He was trying to put my arm around his neck when I deliberately fell on my knees, my butt protruding into the air. He grabbed my wallet and placed it in his inside coat pocket while assisting me to my feet.

Ard and the ship's captain were peeking the whole time. The bartender was caught red-handed; Captian Burke gave me my wallet and escorted the dud to the brig. On the way back, I showed Ard the bartender's stash in the fire extinguisher. He had been very productive since I last checked.

I slept like a rock, waking with my head spinning. We'd already ported in Algiers. I ran into Elaine and her mother having breakfast.

Barry: Good morning, ladies. I'm surprised to see you here. How come you aren't touring the city?

Mother: I just don't feel up to it, today.

Elaine: Mother's not feeling well so I suppose we'll stay aboard.

Mother: Go on ahead Elaine, and have fun with Sam. I'm going to go lie down anyway.

I gulped down a cup of coffee and we accompanied her mother to their stateroom. Then we went ashore. We toured the city in a cab. We necked in the back seat; it reminded me of double-dates I went on in high school. We had dinner and returned to the ship after dark.

Barry: Want to come to my cabin for a nightcap?

Elaine: It's that time of the month, dear.

I got the hint and walked her to her cabin. Then I looked around for the sailor named Tom. I found him in his quarters. We began talking about the thievery.

Barry: Did you hear about the bartender getting busted.

Tom: Sure.

Barry: I was the guy he pickpocketed. I saw him robbing some other dude so I helped set him up

Tom: Congratulations. You want to know something? He isn't the only shady character on this ship.

Barry: That so?

Tom: I've got suspicions about my roommate but I can't prove anything. You know, I've noticed that the *Maid Marian* has been plagued by thieves since I started working here.

Barry: Do tell.

Tom had to leave because the graveyard shift was beginning. I dropped by Ard's place; he already had turned in and was half asleep when he answered the door. I told him what Tom had told me. He responded with an abrupt "thanks and good night."

I found a note under my door when I awoke the next morning. It read: Sardinia, second beach, high noon. I goofed around the shops and docks until then. Ard and Laura were sunbathing when I found them. Bob and Vicky were nearby wading in the sea.

Ard: I'm convinced there's a heist ring on the *Maid Marian*. It's interfering with our pilfering. Unfortunately, the bartender won't talk.

Bob: Let's put them out of business.

Ard: You're way ahead of me, pal.

Barry: I've been hanging out with a crewman named Tom. He said this ship has a history of thievery. I think Tom can help us.

Ard: See what you can find out from Tom. I've already teamed with Burke. Bob and Vicky will maintain a vigilant watch to see if anyone else visits the caches we've discovered.

I returned to the ship looking for Tom.

Barry (to sailor): Have you seen Tom?

Sailor: He's below deck.

Barry: Is it okay if I go down there?

Sailor: I don't care, just don't stay long, it's against regulations.

I climbed down a ladder and found Tom kicking back with a Camel in his mouth.

Tom: It isn't cool for you to be down here, man.

Barry: I just wanted to see if you'd like to go raise hell, if and when you get any time off someday.

Tom: As a matter of fact, the ship took on the remainder of our crew at the port of Algiers, so I don't have to pull double-shifts anymore. I also have some leave coming. Tell you what, let's mess around Sicily and play it from there.

Barry: Sound's good.

I met with Tom as the ship embarked on Sicily. We hit the island with a powerful hunger so we dined at an all-you-can-eat pasta place. Then we dropped into a nightclub that had a live band and lots of women. We danced with different dames until midnight. About that time two foxy women speaking Italian entered the bar laughing; they plunked down at the empty table next to ours. Tom maneuvered to their table the moment they sat down.

Tom: Would you pretty ladies care to join us?

They giggled.

Woman: No espeaky American.

I spoke to them in my broken Spanish.

Barry: Ustedes estan muy hermosas. Me gusta mucho si quieren sentar con nosotros. Podemos comprar unas bebidas para las senoritas?

They giggled again and whispered to each other; they understood enough to accept the invitation. Their names were Sophia and Andrea. I had the hots for Andrea. She was a slim, seductive looking thing with alluring hazel eyes and silky lips. Her wavy light brown hair blanketed her bare shoulders. They were natives of the mainland and were spending the weekend in Sicily. We danced for maybe an hour. Tom suggested we get a couple of bottles of Rosé and head over to the beach. Much to my surprise they accepted. What a great idea that was!

The four of us found a secluded area and built a small bonfire. I opened one bottle and passed it over to Andrea; she took a slug and handed it back to me. Tom opened the other bottle and passed it to Sophia, who had pulled two reefers from her purse. I'd never smoked the stuff before and I was hesitant to try. Andrea persuaded me to indulge. We passed around a bottle and a reefer, another bottle and another reefer. Pretty soon everyone was blotto, having gone through two bottles of wine and two joints in no time flat.

Tom exclaimed that it was time for a swim, so he stripped and bounded out to the surf in the raw. It looked fun and I did the same. The girls watched and howled as we skinny-dipped in the surf. The cool water sobered us up, while the girls enjoyed the show stoned on their butts. After the swim we dressed and sat beside our respective partners, sneaking a smooch whenever we could. Then a policeman chased us off the beach. Tom had very little trouble coaxing them to continue partying at their rented bungalow. Tom apparently knew his way around Sicily as we zig-zagged through empty streets to where they were staying. I determined it was true what I'd heard about Italian women being hot lovers (much like Mexican lovers I might add). Not surprisingly, I had developed a special taste for Latin women.

Midmorning the four of us got into gear and commissioned a grand tour of the island. Unfortunately, Tom and I had to get a move on halfway through because the *Maid Marian* was set to sail in the afternoon. I had an early supper with Tom at the crewmen's table where the conversation worked its way around to the robberies.

Tom (whispering): I'm sure this is a big operation.

Barry: You don't say?

Tom: See that guy over there scratching his head?

Barry: Yeah. Isn't he the first mate?

Tom: Right. I've had suspicions about him. I haven't liked him since he came aboard last fall. He lies as if it doesn't matter. He is a sneak and a cheat.

Tom left after dinner to catch some shut-eye before his shift. I went upstairs to the sundeck and fell asleep on a recliner, spending the night there. I awoke with the sun in my eyes and Tom sitting on a lounge chair next to me.

Tom: Mornin' Sam.

Barry: How long have you been here?

Tom: I just got off work. I saw you crashed out.

Barry: How 'bout breakfast?

Tom: Nah, I'm too beat. Besides, I had a snack a few hours ago. I just wanted to tell you that I followed my roommate, and well, I found one of their hiding places.

Barry: You found some stolen junk? Where?

Tom: I'm not sure I should tell you.

Barry: Come on man, we're buddies, aren't we?

Tom:  Yeah, I guess.

Tom told me the location of the stash. He said he'd look me up after he copped a few zzz's and we'd invade Crete. I went to my room to freshen up. A note was under my door. Ard needed another meeting. I found the gang at the shuffleboard court on the starboard side. It was still early, so hardly anybody else was about.

Ard (standing with a shuffleboard stick): What did you find out?

Bob: Vicky saw one of the maids stuffing her pockets with jewelry while she was cleaning staterooms thinking nobody was looking.

Ard: Hmm. Fascinating.

Barry: Tom has discovered another stash. He also thinks the first mate is in on it.

Ard (shoving a puck with his stick): Time for you to let Tom in on our scheme.

Bob: Are you sure we can trust him, Ard?

Ard: He obviously trusts Barry, and we need him.

Bob: What's the game plan?

Ard: I can't prove it yet, but I believe the first mate is manning the gate. We're competing with a well-established ring; I've a strategy for a sting. After consulting with Burke, I know this will work. We've got positive identification on some players, we've located several drops, we have personnel in tactical positions. But the puzzle is incomplete; missing pieces. I'll figure it out soon. There's a big slice of pie for everyone, including Tom.

Barry: I doubt if Tom will do anything illegal.

Ard: He won't have to.

Barry: What's in it for him?

Ard: A promotion, raise, bonus, vacation, et cetera.

Barry: I see your point.

Tom and I hit Crete for lunch.

Tom: The first thing I'm gonna do is pig-out big time.

Tom's eloquence matched his appetite that's for sure. Next, we visited a bunch of historical sites, art museums, and such. I didn't peg Tom for a cultural enthusiast but the tour was thought-provoking. We were standing among some ruins when I told him about the sting we were planning.

Tom: Are you for real?

Barry: Listen, Tom, I've been meaning to tell you something.

Tom: I'm all ears.

Barry: Well um, have you ever heard about this roving gang, sort of mercenaries, modern-day Robin Hoods if you will?

Tom: Are you kidding? They're world famous! Wait a minute, you're not telling me that you…

Barry: Afraid so amigo.

Tom: Holy cow! What the F are you doing on the *Maid Marian*?

Barry: We're going to expose the theft ring.

Tom: Boy, you people have got balls. They're syndicated. You're talking about the big boys.

Barry: You want a piece of the action?

Tom: Sheesh, I don't know.

Barry: C'mon Tom, you've got balls too, I've seen 'em.

Tom: I want to meet the boss of your operation.

Barry: That can be arranged.

Tom (giving the thumbs up): Now let's locate us some babes.

We were unsuccessful finding any babes, only sleazy whores. It was an off night, I guess. We boozed it up, instead. Then, I helped Tom sober up. After pouring a gallon of coffee down his gullet, and force-walking him back to his quarters, I went to my room and dozed off.

In the morning I found another note. A meeting was scheduled for eleven p.m. in Ard's quarters. Tom had to be at work at eleven. I went to Tom's quarters at ten-thirty and found him shaving. I discreetly informed him of the meeting. He paid his roommate ten bucks to cover him twenty minutes in order to pay a delinquent beer tab. Everyone showed up exactly on time. I introduced Tom to the gang.

Tom: It's an honor to meet you all. Can I get your autographs?

Ard: Look Tom, here's the deal. You get credit for taking down the hoods, we get a third of the recovered goods.

Tom: If you guys fail, my ass is grass.

Ard: If we succeed, you'll pass as brass.

Tom: What do I have to do?

Ard: Nothing, really. I'll turn the evidence over to you. You give it to Burke. The Captain will escort you while you point out guilty parties and drop-off points.

Tom: Why are you doing this when you could have the whole enchilada?

Ard: One should never overindulge just because there's plenty.

Tom: Man, that's heavy.

Tom went to work and I went to bed. The next afternoon Tom and I visited Athens. We went to the Acropolis. It was amazing. Tom had to go back to work but I stayed awhile. I returned to the ship and noticed Becky hanging around my door. Fortunately, she didn't see me. This was no time to be fooling with her. I went down to the engine room where Tom worked; he wasn't there but his roommate was. I didn't want him seeing me and ducked behind some pipes. He was twirling a small bag which he placed in his pocket. I tailed him above deck without him catching on.

He bypassed the swimming pool and stopped near a man sitting in a storage area. He rose and they shook hands; it was the fat dude I'd hustled at billiards. As they spoke, I saw Tom's roomie pass the bag. They parted company. I followed mister red-faced fatso who went straight for his cabin, I kept going to mine and conked out.

The ship was at sea when I awoke so I moseyed around a spell. I spent the rest of the evening playing blackjack in the casino. Surprisingly, fatso and the first mate entered together near the slot machines; they said a few words and went separate ways. He noticed me and approached; we chit-chatted. He asked for a rematch so we traipsed over to the billiard room. I bought him drinks all night and let him win a few games to see if I could loosen his tongue. All I found out was his name, Forsythe. The night wasn't a total loss; I managed to hustle another hundred out of him. I awoke with Tom banging on my door.

Tom: Let's go to Naples and find us some more of those fine Italian chicks.

Barry: Sounds good.

Tom (handing Barry a note): I found this on your floor.

Barry (opening the note): We have a meeting in Naples.

Tom: When.

Barry: Noon.

Tom: Fine, let's chow down first.

We dined on the waterfront, then went to the marina and located Ard, who directed us to a yacht that was docked there.

Barry: I wonder whose yacht this is.

Tom: Who cares?

Ard: Here's the scoop. Altogether we have located four stashes and identified five players.

Barry: Make that six players.

Ard: Who?

Barry: A guy named Forsythe; he's in room 4209. You've seen him, big as a truck and looks sunburned in the face. I saw Tom's roommate handing Forsythe a small purse. Tom fingered his roommate earlier so I followed him. Also, I've seen Forsythe speaking privately with First Mate Oglethorpe three times. But the liaison only lasts for seconds, like it's supposed to appear coincidental.

Ard: Excellent! Now it makes sense. Forsyth is the missing link; and hence, must be the fence. He will be collecting the booty and carrying it off the ship at an upcoming port of call.

Bob: What's our next move?

Ard: Let's see, so far there's six of us and six of them. I need your help, ladies. Are you up to the task?

Laura: Are you kidding? I've been prodding you to let me do something. This is too exciting to be a spectator.

Ard: Vicky?

Vicky: Yes, I would like very much for to help.

Ard (to Laura): Okay Laura, I want you to get friendly with Forsythe. Use your charm. Tease him a little. Loosen him up. Get him to take you to his stateroom for a nightcap and I will give you something to conceal behind the toilet.

Ard (to Vicky): I'll convince Captain Burke to place you on the housekeeping staff. See what you can find out about that chambermaid you saw. I got her name, it's Lucía. She's from Puerto Rico so you two should get along famously.

Tom: I can keep an eye on Greg, well, except when I'm working graveyard. Anyway, he's the the fellow Sam was talking about.

Ard: I'll study Oglethorpe and maintain dialogue with Burke. Bob, you keep tabs on Butkowski, the guy you saw at one of the drop sites. He runs the gift shop and pharmacy. Barry, you keep tabs on Hartmann, the bartender with the handlebar mustache. He knows you by now so you can make friends. Questions?

Bob: Is the pleasure part of this cruise over?

Ard: Not at all. Have fun, but disclose whatever makes an impression. Be subtle and watch your six; trust your instincts and mix it up. You can't watch someone day and night without stirring suspicion. Employ your intuition without compromising the mission.

Ard: Anything else? (Pause) I'll be in touch.

Tom and I partied all afternoon in Naples but again had no luck with the ladies. Tom had to work again, but he had the coming weekend off. I found Hartmann tending bar on the observation deck and got tanked with him. We played chess. He whipped my ass. I followed him after closing time and noticed him at a new drop site. I slept until noon and then rousted Tom out of bed. It was the weekend, and Rome was waiting to be conquered.

We had another feast and looked at the sights. We started bar-hopping about eight. We found a club with a good rock band that was jam-packed. We noticed a pair of comely ladies who were speaking English so we made the moves on them. Their names were Fran and Liz.

I went for Liz. She had amazing violet eyes, with short dishwater blonde hair in pig tails tied with violet ribbons. She had on a ton of makeup. I figured she'd look darn good anyway without all the makeup. I especially liked her accent. She was on vacation with her friend, another looker with long reddish hair, tied in a bow and dangling to one side. They were tailors from Britain and had been saving up for a year to make this trip.

We drank and danced all night. Then we slept with them at their hotel. The next day we watched a nasty Italian flick together. Then we went back to their hotel and switched partners. By the way, Liz was a true blonde and Fran a true redhead. We helped them pack. They had to catch a plane because Monday was a workday. Too bad we didn't get to spend more time with them; they were a blast, with a great sense of humor and genuine as the day is long. Monday was a workday for Tom as well. He said he'd check with me later.

I had dinner in the main galley and went to my cabin. There was another note informing the next meeting would be at noon tomorrow in Ard's cabin. I roused Tom for the meeting. The gang had been productive.

Bob: Vicky discovered a stash in the laundry room.

Barry: I located another stash in a planter among some bushes.

Ard: Great work everyone. I've hidden half the stolen jewelry from the fire extinguisher in Oglethorpe's quarters. Laura's hidden the other half in Forsythe's stateroom.

Ard: That leaves six caches altogether.

Tom: Man alive, you characters do get around.

Ard: After midnight, Bob will grab the stuff in lifeboat four. Barry, you collect the contents from eight. Bring the goods back here to my room; that'll be our third of the take.

[Diary side-note: The lifeboats were the two drop points our gang had been utilizing.]

Ard: Tom, around five a.m. I want you knocking on the door of the Captain's quarters to report the cache Barry discovered in the planter and the one Bob found in the life preserver. Wake up Burke if you must and assure him you have collected critical information that he needs to be aware of right away. Tell him you saw your colleague Greg hiding something in the planter and investigated, finding jewelry, but you left the site undisturbed. Then mention the life preserver and tell him you noticed Hartmann stuffing it with jewelry. Impress upon Burke that you have been keeping an eye out ever since the public address announcement. Burke will have to pursue this straightaway and will take you along as backup. Mention how you've observed Oglethorpe acting suspiciously, occasionally meeting secretly with a guest by the name of Forsythe, as well as swapping something secretly with Greg. Meanwhile, Burke will confiscate the goods in each location and thank you. My guess is he will want to keep you close since he doesn't know who among the staff he can trust.

Tom: No sweat.

Bob: Then what?

Ard: I am meeting Burke at seven for breakfast to brief him on my findings, at which time I will tell him that Vicky discovered a cache in the laundry room. I will accompany him in investigating this and ensure he finds the goods. Along the way I will mention observing the first mate transferring a small bag in a clandestine manner to a guest who looked fat and had a red face. He'll know I'm referring to Forsythe. Burke will have enough evidence to obtain permission to search Forsythe's and Oglethorpe's quarters. He'll find stolen goods in both places, naturally. Most likely Tom will be Burke's prime witness; and Tom will know where to look to ensure discovery of missing valuables. Burke will doubtless stake out the drop sites. Once the announcement is made that numerous missing valuables have been located, the pigeons will return to the coop, and the good Captain should be able to catch Greg, Lucia, Hartmann, Butkowski, and who knows who. It'll only take one or two snitches to implicate the rest of the conspirators.

Bob: Is the business part of this cruise over?

Ard: You're incorrigible, Bob.

Bob: I'm what?

Ard: As soon as you deliver the goods to me you can enjoy yourself for the rest of the cruise.

Bob: Time's a wastin'.

Tom: I gotta get going.

Barry: Adios, Tom. I guess I'll have to invade Monaco alone.

Tom: Get some for me, cowboy.

I bounced from bar to bar along the Monaco waterfront until I got hungry. I stopped at a plush establishment that had a female vocalist. Her voice was sweet music to my ears. I grabbed a table close to the stage.

She was a knockout. She had reddish-brown hair that flipped at the shoulders. She had a petite French nose and bright shining hazel eyes; her lips were ruby red, and she had a dimple in each cheek. I forgot about being hungry, at least for food that is. She finished her set and some wino introduced another act. I went looking for the girl but she had slipped away. I ambled outside to puff on a smoke.

I was leaning against a lamppost when the glamorous young singer strutted out the door. The cigarette fell from my gaping mouth; I panted like a hound dog when I saw her. She asked me in English for a light. I lit her cigarette and fired up another for myself.

Barry: What's your name sweetheart?

Girl (with French accent): Jannette. And you?

Barry: Uhh, Sam, Sam Carter.

Jannette: How did you like the show?

Barry: I think you're fabulous; and I also enjoyed the show.

Jannette (curtsying): Thank you kind sir.

Barry: When do you get off work?

Jannette: I am off work now.

Barry: Are you hungry?

Jannette: A little.

Barry: Won't you join me for dinner?

Jannette: All right, but not here.

Barry: Lead the way, my queen.

She showed me to another plush establishment around the corner. As we entered, she waved at a female performer on stage who nodded back. We sat in the corner. Jannette ordered champagne so I did too. She told me the Quiche Lorraine was excellent and I ordered that; she ordered a chef salad. The singer on stage was her friend, Adrienne; she was a honey and a fabulous singer too. She joined us as our dinner was being served. I ordered a glass of bubbly for Adrienne.

Adrienne didn't speak English so the girls yacked while I ate. Shortly thereafter a handsome gentleman approached and Adrienne left with him. Jannette and I finished our champagne and got better acquainted. Then we went into the lounge, listened to some soft music, and danced a few. I thoroughly enjoyed her company. She was sweet, intelligent, and could read me like an open book; It's like she could hear my thoughts. She definitely was my kind of woman. I couldn't hide my attraction for her and I told her.

Barry (dancing slow with Jannette): I love the feel of your touch, so soft and tender. And you are lovely to look at, and you smell amazing. The sound of your voice is soothing to my ears.

Barry (after a pause): That leaves only one of my five senses that you have yet to titillate; and I bet you taste delicious.

Jannette: Well, that has to be the best line anyone has ever tried on me just to steal a kiss.

Barry: It wasn't a line, my dear. If it was, that'd mean I've used it before.

Jannette: So, you're telling me it is, how you say, original; first time first place?

Barry: It's the truth, chéri; maybe because it's you that is so original, unique and special.

Jannette: You think so?

Barry (kissing her): Oh yes.

Jannette (after a brief, passionate kiss): Not here, okay baby?

Barry: Of course, baby. I was right though, that was delicious (smacking his lips).

We went to another place off the beaten track and danced another hour. I asked her if she believed in love at first sight. She said in her sweet French accent, "It happens." We strode along the harbor walk and I stopped and kissed her again. She emphatically returned it to my delight. We walked and talked, and kissed some more. Then she took my hand and led me to a run-down apartment, and up three flights of stairs. It was her place. She closed the door and gave me another scrumptious lip-lock. I carried her to the bed; we made adoring love. It was out of this world.

I awoke with the early morning sun peeking through the curtains. I looked at the clock. I had two hours to get back on the ship before it left Monaco. I didn't want to go and Jannette didn't want me to leave. Then, she started crying. Suddenly, I got a brainstorm. I asked her to come with me. She looked worried. I got on my knees and pleaded with her. She looked anxious. I concluded that it was now or never. She quickly packed one large case. I grabbed the case, she grabbed an African violet, and we hit the trail. On the way, she left a note on Adrienne's door explaining everything and telling her to pick up Jannette's paycheck.

The ship was just about to shove off. We ran aboard. Fortunately, nobody bothered either of us, acknowledging our haste to depart with the ship. They didn't recognize Jannette as a visitor. She dumped her stuff in my cabin and we went for breakfast. The morning announcements included a special report about the break-up of the theft ring, and the return of many valuables. Eight people were in the brig, including Forsythe and Oglethorpe. Tom was a hero.

Ard and Laura noticed us and invited themselves to our table. I introduced Jannette using our fake names. Somehow, Ard wasn't astonished that I had a stowaway with me; then again, nothing I do surprises him. Laura and Jannette hit it off immediately. We were still drinking coffee an hour later when Tom showed. He was very surprised I had Jannette with me, but he didn't let on who we really were. Jannette and Laura left to the ladies' room.

Tom (standing): I guess you've heard the news. I'm the toast of the ship; they promoted me to chief maintenance officer. I'm not sure I like all the attention but I don't mind the promotion and pay.

Ard: It'll blow over in a day or two. Enjoy it while it lasts.

Tom (giving the A-OK signal to Barry): Nice looking lady. How did you manage to slip her aboard?

Barry: I didn't. We just hurried up the ramp like we owned the place.

Tom: Far out! Later on, my friend.

Ard: Don't worry about Jannette. Let me know if anyone gives her a hard time. Burke owes me a favor. She doesn't know anything, does she?

Barry: Not yet, but I guess I'll have to tell her sometime.

Ard: Wait until we return to Rio.

Jannette and I enjoyed each other's company day and night. Luckily, Elaine and Becky both wrote me off after seeing me with another woman. Jannette and I also toured Barcelona together, where we were entertained by a flamenco dancer. The next day we sailed past Gibraltar and into the Atlantic. It was along the sandy beaches of the Canary Islands, watching the sunset, when I told Jannette I needed her in my life forever. We made love in a cove.

The last stop on the cruise was the Bahamas, where we hopped on a flight to Rio de Janeiro. While in flight, the gang bid farewell to the *Maid Marian*, and to Tom. We checked into a hotel and hit Copacabana. Another official gang meeting had come to order.

Ard (to Barry): Tell her who we are.

I told Jannette everything. She was speechless.

Barry (to Jannette): I hope you don't hate me for deceiving you.

Jannette: I could never hate you.

Ard: Now that's out of the way.

Bob: Wasn't it great the way those chumps did the dirty work for us?

Barry: I'll say; they had a head start, too.

Ard: I estimate the value of our total take to be over a hundred G's, not including the cash we raised. It should be enough to fund our next project.

Bob: Another project, so soon?

Ard: It's not like you haven't had a vacation.

Barry: Fill us in Ard.

Ard: Keep your pants on. First, I've got to unload the merchandise and aggregate our bankroll. While I'm away, play a few days, soak up some rays, enjoy your stays.

The meeting was adjourned and the gang had a free-for-all in the surf. I got a good feel of Laura's ass and someone fondled my crotch. That night, Ard disappeared for two days. Jannette and I kept Laura company. Ard returned with more money than he expected for the hot rocks. He gave us ten grand each, and two weeks to blow it.

We had to split up and lay low for a spell. Ard sent Laura home to spend time with her parents while he ran some errands. Bob and Vicky returned to the Bahamas. Jannette and I moved into a hotel close to Guanabara Bay where the gang was to reconvene in ten days, at high noon. Jannette and I loved it there, and we fell deeper in love.

⌘⌘⌘⌘⌘⌘⌘⌘⌘⌘⌘⌘⌘⌘⌘⌘⌘⌘⌘⌘⌘⌘⌘⌘⌘

## PHASE FIVE

Jannette and I spent every afternoon on the beach, getting a terrific tan. One day she asked when I would take her to the USA. She already had a passport and visa, anticipating making the trip someday with Adrienne. I promised we'd be going to America very soon; I didn't realize how soon that would be.

Late one evening Jannette fell asleep with the television on; I was still kind of wired so I decided to go downstairs for a nightcap. A bulky patron had been telling dirty jokes with the bartender. I listened in; it was hard not to, because the guy was practically shouting. I snickered at one of his jokes.

Man (pointing with his thumb): Bring this distinguished gentleman another of what he's drinking.

Barry (rising from his stool): Your best scotch on the rocks.

Man (extending his hand): JD Luckett's the name, of Revolution Recording Company.

Barry (shaking his hand): I'm Sam Carter, Texas oilman. Do you play pool?

JD: Hell yes.

We smoked cigars, played several games of pool, and kidded around.

Bartender: Last call gentlemen.

JD: Hell, it's only four a.m. Tell you what, Sam, I've got a bottle of this stuff in my hotel room.

Barry: You're speaking my language, clearly well-trained in the art of drunk.

When we got to JD's room it dawned on me that he was a record producer.

Barry (taking a glass from JD): I bet I can make you rich.

JD (pouring from a bottle): Hell, Sam, I'm already rich.

Barry (taking a swig): I'm talking filthy rich.

JD: Now you're speaking my language. What've you got?

Barry: I happen to know a certain French lady who recently played Monaco; sings like a bird and looks like an angel.

JD: I'd be happy to listen to her tapes.

Barry: I can do you one better. How about a live performance?

JD: When?

Barry: I might can arrange for an audition tomorrow afternoon.

JD: That'll work, but I'm leaving the day after. Tell you what, why don't you and your companion join me for dinner?

Barry (downing the drink): Sounds like a winner. Got to go. Hasta mañana.

Dear Diary, I had another strange dream last night, more like a nightmare. I watched an earthquake devastate a city which crumbled around me. I awoke with Jannette shaking the bed. I had a ferocious hangover.

Jannette: Get up, you lazy bones.

Barry: I've got some terrific news.

Jannette: What is it?

Barry: Tonight, you're going to audition for Revolution Records.

Jannette: Don't tease me like that.

Barry: I'm serious. Just one thing.

Jannette: What?

Barry: Remember, my name is Sam Carter, got it?

Jannette (two thumbs up): Got it.

Jannette was so excited she could hardly stand it. We had a snack in the room and played and wrestled on the bed most of the afternoon. I was so zapped of energy I dozed off. I had the earthquake dream and was awakened by Jannette shaking the bed, again. We made ourselves ready and went to the restaurant.

JD was infatuated with Jannette. After some excellent lobster, we went into the lounge where a pianist was playing. Jannette was nervous; I gave her a kiss to settle her down. She asked the pianist if he knew one popular song; he did, so she sang it while he played. JD was pleased as punch, more like floored. After singing a few more partial songs JD was floating on air. He invited us to fly on his private plane to Los Angeles. He wanted to make some recordings for a possible single and maybe an album. Jannette came unglued. Her dreams were coming true so fast she couldn't see straight.

The flight to L.A. was long; regardless, I slept most of the way. JD set us up at an exclusive hotel. Jannette and I spent the evening between the sheets. In the morning JD and his chauffeur picked us up in a stretch limousine. The driver took us down Sunset Blvd. to a blue, rectangular building.

JD showed us around the studio and introduced Jannette to some musicians. They practiced a few numbers on the charts to get loosened up. Jannette gave them the music to several songs in her repertoire. They rehearsed all day with only a short break for lunch. I got bored and walked up and down the strip smoking like a chimney.

Afterwards, JD took us to his mansion in Beverly Hills. It was gigantic. We sat around the swimming pool drinking wine coolers and making proposals. Jannette and I stayed in JD's guesthouse that night. I reminded Jannette that I had to be back in Rio in two days. She was torn between going and staying. I persuaded her to stay and I'd be in touch. She gave me another succulent kiss.

The following evening JD had a party for Jannette. There were quite a few stars there, including me, so I kinda rode in the back seat. If they were to have uncovered my real identity, well you know what I mean. Fortunately, Jannette never let me stray too far, and nobody took any notice of me anyway because she was the newcomer to stardom. JD looked extremely jealous. I hated to think what he would try with my beloved while I was gone.

I had a difficult time saying goodbye to Jannette prior to my flight. All I could say is, "I love you so very, very much." That didn't make it any easier. We rode all the way to the airport gazing into one another's eyes. I never thought I'd ever be able to replace Teresa, but I knew I wanted to settle down with Jannette for life. She was a hard-loving woman; definitely a keeper, Señor Diario.

The flight back to Rio was monotonous. I felt so lonely I couldn't eat so I drank, smoking one cigarette after another. I fell asleep in my hotel room without unmaking the bed, caressing a bottle of scotch as if it were my true love. I awoke feeling weak, like I had a touch of the flu. I sneezed ten times, blew my nose five times, and took a hot bath. I laid there like a cadaver, until I finally shook off the trail dust. I felt better after a few trips to the breakfast buffet.

I strolled along the boardwalk killing time and chain smoking until the rest of the gang showed. All my thoughts were of Jannette, and our last opportunity to be together in that very spot at Guanabara Bay. Finally, Ard and Bob arrived. I told them of Jannette's instant success. They were happy for us.

Barry: So where are your sugar pies?

Ard (sitting cross-legged on the sand): It's a dangerous mission. The less they know about it, the better.

Bob (leaning back with elbows behind his head): Let's have it, Ard.

Ard: Remember reading about the hijacking of a 747, last year?

Barry: Yeah, a planeload of journalists from different countries were kidnapped. They're supposedly being held as political prisoners somewhere in Africa.

Ard: I have it on good authority they're being held at a compound in Kampala.

Bob: What's that got to do with us?

Ard: We're going to set them free.

Bob: Intelligence sources know full well where they are. Why don't the Israelis, or even the Egyptians rescue them? They're good at that sort of thing.

Ard: Because the Mid-Eastern cold war has been escalating. Representatives from mutually hostile nations are among the hostages. A single country acting alone could turn everything into a full-scale blowout, especially if the rescue happened to be unsuccessful, or if certain parties were damaged, injured or killed.

Bob: Right. We're going to bust them out of prison all by our lonesome?

Ard: Not exactly. Instead, we're going to take a hostage of our own and hold him for ransom.

Bob: I don't get it; you've lost me.

Barry: How can the three of us pull that off?

Ard: We're going to have company on this one.

Bob: Who?

Ard: Sims and Southerland.

Bob: How are you going to find them?

Ard: They'll find us.

Barry: Who are they?

Bob: Some guys we knew in 'Nam.

Barry: Who's the target?

Ard: The President-General of Uganda.

Bob: Who's going to pay a ransom for that jerk? He's a notorious dictator. Nobody likes him.

Ard: Always the skeptic, aren't you Bob?

Barry: Sounds to me like it couldn't happen to a more deserving asshole.

Ard: I'm leaving for Cape Town in the morning; if you're not in, don't show up.

I got blitzed again at a nightclub by the coast. I began to fraternize with a local girl named Sylvia. She reminded me of Teresa, with her brown eyes and dark hair. I was so inebriated I didn't know my left from my right. I went with Sylvia to her apartment. We staggered to her door and she fumbled for the key. We both flopped down on the bed, too far-fetched for sex.

I awoke with a migraine and took a shower; I had to get moving. Sylvia slipped into the shower naked as a jaybird, got me going, and we made it standing up with the water pouring on our heads. She had a big ass, but shapely. Although the sex was fine, I became overcome with guilt. I couldn't believe I'd cheated on Jannette after being apart for only two days. I hoped I wouldn't live to regret it. I swore to God then and there that my gigolo days were over. I agreed to play the oil tycoon; it wasn't like I was a novice when it came to oilfields. But that other personality was dispatched forthwith.

It was an arduous flight to South Africa. Upon arriving, we had a prime rib dinner and drank some beers. After dinner, Ard told Bob and me to stay in our rooms while he chartered a plane. The next day we rode a private prop-plane destined for the Congo. The pilot refueled along the way, and finally landed the aircraft on a grassy field just off the coast. As soon as we got out, Ard handed him an envelope full of cash and the jittery pilot returned to the air.

We hoisted our rucksacks and trekked north up the coast until it was way past dark. We camped at a lagoon in the soft sand. I laid on my pack staring at the stars, dreaming of Jannette. I was rudely awakened at sunup, surrounded by several primitives holding spears in our faces. It reminded me of the Tarzan movies I used to watch. The natives were wearing masks; I hoped they weren't death masks.

We were led by spearpoint to their village deep in the jungle. The entire tribe came out to greet us. The place looked like the cover of a National Geographic magazine. We were brought to a shanty where an old, overweight but muscular black man was smoking a long pipe. He smiled through his big rotten teeth.

Chief (with British accent): Good day.

His short Afro hair was gray at the edges and his eyes were yellow and bloodshot. It was apparent that he required some kind of payment for trespassing. He was very disappointed when he saw we were penniless.

They confiscated our guns and our gear. Ard pulled out an old photograph and showed it to the chief. The chief grinned as he put his grubby fingers all over it, crumpled it up, and tossed it over his shoulder. Ard picked it up, unfolded it, and placed it in his back pocket. We were forced to sit around a tree where they tied us and the tree together.

Bob: This part of the plan, Ard?

Barry: What do you think they'll do with us? They could easily kill us.

Ard: Maybe they'll just make us slaves.

Bob: Great.

We sat there the rest of the day and all the night. In the morning a native girl bracketed by two guards brought us some plant-like stuff looking similar to turnip greens. She motioned for us to eat. A guard removed some of the bindings, but left our hands and feet tied. The girl tossed the stuff into our laps. Ard began to eat it like a dog. I didn't see him keel over so I leaned over and took a bite, seeing how I was famished. I chewed it up and promptly spit it out; it didn't resemble anything I'd eaten before, and it tasted raunchier than turnip greens. Needless to say, I passed on breakfast; the only appetite I had was for a drink. Ard said the natives looked pretty healthy and what was good enough for them was good enough for him. Bob just kicked his greens aside after seeing my reaction.

Shortly thereafter, the chief returned with a native woman who resembled a beef trust. She could've been twice the width of the chief and inches shorter. They stopped directly in front of us.

Chief: You likey sister.

Bob: I think he wants one of us to pork the porker.

Ard: Any volunteers?

Barry: Fat chance.

Bob: Hah!

Ard (nodding): Since I got you into this fix, I guess I should fix it.

Ard was set free, and promptly left with the heifer; they tied Bob and me back to the tree. We made cracks about Ard's new wife for a few hours. Then, Ard returned to the tree looking pale as a ghost. He untied us.

Ard: You guys are free to go.

Bob: How was she, Ard?

Ard: I don't want to talk about it.

Bob: The hippo must've worn him out.

Ard: I managed to cloak my compass. Here, take it and go due north for ten clicks and wait for me.

Barry: What's a click.

Bob: One kilometer. Don't worry, I'll figure it out.

Ard: I'll attempt to slip away tonight when most of the natives are sleeping. Give me forty-eight hours to find you if I might. After that you should keep moving northwest.

We were getting ready to haul balls when the chief stopped us.

Chief: You stay, party.

Barry (to Bob): I guess we're supposed to attend the wedding reception.

We weren't excited about hanging around but it appeared we had no choice. Sitting on a log by the chief's wooden throne, some maidens handed us a coconut cup filled with some kind of beverage.

Chief (motioning with his hands): Drink. Good.

We drank. It was tasty, especially because it was fermented. It took the edge off my withdrawal symptoms. As the two teens were leaving, one of them winked at me. She was half-decent compared to the other girls.

Chief: You want marry?

Barry (waving hands back and forth): No, no thanks.

Chief: Ha, ha, hah!

In minutes, the arena was jam-packed and the ceremony began. The bride was dressed in orchids, flowers and such. The natives tugged Ard alongside her. He looked utterly humiliated. The chief handed the happy couple some stuff to eat and drink, recited some indigent mumbo jumbo for twenty minutes, placed ornaments on their garments, and the ceremony was over. A shindig followed. I engorged myself with fruit and what looked like broiled antelope. Whatever it was, it was appetizing enough. Bob and I stuffed all the food we could grab into our shirts, snatched our gear, and ducked-out in the midst of the revelry. Bob led us west first; then we doubled-back a-ways, and headed north. We trekked for hours in the blackness. I used my cigarette lighter to torch a stick, so Bob could shoot an azimuth using a compass which glowed in the dark. He would direct me left or right before stepping-off the yardage. We repeated that who knows how many times until Bob called it.

We awoke with the sun and began exploring our habitat. I found a grove of coconut palms so I shimmied up a tree and batted several loose. I took them to our hideout where Bob sat with a bunch of bananas. We had a nice breakfast and explored our area of operations most the day, but still no Ard. We ate the leftover meat and bread for dinner and went to sleep.

I had another weird dream last night, Diary. It was the dream I'd had before, the one where I'm reaching out from the clouds to touch an angel that looks like Laura and she disappears; only this time it was Jannette. I couldn't get back to sleep. I wandered around thinking; I couldn't get the disturbing vision out of my mind.

Suddenly, I thought I heard something. I stopped still as a church mouse and listened. I heard it again, a faint voice. It had to be Ard. I started hollering out to him. Bob jumped out of a deep slumber. He immediately appraised the situation and began yelling too. Ard located us several minutes later.

Ard: Let's get moving. They'll follow as soon as they notice I'm gone if they haven't already.

We double-timed it in a northwesterly direction, through the bush without stopping. About noontime we crossed a path; we were totally beat up and scratched up. We continued on the path northwest at a fast pace until long after dark. The path eventually led to a small town. It wasn't much, but it was civilization. We traded our remaining supplies for food and a place to stay. The next day, Ard exhibited the photograph to every villager we met. Finally came an official-looking guy who frowned when he saw the picture. Unfortunately, the guy didn't speak any English.

The official led us to a mission. A nurse from Australia was in charge. She helped us communicate with the man. The first thing we learned was that we were in Gabon and not the Congo. The official identified two black guys in the photo as mercenaries. They passed through a year before; they had charges of rape and theft hanging on their heads. Ard convinced our hosts we were bounty hunters seeking justice regarding those mercenaries. The official explained they were last seen in Libreville. Ard asked if we could obtain transportation to Libreville. The official knew someone, adding that it would cost plenty and we didn't look to have the means.

He led us to a trading post. Ard asked the proprietor if he could take us to Libreville. The man acted like he didn't understand until Ard pulled a small uncut diamond from his pocket. The man's eyes nearly popped out of their sockets. He immediately called his helper to fetch a jeep, and to fill it with petrol along with several five-gallon cans. We jumped into the back of the dilapidated jeep and Ard handed over the diamond. We traveled all day until darkness set in. The jeep had no headlights so we stopped at another village for the night. Ard ordered us to take turns guarding the jeep, as the other two slept in it, just to make sure the locals didn't ditch us there.

We continued onward at first light over some rough routes and even cross-country. Finally, we hit a paved road. We were dropped-off in Libreville shortly afterwards. At the village, Ard traded a smaller diamond for a rifle, pistol, ammo, and supplies. We came to a building flying a French flag and moseyed inside. Ard showed a few people the photo; he got no response. After we left, one guy came around the back of the building and stopped us. He spoke English with a heavy African accent.

Man: I maybe help and you pay.

Ard: You see somebody in photo?

Man: Maybe. You looking them?

Ard: Maybe. I trade rifle for what you know, if good stuff.

Man: Try Ghana; but be care. Men bad; they wanted by law.

Ard: How we get to Ghana?

Man: Maybe I know.

The African led us to a big mansion in the middle of a cacao plantation. Ard turned over our only rifle complete with loaded magazine; the man promptly left. A black butler answered the door; he invited us inside and had us sit amongst a bunch of artifacts and animal trophies. I was admiring the museum when the butler returned and showed us to a library where a French man sat in an easy chair, smoking a pipe, with a book in his hand.

Man (closing the book and rising): Welcome to Le Tour plantation, gentlemen. I am Jacques Le Tour. What brings you here?

Ard (showing Le Tour the photograph): We're searching for these mercenaries. Our guide said we could find them in Ghana. Our mission is to apprehend the rascals.

Le Tour: I see. What can you provide for payment?

Ard pulled out his last diamond. Le Tour sprung out of his chair, took the diamond to his desk, flipped on a desk lamp and inspected the gem through an eyeglass.

Le Tour: Hmm. Appears to be two, two-and-a-half carats; good luster; not too many intrusions. Where did you find such a wonderful specimen?

Ard: Call it a wedding present.

Bob and I chuckled under our breath.

Le Tour: I would be happy to take you to Accra, but first, be my guests this night.

We were thrilled to stay. We received the grand tour of the plantation, enjoyed an eight-course dinner, and got a history lesson from our well-educated host. He had some excellent tobacco from Rhodesia to smoke. I lodged in a corner room with antique French furniture and a canopy bed. I slept like a log, dreaming about my dream girl naturally. I awoke at sunrise and found Le Tour reading in the library.

Barry: You must read a bunch.

Le Tour: It's my favorite pastime. Do you enjoy reading?

Barry: I read the newspaper most days but that's about it.

Le Tour: You must have read books. Which is your favorite book?

Barry (pausing to think): Probably *Huck Finn*.

Le Tour: Ah, yes, Samuel Clemens. He also is one of my favorite novelists.

I figured he'd laugh but he sounded impressed.

Barry: Have you read all these books?

Le Tour: Absolutely, some of them more than once.

Barry: My goodness! There must be thousands of books in here!

Bob and Ard came downstairs and Le Tour ushered us to the breakfast table. We feasted on scrambled eggs, crepes, sausage, and mixed fruit; it was excellent. I asked Le Tour if I could bum a cigar from him. He told me to take several, so I helped myself. We followed him to a biplane used for crop dusting. Le Tour took the controls while the three of us crawled on top of each other. The ride was uncomfortable to say the least, but it was not far.

Upon arriving in Accra, Ard resumed the search for his mercenary buddies, but to no avail. We stayed at a run-down hotel that should have been condemned, but it was all we could find or afford. We were crammed into a filthy room furnished with army cots. I was rudely awakened by a jolt on my bed and a rifle looking at my nose.

Bob: What, this again?

Soldier: You are under arrest by the government of Ghana.

Ard: What's the charge?

Ard got no reply. We were taken to the outskirts of town. The truck stopped by some steel gates at what appeared to be a concentration camp. I got that funny feeling in my innards again.

About then a grenade went off nearby and everyone grabbed a bite of dirt. I heard machinegun fire all around and kept my head down. Someone wrenched me to my feet and rammed me into a jeep with Bob and Ard. Before I had a chance to sit, the jeep was smoking down the crude and muddy lane. Several armed men jumped into their vehicles and tore out after us.

The black dude riding shotgun opened fire on the pursuers. He shot one of the drivers and that jeep smashed into a tree; everyone bought the farm, it looked. Then he tossed a few smoke grenades to hide our tracks, and the pursuing truck crashed into the jungle. Minutes later we exited the path and bounded over some rougher terrain. In an hour we came across an abandoned mine. The driver steered right into the mineshaft and hit the brakes. We moved on foot through a maze of tunnels into a cavern lit with lanterns. An Anglo guy approached us. He was pushing fifty years old, gray-haired, but well built.

Man (shaking hands with Ard): Denton, you bloody grunt bastard.

Ard: Southerland, you stinking limey mossback.

Bob (to Southerland): Long time no see, Major.

Southerland (to Bob): Well you certainly aren't the worst for wear, Leftenant.

Barry (holding a cigar): My name is Barry. Have a cigar?

Southerland (taking the cigar): Don't mind if I do, young man.

Ard: Where's Sims?

Southerland: Follow me.

We followed him through a shaft which funneled into a narrow tunnel curving upwards; we crawled on all fours until we were outside on top of a hill. A helicopter was waiting; we climbed aboard and lifted off immediately. The chopper took us deeper into the jungle, far from the mine. We stopped at a miniature fortress in the middle of nowhere. We entered a candle-lit hooch where a black man sat on a rock. He looked like a football player, husky and leathery, but too groomed to be a mercenary.

Southerland: Look what I found.

Man: Captain Denton, as I live and breathe! And if it isn't Lieutenant Frederick!

Ard: Good to see you First Sergeant.

Bob: Where's the mole?

Southerland: Fraser was nailed last year in Sierra Leone trying to pinch some diamonds, the pitiful bloke.

Sims: I always knew he'd come to a bitter end. He was way too rowdy. We gave him a dishonorable discharge after he raped a teenager in Gabon. After cutting him loose, he spiraled downhill.

Sims: Where's Sarge?

Bob: He got wasted during our last mission in South America.

Southerland: Yeah, we heard about that. So Chief Sanchez is the frigging president of Uruguay!

Ard: What do you know?

Barry (approaching Sims): I'm Barry, have a cigar.

Sims (taking the cigar and shaking his hand): Glad to know you, Barry.

Sims: What brings you guys to this neck of the woods? I hear you've been asking all around about us.

Bob: Yeah, you're downright popular.

Ard (puffing on a cigar): I've got a little proposition for you.

Ard explained his plan of kidnapping the President-General of Uganda, while Sims broke out a jug of rum.

Southerland: Sounds like fun.

Sims (passing the jug to Ard): He's got protection up the ass. Whose army are you going to use?

Ard (after taking a belt from the jug): Why, yours of course.

Sims (to Southerland): I don't know Matt; it sounds pretty risky.

Southerland (to Ard): What's in it for us, lad?

Ard: Potentially half-a-million, another half for us.

Southerland: Good heavens old man, you really think he can come up with that kind of collateral?

Ard: Sure he can; out of his own pocketbook.

Sims: Don't mention the ransom to any of our troops; they might get ideas.

We charbroiled some wild ox for supper. It reminded me of the javelina Sarge popped in the Mexican jungle. I fell asleep in place, dreaming about my girl; in fact, that's all I ever dreamed about anymore.

Rollcall was at 0400 hours. We had fruit and coffee for breakfast. Then, ten men loaded up two choppers and we took off, eventually landing in Bangui a town in central Africa. We got some fuel and chowed down on C-rations. Yecch.

Bob: So, there's actually a place in Africa where you're not wanted by the law?

Sims: We've done a few favors for the emperor here.

Bob (to Ard): What's the scoop, Cap'n?

Ard: The president frequently visits the hostages on Saturday. We'll hit before he makes it to the compound.

Sims: My contact in Bangui says he missed his visit last Saturday; chances are he'll make it this weekend. Leslie, he's my man; he was setting up shop there when the hijacking messed it up.

Ard: That only gives us one day to train. Better get some sleep.

We practiced our maneuvers for twelve straight hours. Everyone got their part down pat until they were sick of it. Tomorrow was the big day.

We moved out at dark-thirty. I was still half-asleep until I got some coffee down my gullet. We flew in the dark for hours. Then, Sims parachuted out of the helicopter. In a short while, two flares were lit on the ground and the choppers landed between them. We assembled; then Sims and three others moved out on foot. The rest of us camouflaged the choppers as the flares fizzled. I ate some C's and studied a soldier repacking the chute while I held a flashlight for him. Then we waited. It was well after dawn when Sims returned alone.

Sims: I think it's on, and guess what?

Barry: What?

Sims: We're gonna get some help. I've got to change the plan.

Ard: I'll be the judge of that.

Sims: I think we can stage a riot and cut off the president's motorcade. I've solicited some help in town from the guy I told you has an underground operation.  He'll assist us for free, since it'll be clear-sailing for him without that dirtbag dictator in the way. I think we'll have a much better chance beating him to the compound.

Bob: You told this guy our plan?

Sims: We can trust him. I met him in Saigon. He was at Cam Ranh Bay. He's a fellow "lrrp".

Barry (to Bob): A what?

Bob (quietly): Long range reconnaissance patrol.

Ard: Hmm. If we seize the scoundrel, say here (pointing at the map), just out of range of the palace gates…

Sims: They'll be defenseless.

Southerland: He's got a point, Captain. The hostages are quite well-guarded at the compound and could to respond to a melee, old bean.

Ard: I like it, Top.

Sims: He likes it.

Bob: The plan hasn't really changed that much.

Ard: Only this time the Vulcans stay silent until civilians are safely removed from the area. I don't want harm to come to any innocent bystanders.

Sims: My buddy Les will alert us when the motorcade is moving out. That's when he'll start gathering the protestors.

Southerland (to Sims): The sooner the better, Leroy.

Sims: If I can get back there quickly it should be a go. Otherwise…

Ard: Otherwise, we'll hit them at the same location while the president returns to his palace.

Sims: Sounds good. Watch for a rocket flare in the eastern sky. That'll signal they are either coming or going, and the riot is in progress.

Barry: Good luck, Leroy.

Southerland: Okay, you buggars, let's get this bleeding camouflage off the birds.

At one-fifteen in the afternoon we saw the flare. It was too soon for the procession to be returning so it must have been departing. We boarded the choppers. I flew with Southerland, and participated as loader for the twenty-millimeter machine-gunner. Ard manned the 20mm Vulcan on the other chopper; Bob was his assistant gunner. We were in the air in no time, and over the parade in a flash.

Five limos were stranded amid a throng of angry civilians. As soon as the choppers were in range, the ground team began firing their weapons at the vehicles. Civilians started hurrying in all directions, while others ducked behind barricades. The Ugandan secret police opened fire on the choppers. They subsequently were engaged by the ground team, which successfully dispersed them. One of the friendlies on the ground pointed an M60 machinegun at the president's car motioning for him to exit. He reluctantly did.

Ard dropped a harness from their chopper and we dropped a rope ladder. The ground crew started climbing up the ladder while Sims attached the harness around him. Meanwhile, we had opened up with the Vulcans to keep the entourage at bay. The Vulcans chewed the limos to pieces. Sims had looped a rope around the president's feet, who was on his knees with his hands clasped behind his head. Sims grasped the president's belt firmly then nodded for his pilot to fly. Southerland steered the Huey into the sky, following the other. You could hear the president screaming above the noise of the chopper engine and blades. I bet he was praying his belt would hold up.

We were safely outside the city limits when we landed. We gathered up the prisoner and our troops, then returned to Bangui.

President of Uganda (shaken): You will pay for this!

Ard: No, you will.

We drank rum and ate heartily. Sims had some dynamite jerky that Les had given him. The hostage was allowed to drink rum with us. He drank himself into oblivion, as did I. The next day, Sims left in a chopper with the president. Southerland showed us around Bangui, while a team stayed by the chopper.

Barry: Where can I find a phone?

Southerland: Maybe the airport, or one of the better hotels. You can always try the emperor's palace.

Barry: Very funny.

Bob (to Ard): Should he be making any calls?

Ard: Doesn't matter. The hostage is in good hands.

I located the biggest hotel in town; it had a phone. I called Jannette's private line in the guesthouse, collect. It was late at night in California and Jannette was asleep.

Jannette: Oh Barry, I can't believe it's you. Where are you?

Barry: On safari in Africa.

Jannette: Africa! No wonder you sound so far away.

Barry: Enough about me, what about you?

Jannette: We have a song on the radio.

Barry: Great! Sing it for me.

She sang the first verse over the phone.

Barry: Wow, that's outstanding!

Jannette: The song is about us. It's called, *To Love is to Know*. I wrote it, and our pianist helped me arrange the music.

Barry: It's a lovely song, almost as lovely as you.

Jannette: I'm going to Las Vegas with JD. He wants me to perform on stage to promote my single; he already made arrangements.

Barry: When?

Jannette: In two weeks.

Barry: Maybe I can meet you there.

Jannette: I hope so, I miss you so much my darling.

Barry: I miss you too, sugar. See you soon. I promise.

God, it felt great to hear her voice. We continued camping outside of Bangui while Ard and Southerland worked out the ransom details. We were to meet the head honchos of Uganda along the banks of Lake Victoria. There we would swap our hostage for the money and the freedom of the detainees. Sims was notified over shortwave radio to commence the exchange. The two choppers merged at the meeting site where two military vehicles were parked. We landed in a clearing. They met us about half-way.

Official: I regret to inform you that we could not raise the million dollars you requested.

Sims: The hell you say!

Official: We have agreed to pay a quarter of the ransom and release the hostages, on one condition.

Ard: What's the condition?

Official: You keep the president-general. The republic of Uganda doesn't want him. He is a murderer and a thief and guilty of war crimes. We feel we owe you something for taking him off our hands.

Southerland (laughing): They don't want the son-of-a-bitch back! Doesn't that beat all?

Ard: It's a deal.

Sims: Wait a minute, Captain. What are we going to do with him?

Ard: Sell him again.

We returned to the outskirts of Bangui with 250,000 in American dollars and had a good laugh. The president cried. Ard and Southerland headed into Bangui; we holed up inside the choppers in the rain. Ard returned with a Johannesburg newspaper a few days later. The political prisoners were released, a new Ugandan government was emplaced, and our gang was identified as potentially responsible. Celebrities, again!

Next, our squad left for the hideout in Ghana; Ard and Southerland's squad stayed put. Ard was going to send dispatches to various countries where the hostage was looked upon as an international criminal. After two weeks, Ard and Southerland returned. Ard looked delighted when he slid off the chopper.

Ard: Looks like the Israelis are the highest bidders at half a mil.

Sims: Great.

Ard: We've been invited to be guests of the Israeli government.

Bob: We can't go there, what if they turn us in?

Ard: Come now. They don't want our government to obtain proof they've been dealing with us.

Bob: What then?

Ard: Take another vacation. Tahiti is great this time of year.

Barry: My destination will be Las Vegas.

The Israelis treated us like kings. They allowed me to call L.A. direct. JD's butler gave me a phone number in Vegas. I called there five times before I got hold of Jannette.

Barry: I'm coming home, dear.

Jannette: I can't wait, my love.

Barry: How's your gig going?

Jannette: They adore me. Our song has hit the top forty. My album will be out by Christmas.

Barry: That's fabulous. What a great Christmas present!

Jannette: I love you.

Barry: Will you marry me?

Jannette: You know I will.

Barry: We'll get married in Vegas as soon as I return.

Jannette: Good, because we wouldn't want our child to be born out of wedlock.

Barry: For real?

Jannette: I would never make fun about something like that.

Barry: That's the best gift you could ever give to me.

I told the assembly about my engagement and the kid on the way. They congratulated me and everyone drank to my virility. As usual, I drank myself silly. I was becoming such a lush. I vowed to give up booze forever right after my wedding night (I already quit philandering so booze should be easier I figured).

## PHASE SIX

Dear Dairy, I mean Diary. Anyway, I'm a bit hungover. Yeah, yeah; I know. During our brief stay in Tel Aviv I got to meet several Mideast diplomats, including the Prime Minister of Israel, the President of Egypt, and delegates from Jordan, Syria, and Saudi Arabia. They were very cordial and interesting people. Since they all were affected by the hijacking, they had a common interest in the Ugandan dictator, and in the release of the prisoners.

Sims and Southerland took their share of the proceeds back to Ghana. Our shares went into a Swiss bank account, not including our usual allowance of ten thousand. The gang returned to Rio and promptly split up, each going separate ways. I grabbed the next flight to Vegas without any luggage but wearing a new suit and shoes. I hailed a taxi and made a beeline for the club where Jannette was playing. The place was packed to the hilt. I found JD sitting at a booth in the back.

Barry: JD!

JD (rising from his seat): Hey, Sam, welcome back? How was your African safari?

Barry (shaking hands): Enlightening.

JD: I went on a safari once. Bagged me a few trophies. You've probably seen them in the study.

Barry: Jan and I are getting married.

JD: I heard. Congratulations.

Barry: No hard feelings?

JD: Course not, slick. All's fair in love and war.

The audience roared as Jannette sang her hit song, our song. After the song she came to the table, not knowing I'd be there. As soon as she saw me, she leapt into my arms. We kissed for ten solid minutes. I was anxious to get going but she had another performance. Jannette announced our wedding plans at the end of her final set. The audience applauded all the more. A spotlight shone on our table. I covered my eyes and waved, feeling embarrassed. I was aching to get Jannette alone. I finally succeeded; we made love all night long. It was terrific.

The next morning. I had breakfast and several newspapers brought to our suite. Front-page headlines declared breakthroughs in the Middle East peace talks. Partial credit was given the gang for initiating the discourse. We had picked up a nickname: the media was calling us *The New Crusaders*. I showed the front page to Jannette. She was very proud of me, and the gang.

Our wedding was planned for the following week at JD's place. I sent word to Ard who was still in Rio. Jannette enjoyed making all the arrangements, and picking out a wedding set and dress. I paid the minister to have my real name printed on the license, but to call me Samuel Carter during the ceremony. I wanted it legal without anybody noticing.

It was like a dream come true for both of us. Jannette's violet plant had scads of buds and flowers; she told me that it hadn't flowered the whole time I was gone. Two days before the wedding, Ard contacted me. The gang was coming to the wedding. He'd managed to get hold of Bob and Vicky who were flying in from Tahiti.

The following afternoon I borrowed a car from JD to pick up Jannette's dress which was being altered. I was carrying her dress in a box which I placed in the backseat. I flopped into the car when suddenly I felt a tremor. It was a weird sensation. I drove onto the freeway; the L.A. traffic was bumper-to-bumper. I was nearing Beverly Hills when I sensed a few more tremors. I became impatient. I began weaving in and out of traffic until I arrived at my exit.

Just then a violent earthquake hit. It was so powerful I went crashing through the guardrail and down the embankment, flipping the car which was totaled. I started running to the house with the dress tucked under my arm when it began to pour. Then another major shudder knocked me to the ground, getting the dress all muddy. As I sat in the mud, bewildered, the big one hit. Houses were collapsing all around me; the nonstop racket was deafening for a full minute. I ambled through the wereckage and ultimately made it to JD's place. It was in shambles.

I ran around back. JD was oriented headfirst in the swimming pool, which was filled with the debris of his bathhouse instead of water. I started digging through the remains of the guesthouse, looking for a trace of Jannette. I found her in what was left of the kitchen, with the telephone locked in her hand. She was crushed under a pile of rafters. Her once radiant eyes were colorless, glaring at me. She wasn't moving because her neck was broken. I peered into her vacant eyes one last time and forced them shut. I slumped there with her head cradled in my arms in a downpour. I was in total shock, as stiff as my true love, so I gave no notice to the aftershocks that occurred all night long.

Twenty-four hours later I was still frozen in place, clutching Jannette and the wedding dress. Ard slapped me out of my stupor. He and Bob stood there, reflecting my grief. Bob helped me to my feet. Ard wrapped Jannette's body in a blanket while Bob collected the remains of JD. There was no sign of anyone else in the rubble. Bob and Ard carried them to a pickup and laid them in the bed of the truck. I stumbled along behind them, grasping the droopy dress, feeling completely numb.

We crowded into the cab of the truck. Bob negotiated through the devastated remains of Beverly Hills. Nobody said anything. My only thought, I was supposed to be married to a wonderful woman who was carrying my child. A dream come true had turned out to be a nightmare come true, literally. Finally, Bob broke the silence.

Bob: It beats the piss out of me the rotten luck you've had with your women, Barry. It seems like, whenever you fall for someone, they croak.

Ard: Luck has nothing to do with it.

Bob: I suppose it takes skill, huh?

Ard: Sometimes, a person has to go through hell before they get a glimpse of heaven.

Barry: I've been both places.

Ard: You've a long way to go my friend. You're still having difficulty differentiating the two.

Barry: So, where'd you get the pickup.

Bob: We borrowed it from the motel.

Barry: Pretty terrible earthquake.

Ard: Eight-point-six on the Richter scale. Largest ever recorded in the continental USA.

Bob: Much of Hollywood and Beverly Hills were wiped out. Mud slides occurred all over Southern California. A sizeable portion of west L.A. fell into the ocean. The entire zone has been declared a disaster area.

Barry: Easy to see why. You know I dreamt this was going to happen.

Ard: No kidding? That's amazing. You must always tell me about your memorable dreams, Barry.

I described the two weird dreams I'd had previously as we continued meandering through dilapidated homes. The only vehicles allowed in the area were rescue vehicles. We tried to look official as we drove around roadblocks with our four-way flashers blinking. Finally, we made it to the motel; Bob honked the horn as he parked. Laura and Vicky immediately came out of the motel room. As soon as they'd evaluated the situation, they ran to console me.

Bob and Ard carried Jannette's body to a room and laid her on one of the beds. Bob drove JD to a collection station. Ard poured me a stiff one and I downed it in one gulp. I took the bottle from him trading it for the wedding dress. It didn't take me long to finish it off. I passed out next to Jannette's rigid body. What a lousy way to spend our wedding night, I surmised. When I awoke, Jannette's body had been removed. I staggered to the bathroom where I found Laura in her underwear putting on her face.

Laura (grabbing a cosmetics case): Go ahead Barry, I can do this in the bedroom.

I finished my business and washed up.

Barry (entering the bedroom): Where is everybody?

Laura (putting on eye liner): Ard and Bob took Jan to the morgue to affirm her identification with the coroner. Vicky's probably in her room.

Barry (picking up a pack of cigarettes from the nightstand): These your smokes?

Laura: Help yourself.

Barry: Don't mind if I do.

Laura: I'm so sorry about what happened. Jan was such a great gal. I liked her a lot.

Barry (lighting a cigarette): I know you did. She was very fond of you too.

Laura: If there's anything I can do…

Barry (exhaling smoke): I'll let you know.

Laura: Are you hungry?

Barry: As a matter of fact…

Laura: Let's go get Vicky and have brunch.

I stuffed down a good breakfast while the girls had coffee and sweet rolls. I lit up a smoke from the pack I'd taken from the nightstand. Ard and Bob joined us soon thereafter.

Bob (pulling up a chair backwards): It's standing room only at the morgue.

Laura: Very funny.

Ard: Sorry Barry, but we cannot be seen at a public funeral. They will contact Jannette's next of kin through her friend Adrienne, and probably ship her body back to Monaco.

Barry: I suppose you're right. I'd like to borrow the truck again and search for survivors.

Ard (still standing): Let's do it.

As Bob was hot-wiring the truck, the owner of the motel came running outside.

Owner: Hey that's my truck!

Bob: We were going to use it to search for survivors.

Owner: You're the ones that commandeered my only vehicle yesterday!

Bob: Yeah. Sorry.

Ard: It was an emergency.

Owner: All you had to do was tell me. I'd have loaned you the truck if I knew the reason. I wish I could help, but I've got to mind the business.

Ard: Thanks. I'll make sure we leave you with a full tank.

Owner (taking a key off his chain): Here, take this. And next time try asking.

Ard: Don't worry, it won't happen again.

Barry: Much obliged, partner.

Bob hopped into the driver's seat and switched on the four-ways. After several hours, we had managed to turn up only dead bodies. It was about four p.m. when we came to a particular home with a tree laying in the middle of it. I was rounding the side of the house when I thought I spotted a hand. I started tossing bricks, sheetrock, and two-by-fours aside. A little girl was buried underneath. She was trapped by the tree. I cried out to Ard and Bob.

We grabbed a large beam and used it as a lever. As soon as the tree was lifted, I slowly pulled the girl free by her shoulders. She was in bad shape.

Ard (examining the girl): She's got a compound fracture of the left radius, internal bleeding around the belly and hips, contusion on her forehead, probable concussion...

Barry: Is she dead?

Ard (hand on girl's right wrist): I feel a pulse.

Barry: She's alive!

Ard: Barely.

Bob: I found some oldsters, probably her grandparents. They bought it. I put them in the truck.

Meanwhile, Ard was setting the girl's broken arm and bandaging the contusion. I took a blanket from the cab for a stretcher. We carefully moved the girl onto the stretcher in case she had any trauma to her back or neck. Bob had scavenged a few cushions and thrown them into the bed of the pickup. Ard and I gently laid the girl on the cushions between her grandparents; we rode in the back to keep her steady. Arriving at an emergency clinic, we solicited some medics to bring a gurney. She was wheeled to a triage; they also took the deceased grandparents off our hands. I felt sorry for the child, figuring she would wake up to find her loved ones had perished.

Before resuming our search next morning, we stopped at the clinic. The girl had been transfused with fresh blood and patched up in several places, a cast was on her arm, and her head bandaged. She was still unconscious, being fed intravenously. We continued the search until noon looking for trapped or stranded people. We stopped at a hamburger joint for lunch that was giving out free food to first responders, bought a couple of six packs and a bag of ice at the convenience store, and returned to the rubble. Bob and Ard were placing a dead body by the road for removal. I jammed a broomstick in the ground with a red garment attached to mark the spot. Then I noticed motion in the street. It was a stick bobbing up and down from a manhole cover.

Someone was trapped in the sewer. The manhole cover was too stuck to budge. Bob found a bar made of wrought iron. The three of us finally pried the lid off. A man climbed out of the opening. He looked pretty sallow from breathing the stale air.

Barry: What's your name, guy?

Man (stepping out): Ed. Boy am I glad to see you fellows. I've been down there since the quake. I was lucky. It's probably the only section of the sewer that didn't flood. It was blocked off by a cave-in.

Bob (popping the top of a beer can): Have a beer.

Ed (taking a slug): Ohh, that tastes good. Nice and cold too.

We finished off the rest of the beer with Ed. Then we gave him a lift to an emergency National Guard installation. It was getting dark when we stopped by the clinic to check on the little girl.

Doctor: Her condition has stabilized. She regained consciousness just after you left this morning asking for her grandparents. I understand you found their dead bodies?

Ard: Unfortunately, yes.

Doctor: Poor child. I gave her a sedative; she's sleeping now.

Nurse: You gentlemen saved her life you know.

Barry: What's her name?

Doctor: Her name is Nancy.

Barry: Does she have any kin?

Doctor: We don't know yet.

Nancy awoke and turned to see who was talking, having heard someone call her name.

Barry (leaning over the bed): Hey there, little bunny. How do you feel?

Nancy: Not so good sir. Who are you?

Nurse: These are the men who revived you, Nancy.

We introduced ourselves, giving our fake names.

Nancy (struggling to sit up): I want to go home.

Doctor: Do you have any relatives we can contact?

Nancy (sobbing): My aunt lives in Santa Barbara.

Nurse: What's her name, sweetheart?

Nancy: Grace Flanagan.

The nurse obtained the number from a special operator and dialed it. Nancy's aunt was very grateful. She talked to Nancy for a minute or two. Then the nurse took the phone and explained Nancy's condition.

Nurse (to Ard): Miss Flanagan would like to talk to Nancy's rescuers.

Ard (pointing with his hand): That'd be Sam here.

Barry: It wasn't just me.

Nurse (handing the phone to Barry): Here, talk to the woman.

I spoke to Grace and reassured her.

Grace: I'm coming to L.A. to get Nancy and I'd like to meet you.

I told her where we were staying. The next day she showed up at the motel before we had a chance to resume the search. We chatted half an hour. Nancy's aunt was lovely, with semi-long auburn hair. She was about my age, but the freckles on her nose and below her eyes created the illusion that she was younger. I directed Grace to where we could pick up Nancy. We returned to the motel with Nancy in tow. I pushed her on a wheelchair into Ard's room. Grace invited everyone to stay with her a few days. I didn't think it was a good idea, but Nancy insisted. The proprietor of the motel graciously accommodated Grace and Nancy for the night in his private home behind the motel.

Grace drove Nancy to her house the next day. I bought a used Continental real cheap and chauffeured the gang to Santa Barbara. We located Grace's house and I parked in the street. Grace came out to greet us, inviting us inside. Her place was nicely decorated. There was a little fir tree in the living room with ornaments on it and presents under it. I had forgotten that it was Christmastime. It made me think of a sacred birth, and the birth that might have been, had Jan survived.

Grace served coffee and we discussed the earthquake. Ard requested a phone book so he could find a place to stay the night. Grace demanded everyone remain at her place. She showed Ard and Laura the guestroom. She led Bob and Vicky to a couch in the den that made into a bed. Nancy wanted to sleep with Grace. That left only me. I told her I'd be all right on the living room sofa. Grace brought me a couple of pillows, a sheet and a quilt.

I went into the kitchen to see what smelled so good. There was a pot roast in the oven. Grace came into the kitchen to check on the roast. As she bent over, I gazed at her rear end. It was very shapely, reminding me of an inverted valentine. She noticed me staring at her derriere and smiled. As I looked into her pea green eyes, I felt a surge in my veins. I couldn't stop staring; I was enveloped in her eyes. My adrenaline continued to flow at an increasing rate; I was about to kiss her. Just then, Nancy walked into the room. Grace persuaded Nancy to set the table.

Barry: Can I ask you a personal question?

Grace: Go ahead.

Barry: How come you live alone in such a big house? A fine-looking woman like you should have a husband looking after her.

Grace: My husband left me two years ago for another man.

Barry (coughing): That's terrible. I'm sure you wouldn't have any trouble finding a better replacement.

Grace: There seems to be a shortage of them. Besides, I'm in no hurry to remarry. Are you married?

Barry: I lost my fiancé in the earthquake.

Grace: Oh, my gosh! I'm sorry. I shouldn't have asked.

Barry: Not to worry.

Grace: What do you do for a living?

Barry (hesitating): I'm an oil man. And you?

Grace: I teach fourth grade.

Barry: How nice.

Grace (handing Barry a carving knife): Why don't you slice the roast for me.

Barry: I'd be happy to.

We assembled around the dining room table; Grace said grace. She added a special prayer of thanks for Nancy's safety and asked for a blessing upon her new friends. I hesitated for a moment contemplating how I had forgotten about prayer. I was ready to chuck everything for love, and here I already was in lust. I brushed it off and dug in. Grace was an excellent chef. It was a pleasure to eat a home-cooked meal for a change. Ard and them went for a stroll after dinner in the direction of the beach.

The phone rang while Grace and I were enjoying an after-dinner brandy. It was Grace's parents, Nancy's other grandparents. They were worried. Grace told them the bad news. They insisted on coming to visit for the holidays.

Grace: Your grandparents are coming tomorrow, Nancy.

Nancy (excited): Oh, boy.

Grace: You don't mind do you, Sam?

Barry: No problem. We ought to be clearing out anyway.

Grace: No, don't go! I mean, why don't you stay through the holidays?

Nancy: Please stay Sam. You're my guardian angel.

Barry: We'll see.

Nancy: Let's go to the beach, can we?

Barry: I don't know, Nancy; the doctor said for you to take it easy.

Nancy: I feel fine. I don't need that stupid wheelchair.

Grace: All right, just for a little while; but you are riding young lady not walking. Get your jacket, it's chilly outside.

We walked down to the beach; it wasn't that far. The full moon shimmered on the water and illuminated the crests of the waves. Nancy got up and hobbled along the shore looking for shells. Grace put her arm around my waist; she was shivering. I turned to her and looked into those hypnotizing eyes. She blushed. I kissed her and she responded with fervor. While we were smooching, Nancy called out; we immediately broke the clinch.

Nancy: Are you in love?

Grace: Let's just say I enjoy Sam's company very much.

Nancy: I think it would be nice to have you as parents.

Barry: Slow down, young lady.

Grace: Don't you want to live with your grandma and grandpa?

Nancy: I'd rather stay with you Aunt Grace. I don't like it in North Dakota; it's too cold and there's no beach.

Grace: I'll have to think about it; they will want to discuss it too.

Barry: We'd better head back; it's getting kind of cool out here.

Everybody was ready to turn in early, except me. I sat alone in the dark on the sofa, puffing on a cigarette. Grace turned on the kitchen light and saw me smoking in the living room.

Grace: I thought you were asleep?

Barry: I'm not really tired; wouldn't sleep even if I could.

Grace: Maybe you could use some company.

She sat next to me on the sofa. We started kissing. We gradually worked ourselves into a reclining position. Grace got up and turned off the kitchen light. She returned to my anxious arms. We made love right there; it was nice. Grace returned to the master bedroom afterwards.

Time passed. Christmas Eve was upon us. Ard and the gang didn't want to hang around with the grandparents so I gave him the keys to the Lincoln. We picked up Nancy's grandparents at the airport. They were really over the hill. They must've had Grace when they were in their forties. There was a bundle of packages they'd shipped airfreight so we gathered them and returned to Grace's. She made roast beef sandwiches. That night, Nancy opened all her presents. It was fun watching her; she was such a precious child.

Christmas day I went to church with Grace and the family. This was something I hadn't done in God knows how many years, well, outside of funerals and my marriage in a ramshackle chapel during the Uruguay caper. I felt funny going to church with blue jeans, until I realized I wasn't the only one. I enjoyed listening to the Christmas story once again. I forgot how emotionally touching the event was. There was a luncheon at church afterwards. I didn't want to stay but I was outnumbered. Fortunately, Grace ran interference for me.

I overheard many of the guests gossiping about what a lovely couple Grace and I made. I figured things were moving too fast and it was high time for me to hit the brick. That night, Grace insisted I sleep with her and give Nancy the hide-a-bed. I reluctantly succumbed to her demands. The next morning, I overheard the oldsters talking in the guestroom.

Grandmother: I think it's disgusting, Grace shacking up with that man. They are a bad influence on Nancy.

Grandfather: We've got to get her away from here. These people in California are too immoral.

Grandmother: The earthquake was a warning from God. It's fulfillment of prophecy by Saint Luke, I tell you.

I cogitated on their remarks for a few seconds until Grace interrupted my train of thought.

Barry: Your parents disapprove of our sleeping together.

Grace: They're old-fashioned.

Barry: Still, I think it would be best if I stayed in a motel.

Grace: We'll discuss it after breakfast.

That morning, Nancy cooked pancakes for everyone. She did a very good job. I collected the dishes and began washing them.

Grandfather: I believe Nancy should live with us.

Grace: Dad, don't you think you and Mom are too old. Nancy is awfully energetic. It's a major responsibility requiring tremendous time and effort.

Grandmother: We want her to live in a Christian environment.

Grace: Are you accusing me of not being Christian? The Bible says not to judge others since only God knows one's heart.

Nancy: Don't I have a say? After all, it's my life. You act like I'm a piece of luggage that you can toss around!

Grandmother: Nancy, we have only your best interest in mind.

Nancy: Aren't you at all concerned about my interests? I'm not a kid anymore. I'll be an adult in a few years and then you won't have any say whatsoever!

Nancy teetered out of the room crying. I felt sorry for her. I was about to put in my two cents worth, but instead piped down. The next couple days were boredom-city. I spent most of the time watching the boob tube and chain smoking. The grandparents finally gave in and decided to leave the day before New Year's Eve. I made first class reservations and paid in cash. Nancy agreed to visit them in the summertime. Not a soul said a word on the way to the airport. But on the way back, Grace exclaimed that she was going to organize a New Year's Eve get-together.

Grace spent the entire day on the phone. Nancy and I went to buy groceries, booze, and what not. We stopped by the motel and had dinner with Ard and the gang at the cafeteria. They agreed to make a token visit to the party. I liked most of Grace's friends except this one guy named Elmer, who kept staring at Ard and me. I went to the bathroom to take a leak. Grace followed me in. I did my business and zipped up my pants, turning toward Grace. I gave her a kiss and she started rubbing up against me, then unzipped me. After a quickie, we returned to the party.

About that time, the front door swung open and four tough guys barged in, holding guns. They were feds. They placed Ard, Bob, and me under arrest. Many of the guests were peeved and began to harass the officials.

Grace: What do you think you are doing?

First Agent (putting handcuffs on Barry): We're federal agents. We're taking these men into custody.

Second Agent: They are wanted fugitives.

Grace: What are they charged with?

Elmer: These guys are members of the New Crusaders.

The whole room became silent. Grace looked at me in amazement as the officers led us away.

Nancy (grabbing an agent's hand): Don't take Sam away. He saved my life. Ask anybody here. He's not a criminal!

Third Agent: Sorry honey, but we're just doing our jobs.

We spent two days in jail without visitors. We were finally allowed to talk to a lawyer. He brought excerpts from several newspapers exhibiting our celebrity status. No kidding, really?

We were being extradited to Louisiana. He said he'd request a change of venue, since it was obvious that we wouldn't get a fair trial there. He fed us some other legal jazz and left.

We flew first class to New Orleans. The airline treated us really nice, with complimentary drinks, lunch, and everything. It sure beat the garbage we were getting in jail. The stewardesses knew who we were and waited on us hand-and-foot. This angered the marshals, who were handcuffed to us.

The change of venue was denied. Plus, the government decided to try us in federal court. We appeared before a grand jury the following week in New Orleans; we were indicted. Our bond was set at a million dollars each. The attorney protested but to no avail. Ard fired the attorney, deciding to represent the three of us despite the judge's adamant contradiction.

Ard did a swell job in cross-examination. He made every witness for the prosecution look like a dope or a perjurer. Nevertheless, the testimony weighed heavily against us. Finally, the prosecutor rested his case, demanding guilty verdicts for armed robbery, grand larceny, assault with a deadly weapon, kidnapping, and espionage, to name but a few.

The courtroom was emptied for the presentation of the defense. That's because Ard called several character witnesses to include the Prime Minister of Israel, the President of Egypt, the new President of Uganda, and our own Manuel Sanchez President of Uruguay who was given diplomatic immunity. The place seemed like a United Nations assembly or something. Ard's witnesses made us look more like saints than sinners. Ard also managed to get the kidnapping and espionage charges dropped.

Well Diary, here I sit, pencil and note pad in hand, just like the day we started. Despite the great job Ard did as counselor for the defense, we pled guilty to robbery and grand larceny so they would overlook the rest of the charges. However, the judge took into consideration the extenuating circumstances and gave us reduced sentences. I got five years. It wasn't a bad deal, knowing the last time I sat in an American cell I was facing fifteen years in solitary. Good thing Ard fired the lawyer; the dunce wanted us to cop a plea for eight-to-twelve. Ard appealed the verdict to a higher court. After a year of moving from prison to prison, the verdict was upheld. Ard sent a petition to the Supreme Court, but they threw it out.

I served the remainder of my sentence in a federal penitentiary in the southwest. After a while, I was allowed to go outside the walls on work details. The institution had some corn and cotton fields. During harvest season I remembered what real work was about. I met a guy named

Holt. He had been convicted of conspiracy during a presidential scandal. He was the only real friend I made in the joint.

One Christmas Eve I had a few visitors, namely Grace and Nancy. It was great to see them, but there was nothing I could say to cheer them up. We conversed with each other through the heavy mesh screen separating us.

Grace: The guard said we were allowed to visit only half an hour.

Barry: You shouldn't have come all this way for that.

Nancy: Are you kidding? It was worth it.

Grace: Elmer, you know the cop, he's been bugging me. His wife Mildred dumped him and he thinks I'm interested for some reason.

Barry: He's the ass-wipe that finked on us.

Grace: I wish he'd leave me alone. His meddling could ruin my friendship with Mildred.

Barry: I'll fix his wagon someday. You sure are developing into an elegant and beautiful woman, Nancy.

Nancy: Thanks. You look good too Sam.

Barry: I've been working out, plus I have a job laboring in the fields.

Nancy: Are you coming home soon?

Barry: Sooner than you think sweetie-pie.

Grace: We miss you.

Barry: Don't worry; pretty soon there'll be a man around the house.

Grace's eyes sparkled when I mentioned that. She immediately saw diamonds, I suppose. The guard led them away while I waved goodbye. They were all choked up; you'd think they were the ones in the clangor.

The following summer I was called before the parole board. They granted me an early release for good behavior. They assigned me a parole officer in California. I couldn't wait to get back to the West Coast, which had shifted a bit further east last time I'd seen it. I hopped on a plane to Santa Barbara, hailed a cab and went to Grace's house to surprise her. My Continental was still parked out front; Grace's heap was in the driveway. Another car was parked beside it.

As I approached the house, I heard Grace inviting someone to leave. It was Elmer.

Elmer: What about tomorrow?

Grace: I wouldn't go out with you if you were the last man on earth!

I was approaching up the driveway but they didn't see me between the cars. The argument started getting out of control when Grace slapped Elmer's face. He grabbed her hand, pulled her next to him, and tried to force a kiss on her. I gripped him by the shoulder, spun him around, and gave him a right cross flat on his nose. He bounced on the ground a few times, and slowly staggered to his feet, holding his nose. As soon as he recognized me, he ran to his car. Grace flew into my arms and gave me a big kiss. Nancy was on a date, so Grace and I got-it-on twice.

Nancy returned home just after midnight. She gave me a very warm reception complete with hug and kiss. She was already "sweet sixteen" and protruding in all the right places. We spent the whole night chatting. I nodded off about six a.m. I was awakened by a knock on the door. It was Elmer with reinforcements. They took me downtown accusing me of violating my parole. Then they threw me in the slammer again.

I appeared before a judge the next day. I testified that Elmer had assaulted Grace and tried to force himself on her. Grace corroborated my testimony, adding that I possibly saved her from being raped. The judge apologized to me and Grace and said we were free to go. The judge was furious with Elmer, however, ordering the creep never to harass Grace or me again. We left, holding back the laughter.

One summer day, I was sleeping late. Grace had gone to the grocery store. I was dreaming that I was having sex with a movie star. I awoke to find Nancy stark naked on the bed giving me a hand job. I told her to stop, but she didn't, so I had to make her quit.

Barry (pulling up the covers): What the heck do you think you're doing?

Nancy: I'm really horny.

Barry: That's not my problem.

Nancy: If you don't bang me right now, I'm gonna go out and screw the first guy I meet.

Barry: Now that's plain stupid.

Nancy: Well, then.

Barry: Nancy, I'm old enough to be your father.

Nancy: So what? I've made it with older guys.

Barry: Does your aunt know you're not a virgin?

Nancy: Course not.

Barry: I think you should talk to her. She'll understand what you're going through. You don't want to end up pregnant. If you like, I'll have a talk with her. We'll help you get on the pill if that will work for you. Please don't ask me to be your lover. Get serious. You know that Grace and I...

Nancy: Yeah, forget it.

Barry: You can't go around having intercourse with every Tom, Dick, and Harry. You could get a venereal disease. Besides, you don't want a crummy reputation. Sex should be an expression of love; with someone you might want to marry.

Nancy: I've heard that lecture before.

Barry: Look, Nancy. You know I love you, as much as any father ever loved their own daughter. That's why we can't, you know...

Nancy: I never had a father. My parents died in a car crash when I was six.

Barry: I know, darling, but I'd be proud if you called me Dad.

Nancy: Please don't tell Aunt Grace about this, Dad.

Barry: Believe me, I won't.

Nancy: Thanks for not getting mad.

Barry: Don't mention it, really.

School started the following week so Grace and Nancy were gone most of the day. I got a part-time job pumping gas. I didn't need the money; I was just bored. Nancy was chosen senior class favorite at her school. Every day the house was filled with Nancy's friends. It was tough, having all those sweet young tushies gazing at my crotch all the time.

Nancy had a big bash for her seventeenth birthday. There must've been a hundred adolescents going in and out the front and back doors. I figured a lot of them weren't even invited. There were several kids making out in the back yard. Someone spiked the punch bowl with vodka. Many of the kids got bombed. I got pretty loaded myself, what with drinking punch and all the scotch I downed. We received several complaints about the loud music. The police showed up at midnight and told us to simmer down. The kids finally started clearing out. I had to take several of them home they were so inebriated.

I was returning to Grace's when I heard a scream. I came across a car parked by a park where a girl was fighting off the advances of her date. It was Nancy's best friend Leanne. I opened the driver's side door.

Barry: Back off, dipstick.

Leanne (buttoning her blouse): That does it, Eric, we're through.

Eric: Ah, you're just a frigid bitch.

Barry (opening passenger door): Need a ride home, Leanne?

Leanne (flipping her hair back): Would you please?

Barry: No problem.

Leanne: Thank you. You're such a gentleman. Let's split.

As I was driving her home, Leanne scooted over and ran her hand up my leg. I began to check out her firm body. I couldn't resist her. I was too stoned to think straight. We drove to a secluded area near the beach.

Barry: I thought you were a frigid bitch?

Leanne: What I need is someone who acts and looks mature. Eric is such a wimp.

Barry: I'm not sure this is a good idea.

Leanne: I know it is.

Barry: I don't have any… protection.

Leanne (opening her purse): No problem, I do.

What an experienced woman Leanne was for being only eighteen. When I returned, the crowd had diminished completely. Nancy had gone to bed. Grace was cleaning up. She asked where I'd been. I felt extremely guilty and told her. She was very upset, but she appreciated my honesty. I promised her I'd never do it again. She forgave me and we made it; it was the best sex we'd ever had together. I guess she figured she had her hooks in me all the way, now; we're talking hog-tied and fit for branding.

Guess what Diary, I got a call from Bob the other day. He's made parole. He and Vicky are coming to visit. Santa Barbara will be their first stop on a nationwide sightseeing trip. They will stay with us a few days before heading to San Francisco.

---

## PHASE SEVEN

Nancy and her high school chums were hanging around the house almost every day. Leanne tried to make the moves on me a couple of times but I gave her the slip. The year flew right by.

Just before graduation, Nancy approached Grace and me and said she wanted to get married. She'd been dating this guy named Justin all year. He was voted most likely to succeed. (Not surprising, since his old man was a real estate developer). We knew Nancy was a level-headed kid so we gave our approval.

Nancy got married that summer. I gave away the bride. The happy couple moved to San Jose, where Nancy's father-in-law had given Justin a job in his business. Believe it or not, I missed having Nancy and her friends around. Everything was so quiet. Nancy was the closest I've ever gotten to having my own children, outside of when Jannette carried our baby. The memories continue to haunt me. It seems I wasn't destined for paternity. Grace couldn't get pregnant; she got multiple cysts on her ovaries and had them removed when Nancy was two. I sort of liked that about Grace in the beginning; but I wouldn't drop her for being sterile. In the meantime, Grace and I took a vacation to Hawaii. It was spectacular. But you'll have to see the photo album because I can't explain right now.

We were shuffling through a pile of mail when I came across a letter from Ard. He was finally being released from prison. He wanted to have a gang reunion at our place; I called his number and replied "aye, aye" because we always did what Ard suggested. I mean, if you don't trust your commandant, you might as well quit and find another business. We partied together every day; it was like old times but with considerably fewer miles to drive. Laura and Grace devoted a lot of time to each other during the next few weeks.

One Friday evening, after Bob and Vicky had left for their hotel, I invited everyone for a drink in town. Laura and Grace passed, but Ard took me up on it. Halfway to the bar I realized I'd forgotten my wallet. Ard didn't have much cash. I performed a one-eighty. We entered the front room only to find Grace and Laura making love on the sofa; yeah, the same sofa Grace and I made it on. I became furious. I grabbed Grace by the hair and jerked her to her feet. Then I let go, dropping her on the floor.

Barry: I can't believe this! I thought I was enough for you.

Grace (kneeling): Don't be so vain, Barry.

Barry: Me, vain?

Grace (standing): Look, stud, I was bisexual before you ever met me.

Barry: Well, you sure hid it well.

Ard: For once I am genuinely surprised! Wow that hasn't happened in, forever.

Laura: I'm so, so sorry Ard, please, please forgive me.

Ard: Have you two done this before?

Laura (hesitating, knowing she couldn't lie to Ard): Well, maybe once or twice.

Ard: Then it's later days for you brazen gays.

Laura (balling): No, don't leave… Oh boohoo.

Ard: It's too late now, my dear, you're defiled. Once should've schooled you. Twice or thrice turns spicy into vice.

Barry: Let's unass, Ard. No sense in us pining over a couple of lezzies.

Ard: Right on, good buddy.

We left with the lovers sobbing and begging us to stay. As I shut the door, Grace threw me the finger.

Barry: Give it to your bitch, Butch.

I was confused because I remember Grace telling me her husband left her for a man, and here she was picking a woman over me. Maybe I deserved it. Ever since I lost Teresa, I've not been all that faithful to my women. I cheated on Grace once but that was enough. Somehow, I never let go of the guilt, however, being uncommitted to a fault. Now I was feeling empty as could be.

We laid tracks for a lively tavern and got snockered. I packed my stuff the next day and moved out. I didn't see any point in prolonging the inevitable, but I must admit that seeing Grace's tearful eyes reminded me of some great times. I knew it would be a lot easier getting over her than either Teresa or Jannette. The next evening, Ard had a gang meeting at the restaurant beside the tavern, both of which happened to be across the street from the motel we'd checked into.

Ard: It's time for a vacation.

Bob: Is this another business mixed with pleasure deal?

Ard: How'd you guess?

Barry: Where to?

Ard: Las Vegas. We'll go back to our assumed names and characters.

We put off in the morning; got there after dark. We registered into the hotel, ate a scrumptious meal, and hit the casino, parting company to enjoy some personal time. I played craps and slot machines most of the evening, Bob and Vicky preferred roulette, and Ard was a stud at stud poker. I ended up about a hundred bucks in the hole, so did Bob and Vicky. Ard came out five hundred ahead; that figures. Everything he did was profitable it seemed. Whenever something ceased to be lucrative, he'd move onto another project.

I slept late the next day and lazed around the pool until dark, checking out the scenery. I found Ard looking at entertainment guides. Bob and Vicky had gone to a dinner theater. I was attracted to one of the sexier shows. Ard accompanied me. I've heard of vice but this program took the cake.

The show opened with this guy telling dirty jokes. I laughed at a few of them, but most of the good ones I'd already heard. He was followed by a comedy team that cursed every other word and used vulgar gestures throughout. They played with themselves, each other, and the audience. The way they monkeyed around had me roaring. These fools were followed by a female vocalist. Her singing was half-assed but her stripping was full-assed. Her body was something to behold; it definitely made up for her voice, I'd sooner listen to a frog. She tossed her breasts from side to side as the tassels on her pasties swung around in the air; one went clockwise the other counterclockwise. What a talent, huh? And she was well-endowed, maybe unnaturally. Next was a chorus line of beauties dancing the Can-Can. At the end of their act they stripped completely nude, so when they kicked up their legs you could see their bushes. Then they began to parade around looking for tips, carousing with anyone in the audience, dancing on tables, giving private favors, anything goes. The whole place went berserk.

A couple of knockouts came to our table. I dropped a wad of dough and stood up. We were feeling them up and one began to fondle me with her hand. I stretched her out face down on the table and whipped out my rod. I boned her right there on the table in plain sight. Nobody seemed to notice or care. Besides, one of the girls was humping a guy on his lap a few tables over while another was blowing his companion. Ard was falling out of his chair with hysteria. Now that is what I call wild; sin city was an appropriate moniker if not an understatement. It reminded me of some crazy times in Juarez I'd shared with Skip. I couldn't remember raising that much hell and getting away with it.

The next evening, I decided to go casino-hopping and bar-hopping. Ard chose to do something more mellow. After dropping a thousand bucks at various casinos, I went to a lounge where a woman was singing. It just so happens, this was the same club where Jannette was featured, and my usual booth was available. I sat alone, sipping on Scotch, trying to envision Jannette in a darker body. But I was distracted by the Afro hairdo, not to mention the unquestionable magnificence of this woman and her voice. I was totally enamored; she was sleek as a thoroughbred, a real black beauty.

She must have noticed me staring at her and ogling, because she breezed by my table after her act. Her lipstick was purplish in color, like her low-cut dress. She was wearing a tiny lace bra; her breasts stood firm and round, like a couple of baseballs. I couldn't help undressing her with my eyes; she had the perfect figure. I'd never seen a woman with such beauty, style, and polish. She spoke softly, distinctly and articulately. Her voice was so pure it sent shivers up my spine when she sang or spoke. I was mesmerized.

Barry: You are simply captivating. What is your name?

Woman: Deidre. Most people call me Dee Dee. What's your name, handsome?

Barry: Carter. My friends call me Sam.

Deidre (offering her hand): Pleased to meet you, Sam.

Barry (kissing her hand): Can I offer you something, Deidre?

Deidre: That depends on what you are offering.

Barry: Anything your little heart desires.

Deidre: I'll start with a Bloody Mary.

Barry: So, Deidre, how long have you been performing here?

Deidre: Oh, five years off-and-on, I guess. My first album, entitled Deidre, will be out soon finally.

Barry: I bet it will be as spellbinding as you.

Deidre: What a sweet thing to say.

Barry: When it comes to sugar, darling, I've got nothing on you.

Deidre: Flattery will get you everywhere.

Barry: I'm not that smooth a talker, baby, I'm simply telling the truth.

Deidre: Sure, I bet you say that to all the pretty girls.

Barry: I doubt if my previous girlfriend would agree with you.

Deidre: So, you've lost at love?

Barry: Not with her, but there was someone. You may have heard of her; she found stardom on that very stage.

Deidre: What was her name?

Barry: Jannette. Losing her was the greatest tragedy of my life.

Deidre: Oh my God, no kidding. Everybody loved Jannette. But today let's be happy.

Barry: Yes, let's.

Deidre: Want to go to a party?

Barry: You bet.

Deidre: Shall we, then?

She drove me to a mansion outside of town. A guard stopped us at the gate, then flagged us onward. We glided alongside a fine-trimmed lawn to a large parking area where there was another guard directing traffic. Upon entering the mansion, Deidre introduced me to the host, an

Italian dude everyone called Vito, who also owned the casino-hotel we'd just left. The man shook my hand and told me to enjoy myself. I already was.

Deidre and I wormed our way through the house towards the back yard. We had a few glasses of cognac alongside the swimming pool while she read me in about Vittorio Lombardi. Then she asked about me; I told her I was an oilman on vacation. Luckily, we were distracted right then; guests had started the old throw-everyone-into-the-swimming-pool game. We approached for a closer view. A fat guy tried to grab Deidre by the arm I twisted his wrist behind his back, and guided him to the pool shoving with my bootheel against his buttocks. Another dude was trying to get out while the fat guy went in; the two made a gigantic splash.

I was stooping there, hands on my knees, laughing my ass off when Deidre started pushing me from behind. I twirled around, barely getting hold of her hands in mine before we both went plunging into the water. We stood simultaneously hooting and hollering. She started wrestling with me, trying to dunk me. I put my arms around her and pulled her under with me. We kissed under the water until we ran out of breath.

I helped Deidre out of the water. Her dress conformed to her body's every curve, nook, and cranny. She was ravishing. I walked her into the house where a servant handed us some blankets and towels. We dried off and went back outdoors, carrying the blankets and towels. Roaming around the yard, we stopped by a fence between some trees, where I placed our blankets on the grass. We laid there leaning on elbows, heads resting on hands, facing one another, and spontaneously began making out. I started feeling with my hands and stimulating with my fingers. One thing led to another and we did it on a bed of grass fitted with thick blankets, where we spent the night.

I awoke at sunup. Deidre was still asleep. I pulled a blanket over her shoulders and took a walk. I poured the excess water from my boots, brushed off my bleached-out suit, and pulled out a soggy pack of smokes. I lit up the driest one and tossed the rest of the pack over the fence. There were numerous people dozing, here, there, and everywhere. I was wondering how much alcohol went down last night as I tossed the rank cigarette into the pool. Deidre sneaked up from behind and gave me a bear hug; I turned around smiling and kissed her.

Barry: Your beautiful dress was ruined.

Deidre: That's all right. I know where I can get another one. I'm more worried about your suit.

Barry: What, this old rag?

Deidre: You are too modest. What do you say we cut out?

Barry: I'm for that.

Our first stop was Deidre's apartment. It was very luxurious and exquisitely furnished. She excused herself. I lit up a cigarette from a fresh pack I'd found at Vito's place. In less than an hour, Deidre came out looking brand new. She wore a halter-top and tight jeans. Next, we went to my hotel. In fifteen minutes, I'd shaved, gargled, and changed into jeans, sport shirt, and walking shoes. We had brunch at the hotel.

Deidre drove us around town in her convertible so I could see what Lost Wages looked like in the daytime. It wasn't anything compared to the nighttime; but the hotels and casinos were magnificent nonetheless. Then she drove into the desert stopping at some reddish rock formations. She took me there with the sole purpose of seducing me, and I let her. It was desolate in those ragged hills, but beautiful. The scenery was breathtaking, especially in the back seat of her convertible.

Deidre: I've got to get back. I have a show tonight.

Barry: Can I meet you after the show?

Deidre: Sure, if you want to meet my husband, too.

Barry: Your husband?

Deidre: He's a linebacker for the Rams.

Barry: You've got to be joking.

Deidre: I never joke.

Barry: I didn't have a clue that you were married.

Deidre: Don't worry, he fools around on me all the time.

Barry: Do you fool around on him all the time?

Deidre: Please, Sam, I'm really not that kind of girl.

Barry: You were with me.

Deidre: You are a very special guy.

Barry: You're the one who's special. What makes me different from anybody else?

Deidre: I like the way you are always complimenting me and encouraging me; you give me the kind of attention I desire.

Barry: Your husband is a fool for not being attentive to your desires.

Deidre (sighing): How true.

I had dinner at the hotel. As I was engorging myself, Ard came to the table with a sophisticated looking woman. Her name was Faith. She was a supervisor at one of Lombardi's many casino-hotels. Coincidentally, he owned most of the places I patronized; I'm sure I've dropped tens of thousands into his pockets over time. Anyway, they had a drink while I ate. Then, I was summoned to accompany them to my favorite casino. I saluted Deidre as we walked by the lounge and I blazed a trail to my booth. Dee Dee waved her pinky at me. We enjoyed her first set and had a few cocktails. Then Faith took us upstairs to a private table behind a beaded curtain. Much to my surprise, Vittorio Lombardi was sitting there.

Lombardi: My friends, please sit down. Right on time as always Faith (looking at wristwatch). Gentlemen share some rosé with me, won't you?

Ard: Mr. Lombardi, allow me to introduce you to a friend of mine.

Lombardi: It's Sam Carter if I remember correctly.

Ard: You know each other?

Barry: We met last night.

Ard: Mr. Lombardi has offered me a job.

Lombardi: After he took me for five G's at the blackjack table, it occurred to me I needed another dealer.

Barry: I don't mean to be pushy, sir, but if you have any other available jobs I'd be interested.

Lombardi: I can always use extra muscle, Sam. Tell you what. Go talk to my foreman tomorrow. I'll tell him to expect you at eight a.m. He'll be at the maintenance entrance in the rear of my establishment next door. His last name is Coppini.

Lombardi excused himself and Faith went with him, leaving us alone with half a carafe of vino.

Ard (standing): Good move, brother. You read my mind.

Barry (standing): What's the story on Faith?

Ard (walking towards the railing): She used to be one of Lombardi's prostitutes. She worked her way up the ranks; now she's a madame and runs a house, among other things.

Barry: You know, Faith resembles Laura a little.

Ard: She's about as low rent, too. However, my interest in Faith is strictly for monetary gain. I exchange my company for her information. Now that you belong to Lombardi you must remain in intelligence gathering mode; be vigilant everywhere all the time with no exceptions. That's why I immediately got up; I expect the table where we were sitting is bugged

Barry: Yeah, I get your point. Lombardi has action everywhere; legal and illegal I figure.

Ard (surveying the casino): Precisely. The majority of the action on this part of the strip is his, and he also is a top banana with the Mafia.

Barry: Wow, the Mafia, huh?

Ard: Is this project too precarious for you?

Barry: Don't be ridiculous. You can outwit this guy any day of the week.

Ard: Just remember to be very cautious around Lombardi and his employees. The wrong word could get us into deep you know what. Do whatever he says; they'll most likely ask you to do something illegal.

Barry: I don't want to hurt anybody.

Ard: Tell him that's where you draw the line. If it gets too bizarre, let me know.

Barry: What about Bob and Vicky?

Ard: We'll have to stop seeing Bob and Vicky socially. They will be working the outside while we're working the inside.

Barry: Got you covered Ard.

I arrived in the rear parking lot at the precise time. Coppini appreciated my promptness. First, they had a special identification card made with my picture on it. Next, I was given a handheld radio because I would be on call any hour of the day. Then I was briefed about the job and turned over to a foreman everyone called Tate.

For the next week I took orders like a buck private. I did odd jobs such as delivery, chauffeur, bouncer, and laborer. They worked me to death, but the pay was great, not to mention free meals.

After the first week, Lombardi situated Ard and me in an expense-paid apartment and gave me a company car. It was the same apartments where Deidre lived, which he also owned. When I got there, Ard was in the process of searching the place. I was relaxing in front of the TV nursing a beer when Ard motioned to follow him into the bathroom. He turned on the shower and shut the door.

Ard (whispering): The living room, both bedrooms, the balcony, and the phone are bugged. There's a camera over the front door; do not let anyone through that door. Be careful what you say and do at all times.

Barry: Why the constant surveillance?

Ard: I don't know. Maybe Lombardi knows who we are. Maybe he wants to ensure his employees are loyal. Probably both. Just watch what you say, especially here and in all of his establishments. Sorry, but I cannot emphasize this enough.

Tate radioed me on Sunday night. He needed some help unloading a shipment. I went to the designated location where I unpacked a truck. One of the guys dropped a box labeled "wine". The box went thud instead of crash; I surmised the box wasn't filled with bottles of vino. When we finished, a guy named Louie handed me a note. I was to report to Lombardi at his private table. I went upstairs and waited until Lombardi's bodyguard motioned for me to enter.

Lombardi: What'll you have, Sam?

Barry: A beer would be fine, sir.

Lombardi motioned at Faith to fetch me one.

Lombardi: How's the job going so far?

Barry: Great.

Lombardi: I've got a special assignment for you tomorrow. I need you to go to Chicago and drive a truck back.

Barry: You've got it, sir.

Lombardi: Good. Nine o'clock, same place.

I got a good night's rest. Ard was getting ready to go to work in the morning when I stopped him. I whispered about the case of wine that went thud, and the truck driving job. He nodded and left. I went to work sharply at nine.

Louie: Here's a key. It goes to the blue Chevy parked over there (pointing). In the glove compartment you'll find a map and some instructions. There's also an envelope with your expense money.

I was on the road for several hours. I gassed up and stretched my legs. I tried to open the trunk but the key wouldn't fit. I hoped I wouldn't get stopped or have a flat tire, because I was sure drugs were in the trunk. I drove all day and night until I was in Illinois. I found a phone booth and called a number as instructed at which time I was given directions to a garage on the south side of Chicago. When I arrived, I gave two blasts on the horn and waited. A garage door opened and a man waved for me to enter. Next, I was told to report to Julio at a bar down the way.

Julio was the bartender. He thumbed at a door in the corner. The door led to a supply room. I snooped around until I came across another door. I knocked. The door opened and a big guy gestured for me to sit. There were two guys at a table; one guy had a cigar in his mouth. Cigar face did all the talking.

Man: You made good time, Sam. Allow me to introduce myself. They call me the Cajun.

Barry (shaking his hand): Pleased to meet you, sir.

Cajun: You like "stogies"?

Barry: Yes sir.

Cajun (lighting Barry's cigar): I need you to drive a van back to Vegas for me.

Barry: Signore Lombardi informed me, sir.

Cajun: Good. I'll bet you're hungry.

Barry: Indeed I am.

Cajun: Stubby, take him to the hotel downtown. Set him up with a room. Charge anything you need to the room, Sam. We'll have someone call to pick you up; be ready by nine. Stay in your room after dinner until you receive the call; don't go to the bar or leave the room for any reason.

Barry: Very well, sir.

I ate a slew of crab legs and went to bed. I awoke at eight and called room service for a hearty breakfast. Shortly after nine Stubby rang and said to come downstairs. A limousine was waiting outside the lobby. A door opened and I stepped in. The Cajun handed me a cigar. The driver took us across town. They dropped me off in a parking lot.

Cajun: There she is, Sam. The keys are in it. Have a good trip.

Barry: Thank you, sir.

As I pulled out of the parking lot, I noticed a small tin box on the dash board. I opened it; there were some small pills inside, amphetamines. I swallowed a couple. The pills kept me alert but gave me the jitters. I bought a pint of Schnapps along the way to take the edge off. The van was loaded with cases of cigarettes and unmarked boxes. I dared not inspect them.

I drove straight through to Vegas without taking a break, except for pit stops. Morning had broken when I reached the casino. I parked the van in the back, locked the door, dropped the keys into a mail slot, then walked to the apartment. The pills had worn off and I was blitzed. I fell asleep without getting undressed, which was becoming a recurrent theme.

When I awoke the sun was already down. I went to the casino and found Ard dealing cards. I played a few hands until his shift ended. We moseyed outside along the sidewalk. I told him about the journey.

Ard: What you have told me confirms that Vito's not only running prostitutes, he's running drugs and untaxed cigarettes. Lord knows what else. Keep me posted.

I went to my favorite restaurant and ordered some dinner, asking the waiter to serve me in the lounge. Deidre already had started her show. I enjoyed the show as I wolfed down some Ravioli. Deidre sat down while I was finishing, nudging me under the table with her foot.

Deidre: Where have you been hiding?

Barry: I was out of town. Are you sure it's all right being seen with me?

Deidre: Relax, Willie went back to L.A.

Barry: I'm not accustomed to sharing another man's wife, you know, chivalry and all that junk.

Deidre: Don't worry. It'll be our secret.

Barry: It's not that I don't find you arousing, Deidre, on the contrary…

Deidre: Then what's the problem?

Barry: Well, I sort of work for Lombardi now.

Deidre: Really? That's great.

Barry: (leaning forward and whispering) Yeah, but it's better if he doesn't see us together, you know, intimately. Just between you and me, I don't trust him and I don't want you to get hurt.

Deidre (softly): I get your drift.

She excused herself and I wandered into the casino. Louie found me and told me to see the boss. I went to his private booth.

Lombardi: Excellent job, Sam. They were very impressed with the respect and politeness you displayed.

Barry: Thank you, sir.

Lombardi: How do you feel.

Barry: Fine, sir.

Lombardi: Ready to go back to work?

Barry: Sure.

Lombardi: Have you ever tended bar?

Barry: Mostly on the wrong side of the bar.

Lombardi (amused): That's good enough. I need you to fill in for Vincent, the regular bartender downstairs in the lounge. He's sick, and Faith doesn't know what the heck she's doing back there; I sent Louie on an errand so you're it.

Barry: Not a problem.

It was fun tending bar. I got to drink all I wanted. There were plenty of gorgeous women to gaze at. There were a few people who asked for drinks I'd never heard of, however, so I just guessed. Nobody complained, so I figure they got what they wanted, or they didn't know what they'd asked for. I got adequately juiced that night.

Ard and I had the weekend off. We both slept late. I was watching football and drinking a beer when the doorbell rang. It was Lombardi paying us a surprise visit. Ard let him in; he and his bodyguards took a seat while I went to the fridge and grabbed some beers.

Lombardi: I'm really pleased with the work you guys are doing.

Ard: It's our pleasure.

Lombardi: Now that we're all friends, let's cut through the BS. I remember you boys from your Crusader days, so I know what smooth operators you are. I think you could be a major asset to the business. I'm prepared to offer you executive positions in the organization.

Ard: We're listening.

Lombardi: I'm kickstarting an operation in Arizona, mainly in the prostitution racket; quite a bit of drug action, smuggling, and other enterprises which have great potential. There's chaos among the various families there and we're taking over. My guys in Phoenix can't seem to get organized. That's where you come in.

Ard: What's the deal?

Lombardi: With your experience I know you can get the Arizona operation back on its feet. With a little effort you could turn it into a multi-million-dollar venture.

Ard: I will want free reign, everybody taking orders from me; ability to hire and fire whomever I choose.

Lombardi: Of course you will Jon. Or should I call you Alan, or maybe Captain Denton?

Ard: Whatever floats your boat.

Lombardi:  I will open an account in your name, Denton; we'll start with 500 K. Think carefully boys, won't you? I'll need your answer by Monday.

We had a gang meeting the next day. The four of us drove into the country with a few cases of cerveza. We had a picnic beneath some craggy cliffs, quite some distance beyond the red rocks.

Ard: Well, Barry, what do you think of Lombardi?

Barry: Outside of ourselves, I'd say he's the biggest crook this side of the Rio Grande.

Ard: I always suspected Lombardi was onto us. I still think we can take him for a ride. We worked our way into his family just as I had planned. He knows it, but he likes us and he admires us.

Bob: What's our next move?

Ard: We'll play Lombardi's game. I'll set up his operation in Phoenix. Bob, you'll continue to be our eyes and ears in Vegas. I want you to grow a beard, get some glasses; alter your appearance. Use disguises and mix it up. Keep watch on Lombardi and his high command; I need to know his every move. Vicky, I want you to pose as a prostitute in my organization in Phoenix.

Vicky: I do not want to go to bed with nobody.

Ard: Don't worry, you won't have to; just make friends with the other hookers. I'll have fake dates scheduled for you to make it look authentic.

Barry: How do I fit in?

Ard: You'll be my right-hand man and manage the pimps. Lombardi trusts you. You've made quite an impression. The family likes your humble ways, so don't change your style.

Bob: Is the meeting over.

Ard: Yes, why?

Bob: I have an announcement. Vicky and I got married yesterday, legally. We went to the justice of the peace so now it's official.

Barry: Wow a Vegas wedding and we missed it; that explains the huge diamond on Vicky's finger.

Ard: Well congratulations you guys! Let us toast the bride and groom.

We clanked our beer cans together and chugged the contents down.

Bob: Okay if me and Vicky take a week, maybe go to Mexico?

Ard: Take two weeks. Let your beard grow. We need time to get things started anyhow. Then, you go to Vegas, Vicky goes to Phoenix. I'll set up a private phone with an unlisted number where you can leave messages day or night.

We continued the celebration until we were out of beer and it was pitch dark. We drove back into town and dropped Bob and Vicky at their hotel. Ard and I went to the casino. We found Lombardi at his table.

Lombardi: Join me gentlemen; I'll have some more lasagna and salad brought to our table.

Ard: I've reached a decision. I'm going to do it. Barry has agreed to be my assistant.

Lombardi: That is very good news. Let us drink to your success. Louie, bring a bottle of our finest champagne.

Phoenix was hot, almost all year round. I spent most of the week driving, unloading, moving furniture, and so forth. Ard spent considerable time flying to and from Vegas and Phoenix. On Saturday, we had a meeting in downtown Phoenix to officially kick off the undertaking. Several crime bosses were there, including Lombardi, the Cajun, and a guy from Frisco name Martinelli. There were two black dudes from L.A. who had been holding down the fort in Arizona. The main guy was called Albino; his side-kick was named Clyde. I couldn't figure out why they called the guy Albino because he was black as the ace of spades.

Lombardi: First let me say that I am pleased to have Mr. Denton in the organization. His talent is known world-wide. Albino, you and Clyde will take orders from him. You'll also be working with Barry here; he is a very loyal and productive individual.

Albino: We got two nightclubs, a used car lot, a restaurant, a hotel, and a office building. My man Clyde, here, he got a bunch of ho's down town and some mo' in Scottsdale.

Martinelli: We've also got a slow but steady stream of drugs coming across the Mexican border. We're hoping you can speed up the smuggling operation, and get those drugs distributed to myself and the Cajun. In addition, we have cash that needs laundering.

The meeting went on for four hours. Then we had dinner. Later the big bosses (including Ard) left to sort things out amongst themselves.

For days I helped set up operations in our office building. Ard scheduled appointments with every street walker, pimp, pusher, and creep on the payroll. He fired most of them. We visited all the businesses that Albino had described. They had been mismanaged and in disrepair for so long they were losing money. Ard interviewed numerous potential employees and hired many of them. Ard decided that Clyde and Albino would split up the prostitutes. Clyde would work Phoenix and Albino, Scottsdale. Clyde was not the typical black. He wore blue jeans, a sports shirt, and tennis shoes. Albino was the epitome of a pimp. He wore a white suit with a red shirt, and a white wide-rim hat with a red band around it, plus red socks and white shoes. He spoke with a slight British accent. I learned that he was from Honduras.

After a day of interviews, Ard and I slipped into the back room of our Scottsdale nightclub to talk turkey and review the supporting cast. Clyde was in the process of cussing out a few streetwalkers when we entered.

Clyde: All right ladies, get lost... Sometimes they need a little pampering, know what I mean?

Ard: Absolutely.

Clyde: What's the scoop, chief?

Ard: Many of our ladies have jumped ship to work for the competition. It has reduced our sales tremendously, and this is supposed to be a profitable season.

Albino: We needs to hire some mo' hot mamas.

Ard: We'll offer the ladies ten percent on top of their hourly fee. They'll leave the competition in a hurry to join with us if it means more money.

Clyde: Can do.

Ard: Albino and Clyde, you guys have been hustling the street for customers. I want to work the hotels and nightclubs more. We will be specializing in high-classed call girls. Barry, you'll be working the expensive hotels; the ladies will have designated rooms at our hotel downtown. Let's go after the rich johns with connections and cash. I'm going to initiate an escort service that looks like a legitimate business on the books. It will open soon on the first floor; our offices will be on the top floor, the rest on the second floor. I'll be renting or leasing offices on the other floors. Pretty soon, the ladies will no longer be working alleys and street corners; many will have an office of their own.

Clyde: Outstanding! I'm glad Mr. V sent us someone who knows his stuff.

Ard: Okay, Clyde, round up the girls.

Clyde: My main man has spoken.

Fifteen prostitutes entered the room.

Ard: My dear sweet beautiful ladies. I have an announcement. From now on, you'll be getting a raise when your customer pays. Another way to earn more hay, is to work longer days and hustle more lays. You will be receiving a ten percent raise per customer; so, you take more when you make more.

The girls cheered.

Ard: Don't get excited yet. You're going to have to work your butts off, literally. You chicks may have to turn a few more tricks, and lick a few more pricks, but it's just a temporary fix Pretty soon you're going to see a higher class of clients. I've got this down to a science. Show them how sophisticated you are, by acting like a movie star, and riding like a fancy car.

Ard sweet-talked the girls until they were ready to kiss his backside. They'd do anything for him and he knew it. Albino and Clyde were impressed by the way Ard handled them. It didn't take very long to hire lovelier girls, since the salary was better and so were the benefits and the leadership. About ten girls were added to our employment during the week. One of them was Vicky.

Ard and I spent most of our time on the phone. Within weeks, Ard's escort service was a smashing success. Several local businesses were utilizing the ladies to entertain out of town dignitaries, clients, and buyers. Ard's attitude gradually changed from honey dripper to dictator. He had everyone's respect though, because business was flourishing.

Bob called one evening and left a message with Ard's automated operator. Lombardi was on his way to Phoenix with several others on his staff. We were having a fish dinner in the back room of the restaurant when they arrived. We acted surprised to see them.

Lombardi: Mr. Denton, my congratulations. Word has gotten back to me that your escort service is thriving. You are a very popular man in the syndicate. Even the competition has the utmost regard for what you have accomplished here.

Ard: Glad to hear it. How about a filet mignon or a salmon steak?

Lombardi: We have a plane to catch for Chicago.

Ard: Too bad you can't stay and enjoy yourselves.

Lombardi: Maybe next time. There's just one thing more. We were hoping that the smuggling operation would pick up.

Ard: First things first, boss. I wanted to fix the existing businesses before addressing new business endeavors. The smuggling operation is now my primary concern. Some Mexicans are working the border as we speak; they have been digging tunnels, establishing checkpoints, and renting safe houses.

Lombardi: I understand. Enjoy your dinner, boys; we'll see ourselves out.

The next two weeks we stayed in the office on the top floor of our ten-story building. Each of our businesses was now in the black, and we added several of our own ventures. We also raked in quite a bit more moolah renting out office space, enough to pay rent and utilities on all the properties. One Saturday, Ard threw an office party for employees. I got hammered; but you already knew that. I went to my office to unwind, nodding out in my leather swivel chair.

I staggered over to Ard's office when I awoke. He was on the phone, feet propped up on his desk, smoking a Havana. Vicky was sitting on the couch with a prostitute named Yvonne. I grabbed a cigar off Ard's desk and sat between the two lovely ladies. Yvonne lit my cigar. Ard hung up the phone.

Ard: That was Dennis, the bartender. I don't know why these people call me over such trivial matters.

Barry: What's the problem?

Ard: Some guy has reneged on his loan.

Barry: Big deal. Want me to take care of it?

Ard: I told Dennis if he couldn't handle it, he needs to find another line of work.

Barry: Anyone hungry?

Ard: Yvonne, run and get us some coffee and donuts, please.

Yvonne: Anything you say, dearie.

Vicky: I'm glad she's gone. I must tell you something.

Ard: Go on.

Vicky: I heard the girls talking. Albino, he finds two, como se llama, runaways?

Ard: Are they underage?

Vicky: Yes, that's what I am trying to say. It isn't right, Ard.

Ard: Albino will go down for that. I was going to give him a break. Listen, Vicky, I don't want you to worry. I'm going to help those girls, and they're going to help us. Meanwhile, I will ensure their safety. Thank you for your valuable input.

Barry: Changing the subject Ard, I can't say as I've ever had it this easy before, being waited on and such, but it's getting a little tiresome. I mean, it was exciting at first.

Vicky: I miss Robert.

Ard: I appreciate your positions. Be patient. We're nearing the clincher.

Vicky: What is, clincher?

Ard: Lombardi has used us to pull this endeavor together. He basically got us to do his job for him. As soon as the smuggling operation is fully functioning, I wouldn't be surprised if he tries to eliminate us. After all, he now sees us as a threat, not an ally.

Barry: That's comforting news.

Ard: Bob has turned out to be quite the investigator. He tells me that Lombardi has recently met with crime bosses from around the country. He's made trips to Denver, Chicago, Detroit, Miami, and New York. Bob has been a frequent flyer himself.

Barry: What does all this add up to?

Ard: A merger is in progress. If successful, Lombardi will be in charge of mid-west operations from Vegas to Chicago. The Arizona operation likely will become a gift for another crime boss once the merger is completed, probably the Cajun. Martinelli will keep the Pacific coast, I'm sure.

Barry: It sounds like you're talking a monopoly on crime from the Mississippi River to the Pacific.

Ard: Unmistakably.

Barry: So, Lombardi is going to double-cross us?

Ard: I'm going to beat him to the punch. I've been compiling information about the syndicate all the while, so has Bob. It's just a matter of time for that piece of slime.

Barry: What are we waiting for?

Ard: When the merger takes place, I'm going to blow this case into outer space.

Yvonne walked in with our breakfast, stifling the conversation. I'd lost my appetite but I had some donuts and coffee anyway. Then I took Yvonne into my office. She reminded me a little of Deidre, only nowhere near as luscious.

Yvonne kept me company for the time being, and she loved every minute of it. I guess it's because I was the only trick she had to pull. Vicky remained Ard's female escort. She was very happy about that because the tension was wearing her thin. On Friday, Ard called me into his office for a private session.

Ard: Vicky, Yvonne, take a walk. We've got business.

Barry: Bring back some cigarettes and a six pack.

Ard: Guess what? Lombardi likes little girls.

Barry: He does, does he?

Ard: Martinelli does too.

Barry: How do you know?

Ard: Bob observed them escorting underage girls through the back door of Vito's prized property. The girls spent the night there; were picked up before sunrise.

Barry: And we've got two little senoritas on our staff.

Ard: I know. Isn't that great? They're the bait.

Barry: And Lombardi and Martinelli are the fish.

Ard: They are going to be the catch of the year. They won't just go down for racketeering. Other charges might include child prostitution, indecency with a minor, attempted statutory rape. Let's see... I've got to get the bosses to visit Arizona. I'll throw a party; make them the honored guests. Brag about how every business is running smoothly even though I haven't even begun initiating the smuggling gig like I told them.

Barry: How about a masquerade party on Halloween, week from Saturday?

Ard: I like it. Perfect.

The invitations went out the next day. Ard sure could throw a party. He shut our Scottsdale nightclub to the public, posting a sign that we were closed for the weekend due to maintenance. All the shades had been drawn. He had the place decorated and stocked by nine. Everyone in our employment was there. So were four major crime bosses and several of their employees. I'd never seen so much booze, drugs, and vice happening. Check that; yes, I have. Anyway, I would liken it to a Roman orgy. Albino introduced the runaway girls to Mr. V and Mr. M. The dirty old men were utterly infatuated with the young vixens. The girls had been instructed to coax the two hoods into the executive office at exactly midnight. The entire establishment had been rigged with listening devices and cameras. You'd think the crooks would be accustomed to such eavesdropping, but were not used to being surveilled themselves apparently.

It was approaching midnight when Ard called for a gang meeting in the parking lot. For some reason, he asked me to invite Clyde.

Ard (pointing): Vicky, wait in the back seat of that black car with the tinted windows.

Clyde: What's the scoop, big daddy?

Ard: Have you heard anything on the street about a contract put on me?

Clyde: Only rumors, man.

Ard: Can I trust you Clyde?

Clyde: Are you joshing me? You're my main man.

Ard: Do you like your job?

Clyde: You've really got me worried now, big guy.

Ard: Listen Clyde. I'm giving you the escort service as a present.

Clyde: Oh yeah? Wow, I came out smelling like a rose on that one.

Ard: There's one condition.

Clyde: Rap to me, man.

Ard: Go legitimate. No pimping. No underage girls. What the escorts negotiate on their own is up to them, but they'll have to find their own accommodations if they turn tricks. Stay within the law, and you'll be a rich man.

Clyde: Hey, I'm cool; like I can be totally cool if need be.

Ard (shaking his hand): It's been nice knowing you, Clyde. Now you must run and hide.

Clyde: Say what?

Ard: Trust me my man. Get lost. Take a trip somewhere. Lay low a few weeks.

Clyde: Whatever you say, big daddy.

Ard handed him a box and Clyde took off. Ard opened the passenger door to the sedan and told me to take the wheel. I slipped into the driver seat and noticed Bob and Vicky necking in the back seat.

Barry: Hey, Bob, good to see you.

Bob (muffled): Same here.

Barry: Where to, Ard?

Ard: I've always liked Florida.

I drove the rest of the night, throughout the day, until way after dark. We didn't make it to Florida, but we did make it to Galveston. It was close to my old stomping grounds. We lodged at a hotel overlooking the gulf coast. Ard brought Dallas and Houston newspapers with him and dropped them on the breakfast table. Front pages of both papers were dedicated to the break-up of a major crime conglomerate. The FBI was taking the credit. Honorable mention was given to the Crusaders, only because some news agencies were alleging our involvement.

Ard (reading): Sixty-five arrested on racketeering, conspiracy, and drug charges.

Barry: I would love to have seen their faces when the feds raided the nightclub. To think, they were about to double-cross us.

Bob (reading): Check this out. Lombardi and Martinelli were caught with their pants down, literally, soliciting sex from schoolgirls.

Ard: The runaways agreed to work with me even though the feds were against it. I bet they're glad now.

Vicky: What will happen to las muchachas, Ard?

Ard: I promised them a $25,000 trust fund for college if they'd agree to return home and get family counseling. They were exhilarated and they were relieved. Their parents don't know yet, but when they find out I'm sure they will be surprised, happy, and proud. I checked up on the families; they are decent people. The girls had fallen into drugs, hanging with the wrong crowd. They've learned their lesson.

Barry: I'd say the road to recovery for these two princesses has been paved.

Bob: Were you working with the feds all along?

Ard: No. I brought them in at the end. It was nothing but gravy for them.

Barry: And they took the credit, how typical.

Ard: But we took the profits.

Bob: Ah yes, profits. An excellent topic for discussion.

Ard: Our Swiss account has increased by a mere four million and we still have a Phoenix account with another million.

Bob: Is that all?

Barry: Hey Ard, I've always wanted to ask you…

Ard: Ask me what?

Barry: How come you give us one piece of the puzzle at a time? It seems we're always the last ones to see the big picture.

Ard: Honestly Barry, ignorance can be a virtue. I couldn't bear to hurt you. Look, I made some mistakes; luckily, we got some breaks. Plus, I raised the stakes. Since you are my friends, I must make amends. So, if everything is blown, I go down alone.

Bob: How do you do that?

---

## PHASE EIGHT

We goofed off along the gulf coast for a couple of weeks. Little by little, we made it around to the Atlantic side of the Florida coast. It was there when Bob said he and Vicky intended to settle down. They bought a beach house on ocean drive near Ft. Lauderdale. Ard had a prior appointment in Washington DC; I chauffeured him up the coastal highway.

I was getting dressed in our hotel room when someone knocked. Ard answered the door. The guy at the door wanted to speak to Ard privately. I grabbed my smokes and took a walk for half an hour.

Barry: What was that all about?

Ard: He's with the C.I.A.

Barry: Is that the meeting you mentioned?

Ard: Yeah. They want me to work for them, doing covert operations.

Barry: You going to accept the job?

Ard: I'm considering it.

Barry: Wow, I never figured you going legitimate; especially with the government.

Ard: If I do, it will be temporary.

Well Diary, it didn't take long for Ard to accept the position; he had to report for duty in Virginia. I gave him the keys to the sedan (it looked too much like a federal vehicle anyway). I toured D.C. for three days; it was interesting, but then again it was my first visit to the capitol. However, I became bored; or maybe I was more lonely than bored, they feel about the same. I decided to fly nonstop to San Francisco. I purchased a brand-new Lincoln Continental with cash at a dealership only miles from the airport. I figured on driving south along highway one, I'd heard the experience was something else. I expected on stopping in Santa Barbara along the way to see what Grace and Laura were up to.

I have to say, the drive through Big Sur was unbelievable. I took my time, making several stops to take in the views and shoot some photographs. I rode to Grace's house next. I was dumbfounded when Elmer the cop answered the door.

Elmer: What the hell do you want?

Barry: Is Grace around?

Grace (pushing through to the door): Barry, come on in. How are you? What brings you here?

Barry: I was in the neighborhood; thought I'd drop by.

Grace: What been going on?

Barry: Busting up the mob.

Elmer: You expect us to believe you had something to do with the Cosa Nostra arrests?

Barry: I don't expect you to believe anything. I'm just answering Grace's question.

Elmer: I think it's time for you to leave.

Barry: I'll leave when Grace asks me to.

Elmer: No, you'll leave when I ask you to. I'm the man around here now.

Barry: Is he for real?

Grace: We're married, Barry.

Barry: You've got to be kidding. I thought you wouldn't be with him if he was the last man on earth?

Elmer: Are you going to let him insult me like that?

Grace: Please Barry, be nice.

Barry: Sorry. What do you hear from Nancy and Justin?

Grace: They're expecting a child.

Barry: That's terrific. Say, I misplaced their address and phone number.

Grace: I'll write it down for you; they've moved. Everything has changed.

Barry: Grace, do you know how I can get in touch with Laura?

Grace: Yes, I'll write down her address and phone number too.

Barry: Thanks. Well, I guess I should be leaving. God bless.

Grace: Good luck, Barry. Keep in touch. Let us know how you are doing. And God bless you too.

I vamoosed. Elmer slammed the door behind me. I drove to Laura's place. It was a fairly modern apartment complex in one of the more fashionable neighborhoods. I knocked on her door, but there was no answer. I lit up a smoke and lounged around by the pool. I had the whole place to myself since it was almost wintertime. I fell asleep. It was dark when I awoke.

I went back to Laura's apartment. She was just arriving with grocery bags in her arms. She was trying to get the key into the lock.

Barry (disguising his voice): Can I help you with those groceries, ma'am?

Laura: No thanks I can manage.

Barry: Are you sure? They look awfully heavy.

Laura (turning): I told you I don't... Barry! Why didn't you tell me it was you? What a wonderful surprise. Come on in.

I dropped the groceries on the counter. We squeezed each other and I followed it up with a peck on the cheek.

Laura: It's great to see you. I sure miss the gang.

Barry: What's been happening?

Laura: I'm working as a teller at the bank. Grace and Elmer got married. I hardly ever see her anymore. Nancy is pregnant. That's about it. And you?

Barry: Ard engineered the Mafia bust.

Laura: I thought that was you guys. Pretty gutsy.

Barry: It was fun, actually.

Laura: Barry, about that incident with Grace; it was merely a sudden fling. You know how impulsive I can be; but I've never done that sort of thing before or after.

Barry: Forget about it. I have.

Laura: Are you hungry?

Barry: Let me take you out to dinner.

Laura: Give me an hour to freshened up.

Barry: I could use a shower.

Laura: Let me shower first; then you can have the bathroom while I put on my face.

Barry: I'll get my suitcase.

Laura: Where are you staying?

Barry: Nowhere yet.

Laura: Well you're more than welcome to stay here. The couch unfolds into a sleeper.

Barry: Thanks, I think I will.

We went dining and dancing. Then we went for a moonlight drive. I parked at an overhang near the beach. Laura glided over next to me. I put my arm around her as she nestled close to my chest. Finally, I couldn't resist any longer. I kissed her solidly on the mouth. She returned the kiss enthusiastically. We stayed in an embrace for what seemed like an hour. I drove back to the apartment. I started to take the cushions off the couch.

Laura: There's plenty of room in my bed.

Barry: Are you sure?

Laura: Yes, I am.

She grabbed my hand and ushered me into the bedroom. She began to undress me, and I her. This was like another dream come true (the pleasant one not the ugly one).

Barry: I've had a crush on you for a long time, Laura. I think you are a gorgeous woman.

Laura: I find you very appealing also, Barry.

We made love. It was fantastic. We awoke in the morning and made love again. She was just plain beautiful, even in the morning without any makeup.

Laura: If Ard could only see us now.

Barry: He'd probably laugh.

Laura: You're right, he probably would. What's he doing nowadays?

Barry: I think he's in Russia.

Laura: Surely you jest?

Barry: He's working on some secret deal involving national security.

Laura: I'm really not that surprised, actually. He always did like mystery and intrigue.

We lazed around her pad all weekend, drank some beers, made love, and switched channels on the tube. She was up bright and early Monday morning for another day at work. I was barely moving. She left a note saying she would be home at five-thirty. She also left me her house key in case I wanted to do some running around. I just loafed about the apartment all day, and the next day and the next.

After a week, I asked Laura to quit her job and run away with me. She was delighted. I told her I was more of a Northern California fan, so we drove up the coast to a secluded area northwest of Sacramento. We discovered a neat little cottage on a hill with a view of the ocean; the place was surrounded by five acres of trees. We both fell in love with the place so I bought it.

We celebrated Christmas over at Grace's place. Nancy and Justin were in town with their new baby. I actually managed to tolerate Elmer. He had made detective; his career got a major boost after he pegged us, I'm sure. We phoned Bob and Vicky while we were there. They said they were coming to Hollywood to start working on a film. I guess our notoriety landed Bob a deal with the motion picture industry. They also were expecting their first child.

Laura and I had a housewarming party on New Year's Eve at our cottage. It was like a gang reunion, only without our fearless leader. Ard phoned on New Year's Day. He was back in the states. He had uncovered a plot by the commies to assassinate our President. He was glad to hear that Laura and I were a couple. He said he'd been awaiting the inevitable after I'd told him my dream of meeting Laura in the clouds. He sounded tired. I sensed that it was just a matter of time before Ard would get frustrated with the government and call the gang for another escapade.

Dear Diary, sorry I've neglected you lately. I've been buying and selling real estate; it's a real lucrative business. I guess I'm pretty rich now. Laura told me the other day that she's pregnant; it wasn't that much of a surprise because I agreed that she stop taking the pill. I also told her I would marry her. She was thrilled. We're going to get hitched this Christmas. She should make an impressive bride by then, being with child and all. I thought of Jannette and smiled; it was Laura in the dream before it was Jan. I will never forget her. Male or female, we plan to call our first child Jan.

Bob and Vicky had started a family and now I was starting one. It made me feel very happy, if not old. I wondered if Ard would ever settle down and have kids. You know, I haven't heard from him in months. I sent a lengthy letter to his P.O. box. I hope he can make it for the wedding. Either way, we ought to get together again and party, just for the sake of old times if for no other reason. I know it's just a matter of time. But then again, what isn't?

THIS PAGE INTENTIONALLY LEFT

NOT BLANK

## This is the stupidest book you will ever read !!

But seriously, folks, have you fulfilled your basic psychological need for idiocy? *Dr. Zorch's Encyclopedia of Idiocy* is designed to do precisely that. It's zany, crazy, funny, but above all, it's idiotic. This is adult-oriented off-beat humor for the incorrigible and cynical intellectual. The book is the perfect gift for a recent graduate receiving a diploma or degree, for it will help them to balance their newly acquired wisdom with the proper measure of absurdity.

After all, who wants to be serious all the time? And who wants to be taken seriously all the time? The following text will enable you to develop the skills you will need in life, so that you will never know the difference between the two, and neither will anybody that knows you. Doesn't that make sense? Well it shouldn't, so hurry up and get to work...

# DR. ZORCH'S ENCYCLOPEDIA OF IDIOCY

# Dr. Zorch's

# Encyclopedia of Idiocy

(unedited)

# Hieronymus Q. Zorch

**(1966-1999; revised 2019)**

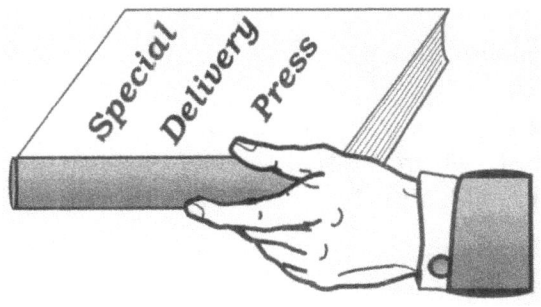

# Dr. Zorch's Encyclopedia of Idiocy

## Prepared by a scholarly consortium of psychologists, psychiatrists, therapists, analysts, scientists, physicians, geeks and kooks led by the honorable

## Hieronymus Q. Zorch, *Ph.D.*

Title: Dr. Zorch's Encyclopedia of Idiocy
Author: Hieronymus Q. Zorch
Illustrator: Baugh B. Tchandtz
Subjects: Humor, Satire, Parody, Weird Stuff
Clipart compliments of Microsoft Corp. (*)

LCCN 99-93613
ISBN 0-9969702-2-5

Printed in the United States of America.

# TABLE of CONTENTS

# DR. ZORCH'S ENCYCLOPEDIA OF IDIOCY

~~~~~~~~~~~~~~~~~~~~~~~~~~~~~~~~~~~~~~~~~~~~~~~~~~~~~~~~~~~~~~

## Introduction

This encyclopedia is a guidebook and training manual for people that are too smart for their own good and therefore need to unlearn everything. It is the ideal gift for any graduate, or those receiving a diploma, birth certificate, driver's license, social security card, haircut, pedicure, or bachelor degrees Fahrenheit, master degrees Celsius, and doctor degrees Kelvin.

You hold in your grubby hands a handbook representing the product of hundreds of painstaking years of scientific research. Within these pages you will discover the perfect, self-contained, and comprehensive course on idiocy. After finishing this vexing course, you, a mere wise scholar, will be fully trained and qualified as an unadulterated ignoramus. Becoming the optimal imbecile requires much practice and experience; but with the help of this text, you can learn sound asinine principles and teach them to others.

The reader is encouraged; indeed, it is demanded that he or she color all diagrams, pictures, and illustrations provided in this book. This is an essential component of the therapy and part of your daily homework. You may use any of the following media: crayons, colored pencils, watercolors, pastels, fecal matter, blood, and cosmetics. It is permissible to use another medium as long as you obtain notarized authorizations from your veterinarian and channelers. Use the standard #2 pencil with eraser, as you may need to refabricate your answers from time to time until you have arrived at the final product.

Due to the juvenile nature of this exposition, it is not recommended for juveniles, largely because Dr. Z was a juvenile when he wrote most of it. Discretion, therefore, is ill-advised since parental guidance is already out the window.

*IDIOCY*: A developmentally hindered, simple minded, or foolish action or state, exhibited in complete seriousness and/or completely unawares.

Or simply, being utterly and ridiculously crass without even trying.

# Foreword

The following fore-word was provided by Dr. Mgabo Nfama Burgerbagger, Prime Minister of Rhozakia, Fujakistan Peninsula (political consultant and translator for the government of Kulawi).

*Dr. Zorch has epitomized the idiotic state of mind in his treatise on mental misfits and "estupiddoes" as we call them in my native tongue. He has couched a most concise and complete definition of lunacy, and its many ramifications. He even expanded the concept of insanity to encompass every dimension of total consciousness, including non-cognitive data processing.*

*Since Sigmund Fraud and Carl Junk, there has yet to enter a theorist or therapist who delved this deeply and accurately into the unconscious realm. Dr. Zorch has identified an area of the brain that no one before him attempted to explain or study. He has advanced the field of abnormal psychology to its ultimate end: uncovering the final and most immense stage of subconscious awareness. Now we can have a thorough understanding of the cause and treatment of uncommon forms of social retardation, brain damage, cerebral disease, mental incompetence, and involuntary foolishness. Like many famous men before him, Dr. Zorch has etched his name permanently into the foundations of mental health, the science and the myth. His name forever will be remembered and awed within the bowels of historical and observational research.*

Note: Excerpts from this exceptional book have been translated into the following foreign languages (listed alphabetically by accident).

| | | |
|---|---|---|
| Arabic | Greek | Portuguese |
| Czechoslovakian | Hebrew | Rumanian |
| Danish | Hungarian | Russian |
| Dutch | Indonesian | Spanish |
| Ebonics | Italian | Swedish |
| Esperanto | Japanese | Swahili |
| French | Jive | Tongues |
| German | Norwegian | Turkish |

This back-word provided by Dr. Zorch was taken verbatim from his best-selling autobiography entitled, *How I Became*. That book is now in its 46ᵗʰ edition (since our favorite philanthropic philosopher has yet to become).

*Without stupidity training, intellectuals are destined to become overeducated egomaniacs. Such a person is inclined to communicate in a condescending manner to what they believe to be an inferior intellect. This behavior is unacceptable in a diverse world, and will reap only animosity and disdain from others. It is henceforth imperative that learned people void themselves of all instruction and understanding before they can begin to apply their knowledge and art. Otherwise, they are destined to become like the crazy fool who wasted his genius locked in an asylum. It is better to be stupid and sane; this I had to learn the hard way, and I am a wiser man for it.*

*How to Use This Book*: paper weight, Frisbee, outhouse supply, door stop, head knocker, sun screen, floor mat, kindling, origami.

*How Not to Use This Book*: term paper, cat food, ear wax remover, passport, fishing bait, bath soap, ice cream topping, legal tender, spare tire.

---

**DANGER**: This book contains concepts and terminology that may not be suitable for young audiences; parental diplomacy is undecided. This book is not recommended for children under the age of accountability. Therefore, if you have virgin ears, do not read this book if you would prefer to keep them.

---

**CAUTION**: Uncontrollable fits of laughter may result from prolonged use of this text. Symptoms include splitting pain in the side, shortness of breath, bouts of crying, and habitual knee slapping. If symptoms persist, contact your chiropractor and/or the nearest straight jacket supplier.

---

**WARNINGS**: Do not consume this material in conjunction with excessive amounts of drugs or alcohol. Do not jump from a plane without a parachute. Do not stick a coat hanger into an electrical outlet. Do not try to beat a freight train to a railroad crossing. Do not light a cigar in a fireworks factory. Do not exit a moving vehicle on the freeway. Do not yell "fire" in a movie theater. Do not insult a crazed maniac holding a loaded gun. Do not drop acid and stare at the sun. Do not leap from tall buildings. Do not pay attention, if it is free.

# Acknowledgements

Dr. Zorch would like to thank the following professional mountebanks for their inefficacious contributions to this work.

| Name and Title | Organization or Field |
|---|---|
| Al B. Awallaby (MD, OD) | Australian Scientific Systems (ASS) – Sydney |
| A. Barber (PhD, LPCC, NCC) | Professional Hair Stylist (Buffalo, WY) |
| Billy Bob ("Bushy") Beavers (ObGyn) | STD Clinic Director (Juarez, MEX) |
| B. A. Boozer (EdD, DeD) | Owner of a Mescal Distillery (Durango, TX) |
| Payne "Indie" Butts (DuD) | Door-to-Door Salesman (LA, CA) |
| Buster ("Red") Cherry (IUD, DNC) | Dir. of Prophylactic Quality Control (Bofo, Inc.) |
| Maria Juana Estonia (ThC) | Drug Enforcement Agent (San Diego, AZ) |
| Barry Dee Hatchett (Ma) | Assn. of X-Ray Examiners (AXE) (Ow, IA) |
| Lou Nat Hicks (MAd) | Mental Asylum of Delaware (MAD) |
| Jack N. Hoff (Cum Laude) | Self-Employed Handyman (state of CON) |
| Tai Won Hon (DMZ) | Mongolian Regimental Commander (Gobi Desert) |
| Shirley U. Jest (QRS) | Mayor of New Guinea |
| Mick E. Mouse (XYZ) | Advisor to the President |
| E. Z. Pickens (EKG, GSR) | Garbage Collector (NY, NY) |
| Petunia P. Pugh (CIA) | Lesoto Sanitation Dept. (LSD) – Joto County |
| Oedipus ("Eddie") T. Rex (Jr.) | Paleontologist (Little Ark, Rockansaw) |
| Chuck M. Spears (NFL) | Acupuncturist (Decatur, USSR) |
| Frank N. Stein (RIP) | Transylvanian Mortician (Riga, Latvia) |
| Moe Joe Tallywacker (SoS) | Private Dick (Chicago, ILL) |
| Will U. Schuttup (KKK) | Political Lobbyist (Washington, DC) |
| Simba ("Bif") Ungowa (GNU) | Afro-Engineering Chair, Institute of Kenya-Nairobi |
| Chu Mei Wang (YUM) | Chinese Univ. of Nature & Technology (CUN&T) |
| Eg Fu Young (BFD) | Sue M. Bigg Associates (Attorneys at Law) |
| Z. Ziggy Zilchman (ZZZ) | Sleep Therapist (Sleepy Hollow, MASS) |
| Mr. & Mrs. Zorch (Deceased) | Dr. Zorch's parents, without whom, etc... |

We now pause for a moment of silence. *Please* keep the following books, scoundrels, and related unfortunates in your thoughts: national leaders and assorted scallywags; road kill; family members and cartoon characters; popular magazines and tabloids; news reporters and foreign correspondents; draft dodgers and conscientious objectors; fetuses, embryos, zygotes, and one-celled animals; multiple and absent personalities, and their various ego states; paraprofessionals. *Please* do not keep the following persons in your garage: in-laws, outlaws, lawyers, and alternate ego states.

# Endorsements

Here are some quips from popular newspapers, magazines, publishers, editors, agents, authors, and critics regarding this fabulous book.

*A work of genius...* Caracas Globe

*Bound to be the #1 best seller of all time...* Zanzibar Traveler

*Dr. Zorch has outdone himself in this great work...* Qatar Times

*Marvelous, simply marvelous...* Beijing Explorer

*I'll take it with me to the grave...* Death Magazine

*Should be on the desk of every graduate...* Chihuahua Herald

*You'll want to read it over and over...* Baghdad Frontier

*Excellent source of entertainment and knowledge...* Kola Post

*Selected as best non-fiction of the decade...* Lame Magazine

*Required reading for Freshmen...* Chernobyl University Press

*Words of wisdom for the one seeking truth...* Cambodian Journal

*America has the best politicians money can buy...* Will Rogers

*By persuading others, we convince ourselves...* Junius

*He not busy being born is busy dying...* Bob Dylan

*I think, therefore I am...* Descartes

*Shazaam...* Gomer Pyle

*A rolling apple gathers no worms...* Me

*It's better to know nothing than to know what ain't so...* Josh Billings

This book is dedicated to YOU!

# Chapter One

## Establishing Your Entry Level Aptitude

~~~~~~~~~~~~~~~~~~~~~~~~~~~~~~~~~~~~~~~~~~~~~~~~~~~~~~~~~~~~~~~~~~~~~

First you must take a test to determine your potential for idiocy and your current level of stupidity functioning. Please be as stupid as you can when responding to each examination item. For correct answers, simply turn the page upside down and read backwards. Give yourself a score of +/− 0.00 for each incorrect answer you provide. If you cannot find the appropriate answer on the answer sheet, you are free to pull an answer out of your butt. However, do not wipe said butt with the answer sheet or you will receive a demerit. Ensure your responses are final before turning each page.

Never should you attempt to study for this examination, because the harder you try the worse you will perform. Instead, allow yourself to draw a complete blank prior to responding to each item. This is the only kind of practice that can help you to excel. Erasing your data banks of all non-extraneous information is very beneficial to your mental incompetence. Eventually, after much rehearsal, you will progress from bad to worse. You will find yourself much happier during the latter stages of redevelopment as you delve into the mysteries of brainlessness. Be patient, it will come: project.

> Note: It is critically important for you the student to circle relevant answers. Upon completion, splice these answers into one continuous stream of plegm, and you will have a comprehensive exhibit of your personality and issues, so that you can relate this to your shrink, as this is vital to his or her diagnosis.

won

# Scholastic Ineptitude Test

## Part One – *Multiple Choice* (circle the correct response)

1. Are you...

    a. yes and NO ?
    b. perhaps later ?
    c. maybe ?
    E. in pain ?
    F. somewhere ?

    f. None Of The Above ?
    G. nonE oF thE beloW ?
    D. 2749386018 in light years ?
    h. is it disheveled or deshoveled ?
    I. over the rainbow ?

2. Why is it called a "crane" ?

    A. for reasons only a mind can conger
    V. Because It Is There, Psychologically
    B. because it goes "crane, crane"
    d. bang a gong in a kong song
    E. Same As 7 Across
    f. for the same reason they call it a "snipe"
    III. The familiarity of inaccessible intentions are
        beyond jurisdiction of the withholder.

3. What is the difference between a duck ?

    a. false
    b. sometimes
    c. the legs aren't the same
    D. 20 years for bestiality
    Ee. One spelling only

    F. 99 quacks
    ff. 700 French Ticklers
    G. to confuse people
    h. Not negative, nor none,
        no neither nothing

4. If someone robbed a bank and went to Baja, he would...

    a. Pass GO and collect $200 ?
    c. Get out of Jail Free ?
    D. Marry a girl named Lupe ?
    ff. Spend it on Oranges ?

    B. STOP ?
    C. EAT OUT ?
    eeeee. eat in ?
    G. read the comic section ?

5. Imagine you are in Washington running for U.S. Senator. You are in the shoes of the
   favored candidate and you are *not* elected. What do you do next?

    z. fly to Africa.
    x. buy new shoes.
    v. draw a blank.
    t. run for cover.
    r. run guns.

    y. HIRE A BOOKKEEPER.
    w. Flip the Birdie.
    u. Marry a girl named Chata
    . s. run for president.
    q. run away from home.

6.  If you wrote a book it would be on what ?

    A.  some paper, or is it pages
    b.  the spread of venereal diseases among gorillas
    L.  your autobibliography
    M.  books
    IV.  the visible spectrum of dichromatic wombats
    XI.  Seven Lame Nomads Going South Along the Sahara
    jj.  Idiocy

7.  If you had a million dollars you would spend it on which ?

    7.  A new Flyrdwimple          7.  Prune juice
    7.  100,000,000 pieces of gum  7.  $ 1,000,000.00 in U.S. currency
    7.  a million lottery tickets  7.  Hookers
    7.  night watchmen             7.  bricks
    7.  DOOR PRIZES                7.  door women

8.  How would you describe your life ?

    a.  True & False                        b.  comical
    h.  un-anti-irr-con-ex-dis-interestingless   i.  flamboyant
    w.  SYGNOMINOCYNCT                       ww.  whit
    X.  True or False                        XX.  is it boring or booring

9.  If and when you marry, it will be for...

    A.  Eccentricity.    T.  Nose.       F.  By Laws.
    M.  other-in-law.    Q.  quartz.     I.  fish scales.
    G.  Feet.            Z.  PRESTIGE.   3.  shoelaces.
    19.  toe jamb.       Next            nth.  awhile

10.  When you dream is it on...

    a.  Your Bed ?
    A.  becoming an illegal alien ?
    b.  DREAMS ?
    B.  Trying out for the gay Olympics ?
    c.  Centrifugal force ?
    C.  Centripetal force ?
    D.  becoming a professional transvestite ?
    d.  biological chemistry of anteaters ?
    e.  answers f. and g.
    fig.
    gaffe.
    Giraffe.

## Part Two – *True or False* (circle the correct response)

1. It is now 14 o'clock ?        true        false

2. This test is fun ?        TRUE

3. Booze is for lovers ?        tre        fale

4. Why are there emus ?        eurt        eslaf

5. Stoker's cough ?        false        true        maybe

6. Mountains ?        yes        no

7. Traffic Jelly ?        no        yes

8. I'm in love ?        nope        yep        wishful

9. True, False ?        false        true

10. I am attracted to the opposite sex ?        yes        no        no kidding
       which one        all or none        anyone

## Part Three – *Matching* (draw a line to connect the left column item to the appropriate match in the right column)

| | |
|---|---|
| 1. Creampuff | A. Vat |
| 2. Cream | B. Crab Livers |
| 3. Puff | C. WOOK |
| D. Birdies | 4. Applesauce |
| E. with your mouth closed | 5. Apple |
| F. Menudo | 6. Sauce |
| G. Zilch | 7. Seven |
| H. The Ides of March | 8. thgie |
| J. JAY | I. Obese harlots |
| 11. Antidisestablishmenterianism | 9. Gristle |
| 10. Anybody, Anywhere Anytime, Anything | Y. Nobody, Nowhere Never, Nothing |

## Part Four – *Fill in the Blank*
### (write the correct responses in the blanks provided)

2. There are _____ (number of frogs in Zimbabwe).

1. Then he said _____.

3. Shoot the _____!

4. Lithuanian lemurs are likely _____.

5. The person reading this is an ___.

6. When I grow up _ will be a copper.

7. This test __ neato, keeno, etc...

8. _____   _____   ___   _____   _____   ___.

9. There will be no number 10 because _____.

11. Blankity, blank, _____ blank, _____ __, blankity, blank?

12. Four score and seven years ago our fathers brought forth on this continent a new nation,

_____

_____

_____

_____

## Part Five – *Essay*
### (write a full paragraph on each topic)

1. Write an essay, in twenty-five words or less, about your life story.

2. Write an essay on essays.

3. Write an essay on germs (include mono, syph, clap, etc.).

4. Write a simpletons on essay.

5. Write an essay on LLRMSDGWYNMBXZ.

6. Write an essay on your toenail.

7. Write an essay on this test.

8. Write a 10,000-word essay on the interplanetary insolubleness of a fricasseed rabbit.

9. Write the biography, in one word or less, about one Richard Milhouse Nixon.

10. Write an essay on a grain of sand.

## Part Six – *Comprehension*
## (circle the choice that correctly identifies the picture)

1.

a. an upside-down M
b. a backwards W
c. a piece of cheese
D. a thing
e. a smelt
f. who cares ?
G. I cares ?
i. Boatman

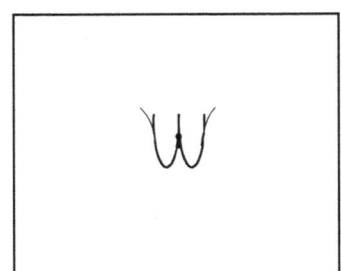

2.

A. the Empire State Building
B. a map of Alaska
c. wood
d. Dee
E. product Dr. Zorch lives for
f. a spaceship
G. a baby's toy
I. Belt, Man

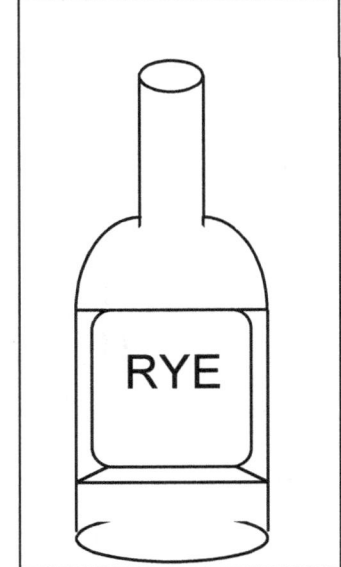

3.

a. dog mess stuff
B. a squashed bug
c. a carrot patch
D. a straight line from you to yesterday
e. the path of a transcontinental tricycle
f. computer diagram of the immigrant crisis
g. the answer to the energy crisis
H. provide your own best answer

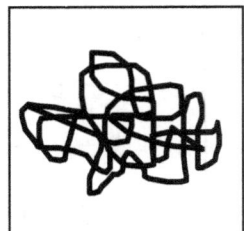

4.

a. a birdie
B. a peace sign
C. a piece sign
D. a pee-pee sign
e. apiece, signed
f. your IQ
G. direction in degrees longitude
i. H

5.

Z. a pansy
Y. a flour
X. a gun
W. a booger
V. a tropical fish
H. daisy chain

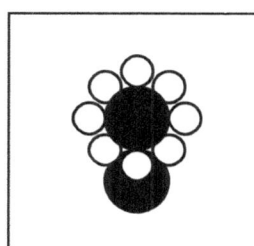

6.

a. a star
b. an asterisk
c. a *
D. a flower
E. a general
f. The Pentagon
g. a diamond-back rattler
I. County Sheriff Sharif

7.
a. Dr. Zorch's prized possession
b. a rubber nickel
C. a nickel rubber
d. SQUARE
e. TRIANGLED
F. this end up
g. top secret
H. foot long hot dog

8.

a. China writing
b. English writin'
c. Greek written
d. Hieroglyphic Rightwing
E. MARS RIGHTY
f. a crock of crap
G. see answer to G39

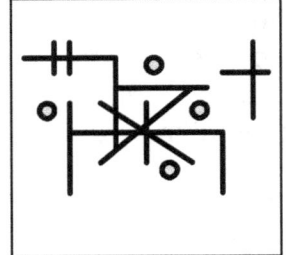

9-10.

A. an orangutan
B. a Circles
c. A BALLS
d. A testes
e. a testicles
f. a nut
g. a pill
g. a scrotum
h. a lieu, hump, scrotum
K. a Tasmanian devil
l. what goes around comes around
S. your IQ
x. your grade on this test
n. the third eye
w. the egg of a retarded dodo bird

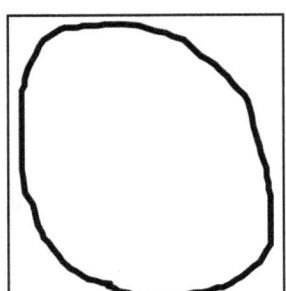

Bonus Item.

a. Reach out and touch someone
b. Reach out in the dork-ness
c. Reach for the stars
d. This is not a true bonus item
e. This is not a true bones item
f. A bone in the hand is not worth two in the bush
g. No bones about it
h. I'm a natural bone lover
i. I'd like to pick a bone with you
j. I'd like to boner you too
k. The hand bone's connected to the ham bone
l. Napoleon, Bone Apart
m. Let your fingers do the walking
n. Let your bone do the talking
o. Bone APPÉTIT
p. Daniel Bones

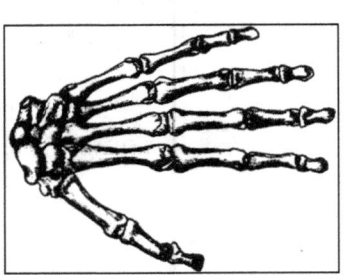

ANTHOLOGY                    ached

# Etiquette Section

## Part One – *Multiple Choice* (circle the correct response)

1.  The correct way to introduce a man and a woman is :
    a.  John Doe meet Jane Doe
    b.  Mrs. Doe meet Miss Doe
    c.  Mr. Doe meet Mistress Doe
    d.  Madame Doe meet your John
    e.  Mr. meet Ms., Mrs., Miss, Mama Doe
    f.  woman meet man, man meet woman
    g.  doe meet stag
    h.  penis meet vagina

2.  A woman should rise when greeting a man only when :
    a.  her girdle is showing
    b.  she isn't wearing any undergarments
    c.  the man is three feet tall or less
    d.  the man is nine feet tall or more
    e.  the man is holding a gun
    f.  the woman is holding a gun
    g.  the woman is holding the man's gun
    h.  the man is sitting down

3.  A man should rise when :
    a.  his pants fall down
    b.  he has to piss again
    c.  he sits on a tack
    d.  his girlfriend has had enough
    e.  his girlfriend is waiting in the missionary position

4.  At a wedding reception, the groom should spend his time :
    a.  is it beside his wife or beside his mistress
    b.  is it on top of his wife or under the table
    c.  getting acquainted with the female guests
    d.  shaking hands
    e.  shaking fists
    f.  asking his father-in-law for money
    g.  making out in the back seat
    h.  hog-tying his mother-in-law
    i.  wouldn't you like to know

5.  A bread-and-butter letter should be written :
    @.  on toast
    #.  on toilet tissue
    $.  in green
    %.  in blood
    &.  to the grocery store
    *.  to the mortuary
    +.  by the bride
    /.  by the milkman
    ).  by the bank

6. In a business letter, a woman should sign herself as :
     a. M. Doe                                    4. Jed Clamp It
     b. Old Mother Hubbard                         h. Aunt Jemima
     c. Madame Doe                                 i. Buckwheat
     d. Doe Dee Doe                                8. is it bitch or butch
     e. Ms. Smiff                                  k. a good Catholic always does
     f. Piggy Zilchman (Ziggy's wife)              l. if she wrote the letter herself

7. Which is the most formal way to open a letter :
     a. Dear Miss Bigham
     b. My Dear Miss Bigham
     c. Dear Bigham
     d. Eat my Bigham
     e. Dear Sir Bigham
     f. Tyrus Goon is a Fizz

8. What does RSVP mean ?
     a. Roman Senators are Very Peculiar
     b. Rotate Seven Vampires Painfully
     c. Raccoons, Skunks, Voles, and Possums
     345. Royal Service for Visiting Penguins
     e. Rob Someone if Vacating the Premises
     f. The Rolling Stones are Virtual Psychotics
     9. Rapists Seldom Violate Porcupines

9. A man should ask a woman to dance only :
     a. if she doesn't want to dance with him, even if he was the last man on Pluto
     b. if she is married to someone else but likes to fool around
     c. if he brought a broom
     d. if he plans to take her to his apartment, or is it her apartment
     e. if he plans on writing her a bread-and-butter letter
     00. if they don't know how to dance and would like to make fools of themselves
     iii. if she is having her prosthetic limb overhauled, or is it broken in

10. Should a boy ask a girl for a date who is interested in someone else ?
     a. yes, if she likes to fool around
     b. yes, if he is married to her
     c. yes, if she wants to make someone jealous
     44. yes, if he wants to get something
     T. yes, if he likes to fight
     G. no, if she asked him first
     6. no, if she is married to the district attorney
     P. no, if she put out for Lxx Vyshniff
     5. no, if she is dead

11. A tuxedo is considered appropriate dress only when :
   a. underpants are worn on the outside
   b. trousers are optional
   c. a penguin gives the okay
   5. accompanied by moccasins
   6. a hand-me-down from Dr. Zorch
   56. his fly is open and he is waving his flag

12. A boy scout should help a granny cross the street when :
   a. the traffic is heavy
   b. her seeing eye dog has been run over
   c. she doesn't want to cross but he needs the merit badge
   d. the granny is horny and the scout is desperate

13.78329480663819. When going for a stroll with a woman, the man should :
   a. walk on the curb side
   b. walk on the curb
   c. walk in the street
   16. walk down the center isle of traffic
   d. walk on the grass
   e. smoke the grass
   f. walk three steps behind the woman, or is it in front
   g. jog in place

## Part Two – *Fill in the Blank*

### (for the following items, put "F" for fork, "S" for spoon, "K" for knife, "R" for rake, "P" for pick, "T" for tongue, or "Fingers" for fingers)

1. Asparagus boiled in buttermilk is eaten with _____.

2. Rhubarb and broccoli salad is not eaten without _____.

3. Platypus pufrye is eaten from _____.

4. Glue is eaten _____.

5. Bugs are never eaten under _____.

6. Scummy slime balls are not eaten in absence of _____.

7. Fox pee can be drunk with _____.

8. Greasy, grimy, gopher guts are seldom eaten during _____.

9. Mutilated monkey meat, marinated in murky mire mandates _____.

10. An orgasm is eaten with _____.

# Part Three – *True or False*

## (indicate the correct response with a "T" or "F")

1. A woman should never remove her overalls when attending a shower.

2. A woman should bring her own shampoo when attending a shower.

3. A woman should remove her battle boots and pistol belt when attending a sauna.

4. A woman should always remove her clothes when attending a love-in.

7. A woman should remove her helmet when attending a hockey game.

8. A woman should never remove her sombrero when sexually assaulting a chili pepper.

9. A woman must salute a man of her own age.

10. A man must perform a scratch-and-sniff test on every date.

11. A man should always remove his jock strap when attending the dry cleaners.

12. Men must remove their rubbers when attending an abortion clinic.

13. A man does not have to remove his goggles and snorkel when attending an orgy.

14. A man must remove a woman when attending her funeral.

15. A man must remove a woman when his wife gets home.

16. A man must remove his pants when requested by a woman.

17. A man must shave his nuts when requested by a squirrel.

18. A wolf must not share his bone with a dog unless that dog is a total bitch.

19. A vampire must not bite a woman who is in her period.

20. The person inventing this examination is sick.

21. The person taking this examination is sick.

22. Everybody else is sick.

23. I am sick, you are sick, everyone is sick, sick; Old MacDonald bought the farm, E-I-E-I-O.

# Part Four – *Marking*

## (Check-mark the situations in which improper etiquette is being employed.)

1. Blowing your nose at the dinner table using the hostess's fine linen napkins.

2. Providing bacon sandwiches, hot dogs, and pork rinds to munch on at a Bar Mitzvah for the rabbi's son.

3. Displaying your filthy soiled underwear during Flag Day.

4. Placing your used sanitary napkin in a Salvation Army collection box.

5. Coughing up a green loogie on the Pope's hand as you attempt to kiss his ring.

6. Wearing a tank top, cut-offs, and sandals to the Presidential Banquet.

7. Spitting on each hamburger you make at a fast food eatery.

8. Squeezing your pimples during your business presentation to corporate executives.

9. Throwing up on your date as he attempts to steal a good night kiss.

10. Farting aloud during a wedding ceremony.

11. Sneezing repeatedly over a salad bar, then wiping your nose on the lettuce.

12. Combing your hair in an operating room.

13. Asking a door salesman for free samples and a $50 loan.

14. Urinating in the punchbowl at an office party for VIPs.

15. Laughing hysterically during a funeral.

16. Inviting your clergyman over to watch skin flicks.

17. Throwing rotten tomatoes at a New Year's Day parade procession.

18. Asking a homeless person if he can spare some change.

19. Dumping your garbage in the neighbor's swimming pool.

20. Leaving a dirty dripping diaper in a public wash basin.

21. Singing the *Star Spangled Banner* at a Muslim mosque.

22. Flicking boogers at a substitute teacher.

23. Leaving anonymous phone calls on your own answering machine.

24. Cleansing yourself in the neighbor's birdbath.

25. Shaving your underarms at the theater.

# Chapter Two

## Lessons in Idiocy – Program of Instruction

~~~~~~~~~~~~~~~~~~~~~~~~~~~~~~~~~~~~~~~~~~~~~~~~~~~~~~~~~~~~~~~~

Lessons in Civics, Philosophy, Mathematics, Science, Engineering, and Literature are provided. You will find these lessons invaluable and unvalued. At the end of the lessons, retake the previous examination and compare your answers to your entry-level scores. If this doesn't make you feel stupid, nothing will. You will realize that you now have been duped into becoming the ultimate nincompoop. You will become overwhelmed with pride and motivation. You will definitely want to continue your studies in the art of idiocy for years to come, until your mind is entirely devoid of any semblance of reasoning.

Once you have completed the entire course on obtuseness, you will have earned the equivalent of a doctorate degree in Imbecilic Theology. Impress your friends with your newfound scatterbrain; they will surely consider you to be the dimwitted dolt you have striven to become. People will undoubtedly ask you to school them on the intricacies of inanity so that they too can become deliriously dopey like yourself. But don't let this go to your head, or you may replace the emptiness that is already there.

Disclaimer: *Middle Leg Society* members and their escorts may test out of the Civics Lesson if they have completed the final phase of initiation and indoctrination (i.e., if they have reached the 33 1/3 level of climax or above). To test out, you must be able to score 33 1/3 times within the next three periods; otherwise menstruation will likely prohibit any further participation as a blood brother or sister, and dismemberment will result. Remember, members, you must renew your membership by placing your third leg candidate into the squeeze box before the new moon, or there will be an additional charge. Escorts may come for free as many times as they wish. And please, support your local 4-F Club.

# Civics Lesson: Dr. Zorch's Believe it or Bust

The following is a lesson in civics, based on obscure events from world history and geography. Not only are the phenomena absolutely, positively, unquestionably, indubitably true, but they are extraordinarily trivial. Dazzle your friends with these little-known facts; and, believe it, or...

Prince, Duke, General, Professor, Doctor, Reverend Paul A. Poopdeck the 9th made a key from his deceased wife Crawdad. It was a skeleton key, of course. The key opened his vault of bile salts tablets.

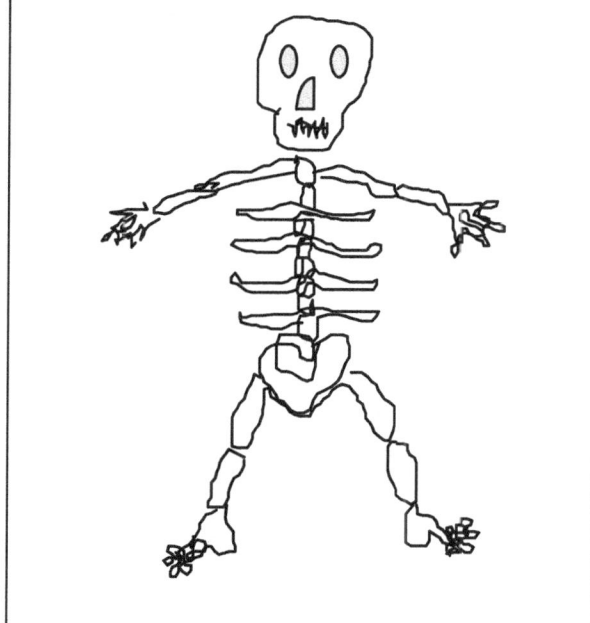

This ant hill in Ramratty, Ireland is made entirely out of ants.

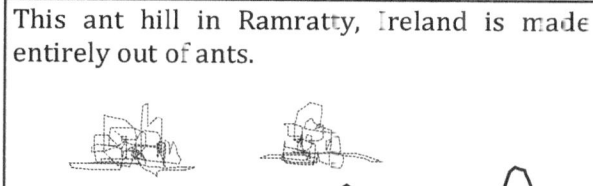

This natural stone formation in Eraserville, Swaziland was made entirely by man.

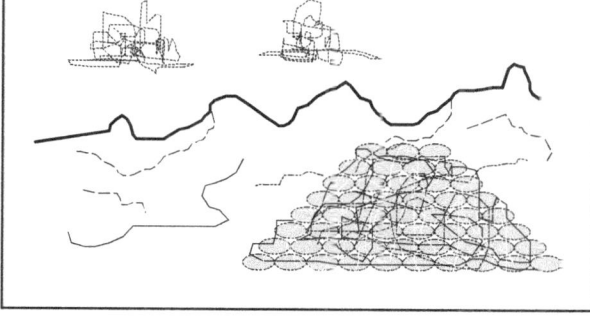

Corobi Tribes in Sockeetoomee, Lithenburg make their fifteen-year-old youths stretch four hairs on their heads until they are exactly as long as their erection. Of course, the males with the longest, straightest bangs are considered a prize catch among the females of his harem. The penalty for fudging is wearing togas without athletic support. As legend has it, this can get quite hairy at times.

Bullwinkle T. Irvington the IIIIII was so convinced that he could not defecate properly, that he pulled out a revolver and shot himself in the butt. Later, he puked up the bullet. It had traveled through his intestines. Bowel movement was restored.

Long John Silver got his name from Ichabod Doolittle, the shoemaker. Ichabod provided specially made tennis shoes to the famous pirate, said to be size 19B.

King Claude the Clyde III was so superstitious, on his thirteenth birthday he threw up in his oatmeal.

sick team

Gruesome, Formosa is the only city with 222 members, yet it doesn't have a population. Newspapers in Gruesome do not provide the news, they only have lines on them.

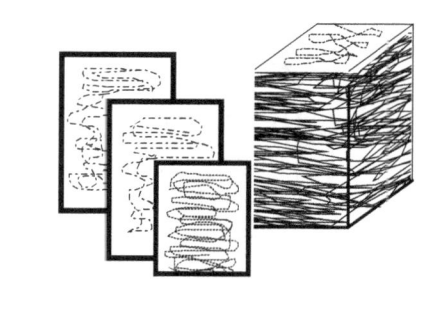

In Crawvittle, Spitland on the Island of Ubawangy, the letters "WORD" mean "Your Grandmother wears combat boots." Thus, nobody says a word in Ubawangy, or it will be taken as an insult. So WORD to you; and good day.

**WORD**

Dracula X. Foxx, of Gaytowria, Queensland was born on his ass.

Boris ("Dad") Farmer of Nebraska, Illinois accidentally shot himself in the toe while cleaning his Lugar. When he took his shoe off, his toe fell out of the shoe and Boris keeled over dead.

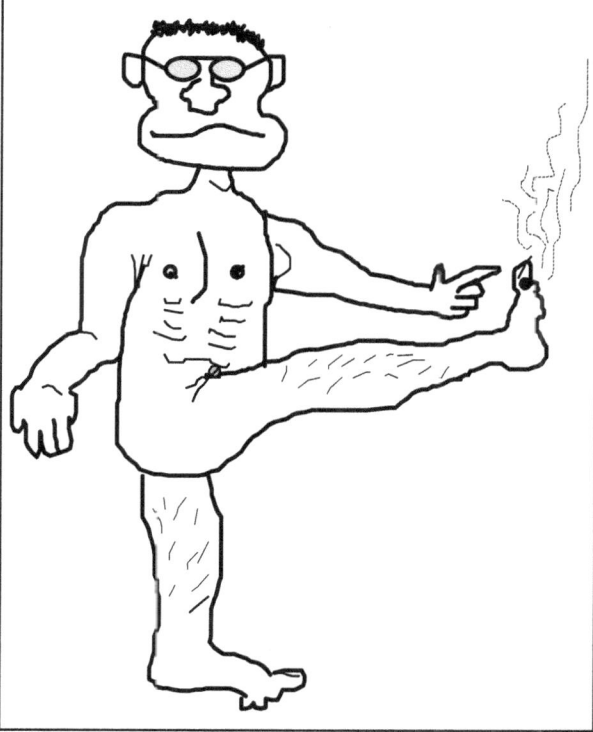

Did you know that a hummingbird does not hum when it has been squashed? Coincidentally, this is also the only way to spay an ant.

Noug Vadren was expelled from the Monastery of Her Golden Streams for losing his 68th antelope.

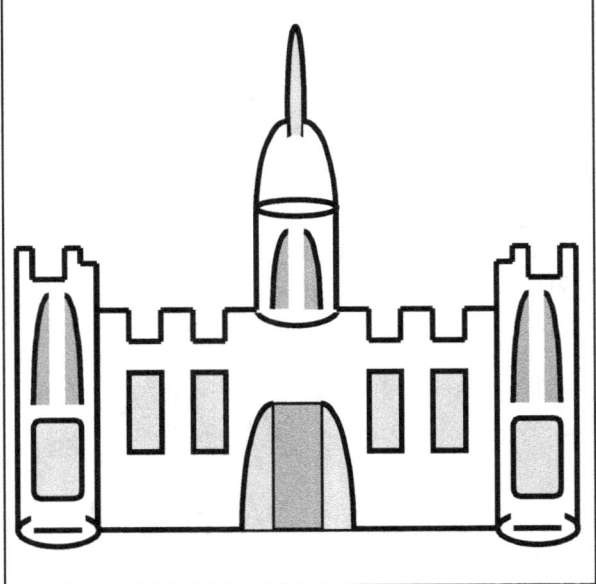

Czar Ivanivov Kobonov Rippov of Kamchatka ruled from six o'clock to eight o'clock on February 30, 1299. He was the longest reigning czar ever to rule that region, and still have time to get in a game of sploshtzky.

Nero K. Pus, from Dogwood, Pennsyltucky has been the only one to make a seventy-foot clay dinosaur since 1427.

Ebeneezer Disraeli of Deadguts, Afghanistan has a store featuring Disraeli Idiocies. (He comes from a long line of Disraeli idiots). It is the only store in the world that serves grits pie.

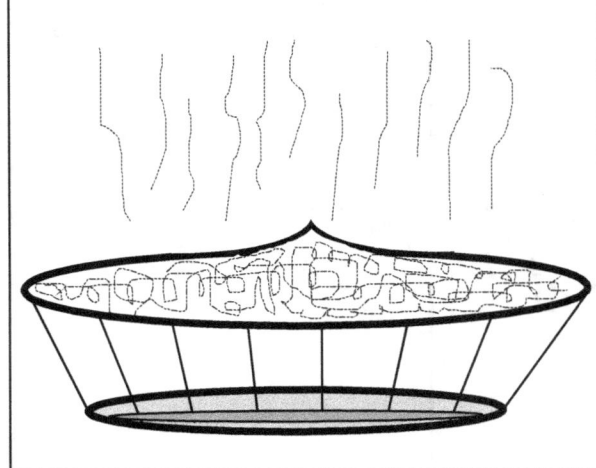

Stamps from Yugovakia bring the highest value known to collectors. There has only been one stamp ever made there, in a small town called Kimchowsk. The stamp is made out of pulverized opossum pelts.

The sign for pi in Hillybilly Yokum Center, in Pottsdam, Arkantstandus means "Big Deal." This is the same symbol used as a logo for the convention center in Pottsdam, as well as the emblem adorning City Hall. Thus, we can arrive at one and only one conclusion.

P. P. Peabody of Crapperton Straits, South Disgusta was the first person to actually observe a snake taking a dump. It was documented in the year 1902, and the specimen still resides in the Smythstonian Institute.

If you pet a cat 9,086,483 times, you will generate enough electricity to kill the cat (Not recommended for people over the age of sixty-nine).

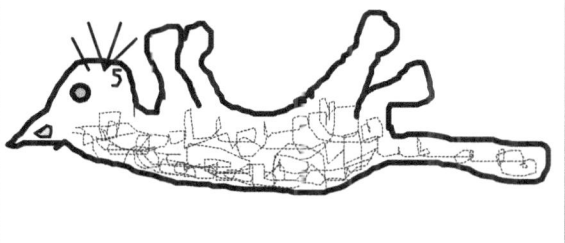

This painting by O.T. Fudd was intended to be a portrait of F.D.R. Fudd considered the famous president to be a nut, so he painted a walnut. He traced this pattern off the wall.

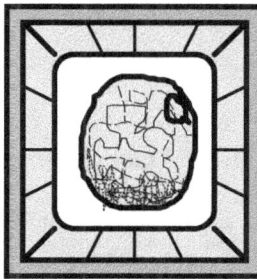

# Bonus Item: Double Dog Dares:

"What're you burning kid?" "My neighbor's dog." "What fur?" "He's protesting the visit from the shah."

"Don't flush the cat down the toilet." "But she's not letting me use the cat box."

Apply to patent the rat lift.

Ask the attendant to dry clean your hamster.

Go to work at a new international cuisine cafeteria. Place this sign outside: We Serve Pets: teriyaki dog, parakeet parmesan, and cat meat flautas. When you come to work, put on a grass skirt and place your dog in the microwave. Use a piece of bread to wipe the tables. If someone asks "what's the deal" tell them, "I know what I'm paid to do."

Pop a guy's hood as he waits at the traffic light if he drives an older model car. Remove the distributor cap; shut the hood. Go to the window and present it to the driver, demanding, "That'll be five dollars."

Take a dump in the back of a new pickup truck; leave a quarter there. If a pedestrian begins to protest answer, "It's a rental."

Take your family to any chapel displaying a steeple; go dressed up in a collar like the pastor. When greeted, order chicken.

"Do you serve undocumented aliens here?" "Yep." "Bring one for my alligator, please" Waiter rips someone from their seat and dumps them on the floor.

Empty an ashtray on the sidewalk. "Looks like a lot of smoking was done here."

Handmade Indian: Chief Sitting Duck.

Drag-ass (new police show).

Garage Sale: Tell customers you're selling the garage.

Counseling Practice sign: We use only genuine pine 2x4s.

"Can I borrow your handkerchief a moment." Wipe crotch with it.

Tell the judge he looks like a frog, so he must be ready to croak.

Develop new dog food product made from dogs, eaten by people. Advertisement: "How about a steaming thick bowl of pooch?"

New product: Box in a box pussy powder, just add lubrication.

Do a science class project on your anus, or is it urinesque, or you rain piss, or that planet named after some god.

Spot a cop: follow the patrol car to the traffic light. Pin tail on car bumper and kick like a donkey.

Xmas presents: stovepipe for dad, car muffler for mom. Clang.

Put sticky note on menu: Special today is fur burger. Tell waitress, "I'll have this."

ANTHOLOGY                                   twiney

# Philosophy Lesson: The Prophecies of Nosdriponus

The infamous philosopher Vomitian Nosdriponus lived during the thirteenth century in the region currently known as Vatican City. Exiled from his native Crete for his outrageous predictions, he became the mentor and educator of a passel of Greek and Roman philosophers, scientists, monks, and chimps. Many of his profound works have been discovered recently by amateur archaeologists in caves near the Adriatic Sea, funded under the auspices of the Dr. Zorch Foundation. A remarkable number of his prophecies have been found to be false, but some actually came true.

A serendipitous finding was the amount of surprise predictions applicable to 21st century man. While many have yet to come true, you will, without a doubt, be flabbergasted at the insight and unmitigated impertinence evident in this seer's revelations.

These Prophecies of Nosdriponus have been paraphrased in modern English.

------------------------------------------------------------------------

I had a dream about a new religion called Boot Ball, practiced on a field of false grass by men of extraordinary stature. I see them dressed in exotic garments, doing one of two opposite things: attempting to cream the other worshippers, or giving them a warm embrace, often followed by a pat on the buttocks. Every so often the members will stand in a circle and tell dirty jokes. They applaud whenever the joke is a good one. Frequently they will chant and pray, sometimes kneeling and other times falling prostrate on the ground. The synagogue bears a giant sideways cross at either end. They worship a ball that looks like a water buffalo dropping; this ball serves as an object of the opposing emotions of affection and disdain. The elders often fight over possession of it, making love to it if they can; or they give it a giant toss, and sometimes, the great boot. The congregations change their names every few years, but the idols they adore always remain constant. I have seen temples with the following unusual names.

| | |
|---|---|
| Buffalo *Rams* | New York *Cowboys* |
| Baltimore *Cardinals* | Beverly Hills *Bills* |
| Detroit *Oilers* | San Francisco *Packers* |
| Saint Louis *Saints* | Washington *Stealers* |
| Indiana *Chiefs* | Los Angeles *Browns* |
| Phoenix *Dolphins* | Green Bay *Buccaneers* |
| Tampa Bay *Buffaloes* | Cleveland *Beavers* |
| Miami *Forty-Niners* | Tennessee *Yankees* |
| Philadelphia *Texans* | Canadian *Patriots* |

------------------------------------------------------------------------

I see games being played by people of all genders, ages, and nationalities. These games are usually played alone, but often they are played by several males simultaneously.

| | |
|---|---|
| Pinching a Loaf | Hocking a Loogie |
| Draining the Lizard | Hunching a Wizz |
| Springing a Leak | Dumping a Major Load |
| Grinding a Grunt | Fertilizing the Fauna |
| Bleeding the Bologna | Purging the Pooper |
| Blowing the Ballast | Liquidating the Assets |

I see men and women engaging in a number of silly adult pastimes with funny titles (listed below). Any number of men, women, and animals are allowed to participate. Further, the activity can be executed in solitaire (usually by the male of the species). Different props and equipment are employed in strange circumstances. Players often assume positions that require considerable agility and dexterity.

| | |
|---|---|
| Spank the Monkey | Bite the Beaver |
| Slam the Salami | Blow the Man Down |
| Jerk My Crank | Flog the Floozie |
| Pack the Pork | Choke the Chicken |
| Corn Hole the Heifer | Crank the Cockatoo |
| Shake Your Bacon | Squeeze the Lemon |
| Pound the Pud | Eat at the Y |
| Bust a Nut | Whack Your Jack |
| Juice the Rooster | Pulverize the Pecker |

---

I see large groups of human beings crowded around a glass box; I believe it is referred to as a Tubular Boob. A small man is inside the box, pointing to his head; this man must be an instructor. Three miniature people sit at a table pounding on a plate of rhubarb. They are taking an examination that will promote them to a higher position in the box. Contestants attempt to ask questions for which the answers are already supplied. The test categories are different every day, which include the following.

| | |
|---|---|
| Four Letter Words | Beatniks and Hippies |
| Famous Idiots | Double Dog Dares |
| Biting Beavers | Dead Letters |
| Religious Fanatics | Aardvarks and Anteaters |
| Memorable Highs | Lawsuits and Rip-offs |
| Bloopers and Gotchas | Prophecies of Nosdriponus |
| Favorite Martians | Presidential Scandals |
| Vice and Advice | Device and Crevice |
| Fairs and Affairs | Balls, Balloons, and Baboons |
| Tough Titties | Bassoons and Buffoons |
| Untold Secrets | Sassy Assassins |
| Guttersnipes | Daily Doubles |
| The Grim Reaper | Dimwits and Dolts |

---

DR. ZORCH'S IDIOCIES

# Signs Indicating the End of Times

I have determined that in those days there will be fifteen different words or phrases that describe the act of vomiting. The same will be true regarding the act of pharting.

Astonishing assassination assignments are allowed as an approved and aesthetic activity. (Interpretation: Murder will be permitted under most circumstances.)

The authoritative chain of command will be determined by penis size. Note: Women will be among the highest-ranking officials.

The most common occupation will be getting paid to do nothing. The less a person works, the more they will earn. This will be particularly true for those who are employed by the government.

Slow, selective, or secondary suicide serves certain citizens as a source of security and serenity. (Also, an altruistic activity among adolescents.)

---

Nosdriponus foresaw a new nation of various races, kindreds, creeds, and colors. He determined that the world would be integrated into a single military and economic power. Anyone could run for public office, as indicated in his vision (below) showing the candidates for supreme ruler at the dawn of the 22nd century.

---

A number of Nosdriponus's visions were recorded by his loyal scribe and illustrator, Inormus Ignoramus (Iggy). A few are recreated below.

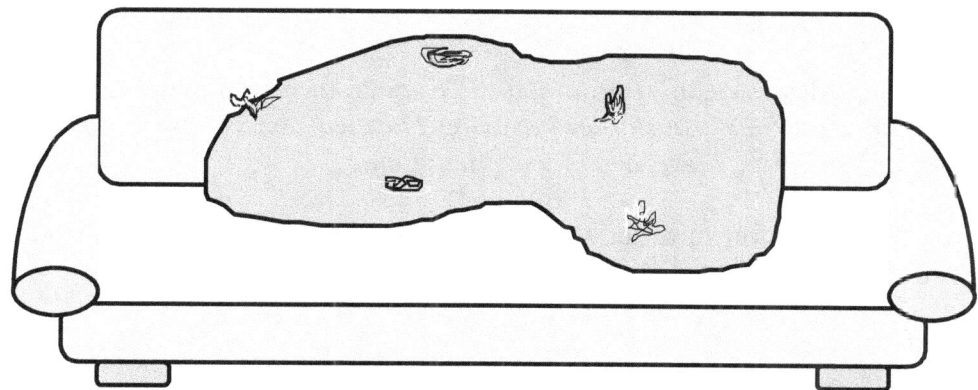

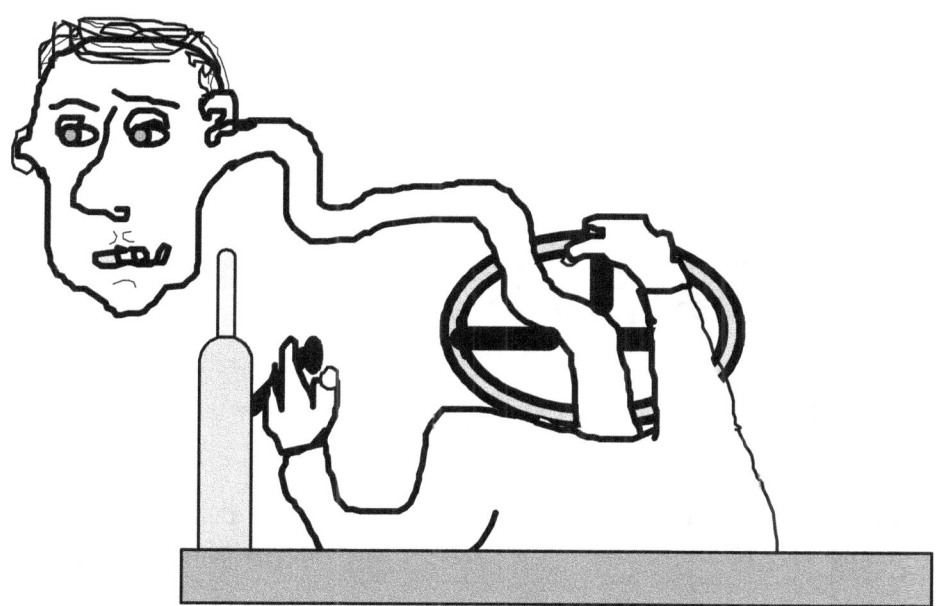

No doubt you will agree; not only were his prophecies incredibly profound, they also were downright absurd. The contributions Nosdriponus never made to the field of epistemology likely will not be unforgotten for no more centuries to pass, not to mention the lifetime of a cocoon.

# Mathematics Lesson: Theory and Application

Metaphysical Mathematics with emphasis on Trigono-calculo-algetry.

-----------------------------------------------------------------------------------------------------

1. The great Ludicrous Alexei Vestovft proposed the original theory of simplification in 1678 as follows: *The only possible translation involving clarified conclusion is remaining in a state of discomfort to confirm a leverage of incapacitation.*

2. In 1724, Tyrus Qat Simpleton surmised that, if Vestovft was correct, then it follows that the formula for velocity can be simplified into five easy steps, as follows:

$$\frac{\sum (472 \times \text{Latitude})^3 + \overline{(4\sqrt{72.8}\ \pi)} - \text{Longitude} = \overline{8\sqrt{S}}}{\text{Circumference of Uranus when Venus is in Sagittarius}}$$

$$\frac{\beta\,(S+67.9823) \times [\,(380 + \pi + (\text{Radius of Neptune})\ {+\!/\!-}\ 72\,]}{\text{Speed of Transylvanian Vampire Bat Heading West at Dusk}}$$

$$\frac{T\{[(2.33 \times 4\pi)^3 \times .002] + \sqrt{14.3} + (S^2\sqrt{6969})\} - 94839}{\text{Speed of Impala with Hyena on its back}} = N/\infty$$

$$\frac{N - [(49+8)\sqrt{89/\pi}\,] + [(447 - \text{Windage}) \times (7\sqrt{7})\,]^7}{92929292929292929292929} = Z^3$$

$$L + 29 = V^2 = \text{Velocity}^2$$

3. Zid Sklitz-Blrdnitz, in 1967 at the age of fourteen, determined that the result shows velocity equal to –0.29 so the original equation by Simpleton must be incremented by a factor of 11.110011.

4. Dr. Zorch updated the theory; his findings appear in the current *Journal of 71st Grade Arithmetic*. He concluded that Vestovft, who was off by a factor of $0^{-9}$, was wrong; so his theory must be discarded.

5. Application: Employ this theory arithmetically to describe a major cataclysm in your life.

   Send submissions for proposed publication of your properly applied mathematical proof.

# Psychology Lesson: Optical Illusions

Which is the longest, AB or BC? Did you guess AB? Well you are wrong, because neither is the longest. AC is, in fact, the longest.

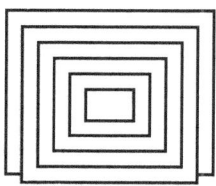

How many squares are there in this picture? Did you count six? Well you are wrong again, because none of the above figures are squares.

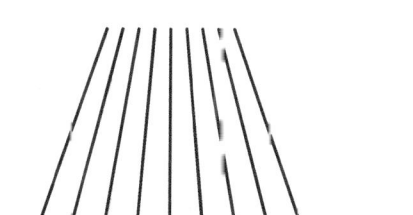

Are any of these lines parallel? You don't think so? Well, you are wrong again. The <u>vertical</u> ones might not be, but the <u>horizontal</u> ones used as <u>underlines</u> are parallel.

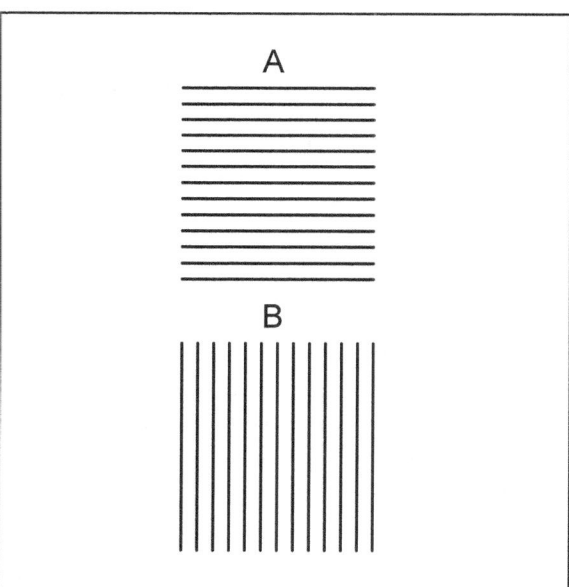

B appears to be longer than A doesn't it? Well measure it, and you will see that it is.

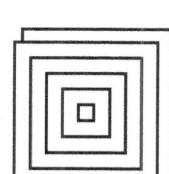

How many squares are there in this picture? Did you count six? Well you are wrong, wrong, wrong; because there are eight. You forgot to count the one surrounding this text box, not to mention the invisible one appearing as an afterimage.

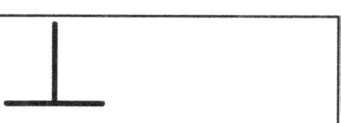

Is this as tall as it is high? Well, of course it is, tall *is* high.

# Biology Lesson: Fundamentals of Discovery
## Topic 504A The Alligator Lizard

### HISTORY

Being one of the living reptiles from the Jurassic period, the Alligator Lizard spends the majority of its time eating. The basic diet consists of tern excrement, llama upchuck, sphinxes, and anything it can get its hands on.

This creature should not be confused with its cousin, the Crocodile Chameleon, which is a descendant of the Alligator Lizard. There are some distinct differences between the two. For example, while the diet of the two reptiles is similar, the Crocodile Chameleon draws the line when it comes to tern excrement.

Below is a diagram of the Alligator Lizard Rex species, which has been dated as far back as the year 100,000 B.C. The illustration is drawn to 1/2 scale of actual dimensions.

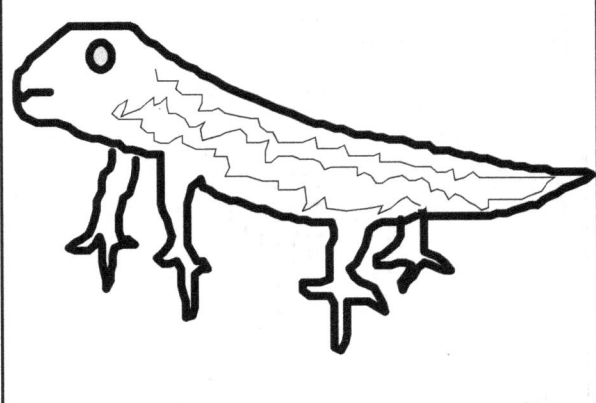

In this diagram we see a close-up of the Alligator Lizard's mouth. This feature is the single, most positively identifying characteristic distinguishing the species from all other reptilians.

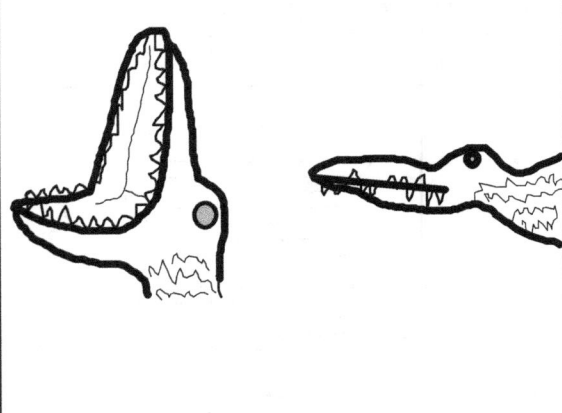

Be sure to stay tuned for our next feature presentation when we will be studying the evolution of the hilarious laughing hyena. It's a positively howling experience as we carouse with the crazy canine impersonators while they frolic with feisty ferrets in a quagmire of quaking quicksand.

Keep in mind that animals are never harmed during the shooting of our film. This, however, is not the case during any pee shooter operations. Thank you all so much for your contributions which help us to maintain quality programming like our nature series. It's people like you that make the world so nice. We just love you to pieces. You are so intelligent and beautiful. Please donate another $100 at your convenience to keep quality programming like this on the air.

# Engineering Lesson: The QRZ-2575LV Countertrap Engine

## (Designed by Grossly B. Dilk, 1971)

**Control Steering Lead Stick Assembly**

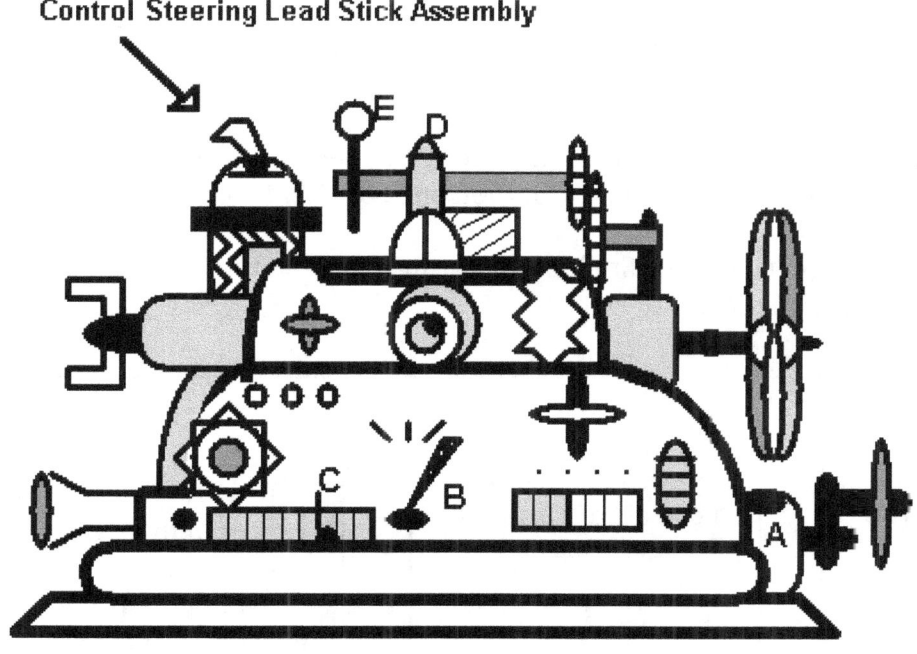

Engine Ignition Procedures

(please refer to diagram above for reference points)

1. Squeeze 1/2 ounce of Type FID manipulating fluid into the Exhaust Manipulation Grease Fitting (A).

2. Verify that the Sprocket Readjusting Lean Arm (B) is in its most forward position.

3. Make positively sure that the Crankcase Lubrication Indicator Gauge (C) is on "Normal," or add six oz. of Muffoil into the water reservoir.

4. Press the Recoil Vulcanizing Igniter Switch (D) while holding the Backfire Modulating Tolerance Ring (E) all the way out.

# Control Steering Lead Stick Assembly Procedures

(refer to diagrams below and on the previous page).

1. Inspect the Control Steering Lead Stick to ensure it is exactly 1/4 inches more than the two left-hand sides.

2. Align Control Steering Lead Stick (A) with Control Steering Lead Stick Retaining Hole (B).

3. Push Control Steering Lead Stick into Control Steering Lead Stick Retaining Hole verifying that it is completely forward; then back off 1/4 inches.

4. **Secure Control Steering Lead Stick by inserting Control Steering Lead Stick Retaining Hole Guide Pin (C) from left to right.**

Right View of
Control Steering
Lead Stick

1/4 inch

Configuration Diagram of
Control Steering Lead
Stick Assembly

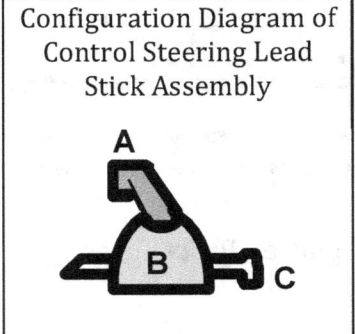

WARNING: Ensure assembly is executed in accordance with performance standards. If Retaining Pin is inserted from right to left the engine will blow upon ignition.

Note: Use Formula DD116 Glycerin-Quinine made by Cilstex Manufacturing of Podunk, Ohio for use in lubricating Vestlid Operating Contlest. Danger: Do not use Glycerin-Quinine manufactured by Haberdashery Chemicals of Flurffield, Ohio, or risk of death will be certain for the next operator to start the engine (Control Steering Lead Stick will be jettisoned).

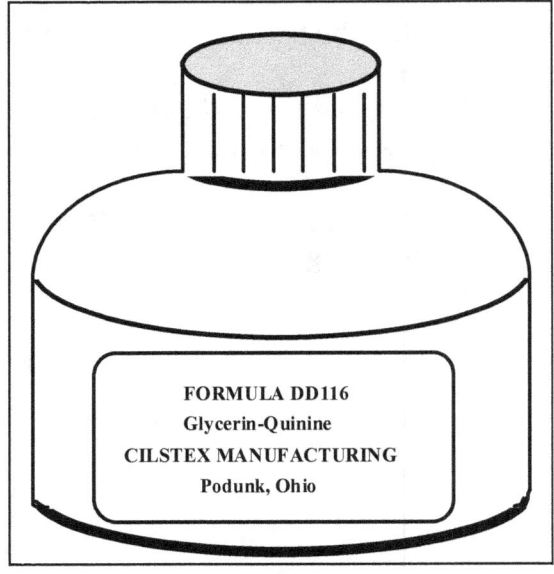

FORMULA DD116
Glycerin-Quinine
CILSTEX MANUFACTURING
Podunk, Ohio

# ADDENDUM TO R-278
## FORM AA64 / CLASS B – PART O

# MODIFICATION GUIDE AND LOG BOOK FOR
# QRZ-2575LV COUNTERTRAP ENGINE

| No. | Stock No. & Item | Oil | Gas | Water | Miles | Defects | Status Symbol | Signature |
|---|---|---|---|---|---|---|---|---|
| 1 | #483 Cylinder Class Z-Bar | 1/2 | 0 | 1 | 33 | Loose | ☼ | *J J Fudd* |
| 2 | #117 Scorch Plate Carburetion Tensioner | 1/3 | 2 | 1 | 76 | Busted | | *me* |
| 3 | #88 Slip Fastening Chassis Lasp | 1/4 | 1 | 9 | 89 | Missing | ? | *Duck Muck* |
| 4 | #9428376 Pushpull Counterbalance Alignment Bushing | 1/9 | 9 | 0 | 44 | In 14 Pieces | ☺ | *Dill Bund* |
| 5 | #1009 Vestlid Operating Contlest | 1/8 | 0 | 9 | 45 | In Podunk for repairs | | *MANDRAKE MARPLE* |
| 6 | #336 Engine Block | 1/7 | 8 | 9 | 46 | Rotten to the Core | | *tom trix* |

## Comments from the Peanut Gallery

1. Class Z-Bar is in constant disarray
2. Underwear in Carburetor
3. Lasp stolen during preventative maintenance checks and services
4. Person inventing this form was insane
5. Person reading this form is insane
6. Insane until further notice

DR. ZORCH'S IDIOCIES

# Liberal Arts Lesson: Musicians

See if you can identify the classical artists responsible for the following lyrical scores (voted best modern lyrics last year).

"I jumped him, I pumped him, I humped him, and I dumped him."

"I played her, I ate her, I laid her, and I paid her."

"I made her get my gator and I weighed her taters later."

"I was goin' down to Hong Kong, gonna play some ping-pong, uh huh.
I met her watching King Kong, staring at his long dong, uh huh.
She was longing for the wrong song trying to get her gong rung, uh huh.
Now I'm swingin' my ying-yang, singin' bout a gang-bang, uh huh."

"I'm dreaming of a black mistress. Just like the one in Kokomo.
Where she would peek out, and I would sneak out, to make mama buck and crow."

"Oh Mickey, he's so tricky, I'm so icky for his dickey.
Oh Mickey, he's so picky, gives me hickeys, licks me, sticks me.
Oh, Oh, Mickey. Yeah, Mickey.
Hey Mickey, take a lookie at my cookie; you're no rookie, have some nookie.
Kinky Mickey, you're so slick, have a quickie, make me kick.
Yay, Mickey! Ooh Ahh, Mickey."

"Crazy Daisy, give me your money, too. I'm so lazy, I will not work for you.
I'll never be sane or stable, or put any food on the table.
But take your place upon my face and you'll know why you said I do."

"Nobody likes me, everybody hates me, I'm gonna eat some worms.
Long, skinny slimy ones; short, fat juicy ones; itsy-bitsy, fuzzy-wuzzy worms.
First you bite the head off, then you suck the guts out. Oh, how they wiggle and squirm.
Long, skinny slimy ones, short fat juicy ones, itsy-bitsy, fuzzy-wuzzy worms."

"Yankee Doodle went to town, looking for a trollop;
Stuck a dollar in her blouse, she gave him quite a wallop.
Yankee Doodle what a dolt, boy he pulled a doozie.
Next time, don't mistake the mayor for some flea-bitten floozie."

## Bonus Item: Name That Artist

## Stupendous Rock and Roll Stars

He began playing at an early age; his parents and grandparents all were talented musicians in their own right. His leap to stardom began in the early '60s, when he led the infamous *Tin Weed*. Later that decade he formed the super-group *Filberts Bottled Inks*, which evolved into *Nemesis*, before reorganizing into *Melted Shelter*. Some of his hit songs have included *Ugly Girls Have Got It Made*, *SOMF*, and *Tease Queen Boogie*. Hint: He is one of the band members portrayed in the live photograph which can be found in the Appendix (reproduced by permission from the Hillmore Auditorium, SW).

## Treasures of World Literature

This series presents the cream-of-the-crop in international prose, poetry, and non-fiction, comprising the top best-sellers of all time. Nowhere in the world has such a wealth of literature been aggregated into such a pleasant potpourri of preposterous poppycock. Delve into the dreamland of dilapidated drivel, from our tasteless treasure trove of intriguing, albeit intrusive, intercourse.

Today's presentation is the blockbuster of modern non-fiction, written by the late Bosco B. Bufferin, and entitled, *To Kill a Burd*. This short story and screenplay can be considered one of many based on actual case files from Sir Samson Floyd Rodneyvelt, private investigator.

You also may want to obtain the other great works available through our "Treasures" program.

*Literary Treasures* are available upon request by sending a self-addressed, stamped envelope, and check or money order for $10 each, to:

> The Dr. Zorch Foundation
> Literary Treasures Series
> P.O. Box Z-70
> Munchkinland, OZ 77777

The following presents a list of outstanding prose available through this series.  No doubt, you will recognize most, if not all, of these legendary gems.

| Title | Author |
|---|---|
| The Teeny-Weeny Bikini | Seymour Hairs |
| Under the Grandstand | Seymour Butts |
| The Ruptured China Man | Won Hung Lo |
| Antlers in the Trees | Hoogoose De Moose |
| The Gilded Stream | I. P. Freely |
| Spot on the Wall | Hugh Flung Dung |
| Lumps in the Road | I. Squatt & U. Leavitt |
| Fifty-Yard Dash to the Outhouse | Willie May Kitt & Bette E. Doendt |
| Advanced Proctology | Drs. Ben Dover & Cray K. Smyle |
| Lesbian Lovers | Lezlie Sweats & Butch Dykes |
| Suicide Skunks | P. U. (Pepe) Le Pew |
| Dream of the Nymph | Won Long Dong |
| My Faithful Wife | Mary A. Skuzbucket |
| Eating Out at the Y | Harry S. Bush & Likki T. Splitz |
| Frigid Women | I. C. Kuntz |
| Fun on the Farm | Ima Hogg |
| The Politician | U. R. Fullervitt |
| Queen of the Corn | Dick Browner & Peter Lipschitz |
| The Procrastinating Pimp | Johnny Come Lately |
| Lucifer's Travels | Miss Bea Hay Van De Mann |
| Tiger's Revenge | Claude Balls |
| Make-Believe Buzzard | Yuplaigh Dedd & I. Lee Tiue |

# To Kill a Burd (by Bosco B. Bufferin)

Finally, the lights dimmed, the curtain was lifted, and the stage lights were illuminated. The audience roared as the announcer walked on stage to introduce the first contestant.

Announcer: And now, to comment on racial strife in Alaska, Mr. Dill Burd. Ladies and gentlemen, Dill Burd.

The crowd applauded as Dill Burd staggered onto the stage. He fiddled with a group of index cards and began...

Dill Burd: My fellow Americans...

All of a sudden, a shot rang out from the bleachers and Mr. Burd bit the floor. General Lovey Lood ran to the front of the stage and announced...

Gen. Lood: Hey, there's been a murder; someone send for the sheriff.

So, someone sent for the sheriff. The sheriff came out on stage with his top-hat and cane, twirling his six-gun. He strolled up to the microphone very casually and uttered...

Sheriff: As sheriff of this continent I would like to send my posse on the case. Ladies and gentlemen, all the way from Alder Blight in North Dobraing, please welcome Sir Samson Floyd Rodneyvelt.

The crowd screamed and cried as Sir Rodneyvelt hit the stage. He maneuvered up to the mike and whispered in a deep voice...

Sir Rodneyvelt: Thank you.

The audience almost died when Sir Rodneyvelt left the stage to chase down the murderer. As he was leaving, Sir Rodneyvelt tripped over the microphone cord, sailed into the corridor, and flew out the window. He landed outside on his bicycle and sped to his office. On the way, he hit a bird.

Sir Rodneyvelt stopped for lunch at Homer Johnson's Funeral Parlor. Homer was the neighborhood mortician and happened to be a good friend of Sir Rodneyvelt.

Homer Johnson: I witnessed the entire tragedy watching television. You are aware of my extensive experience with corpses. Based on my observations I can unequivocally assert that Mr. Burd has certainly kicked the bucket.

Sir Rodneyvelt: Thank you for your expert opinion. Good day.

When Sir Rodneyvelt arrived at his office he reclined on the couch while the psychiatrist took notes. The doctor proclaimed that Sir Rodneyvelt was a paranoid schizophrenic. This made Sir Rod very happy, so he peeled rubber out of there.

It had been a hard day for Sir Rodneyvelt so he went home to bed. He went to sleep thinking it was a distinct possibility that he might awaken. What he did not realize was that he would be drugged in his sleep. Sir Rodney awoke in a purple room with a boiling mad, young fat man drowning him in a bucket of warm spit. Ugh, so gross, ish gruck, mnng brrr, glish ragg gurgh, retch.

If you liked the sound effects, send fifty bills to:

Health and Welfare Corps
Box 2222222223
36-24-36 Lush Street Corner
Bilgewater, Missouri, 493762 Zip

Sir Rodneyvelt knew he could not overpower his opponent so he pretended to be dead. Homer Johnson had taught Sir Rod a most skillful way to accomplish this, and it appeared to work. As the fat man loosened his grip, Sir Rod whipped his elbow around, catching fatso in the eye. Sir Rod grabbed the bucket and sloshed the contents into the fat man's face. Sir Rod hurriedly got his rocks on the run.

When he departed the purple room and entered the hallway, Sir Rod was met by more opposition. Four karate experts were approaching our hero. But Rod was quite familiar with the karate yell. In fact, he screamed so loud the bulb in the light fixture shattered, leaving the hallway in complete darkness. Sir Rod stood perfectly still while the aggressors searched frantically for him. They began fighting amongst themselves while Sir Rodneyvelt escaped. But not for long. He opened the door at the end of the hallway only to find a 155-millimeter howitzer staring him in the face. Rodney reluctantly surrendered.

They took our hero down eight flights of stairs to a large balcony. They tossed Sir Rod over the banister into a fifteen-foot vat of swarming macaroni. Sir Rod attempted to swim, but to no avail. The macaroni was too slippery and he sank to the bottom, as if in quicksand.

The sinister gang scampered away laughing, figuring that the ace detective had finally met his doom. But they underestimated the crafty cognizance of the dauntless dick. He was sitting at the bottom of the vat, entirely breathless, when one large strand of macaroni slapped him in the face sticking to his nose. When Sir Rodney proceeded to jerk it loose, he took a deep breath of air through his nostril. Apparently, this particular noodle was long and hollow, enough to reach the surface of the vat. Sir Rodney sat patiently at the bottom breathing through his noodle.

He was in the simmering vat all day, during which time he thought plenty. He also lost about eight pounds of lard in his backside. Sir Rodneyvelt concluded that he was being held captive in a world-famous pasta manufacturing plant. This plant produced a variety of food products, most notably Dungetti's Spaghetti. Dungetti, Sir Rodney's arch rival, was a top boss in a nationwide crime syndicate. Sir Rod knew that Dungetti would stop at nothing to continue his web of evil.

Finally, the vat of macaroni started moving. After the water was drained, the cooked pasta was poured onto a conveyer for additional processing.

The macaroni would be chopped to shreds before sliding on the conveyor belt into another vat of cheese and tomato sauce. Naturally, as soon as Sir Rodney was dumped, he hopped off to make his getaway. This was not such an easy task, since his sneakers were slippery and he was not accustomed to so much starch in his breeches.

He climbed back up the seven flights of stairs where he noticed a door marked *Top Secret*. He went inside looking for clues, hoping that Burd's murder could be traced directly to Dungetti. Unfortunately, the room had been cleared out recently, except for a file cabinet and a desk.

Sir Rodneyvelt searched the desk and found a book that had been hollowed out. It was entitled *Ebeneezer's Book of Disraeli Idiocies*. Sir Rodney was aware that Ebeneezer had come from a long line of Disraeli idiots. He knew of Ebeneezer's store in Deadguts Afghanistan that was famous for its oddities and relics.

Sir Rodney continued his investigation in the file cabinet. The cabinet was empty except for a single photograph that was stuck inside the front of the top drawer. The photograph was of Huge Heaver and the Bunnies, one of the top rock-and-roll groups of the era. Sir Rodneyvelt surmised that Dungetti had made two grave mistakes in leaving behind these valuable pieces of evidence.

Rod figured there were no more clues to be found at the plant so he hailed a bus and returned to his office to contemplate the situation. On the way, the bus hit a bird.

Rod decided it was time to call his investigating agency and have the laboratory inspect the book and the photograph. He picked up the phone and called, but got a recorded message saying he had dialed a non-working number. He called the operator to determine the problem, well aware that the secret number had worked in the past. The operator informed Sir Rod that there were no working numbers with forty-three digits. Rodney judged that the secret number had been changed.

Sir Rod got off his lazy carcass and went outside and around the corner to the agency. As he arrived, he noticed many of the rookies were practicing with several new classified weapons. He observed as one of the weapons backfired, projecting a bean in the rookie's right eyeball. Sir Rodney scolded the novice.

Sir Rodneyvelt: You are very fortunate that you were using blank rounds of ammunition.

Sir Rod was showing the rookie the correct way of firing the shooter when Bull Dinky, head of the agency, came downstairs to meet him. They both went to Bull's secret office, which doubled as the local sandbox. Rod was wrapping up the explanation of his daring escape from Dungetti when the lab technician, Lynx Filtzhouser, returned with the results of his forensic experiments.

Lynx Filtzhouser: The copy of Ebeneezer's book is an original, of which only nineteen are in circulation. The only thing unusual about the photo of the Bunnies is that it is not recent. One of the band members in this photo quit the group last year.

Sir Rodneyvelt: Which one?

Lynx Filtzhouser (pointing): This man here.

Sir Rodneyvelt: I recognize that man, he's Dracula X. Foxx, a hit man for Dungetti. He also plays bongos on the side.

Bull Dinky: But why would Dungetti want Dill Burd dead? And why would anyone hollow out an original copy of Ebeneezer's book? It doesn't add up.

Sir Rodneyvelt: I think I'll go to Afghanistan and pay our friend Ebeneezer Disraeli a visit.

Bull Dinky: Have a nice trip.

A trip is what Sir Rodneyvelt got all right. As he was boarding the plane, he was stung by a bee that was high on pollen. Immediately, Sir Rod was thrown into a world of kaleidoscopic turmoil. Psychedelic fiascoes burned a ruby hole in his corpus callosum. Rod was weary when he disembarked, informing the pilot...

Sir Rodneyvelt: This has been the worst flight I have ever been on, and the last time I ever fly Afghan Airlines.

Rod left in a huff. He boarded the bus for Deadguts, arriving late in the afternoon. Indeed, the bus hit a bird along the way. Rod took it as an omen. Ebeneezer was closing up shop when Sir Rod appeared. Rodney was surprised to see all the interesting things which Eb had collected throughout the years. As Rod was deep in wonder, he was shocked out of his stupor by Ebeneezer himself.

Ebeneezer: May I help you sir?

Sir Rod showed Eb the vintage private investigator's badge he had acquired years earlier from a box of creamed wheat.

Sir Rodneyvelt: Affirmative. I am interested in your book of idiocies, published last year.

Ebeneezer: Ah, yes. I already have sold nineteen copies.

Sir Rodneyvelt: I would like to see a list of those who purchased the book.

Ebeneezer: As you wish.

Sir Rodneyvelt (inspecting the list): Who are these people?

Ebeneezer: They are all relatives of mine except one.

ANTHOLOGY

Sir Rodneyvelt: Of course, Mr. Dill Burd. What do you remember about Euro?

Ebeneezer (nervously): Nothing, not a thing.

Sir Rodney was convinced that Eb was lying but he couldn't prove it. Sir Rod bought a copy of the book, thanked Eb, and left. Rod finished reading the book just as the long return flight was touching down in Creepsville. Rod rode a cab home, trying to establish a connection between the contents of the book, Dill Burd, and the murderer. On the way home, the cab hit a bird.

It had occurred to Rodney that Dill Burd was the only American on the list. Sir Rodney wondered how Dungetti could have obtained a copy. Rod deduced that Dungetti had stolen the book from Burd. But why hollow out the pages? Was there something in the contents that would implicate Dungetti? There were still too many missing pieces to the puzzle. Sir Rodneyvelt called it a night.

## Curtain

Note: If you want to see how Sir Rodneyvelt unwraps the mystery, read Volume II. The end, Volume I. Note: Volume II can be found on the other side of this page. Side-note: Hangovers do, in fact, make the world go round. This has been scientifically proven.

## About the Author

Bosco B. Bufferin was born in a brothel in Botswana, where the bastard baby was abandoned by the barbaric tribe because he was basically a bit blonder than black. A bowlegged Bushman brought the dribbler to Bujumura Burundi, where a benevolent but bribable British barrister named Bubba Bufferin, and his bubbling Belgian bride Babs, bought the baby for a bulging bag of big brown beans. Brainy Bosco began scribbling brilliant babble as a bouncy boy, before becoming a budding and able bard, barely before puberty began. By and by Bosco published an abundance of bibliographies, biographies, brochures, handbills, and fables, and was a brilliant bookbinder before becoming an absolute nobody and ebbing into oblivious obscurity.

## Please stay tuned while we pause for these important commercial messages.

Do you have difficulty getting to sleep at night? Maybe you suffer from insomnia. If you can't sleep even though you feel dead tired, here's a product that will get you dead asleep. From the makers of *Frozen Stiff* comes a revolutionary new remedy called, *Rest in Peace*. Their instant cyanide formula is easy to use. Simply open one packet, stir the powder into your favorite beverage. Drink up and sleep, sleep, sleep. There are no side effects, and the product can be taken along with any other medication. For your free sample write to Rigormortis Inc., Pine Box 100, Death Row Lane, Saint Cloud, MN. Money back guarantee if not completely satisfied.

Do you wish you could remove those ugly old-age splotches, unwanted freckles or moles, unsightly pimples, and other varieties of skin blemishes? Erase them the easy way with Super, Concentrated, *EAT AWAY*, made from a secret patented formula called $HClO_4$. It only takes three easy steps. Just place a few drops on the area you wish to modify, let set for ten minutes, and then wash. If symptoms reappear, simply repeat the application. Only $19.95 per bottle; order now and get an extra bottle absolutely free. Call the A. C. Burns Co. now, at 1-800-EAT-AWAY. Mention this advertisement for an extra 0.01% off.

This notice is for you ladies out there. How much time do you spend every day applying your makeup? Twenty minutes? Two hours? What if you could have that time back, and still look your best all the time, even when you wake up after a long night of partying? Does that sound like a dream come true? Well Tintoretto's Tattoo Parlor can make that dream a reality. No more lipstick, no more eye shadow, no more blush. That's right, your favorite color combinations can be permanently etched into your face. Come by for a free estimate, you'll be glad you did.

Are you tired of the same old fast food every night? Then come to *Falindo's* and try some of his world-famous goat brain gorditas for something new in fast food gourmet eating

The humble dumbbell fumbled, stumbled and tumbled into crumbled jumble, rumbling, mumbling, grumbling and bumbling. Does that ring a bell? Yeah, me too. If it doesn't ring your bell then listen carefully to this public service announcement. Yes, you too could smoke Datura Stramonium flowers and get the weirdest high you have ever experienced. Warning, excessive use has been known to cause laboratory bovines to go loco, so use only as directed and prescribed by a shaman. Produced by Jimson Pharmaceuticals. DS has been approved by the PTA for recreational use by natives. You are welcome to join the tribe simply by undergoing the hazing process. To learn more, write to J. W., c/o Killer Weed Inc., Tombstone, BC.

In case you didn't know...

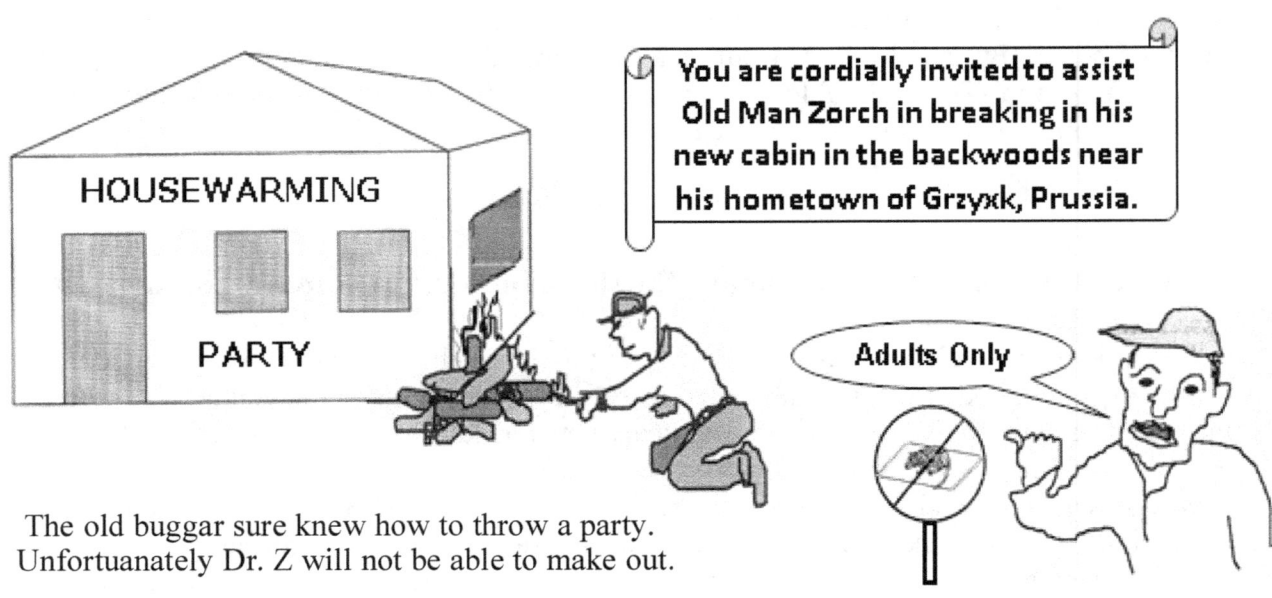

The old buggar sure knew how to throw a party.
Unfortuanately Dr. Z will not be able to make out.

# Chapter Three

## Psychological Profile Analysis

~~~~~~~~~~~~~~~~~~~~~~~~~~~~~~~~~~~~~~~~~~~~~~~~~~~~~~~~~~~~~~~~~~~~

### Mental Sobriety Examination

Now that you have purged your brain of any sign of sagacity you must be re-examined to ensure that you have not lost your marbles as well. Dr. Zorch, renowned psychotherapist and diagnostician, has developed a simple process that enables self-diagnosis. You must be completely dishonest with yourself for the results to be fabricated. Self-appraisal techniques can provide more answers to your questions than the M.D. in Psychiatry or the Ph.D. in Psychoanalysis. It could take a team of professionals such as these decades to tell you what you can determine in just ten minutes using this simple and proven technique compliments of Dr. Zorch.

A complete psychological evaluation is provided. The procedure has been approved by the APE (Association of Psychological Examiners). It is recommended for clinical use by the MUD (Medicine Underwriters Dispensatory) or the CRAP (Coalition of Researchers, Analysts, and Physicians).

## Psychological Profile

Any course on ignorance must be followed by a psychological appraisal. You must be examined, not just from a lack of intelligence standpoint, but also from a lack of consciousness, not to mention an absence of incense.

This section provides an incomprehensible analytic in order to provide patrons a complete psychological profile. The examination is timed; you must complete every test item as quickly as possible in the same order presented. Be perfectly pure and precise if you wish to receive an unreflective rendition of your knowledge, abilities, attributes, and personality. Your psychological prohpylactic can be repropagated periodically.

Be assured that these tests were designed, calibrated, and validated by experienced and trained research scientists and shrinks, working under the direction of Dr. Zorch himself, who also consulted his collection of cretins and agnosticistic and antagonistic gnomes and genomes.

# Scoring Rules (Note that lower scores are desired on all scales).

*Intelligence*: Derive the sum of all your responses to the items below. (If your response was number 3, add three to the sum, and so forth). Divide the total minutes to take the test by the number of items and add this number to the sum. The higher the total score, the greater the IQ. This score correlates with known psychometrics ($r = -1.0$, $p < 0.1$).

*Ability*: Sum the responses to all odd-numbered items and divide by the logarithm of the total, in order to compute the degree of *Cognitive* ability. Repeat this procedure on all even-numbered items for a measure of *Perceptual* ability. The total time, multiplied by the arc sine of 60, plus the product of all items ending with the numbers 5 and 0, computes the measure of *Motor Coordination* skill. This battery is still used to assess millitary inductees.

*Attributes*: Every test item directly taps into a particular characteristic of each person, but in a different way. Thus, different people will have different scales. To determine your archetype, you must review each item ending in the same number as your social security number. (If your SSN ends in 4, examine all item responses numbered 4, 14, 24, etc.). The responses you selected to these items will collectively produce a profile of your personal attributes (physical, mental, and emotional). Simply copy each response into sentences and paragraphs which will reveal your unique prototype, archetype, and typo.

*Personality*: Use the scale below to determine your personality topography.

| Total Score | Stereotype |
| --- | --- |
| -100 | Dead |
| 01 - 50 | Completely normal in every way (i.e., Abnormal) |
| 51 - 100 | Neurotic; Depressed; Hysterical Hypochondriac |
| 101 - 150 | Obsessive-Compulsive; Regressive Denier; Faker |
| 151 - 200 | Manic Depressive; Delirious Yo-Yo Brain |
| 201 - 250 | Paranoid Schizophrenic; Delusional; Psychotic |
| 251 - 300 | Psychopathic Deviant; Demented; Nut Case |
| 301 + | Insane; Bonkers; Flipped Out; Off Your Rocker |
| ∞ | Catharsis; Nirvana; Invalid (Retake Test) |

Part One: *Free Association* – Respond as quickly as possible to each item with the choice that comes closest to the way you are currently feeling.

*Road Signs I* – Which response resembles your interpretation of the road signs depicted?

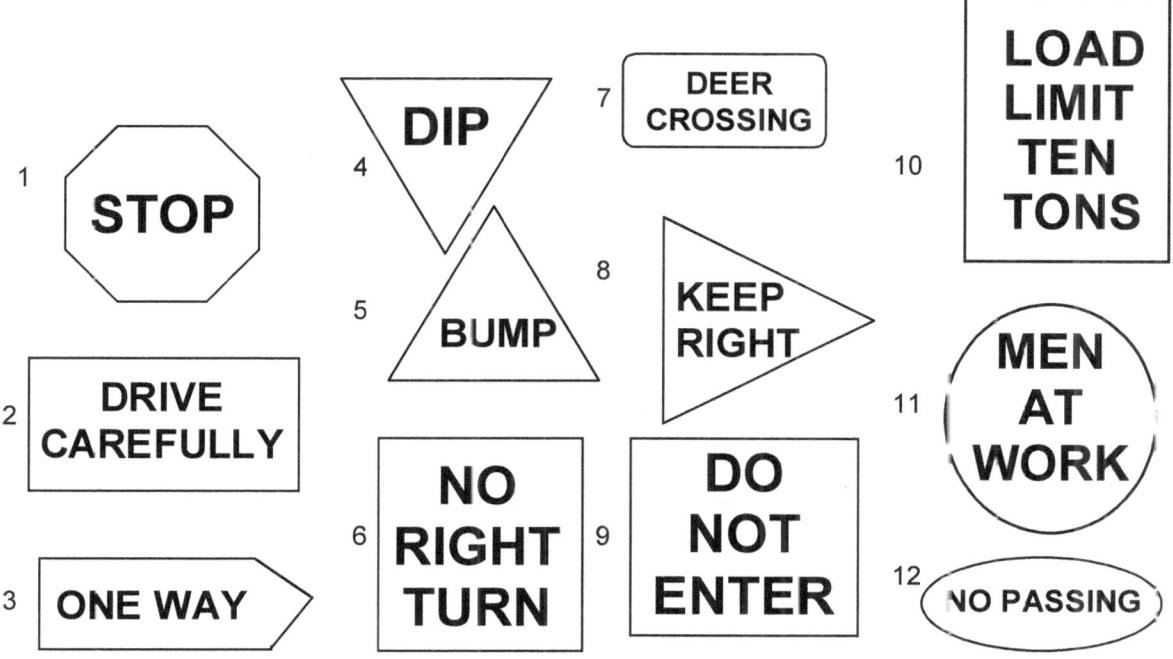

1.  1 = Pots; 2 = Hands Off; 3 = Pull Over; 4 = Bend Over; 5 = Not Here
2.  1 = Construction; 2 = Production; 3 = Instruction; 4 = Obstruction; 5 = Destruction
3.  1 = Underway; 2 = Underwear; 3 = Won Eay; 4 = Win One for the Gipper; 5 = Whoa, Neigh
4.  1 = Lid; 2 = Who Is This Guy; 3 = Who Am I; 4 = Where Am I; 5 = Who Are We
5.  1 = Pimples; 2 = Hickeys; 3 = Mickeys; 4 = Lickies; 5 = Plumb Plump
6.  1 = It's All Right; 2 = Lefty; 3 = Detour; 4 = Stay Stoned (Don't Go Straight); 6 = My Turn
7.  1 = Dear John; 2 = Venison for Free; 3 = Street Crossing; 4 = Dreary Day; 5 = Distrusting
8.  1 = Keep Your Shirt On; 2 = Keep Still; 3 = Keep Your Cool; 4 = Deep Sleep; 5 = At the Wheel
9.  1 = No Parking; 2 = No Necking; 3 = Cherry Lane; 4 = Enter at Your Own Risk; 5 = Reentry
10. 1 = So What; 2 = Want to Bet; 3 = No Elephants; 4 = No Sweat Hogs; 5 = No Pipsqueaks
11. 1 = Men in The Sewers; 2 = A Good Man Is Hard to Find; 3 = A Hard Man Is Good to Find
     4 = No Females, Felines, or Fairies Allowed; 5 = Your Mind Is In the Gutter
12. 1 = No Smoking; 2 = No Smokeys; 3 = No Smokey the Bear; 4 = No Pissing; 5 = Pass Out

*Road Signs II* – Which response resembles your interpretation of the road signs depicted?

1.  1 = Hard Headed; 2 = Hard Head Ahead; 3 = Hard Up; 4 = Hard On Me; 5 = Hard Pressed
2.  1 = No Way; 2 = Speeding Is Fun; 3 = Watch for Cops; 4 = What Sign; 5 = Signs of the Times
3.  1 = Narrow Escape; 2 = Bridge to Tomorrow; 3 = Me First; 4 = I'm Not Backing Up; 5 = Back In
4.  1 = Watch for Falling Kids; 2 = Watch for Failing Kids; 3 = Speed Up, Five Points Each; 4 = Kids Cramming; 5 = Dunce Driving
5.  1 = Train Time; 2 = Beat the Train; 3 = Pull a Train; 4 = Trains Win; 5 = Railroaded Again
6.  1 = What 35 Mile Speed; 2 = I Can't Drive 35; 3 = Speed Kills; 4 = Miles Speeds; 6 = It Ends at 35
7.  1 = Where's the Map; 2 = Petticoats; 3 = Junk in the Road; 4 = No Junkies; 5 = Gumption
8.  1 = Arrow Ahead; 2 = Arrowhead Ahead; 3 = Dead Ahead; 4 = Dead Head; 5 = Curvaceous
9.  1 = Say What; 2 = Watch for Ocean Going Liners; 3 = Line Up Here; 4 = Which Line; 5 = I Dare You to Cross This Line; 6 = You Are Already One Toke Over the Line
10. 1 = You're Telling Me; 2 = Don't End Up Dead; 3 = Dead on Arrival; 4 = This Blasted Map; 5 = Are We Lost or Are We Lost
11. 1 = Bars Closed; 2 = Town Closed; 3 = You Missed Your Turn; 4 = Load Crosed; 5 = Junction, U.S 40, Loop 80, Spur 120, Farm Road 480
12. 1 = Not Again; 2 = Three Lefts and Two Rights; 3 = You Left the Oven On; 4 = Routed or Toured; 5 = Why Didn't We Skate the Interstate

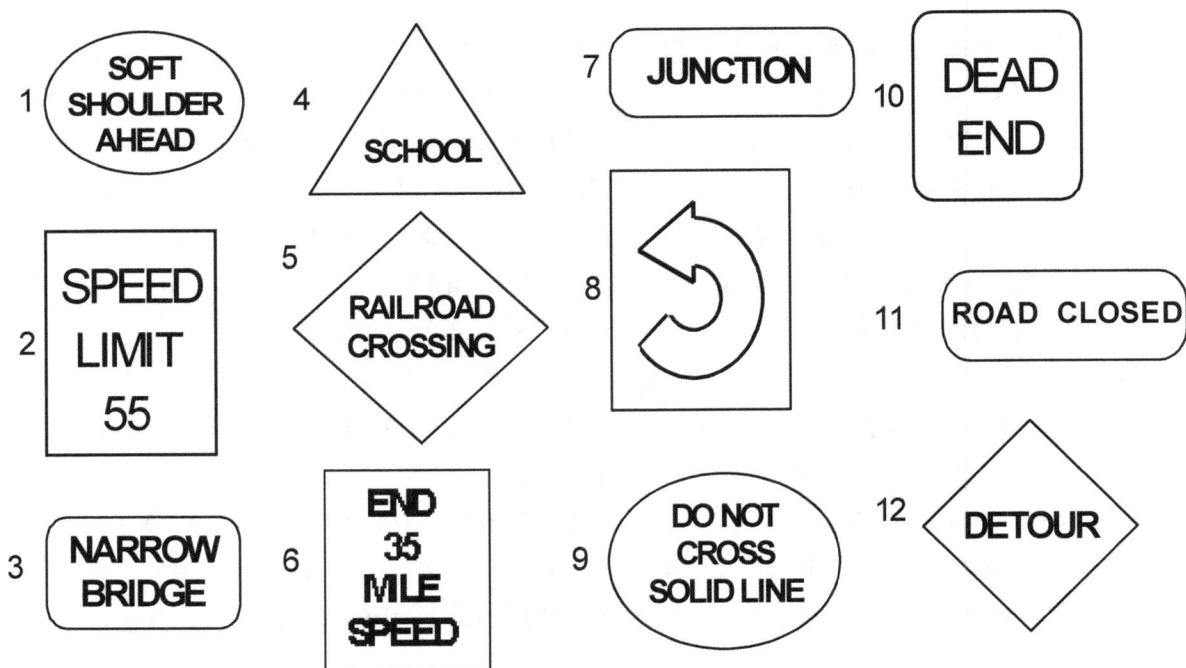

*Road Signs III* – Which response resembles your interpretation of the road signs depicted?

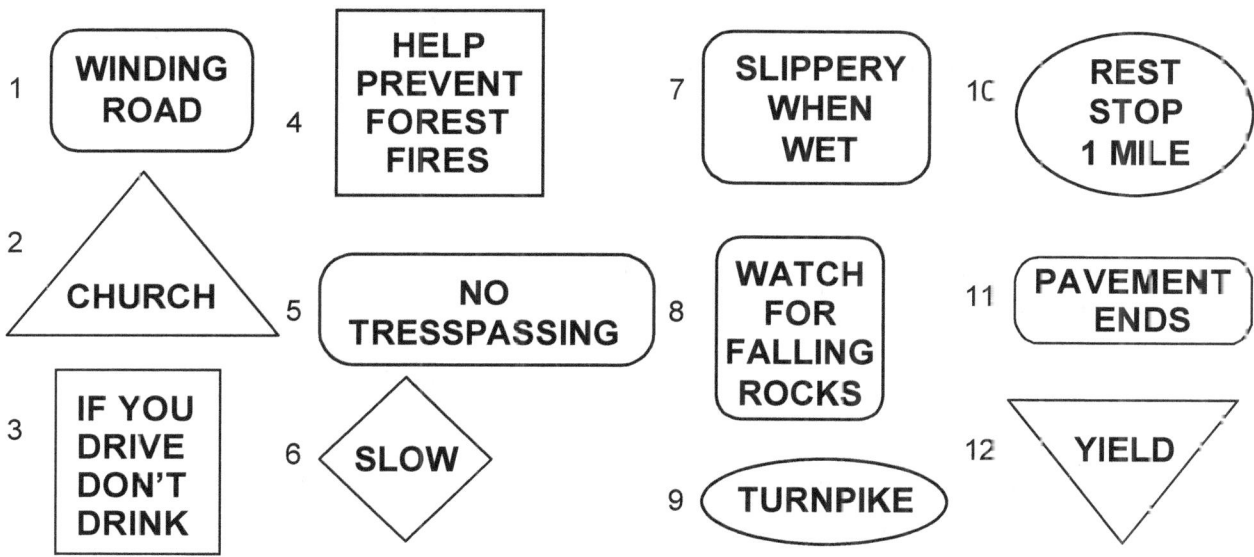

1.  1 = Dizziness; 2 = Snakes Like You; 3 = Curvilinear Road; 4 = Winding Down; 5 = Wound Up
2.  1 = Pray; 2 = Ghosts in Road; 3 = What's That; 4 = Look, St. Christopher; 5 = Crush or Crutch
3.  1 = If You Don't Drink Start; 2 = If You Drink, Drive; 3 = You Drive Me to Drinking;
    4 = Drinking Drives You Nuts;   5 = Nuts Drive Your Crank
4.  1 = Watch for Smoking Bears; 2 = Watch for Smoldering Bears; 3 = Watch for Tokers;
    4 = Bear Crossing; 5 = Fire Brer Bear and Hire Brer Rabbit
5.  1 = Great Hunting Area; 2 = Swimming Hole in The Woods; 3 = Trespass at Your Own Risk;
    4 = This Is the Place; 5 = Crossdressing; 6 = Don't Worry About Dog, Beware of Shotgun
6.  1 = Slow Cars Are Old Fashioned; 2 = Merging Kids; 3 = Floor It; 4 = Get Moving Granny
    5 = Get Mowing Granny
7.  1 = What Isn't; 2 = Slick Chick 3 = Don't Wet Highway; 4 = My Wipers Don't Work; 5 = Slide
8.  1 = You'll See the Rock but Not the Oncoming Car; 2 = Rock and Roll; 3 = Rocky Falls;
    4 = Asleep in the Wheel; 5 = Frolicking
9.  1 = Not Again; 2 = This Highway Isn't Worth It; 3 = Turn Green and Puke;
    4 = Pike Fishing; 5 = Punk Tripe
10. 1 = Keep Driving and You Might Make It to a Service Station; 2 = Man I Got to Go Now
    3 = I Can't Make It, so I Might as Well Just Take It; 4 = Shut Up; 5 = Arrest Stop Ahead
11. 1 = I Am; 2 = That What You Call It; 3 = Get Out and Walk; 4 = Peeving Begins; 5 = The End
12. 1 = Don't Tread on Me; 2 = Merge Faster; 3 = Trucks Have Right of Way; 4 = Lied or Lyed
    5 = Disregard Signals, Road Signs, and This Section

Part Two: *Internal Response Set* – Often, people will think of a variety of answers they can give to a ludicrous question. A person usually gives a tactful, if incorrect answer when they wish to be polite; sarcastic answers are often kept to oneself. Read the following stupid questions and select the response that most reflects your true inward expressions or feelings. Be spontaneous at all times. Do not be afraid to tell the truth no matter how false it is.

1. You have been on a date that is not working out and your companion asks, "Is it just my imagination or are you bored?"
    a. Why, are you practicing to be a drill?
    b. Why does my complexion look plywood?
    c. Not any more, now that I've been bored to death.

2. You have uninvited guests that refuse to leave. Finally, one of them asks, "Are we keeping you awake?"
    a. No, we're paranoiacs; we sleep with our eyes open.
    b. You are actually keeping us asleep. Thanks for curing our insomnia.
    c. Not any more, now that we've been bored to death.

3. You are leaving for a family outing when a family member asks, "Are we going in the car?"
    a. No, I've chartered a greyhound.
    b. No, an airplane is picking us up at the gate.
    c. No, I thought we'd hitchhike this time.

4. You are walking into the polling center when the attendant asks, "Would you like to vote?"
    a. No, I was hired to pull the levers and punch the cards.
    b. Yes, I'm voting for you for county garbage collector.
    c. No, I'm going golfing. Isn't this the Kentucky Derby?

5. After several years of marriage, your spouse asks, "What's new?"
    a. Same thing that's old.
    b. Yesterday was Lyndon's birthday.
    c. I've ordered a new yacht.

6. You are dragging yourself home late from work and your spouse asks, "Is that you, darling."
    a. No, it's me, Myrtle Snodgrass.
    b. No, it's me, your friendly neighborhood burglar.
    c. Who?

7. You are entering a rest room when a companion asks, "Why are you going in there?"
    a. I forgot my sex.
    b. To watch a hockey game.
    c. I've never seen the inside of one before.

8. Your hard work pays off when your business finally turns a profit and an associate asks, "What do you owe your success to?"
    a. To a wild night spent by my parents.
    b. To Groucho F. Zitz
    c. To idiots like you who ask stupid questions.

9. You pick a fight with the bouncer at your favorite bar, who beats the daylights out of you, and then asks, "Had enough?"
    a. Yes, but you might as well finish off the bar.
    b. Not yet, I think I'll go play in the traffic.
    c. Now that you mention it, I've been meaning to cut down.

10. You are bringing your kid to the doctor for booster shots and the nurse asks, "Is this your child?"
    a. No, this little brat ran up here and grabbed my hand.
    b. No, it's the President of the United States; I'm taking him to his State of the Union address.
    c. No, it's an undocumented illegal alien from outer space.

11. After a few hours of small talk your mother-in-law asks, "Are you ready for supper?"
    a. No, I'll have breakfast now and my supper in the morning.
    b. No, I already ate at the Y.
    c. No, give mine to the dog and I'll eat his supper.

12. Your great-grandmother has a heart attack and lies dead on the floor, eyes bugged and mouth gaping. The ambulance arrives, and the medic asks, "Is she dead?"
    a. No, she's asleep, our bed was repossessed.
    b. Yeah, you got here just in time.
    c. No, she always lays sprawled on the floor when she's ready for sex, and she's been waiting for you.

13. While standing at the soda machine in your office building, someone asks, "Can you change a green-back."
    a. Why, does my complexion look chameleon?
    b. Yeah, from your hand to mine.
    c. What shall I change it into, a frog?

14. You are about to check into your hotel and the receptionist asks "Do you have a reservation?"
    a. I have reservations about my reservation.
    b. I reserve the right to remain silent.
    c. I left the reservation so I could come here.

15. We regret to inform you that number fifteen has been banned.

Part Three: *Memory Teasers* – As we get older, we tend to forget things more easily. See how well your memory holds up to these mind benders. Circle the correct response for each item. Then see if you can forget it and measure that.

1. Which is smallest:
   - Number of days in one eternity.
   - Number of phrases or terms for the act of fornication.
   - Number of lies told by the current president during the past year.
   - Number of weight loss programs available.
   - Number of times you've been flipped off.
   - Number of phone calls you've received from telemarketers.
   - Number of flies you've swatted.
   - Number of times you've picked your nose while driving a car.
   - Number of times you've bitten off more than you can chew.
   - Number of television reruns you've seen.

2. Which is greatest:
   - Number of times you've inherited a winning lottery ticket.
   - Number of times you've orbited the globe in your bathtub.
   - Number of times you actually scored with your dream lover.
   - Number of blackbirds you have baked in a pie.
   - Number of times you've been struck by lightning in wintertime.
   - Number of times you've shot par at golf and bowled 300 in one day.
   - Number of times you've attended a Dr. Zorch motivation seminar.
   - Number of times you've eaten raw squirrel meat.
   - Number of frontal lobotomies you've received.
   - Number of times the cows came home.

3. Which is fatter:
   - Friar Tuck
   - Orson Wells
   - Henry VIII
   - Santa Claus
   - Fat Albert
   - Jabba the Hut
   - Piggy Zilchman
   - Pregnant hippo

4. Which is skinnier:
   - Bony Maroni
   - Twiggy
   - Amphetamine Annie
   - Bangladesh woman on a diet
   - Grandma Moses
   - Neanderthal Man
   - 98-pound weakling
   - Anorexic Gumby

Part Four: *Definitions* – Circle the responses that most resemble your interpretation of the following phrases.

1. In the groove
    a. In a trance
    b. Sexual intercourse
    c. In a rut
    d. Satisfactory

2. Up yours
    a. In the groove
    b. Sexual intercourse
    c. Poker phrase
    d. Unsatisfactory

3. Crack up
    a. In the groove
    b. Sexual intercourse
    c. Suppository
    d. Laughter

4. Up tight
    a. In the groove
    b. Sexual intercourse
    c. Suppository
    d. Unsatisfactory

5. Out of sight
    a. Not within visual range
    b. Sexual intercourse
    c. Suppository
    d. Satisfactory

6. Far out
    a. Out of sight
    b. Refrain from sexual intercourse
    c. Suppository removal
    d. Satisfactory

7. Cram it
    a. Sexual intercourse
    b. Suppository
    c. Study hard
    d. Unsatisfactory

8. Bite me
    a. Reference to cannibalism
    b. Sexual intercourse
    c. On a diet
    d. Unsatisfactory

9. Get bit
    a. Reference to cannibalism
    b. Sexual intercourse
    c. Off the diet
    d. Unsatisfactory

10. Screw you
    a. In the groove
    b. Sexual intercourse
    c. Carpenter's term
    d. Unsatisfactory

11. Totally cool
    a. Ice cold
    b. Frigid
    c. Not lukewarm
    d. Satisfactory

12. Take a hike
    a. Mountain climber's dream
    b. Refrain from sexual intercourse
    c. Go fly a kite
    d. Unsatisfactory

13. Eat my shorts
    a. Dietary term
    b. Take a hike
    c. Tailor's phrase
    d. Unsatisfactory

14. Get a life
    a. Piss up a rope
    b. Go fly a kite
    c. Jump in the lake
    d. Become pregnant

Part Five: *Pattern Matching* – Match the object with the appropriate Presidential Candidate or First Lady.

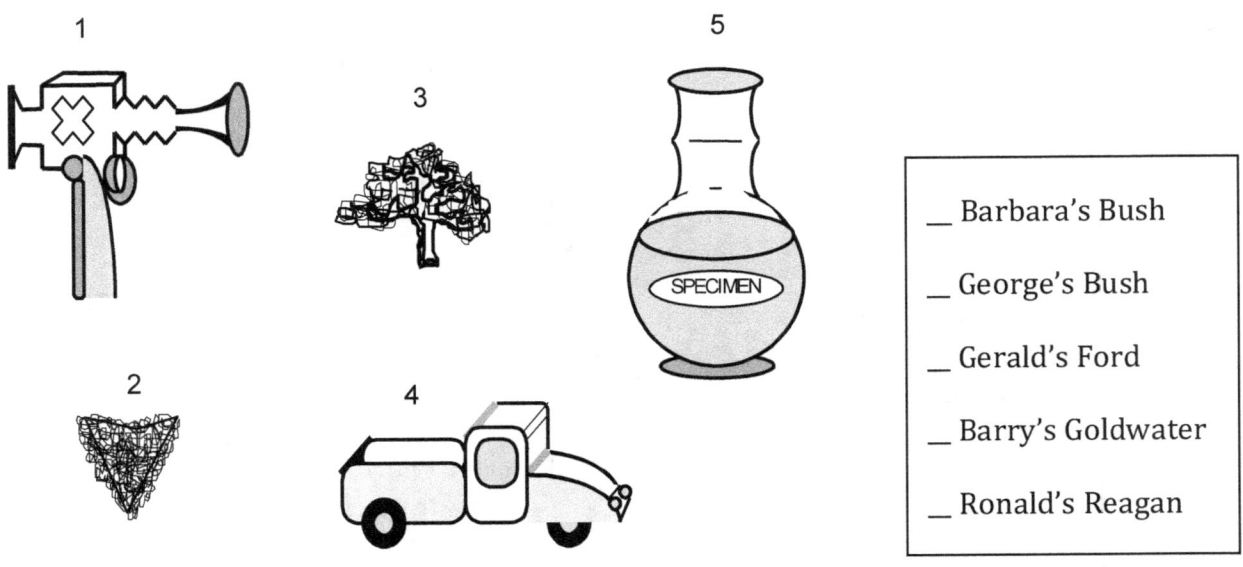

\_ Barbara's Bush

\_ George's Bush

\_ Gerald's Ford

\_ Barry's Goldwater

\_ Ronald's Reagan

Part Six: *Concept Matching* – Match the catchy phrases below with the appropriate picture on the next two pages.

\_\_ 1. Paying in Cold Cash

\_\_ 2. Shooting the Bull

\_\_ 3. Breaking a Promise

\_\_ 4. Catching the Flu

\_\_ 5. Blowing the Deal

\_\_ 6. Getting a Case of the Butt

\_\_ 7. Totally Smashed

\_\_ 8. Fighting a Cold

\_\_ 9. Driving a Point

\_\_ 10. Calling One's Bluff

*Drink*

Flusher's Beer
~~~~~~
Recommended by
physicians everywhere.
~~~~~~
Remember, it's the same
color going in as it is
coming out.

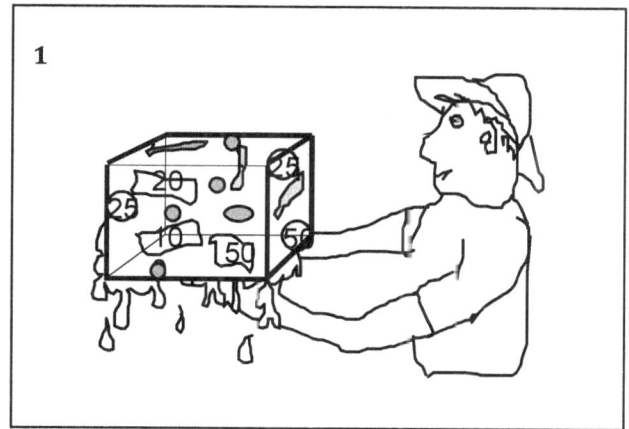

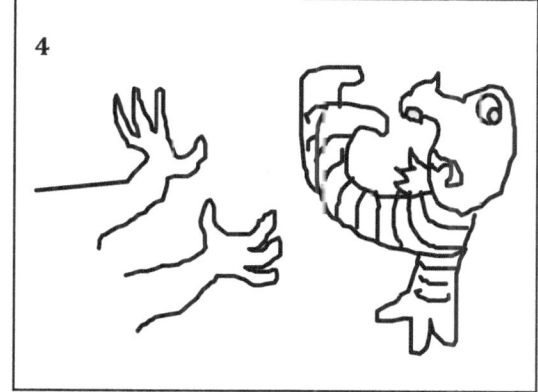

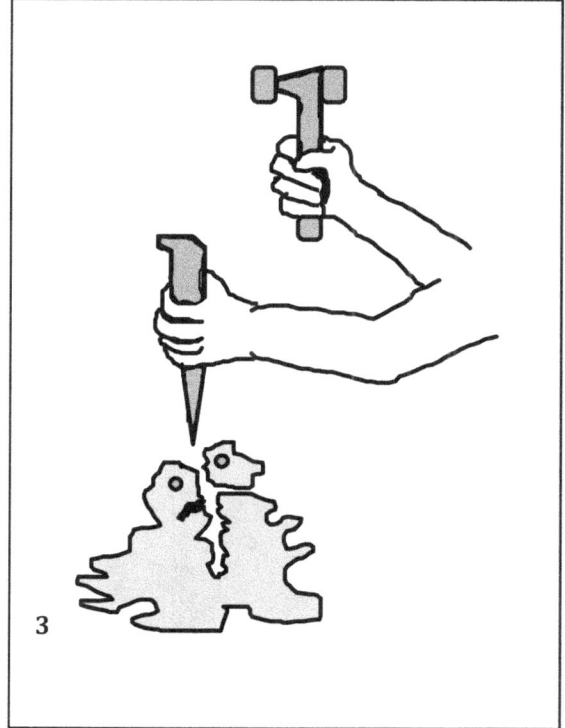

Part Seven: *Dream Interpretation* – Have you ever had any of the nightmares listed below? If not, you will. Simply dwell on the dream of your choice for three hours. Then write your master thesis on what the dream meant. Hint: no dreams are about sex so keep your dirty mind to yourself.

1.  Treading water in the middle of a lake and everywhere are leaping lizards swarming towards you.

2.  Reaching into the bathroom cabinet to gargle with mouthwash and discover you've just gargled with rubbing alcohol.

3.  Drinking a gallon of sauerkraut juice and not being able to throw up

4.  Having the object of your secret admiration phone only to inform you that the grossest scuz-bucket in your class has a crush on you.

5.  Flicking a booger and having it land on you somewhere unknown.

6.  Being trapped in a record store and all there is to play are 45 rpm records, but the one turntable plays at 33 1/3 rpm speed.

7.  Masturbating to the point of impotency and then getting the offer you've been waiting for from the sexiest babe in school. (No sexual identities are to be excluded.)

8.  Being stranded alone on a deserted island and finding only skunk cabbage to eat.

9.  Having someone step on your new hedgehog.

10. Falling and falling endlessly through space, and then landing in a cesspool.

11. Waking up just as you begin to breach the threshold of making love to the person of your wildest dreams, then noticing your partner is snoring.

12. Dreaming that you have creepy crawly insects and other critters all over your body, and then waking up to find it wasn't a dream.

13. Dreaming that you are a multi-millionaire, then waking up to find the electricity and water have been shut off, and an eviction notice is hanging on the front door

14. Finding a mousetrap in your underware.

# Chapter Four

## Psychotherapy and Emotional Growth

### Dealing with Unfinished Business

Dr. Zorch, acclaimed Psychologist, Scientist, and Goofball, has developed exercises that will restore you to utter dumbfoundedness. Having studied extensively on how to incapacitate the already mentally deficient mind, Dr. Zorch has stumbled upon a fortuitous discovery, in conjunction with the theoretical construct of Unfinished Business. Our own Dr. Zorch has determined, through his association with orangutans, that anxiety can be removed by simply allowing the patient to bring his or her unfinished business to completion. Dr. Zorch has invented exercises to perform this function, thereby replacing one's anxiety with total completeness.

The exercises provided herein present excerpts from television shows and commercials which typically create confusion, frustration, anger, and hatred among viewers exhibiting acute anxiety. The clips have been modified, however, to change the climax to a more suitable ending, one more acceptable to the primate intellect. By studying the finished scenarios, one can find pleasure, fulfillment, and lasting joy, where there was once only chaos and turmoil.

Feel free to review the clips as often as necessary to replenish your mental disability with nonpareil nonsense, instability, and/or incapacitation. We thank Dr. Zorch for donating this therapy free of charge, in the interest of Clinical Pathology and Demented Health. However, donations to the Dr. Zorch Foundation are welcome, as long as they do not exceed the amount of $25MB.

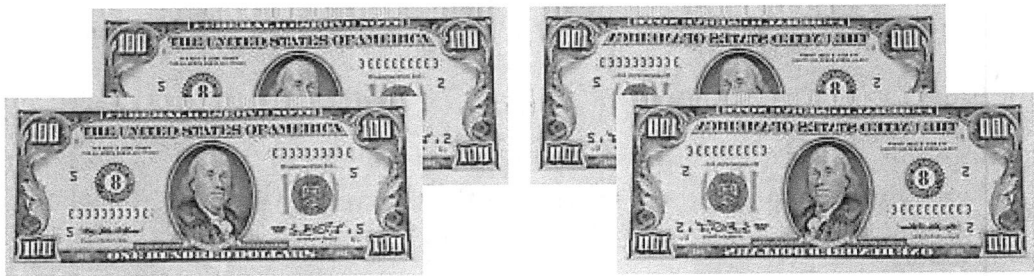

**1**

**2**

**3**

**4**

Instant
Replay

DR. ZORCH'S IDIOCIES

1

2

**1**

**2**

**3**

**4**

femti-opt

DR. ZORCH'S IDIOCIES

# Smoking Section

This section is provided for those of you who smoke, especially if you feel discriminated against just for being a smoker. Here's to your health.

DR. ZORCH'S IDIOCIES

# Dealing with Love-Hate Relationships

If your cerebral incompetence has not been fully restored by now, here is another mind-wrenching exercise that will help you achieve demoralization. This exercise allows you to overcome your hatred for certain people. Often, we love to hate someone because of something they have said or done. This can cause considerable consternation if not constipation, resulting in acute anal agnosticism. Dr. Zorch has developed a nuanced and innovative technique for constructively expressing negative affect, and regurgitating the residue of repressed resentment. The disreputable doctor has provided a revolutionary therapeutic process in the interest of insipid banality and multidementialism, for all you winsome wackiverts.

Read each of the scenarios below. After reading them you will discover your dander is up and your blood is boiling; but you can vent this anger in a constructive and beneficial way. Simply rip these pages out of the book, crumple them up, tear them into shreds, throw them to the ground, and stomp on them. This procedure enables you to direct your bad feelings toward the appropriate target population. You will feel like a new person by dumping that bucket of manure you've been keeping inside you and carrying all your life, and refilling it with positive vibes. If you are not entirely satisfied with the results, repeat the exercise six more times, and then consult a sanitation management physician.

## Scenario 1 – *Driving.*

Driving on the highways and freeways is always a thrill, no matter where you live. It seems that the vast majority of "other" drivers turn relentlessly ruthless the second they sit behind the wheel.

There are those who slow down to block you in then speed up so you can't pass; those who put on their left turn signal and then turn right from the left-hand lane; those who stop five car lengths from the car in front of them, and later blast their horn at you ten milliseconds after the light turns green; those who ignore the traffic signs and signals while they talk on the phone or put on their make-up; those who are the fourth person to run a red light, until you are behind them, and then they slam on their brakes the second the light turns yellow; those who wait at a four-way stop until sixteen cars have proceeded, but will do a Hollywood stop in front of you if it's your turn to go; those who drive with their bright lights on during the daytime, but use only their parking lights at night; those who drive for twenty miles with their right turn signal going, and then come to a complete stop in the fast lane to observe cars parked on the opposite side shoulder; or diesel trucks riding your tailgate, passing, then taking the next exit just to be first. And the list goes on.

Is it any wonder why people pack a firearm when they drive? It's a miracle that more people don't die on the highways from gun shot wounds than from car accidents.

## Scenario 2 – *Parking*.

With the proliferation of automobiles, parking your vehicle has become an insurmountable task. Some people seem to have great difficulty parallel parking. Invariably, they leave enough room behind them to park a semi, but not enough room in front of them to park a beetle.

It is especially irksome when you discover a car using more than one spot because the retard didn't know how to get the vehicle between the lines or deliberately did it to protect their paint job. It makes you want to take out your car keys and scratch the paint from one end to the other. Or worse yet, how about creeps who use multiple parking spaces to protect their broken-down jalopies? It's times like these when you wish you had a case of dynamite in your trunk. Or how about the privileged characters who double park, or otherwise block your car from getting out? You call a wrecker, which arrives the minute the low-life drives off.

When a parking space opens up, full-scale warfare breaks out, with the biggest or fastest cars winning the battle. Don't you want to assassinate the scum bag who grabs the space you've been waiting for as you politely and patiently allowed another driver to exit, with your indicator blinking? Don't you just want to wipe that grin off their face with a chain saw? And it's a life-threatening venture walking through a parking lot. Make sure you wear your track shoes before trying that!

## Scenario 3 – *Working*.

Working in an office is great fun, especially when you work long hours with no overtime.

It seems the coffee pot is always empty when you need a cup. Of course, the blabbermouth who drinks the most coffee never takes time to make a fresh pot, and always leaves a third of a cup in the bottom of the pot, pretending that the pot hasn't been finished yet. Then the coffee cooks until it hardens on the bottom of the pot, looking like coal, and making the place smell like burnt potatoes.

There's the guy who always butters up the boss but never does a lick of work. You remember him, he's the son of the boss's wife's cousin. Then there's the middle manager who always takes credit for all your brilliant ideas and your masterful performance. Perhaps you are that secretary who's forever pounding on the keyboard, while the other secretary, who has been there three months longer than you, does her nails.

The gossip that goes on behind your back is atrocious, but those liars become like honeycomb as soon as you enter the room. There just isn't enough space on Mars to house all the buttholes and their rotten garbage that you have to put up with day after day. Is it not every hour of your labor that you want to declare to the entire office, "Take this job and shove it?!!" Well, not until after you've urinated on your desk.

When you finally get the nerve to retire, the office has a going away party in your honor, as if they really cared and as if you once considered them to be your pals. Don't you just want to take the party cake and mash it into the boss's wife's cousin's face; pour the pitcher of punch down the gossipy secretary's blouse that never does jack; dump the coffee pot along with the burnt dregs down the blabbermouth's pants; and take your token pen and pencil set and impale them into the office manager's skull?

## Scenario 4 – *Shopping*.

Grocery shopping is another entertaining and relaxing nightmare. It seems that people become deliberately inconsiderate when armed with a shopping cart.

People will block the aisle with their cart and pretend that they don't see you trying to get around. There are those who want to yackety-yak with the cashier while the line extends around the block; those who wait until the groceries are sacked before preparing their check or getting out their money or credit card, or go fishing for pennies to provide exact change; or those who forget an item or didn't get the one on sale and go back and shop while others wait impatiently.

When another cashier opens, there's a mad rush. You, holding a mere two items, get beat out by the obese lady with two shopping cartfuls, who won't let you ahead of her because she's in a hurry. Then the cashier has to sack the two cartfuls of groceries because the bag boy went to help the foxy lady with her single bag of groceries. Of course, the express lane is either closed, or the limit on items is not being enforced.

The supermarket always advertises sales for items that sell out during the first minute, or they pull a "bait-and-switch" on the item you really wanted. The price that rings up on the cash register is seldom the one printed on the product or on the shelf where you found it (which is always lower). Plus, you have to go to three different supermarkets to get all the items on your list because managers are untimely when it comes to reordering and restocking them. Is there any doubt why some people become arsonists?

## Scenario 5 – *Excreting.*

Public rest rooms are a public nuisance. Even the most cultured and sophisticated people become total slobs in a public rest room.

A person needs to be equipped with rubber gloves, a scrub brush, and disinfectant before taking a chance on sitting upon a public commode. A man has to wade through a puddle of piss to take one himself. And there's always urine on the seat when you want to do number two, regardless of your sexual identity. And why don't people flush for crying out loud? It ain't their water.

There is seldom enough toilet paper, paper towels, or soap. The mirrors are always broken or missing. Surely, people don't act this irresponsible at home. Wouldn't you just love to grab one of those inconsiderate, lazy, discourteous, and anal-retentive ingrates by the scruff of the neck, rub their face in the mess they left behind, and then swat them where it hurts with a rolled-up newspaper? It's the best way of toilet-training them. I mean, it works with house-breaking your dog doesn't it? Certainly, the doggie is magnitudes more sophisticated than these other douchebags.

## Scenario 6 – *Flying*.

Flying cross-country can be a breath-taking experience. First, before checking your baggage someone will ask if a person you don't know packed your luggage. Just for laughs, tell them you think a crazed Iranian terrorist bellhop might have packed your bags at the hotel, because you cannot locate your derringer. Prior to boarding the plane, you will be inspected by a security person and they will sift through all your carry-on stuff whenever they want. Forget about bringing along your fingernail clippers because they will be confiscated; after all, you might use them to hijack the airliner.

The stewardess and/or the pilot on your flight always broadcasts, "Now sit back, relax, and enjoy your flight." These numskulls know full well that you cannot sit back, since the seat reclines only .0003 inches; they know you cannot relax, because you have a blubbering and wheezing sweat shop sitting on either side of you; they know you cannot enjoy the flight because you've been packed into a tin can like a bunch of sardines, with your knees in your face and your elbows under the armpits of your neighbors. They know that you are terrified of flying, the turbulence makes you ill, and the food is worse than you ever received at your grade school cafeteria. Yet they think those stupid clichés will comfort you? What public relations fool came up with that crap? Don't you just want to slap the taste out of their mouth with the fire extinguisher, then pull down their slacks and cram a bag of peanuts where the sun don't shine?

Speaking of flying, don't you just love to hear about the various catastrophes that may occur which require you to breathe through an oxygen mask, employ your seat cushion as a flotation device, or open the emergency exit/escape hatch? The stewardess repeats these wonderful scenarios every time you set foot on a plane, knowing full well that if there is a catastrophe, your chances of survival are poorer than winning the lottery three consecutive times. They lift your spirits in this manner, only after insulting your intelligence by providing instructions on how to operate a seatbelt, knowing full well that even a certified moron with degenerative brain disease can perform the task. Don't you just want to tell them to shut up and sit down; or better yet, jam their head into that lame excuse for a toilet?

*Postlude.*

Here are some more old favorites that we all just love to hate.

| | |
|---|---|
| Telemarketers | Politicians |
| The Mafia | Unsupervised Children |
| Wall Street | Drug Cartels |
| The IRS | Cults |
| Procrastinators | Dictators |
| Lobbyists | Aggressive Salespersons |
| Bullies | Gluttons |
| Blabbermouths | Snobs |
| Commercials | Commentators |
| Falsies | Prophylactics |
| Vaginal Deodorants | Suppositories |
| Carpetbaggers | Long Winded Orators |
| Sluts | Pushers |
| Stray Cats | Panhandlers |

Dr. Zorch during a full moon
Dr. Zorch hanging a full moon

And, of course, Dr. Zorch's favorite: You and your mate discovering that what you thought was lubricating jelly turned out to be deep-heating rub.

## *Prescribed Activity*

At this point, you are probably so raving mad you could just spit. Simply follow Dr. Zorch's easy and fulfilling steps. Rip these pages out of the book, crumple them up, tear them into shreds, throw them to the ground, and stomp on them. Now take a deep breath... Oh, and you can put away the firearm now.

Don't you feel better? Now you can go out into the world with love in your heart and your fists clenched. I said you could ditch the gun already. Hey there, what the hell is going on? Are you crazy? No, no please don't. I'll do any

Due to technical difficulties beyond our control we were unable to terminate the discussion. Check your local listings for the next telecast or disregard the last transmission. You're free to complete the assignment.

# Mental Health Guarantee

If you have read the scenarios and completed the prescribed activity, you are now a self-actualized person. You can believe this because Dr. Zorch provides his personal GUARANTEE! Where else can you obtain such a valuable gift, absolutely free?

If you are not entirely satisfied with the results, you will receive a full refund on your subscription to *Psychology Yesterday*.

(Note: Dissatisfied customers must submit a notarized letter from their clinician attesting to the fact that they are still exhibiting non-maladaptive behavior. To be acknowledged as fit to practice psychotherapy, your clinician must have undergone the mental health exercises contained herein, as well as being certified by the Dr. Zorch Foundation as incredulously incoherent.)

---

Before you begin you need to be hypnotized. Just follow these simple steps and you will go into a deep trance. First, you must memorize the following paragraph so you can recite it as you concentrate on the image below.

State your name. Gaze at the image. Keep it in focus. Do not shift your eyes. Yes, your eyelids are getting heavy. But the image is enticing and you cannot stop staring. After a while, your eyes will want to close so bad you must give into them. As soon as they close you will notice that the afterimage remains. Focus on that image now projected onto the inside of your eyelids. Continue until you fall into a deeper state of consciousness.

You will awaken the moment you turn the page. Henceforth, you will be able to walk up the stairs and onto the stage, quacking and waddling like a duck if that is your desire. Practice Dr. Zorch's tried and true technique and you can hypnotize yourself at will. Happy stupors.

---

We would like to take this opportunity to express our sincere gratitude to Dr. Zorch's professional staff (and some of our best fiends) who contributed their time and talents to the development of these psychometric measurement tools now being utilized worldwide. Let's give them a heartwarming applause as we chant, "Hip, Hip, Hooray!"

Dr. Gertie C. Birdbreath

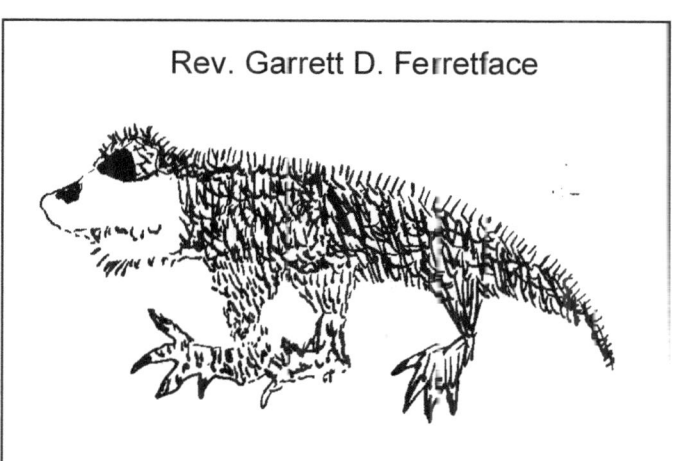

Rev. Garrett D. Ferretface

Fuzzy W. Moosehead, PhD

Professor Magilla Apeschitz

# *Chapter Five*

## For Your Reading Displeasure

~~~~~~~~~~~~~~~~~~~~~~~~~~~~~~~~~~~~~~~~~~~~~~~~~~~~~~~~~~~~~~~~~~~~~~~~~~~~~~~~~~~~~~~~~~

Dr. Zorch has added this bonus bogus chapter at no charge, to farther expand the vacuum above your shoulders, and to further depredate the wasteland that has become your mind. The literary gems which follow were personally selected by Dr. Zorch and exhibit the highest quality of prose and poetry ever assembled in one book. You'll want to read them over and over again. Reading them backwards and upside-down will no longer work. You must now test your comprehension, or RGL: count the number of multisyllabic words and divide by milliseconds. Your mental age should be lowered systematically with each reading. There is no limit to the enjoyment that awaits, as you continue your journey in the land of idiocy.

To misquote the President of the United States of America.

*Dr. Zorch's book has been a priceless resource to me. I take it with me everywhere I go. It should be required reading for all who are in a position of authority in this country and abroad. I especially enjoyed the interesting and entertaining literature. Each selection is perfectly timed to coincide with my morning constitutional. Unfortunately, I managed to get a few streak marks on the pages, but what the heck! Thank you Hieronymus, my auld acquaintance.*

(If you can't trust the President, who can you trust?)

Also, please heed the words of Confucius who was once quoted as saying, "Man who ride bicycle upside-down have hairy crack up." Many thanks to the Confucian Theological Seminary of Georgian Monks for this excerpt and its translation.

Enter at your own risk unless you are an accredited ratfink.

# Prose Section

## The Continuing Adventures of Randy Raccoon and the Fuzz Busters

Episode 1: *Rookie Raccoon*

It was hot in Los Angeles. I was working the day-night watch-check scope-out in juvenile-adult homicide, a division of the Law-busters special forces detachment. My Partner is Randy Raccoon; my name is Detective Thursday. I had just been assigned my new partner last week. In fact, all the veterans of the force had to break in a rookie from the academy. Randy Raccoon was about as green as they come. Of course, it just might have been accentuated by the grass stains on his overalls, and the yellow-green matter that would dribble down the coon's chin during breakfast.

Night had fallen, causing me to stumble. I struggled to my feet while the phone rang with uncompromising persistence. We were alerted to take control of a riot that was brewing in the baddest part of town.

At the end of our journey to the unknown frontier, we witnessed a mob of slithering slobs hanging a marten by the toes on a dome-shaped clothesline. As we approached, the carousing crowd dispersed in differing directions. We tried to chase them down, but they all escaped with eludesome evasiveness. However, one of the intrepid instigators lost the pink polka-dotted hood that he was wearing. I recognized him as a practicing vampire who lived uptown.

I knew he was up to no good, so we staked out the home and office of Vladimir Vanderbilt, the vampire from Valencia Venezuela. After several hours with no movement I decided we should search his palace. It was rumored that the house was horrifyingly haunted, but I didn't believe in such nonsensical balderdash. As we walked up the splintery steps, Randy's paw crashed through the termite-eaten boards and became ludicrously lodged. His toes plunged into a mountain of molten mole manure. While extracting his foot, Randy had to leave his shoe behind to the wrath of the unborn plastic. The superstitious Randy buried the other shoe under a sycamore tree.

I knocked on the door and it opened by itself. We slowly entered the creaking, cobwebbed interior. Randy was creeping along on his bare paws and I followed behind him with my pistol drawn.

Suddenly, we saw an intense vision of a demonic creature beyond imagination. It disappeared, being replaced by a swarm of nine-hundred silver locusts. Randy made a beeline for the bathroom and regurgitated his lunch of turnips and prune juice. As he was washing up, he placed his Hercules ring on the bathroom sink. The ring got up and rolled down the drain all by itself. Randy became so upset I had to slap snap him out of it.

I was busy combing my hair when a million and one black-stringed lyres appeared in the mirror. I kept combing my hair, hypnotized by the image, as I was buried in a snowstorm of dandruff. I fell into a turquoise involvement with butterflies, surrounded by a maze of tulips.

The sound of a hoot owl tripped me out of my momentary mesmerization. Randy pointed to the attic. We climbed the circular staircase. When I opened the attic door, a monolithic mass of mothballs plummeted down upon us. I knew we were not up against any ordinary barn owl. The hoot got louder and louder, as did the ringing in my eardrums. I was nearing the end of my endurance when Randy finally answered the obsessive-compulsive phone. The operator informed Randy he had the wrong number.

Randy slid down the banister, bounced on the floor, and tumbled through the door marked exit. I hurried after him. As I opened the door to the smoke-filled room, I was trampled by a herd of rampaging buffalo. Randy peeled me from the brown-sheeted escarpment, and we got the hell out of there. Randy was in a hurry because he didn't want to miss the last episode of *Muskrat Ramble*, the story of Marvin Musquash in the wilderness of Montana; the title became a number one single on the badger circuit.

We went over to Randy's place. He offered me a drink. I had some dry ice on the rocks. Randy watched television while I finished writing my last will and testament on my three-by-five notepad. Randy couldn't hold back the tears when the show ended. I couldn't hold back the vomit as I puked to my stomach's delight. I fell asleep on Randy's couch with the music of locust buzzing in my ears and the smell of peppermint suckers on my breath.

## Episode 2: *The Salami Calamity*

Randy Raccoon looked as if the world had turned into a wasteland of wet washcloths when he heard the news of his mother. She had been in the hospital with a hieroglyphic hemorrhoid. The doctor thought from the beginning that it would be fatal, but it turned out not to be. Randy was depressed. He hated that fiery furnace of frenzy, who always opened the gates of self-righteous rhinoceros, and smelled like a lasting contraption of tactless cat breath.

Upon arriving at the office, I found a note on my desk and two airline tickets. We were to fly to Turkey. Randy was practically pleased as punch with the opportunity to get away from his mooching mamasita. The plane went through a screaming cistern of cloudy endurance. Randy stepped outside for a breath of fresh air and fell into an inalienable concordance of Scottish hopscotch.

Dazed, he walked into the auditorium where the speaker announced the arrival of Brandy Bones Backer, a singer of Egyptian philosophy. Randy stayed for the program, hoping the artist would sing *When the Lights Went Out in the Barn* or *Watching the Pigs at Night*. These were his favorite songs. I caught up with Randy afterwards.

We were strolling along the avenue when we saw it. It was a giant salami, coming toward us with peppered intolerance, holding a knife as sharp as an opera (operas to Randy are as dull as my toothbrush). The salami was overtaking me when Randy set a pack of biting bulldogs loose. The carnivorous canines cordially completed their consumption of the stoic salami with undue lack of ravishing restraint. With great valence of velocity, we vamoosed with vanishing vilification, or we too would have become victims of the rearranged animals.

Istanbul was a beautiful town to Randy, but he still liked his hometown of Mush Rat Falls, Kentucky better. Not only did Randy fall in love with Istanbul, but he also fell for a lady squirrel full of briskness and folly; what he really wanted was a piece of her whisker-biscuit. The captivated raccoon crawled forward on his belly and asked for her paw in marriage. She responded, with inspirational persuasionality in a demonstration of exasperating maladoration, by saying "No Way Bucko!"

Randy cried a river of glistening eyelashes because he needed her for better or worse. When he got to the worse part, she changed her mind with intense italics and they were married the next day. On their honeymoon they went to Dirty Springs, Utah and stayed at the Catastrophe Hotel. During dinner, Randy ordered what everybody else was eating. The other patrons looked ill, but Randy thought the mishmash looked appetizing. His sylvan spouse let out a blood-curdling retch and left Randy with no good-byes, only a plate of delicious looking marital excretion. Then Randy broke down and wept to his bladder's delight. He faded away into a night of goofy gray gophers meddling with mellifluous melancholy.

## Episode 3: *The Underwear Affair*

After the dance in the civic auditorium, secret undercover agent Randy Raccoon marched straight home and hit the sack. He had a dream about a giant stork stalking the town. As the stork flew over the Yellow Press building, it let go of something. Randy began to run, afraid of being bombarded. As the stork's payload neared the earth, Randy noticed it was a blanket full of half-nude babies. The entire package exploded as it hit the ground, knocking Randy out of bed.

Randy arrived at the workplace with his unusual internalicious turmoil. I told Randy we were on a case that was likely to be the most dangerous of his career. Then I played a recorded message from the chief of police.

"It seems that Furina Fadinzel escaped from the penitentiary. Fadinzel vowed that he would assassinate Idaho "Fido" Collido, the owner of Universal Underwear Unlimited, if he ever became free. Collido was the key witness for the prosecution in placing Fadinzel behind bars for grand theft and attempted murder. Fadinzel must be brought back alive to the penitentiary. If you choose to accept this case say YES into the microphone."

Randy pranced up to the microphone with casual advancement and abruptly announced, "You wish!" The recording continued, "Good, this tape will self-destruct you in five seconds. Good luck Randy." "But I meant, no," Randy assured the machine. Then the recorder went "Arrgruffshputtsooy." Randy slumped into his chair with sorrow in his marrow and woe in his toes. He felt he must solve the case because he respected the last wishes of the machine, even though he didn't approve of suicide.

We went to the garage and requisitioned a squad car. Outside, it was raining cats and dogs, and the cats and dogs were raining something else. It was a real mess, sort of like a burning oil field of cold sawdust. Randy swerved to miss a rat in the road and crashed into a barricade. As he got out of the car, a humongous stork swooped down and grabbed Randy with his giant beak, flying off into the sunset. The brazen bird dropped the remains of Randy onto a platform loaded with crates of marshmallow flavored chewing tobacco. Randy was in severe agony as he limped along, inspecting the symmetric swastika that the beak of the great bird had carved into his abdomen.

Randy stumbled and stamped only to meet face to face with a short skinny man who was wearing knee-high boots with little red hearts engraved in them. Randy knew this had to be Fadinzel, or some weirdo from Nuts Farm Plaza disguised as the mischievous midget, who had recently escaped the town's insane asylum. Fadinzel attacked Randy with a switchblade knife, but the cunning coon pulled out his trusty pocket ax and nailed the scum bum in the neck. Fadinzel fell with a musical thud.

The chief was furious with Randy for not bringing Fadinzel in alive. Randy was severely reprimanded by the chief and given a thirty-day suspension from the force. It was an obvious case of self-defense, and I testified as such; I mean, everything Randy ever did was out of self-defense. But the board wouldn't buy it. On the way to the bar to drown his sorrows, Randy slipped on some axle grease and flew into an elevator shaft. As he was climbing up the laundry chute, he slipped again and slid back down another chute, landing in the chief's lap. At that ungainly strife, the chief said with calm, cool, collected clarity, "You're fired." This was because Randy had interrupted a card game at the Red Robin Club. Randy stompeded out of the building's rear entrance, vowing to get revenge.

I waltzed up to Randy with love and passion in my heart, for it was Tuesday, and Wednesday was my day off. I tried to console my persnickety, but persistentful partner. I told him that in a few weeks the chief would simmer down and might ask Randy to come back. I explained to the masked malcontent that, just because raccoons looked liked bandits didn't mean they made lousy cops. Of course, in Randy's case it did mean precisely that. The rowdy rodent replied with simple soliloquy, "The chief is toast!"

I explained to the indignant rodent that turning to the wrong side of the law would be a permanent condition; a mistake that could never be reversed or overturnable. But do you think Randy gave a rat's ass? Yeah right, it was the only ass he had. But every time the rambunctious rodent tried to do the right thing, he got screwed; first by his wife and next by his boss. It appeared that doing the right thing meant hanging around the wrong people. It was an irreconcilable dilemma of propitious proportions that neither Randy nor I could calculate the corresponding consequences. We decided to flip a coin. Heads, Randy wins and becomes and outlaw; tails I win and I take him to the hoosegow. He could easily locate an attorney who could argue an insanity defense. Let's face it, you have to be a mental case to make it through all that bureaucratic bullpucky alive, not to mention being constantly if not charmingly chastised to the degree of debasing, degenerate, detrimentalization.

I handed Randy my lucky penny, declaring "Indian side I win, Buffalo side you win." Randy flipped it high as he could, while he flipped me off with his other hand. The rare coin landed, twirled, then rolled down the sidewalk, bounced out into the street, got smacked by a car, and hopped into the thumb hole of a manhole cover, dropping into the sewer. Now if that wasn't an omen, I don't know what else to call it.

## Epilogue

When the lady who lived in the shoe returned home, a sunset of soaked celery was falling in jubilant jerks. I gave that lady a kiss that would give a lovesick castaway cringing from thirst a swollen ocean of substantial slobber. I went to the closet and envisioned a deep, dreary darkness of forgotten lore while I disrobed.

I reclined on my bed, exploring my nudity and contemplating my navel, as the wife turned on the tube. Then I heard the news. Randy, the tough tempered torrent, had taken his service revolver and cleaned the chief's chimney.

Back on the raunchy ranch, all the creatures were sorrowful because Randy was on the lam, destined for death row. The lark in the meadow, the lizard in the bush, the tadpoles in the marsh, the skeeters in the sky, the mother of the toad, the warmth of a bug, the smell in the air, the rustle of the woods, the rumble of a quake, the lighting of the lights, the storming of the mind, the wastefulness of this paper, the hurting in my head, the aching in my guts, the heaving from my intestines—all are found in a wonderful panorama of silky sickness.

A moronic mob of blood-lusting stormtroopers, led by Vladimir the Vampire of all people, accosted Randy, took him out to yonder oak tree, and lynched him. Nobody did anything to stop it. And what could I do? It was my day off and my police radio was on the fritz. It just goes to show how everything that happens in this life is predestined, and there isn't a doggone thing you can do to change it.

After that fateful day, the chief's wife and that decrepit vampire became the closest of friends, possibly lovers. I suspected they had a thing going when she started carrying his pet snake every place she went. But who am I to complain? I've got a swell job, a shiny brass badge, and a greasy gun that'll blow gaping holes in anyone who looks at me cross-eyed. We got a new chief who was more corrupt than Vlad who'd payrolled his campaign.

I called in sick to attend the funeral. I was the only one there from the force. Randy was buried by wigwagging waters with mysterious mirages, in exuberant eminence, under glorious ground. I pissed on his grave afterwards. Randy would have wanted it that way.

The story you have just read is true. The names were not changed because nobody was innocent. Dung, dung dung dung ... Dung, dung dung dung. All done! For now. But what if ... Makes you wonder, when wandering into the wetlands of warped witticism. And which makes more sense when everything makes no sense? Meaningless, all is meaningless. You can quote me on that even though I don't believe it myself. As for now, it's Thursday signing off. So, keep your head down and your powder dry. And give a cop a hug today, because someday he may have to shoot you. Unless it's a female cop then you might want to proceed with caution or she'll shoot you first. But anyway, I don't know what ...

# Poetry Section

Some of the most lackluster poetry of all time is featured in this section for your reading disenchantment. These poems were penned by anonymous authors (the authors wished to remain anonymous for obvious reasons). All selections were award winners in the Dr. Zorch artist search, to be held next year.

First Place winner in the *Sea Faring* category.

## Ballad of an Old Seaman

When oy wuz en me teens oy had me a dream
To someday become someting new.
Oy wanted to be on a ship on de sea
An' to sail on de ocean blue.

A few years later, wen de dream got greater,
Oy finally got to de quick.
Oy stowed on a boat dat sailed wen afloat,
An' found wat is wuz to be sick.

Became de first mate on another ol' crate,
When sooner or later, it sunk.
Oy liked it de least so oy traveled far east,
An' landed meself on a junk.

We sailed to de mouth of de sea in de south,
But livin' in China 'twere dull.
Oy also ate 'erds o' sea-farin' birds;
Me main meal wuz usually a gull.

Oy ended me fears 'bout wastin' ten years,
Cuz now dat oy made me a man,
One thing oy could be 'twas a gob on de sea,
Oy couldn't live back on de land.

Oy traveled so high dat oy found Captain Bligh,
But oy didn't agree wit 'is kick.
Next oy traveled remote, to a small whalin' boat,
To be ate by de great Moby Dick.

First Place winner in the *British Intellectual Society* category.

## Once Upon a Log (To My Dare Rover)

i had a dog, he was a frog,
  played in the bog, in the fog.
    once had a cog o' cherry sog,
      'n that blame dog drunk the grog.

while iwuza jog, up came da dog, and his tail he wog.
  den allova rog, me dog
    ran straight on an' busted 'is nog on a log.

so my dog died of a log in 'is nog . . . endsville


First Runner-up in the *British Intellectual Society* category.

## Bloody Red (Dedicated to Ted)
(Cinematography by Zed. Coming soon to a theater near you.)

a bloke named ted broked his 'ed
when he fell outa bed.
oh, how it bled, pretty drops of red, on a bed.

now ted is ded; but don't dred what i sed about ted.
insted, consider the girl ted was to wed.
she pled until she bled; bloody red.

doc ned fled to get fed; this misled ed,
who sped to tred near the bed that kilt ted.
but ted din't have no bred so ed din't bury ted.

epilogue

ted broked his hed climbing on 'is bed. oh,
how it bled; the bedspread painted red.
now ted is ded; my story has been sed;
mebbe you might dred the deathe of ted.

gnight fred... thanks jed...

First Place winner in the *Rap Music* category.

## Slalom

The tone from her shrug bugged my juggling things. Spring mingled to build the killed stillness. I drilled, indeed, I fulfilled a skilled and scheming queen; her hilly tree, be it unseen, unclean. Meanwhile, my jeans full of bean sprouts, about outmoded, were ready to explode from my hold; but so bold as to be colder than her older fur. Were there germs or worms in a thermos? Or just lust, gusting to bring things flinging, or bubble into an able labor?

What a sight it had been then; when one right night she might frighten ten blighted men. Showing rare flair, the mare scared the bare bear, by the glare from her lair upstairs. I didn't care; aware that a fair share of dare was in the air (in sheer beer as to taste of haste). Here, a dull and wasteful place, full of appalling gall would pull all my nickels from the fickle tickling of my pickle.

I could stack thick bricks upon the dawn; or con the blamed pawn from his chessboard game, as sore as he bore my shameful name. But the same fame, being unclaimed, remained in my lame brain. Undressed, stressed, and oppressed with the quest, I'll refrain from further plumb clumsiness, I guess, and clean up the rest of this unimpressive mess.

First Runner-up in the *Rap Music* category.

## Zack's Rap

Met her by the railroad track,
Hanging with the wild wolf pack.
Eyes of brown and hair of black;
You could say that she was stacked.

She was going yackety-yak;
Guess her mind was a total vacc.
So I didn't cut no slack;
And she didn't give no flak.

All the sluts were shooting smack.
While the pimps were smoking crack;
Then one took another whack;
Next he had a heart attack.

Guess he didn't have the knack;
So they took him to a quack.
She led me back to her shack;
Put away a full six-pack.

After that we drank some Jack;
She passed out upon the rack.
I undressed her; she was lack.
I unzipped and took a hack.

Next I pulled out of her crack,
Then I put her tampon back.
I went home and hit the sack.
I ain't never going back.

First Place winner in the *Foreign Artists* category.

## Yaenleckers

> Bingdom fistol lisk debornac
> Seldor meef corbrel genloap.
> Bengst eld twift brezoan arrildif;
> Scortil, selotovix, deasim felops.


First Place winner in the *Western Folklore* category.

## The Tale of an Old Cowboy

> When I was a kid, I had me a dream
> To be a big sheriff and wear a big frown.
> I'd shoot lots of bad guys who showed too much steam;
> And I was a cop in a big western town.
>
> People would cry from the things that I did;
> Others would laugh when they heard of my claims.
> They praised me for gunning down Billy the Kid;
> Were even more pleased when I shot Jesse James.
>
> Were too many gunslingers after my ass.
> So got me an eight-shooter plated in pearl.
> I drew against many, but they weren't as fast.
> Became the best fast draw from West to the world.
>
> I had lots of fun spending all my time killin'.
> I killed Al Capone, and Billy Sol Estes;
> I killed Jack the Ripper, and yes, Marshall Dillon,
> Miss Kitty, and Doc, but was gunned down by Festus.

The Endus

First Runner-up in the *Western Folklore* category.

## The Man that Didn't Die

In those days of old when dudes searched for gold,
From out of the cold came a man very bold,
Whose face I've been told was fungus and mold.
But somebody sold a gun to his hold,
And with it he rolled some forty-eight-fold.

They called the guy "Gil" and he had his fill
Of making the kill. It gave him a thrill,
Though only until he went to Boot Hill.

One day ten years later, another known hater
Tried to grow a pertater; but the root didn't grow.
So he pulled out his hoe and he dug up a toe.

Well it seems underground that a body was found
By the smell of a hound. And the hound made a sound;
Then the hound came unwound. That meant it was bound
To be close to the mound where Gil's corpse was around.

And when they found out there wasn't a doubt.
It was Gil down in there, with a big shiny pair
Of guns on his hips, and sand on his lips.

The dud had been dead with pounds of hot lead
Shot into his head. But all that he bled
Of the blood that was red, wasn't there it's been said.

His form didn't rot from the treatment it got;
Yet with his ten-year nap, Gil's face still looked like crap.

# *Chapter Six*

## Final Examination and Evaluation

~~~~~~~~~~~~~~~~~~~~~~~~~~~~~~~~~~~~~~~~~~~~~~~~~~~~~~~~~~~~~~~~~~~~

## The Grand Finale

If you have made it this far and have not been institutionalized and/or committed, then you will probably survive the final test. If you cannot make up your mind about any of the questions on this examination, then there is hope for you. If an answer to an item seems vividly clear, obvious, and/or intuitive, you have failed in your mission to become an ignoramus. But it is not hopeless being helpless. And worthlessness isn't all that bad either, then again nobody really is.

If you are confused, disoriented, and/or hypnotized by the test items, you must cease taking your medication at once and check into an inpatient clinic immediately. If you fall asleep while taking the test, you are probably too old or too young to benefit from mind emptying and thought constriction.

If every response seems equally as valid and therefore stupid, then you have successfully surpassed the initial stages of incomprehensible, idiosyncratic idiomania, if not ophidiomania. When you can think of additional answers that appear likewise engaging and stimulating as those provided, then you are thinking entirely too much and should repeat the course. If you are compelled to develop a guide to idiocy all by yourself, you should contact Dr. Zorch on his private line (202-555-1212) before you are detained and interrogated by the KGB.

If your mind is so compressed, empty, and/or shallow, that mundane tasks become overwhelmingly interesting and challenging, then you are ready for Phase II. Look for Phase II on the best-seller list next year. Also, plan on attending the Dr. Zorch motivation seminar coming soon to your convention center. Price of admission is $500 and includes a free pass to the lecture. Order now and receive your Dr. Zorch beanie and associated tattoo at no extra charge. It has been a pleasure to serve you in marrying incapacity and integrity, and reproducing incomprehensibility without dillydallying.

If this, then that; if that then though; if though then they; if they then this.

The following public service announcement has been brought to you by Dr. Ing Z. Books and his wife, Robin M. Blighn, Certified Public Accountants.

*Make sure you get out and vote, or else those numbskulls in power will continue to fold, spindle, and mutilate this government. Ensure that you punch the card all the way through or you will create a hanging chad. If this occurs, consult your pharmacist immediately and request salve for the treatment of dingle-berries.*

Paid for by the committee to reelect Ismael A. Skunk congressman, Helen Back chairwoman, Miss Dee Ling treasurer.

Thanks for sharing Zed.

# Liberal and Fine Arts Aptitude

**Part One:** *Music* – Determine which of the following are bona-fide Rock Groups by circling the name of the group. The number you identify correct, divided by five, time 100%, equals your score on Rock Trivia.

Lizard Breath

Fever Tree

Skin Flute and the Bonaphones

Strawberry Alarm Crotch

Stonehenge

Fur Burger and the Whisker Biscuits

The Blow Monkeys

Skid Marx and the Dingle-Berries

Filbert's Bottled Inks

Leopard-Skin Pillbox Hat

Fine Young Cannibals

Joe Bonanno and His Bunch

The Boston Patriots

Hang N. Wang and the Gang Bangers

Felatio Hornblower and the Gay Sailors

Mount Rushmore

Curly, Larry, and Moe

Sly and the Family Jewels

Pikes Peak and the Puke

Dr. Zorch and the Geeks

Little Dick

Screamin' Dreamers

Part Two: *Painting* – Study the priceless painting below entitled, *Nude Nun*. Identify the correct artist from the list provided. Do not masturbate to the painting unless you found this book in the restroom at the sperm bank.

Jacopo Bazongas
Camille Boobies
Dieric Bust
Alexandre Deecups
Bernardo El Blotto
Flippy Lips
Domenico Ghirliesendowed
Hellbent the Younger
Winslow Homo
Ric Hooters
Tomaso Massuccory
Henri Matittse
Edvard Munch
Pablo Picassole

Camille Pissory
Nicholas Pussery
Rambent van Ream
Peter-Paul Rawbuns
Jose de Ribarea
Paul Shazaam
Tiziano Titman
Jacopo Tittorita
Too Loose la Trick
William Turnher
Jan van Ecch
Onecent van Gouge
Antoine Whatho
Hans Whorebait

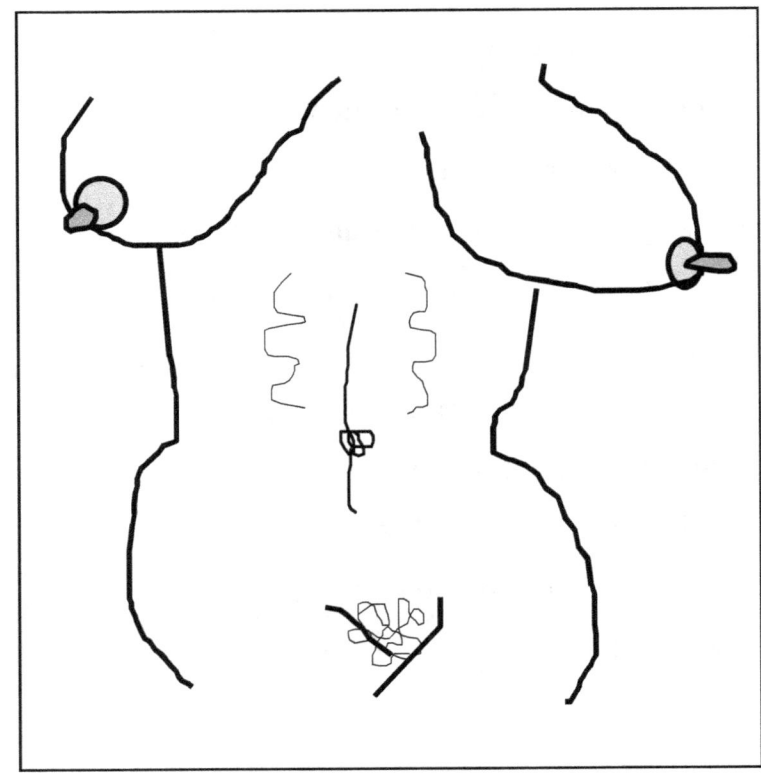

Part Three: *Prose and Poetry* – Identify the correct match involving well-known works and authors from the archives of American and English Literature.

1. Who wrote *Stopping by Woods on a Snowy Evening*?
   a. C. P. Snow
   b. Jack Frost
   c. Alfreds Long Tennishoes

2. Which of the following were written on John's Headstone?
   a. The Cemetery Tales
   b. The Cremation of Sam McGee
   c. Death Be Not Proud

3. Which of the following were written by Cotton Mouther?
   a. The New England Viper
   b. Life on the Mississippi
   c. The Jungle Books

4. Which of the following were written by Edgar Allen Poo?
   a. It Wandered Lonely as a Cloud
   b. The Sleeper
   c. Gone With the Wind

5. Who wrote Mobile Dick?
   a. Johnny Wadswork Longfellow
   b. Emily Dickinsome
   c. Boner W. Overstreet

6. Which of the following were written by Pussey Bitche Chilley?
   a. The Scarlet Underwear
   b. The Red Badge of Coagulate
   c. A Tale of Two Titties

7. Who wrote *For a Mouthy Woman*?
   a. James Throbber
   b. Oh Henry
   c. E. E. Cummings

8. Who wrote *To my Dear Husband*?
   a. Anne Broadteats
   b. Pearly Buttocks
   c. Margaret Widemouth Jaqueoff

9. Which of the following were written by John Bunions?
   a. I'd Like to See One Lap the Miles
   b. Pedestrian's Progress
   c. The Velvet Shoes

10. Who wrote *Twixt Two Tails*?
    a. Markus Twain
    b. William Wordsworthless
    c. Sir Walter Rawthighs

11. Which of the following were written by Sir John Suckling?
    a. The Hollow Men
    b. The Man with the Ho'
    c. The Call Girl of the Wild

12. Who wrote *The Yellow Violet* and *Ode on a Grecian Urinal*?
    a. Rip Van Pinkle
    b. William Shakesbeer
    c. Willa Catheter

13. Who wrote *Poor Richard's Ailingbad*?
    a. John Strainback
    b. Conrad Aching
    c. Carl Sandbag

14. Who wrote *Vatican Pond*?
    a. Alexander Pope
    b. Elizabeth Bishop
    c. Siegfried Baffoon

15. Who wrote *Billy Butt the Sailor*?
    a. Robert Browning
    b. John Dung
    c. Ring Lardass

16. Who wrote *The Dirty Old Man and the Sleeze*?
    a. William Fornicator
    b. Whoreman Cousins
    c. Geoffrey Chaser

17. Which of the following were written by Francis Bacon?
    a. Omlet
    b. Because I could not stop for breakfast
    c. Choose something like a sty

## Foreign Languages Aptitude

Part One: Identify the expressions below that accurately describe or define the act of passing gas, as spoken in the language of Jive. Then use each of them in a sentence.

"Broke wind."                          "Stepped on a frog."

"Let an air biscuit fly."              "Cut one loose."

"Sliced the cheese."                   "Silent but deadly."

"Toxic attack."                        "Pull my finger."

"Mus-turd gas."                        "Someone died here."

"Methane drain."                       "Blow it out your ass."

"Stale breeze."                        "Music to my intestines."

"Raising a stink."                     "Pooper blooper."

"Those barking cockroaches."           "Flatulencial."

 "It wandered lonely as a cloud."

"Catch that, tack it to the wall, and paint it green."

Part Two: Identify the expressions below that accurately describe the act or command to depart, as spoken in the language of Jive. Write a single paragraph in which all valid expressions are used once.

"Make like a tree and leave."

"Make like a buffalo turd and hit the dusty trail."

"Make like a banana and split."

"Make like an onion and peel."

"Make like dandruff and flake off."

"Make like an airliner and take off."

"Make like Columbus and get lost."

"Make like a gay bat boy and shag ass."

"Make like a bee and buzz off."

"Make like a drunk driver and hit the bricks."

"Make like a gigolo and get a move on."

"Make like a prude and bust a move."

"Make like a mountaineer and take a hike."

"Make like radioactivity and fall out."

"Make like a back door man and high-ball the gates."

"Make like a retired proctologist and un-ass."

"Make like a library and book."

"Make like a blender and beat it."

"Make like Wild Bill and get the heck out of Dodge."

"Make like a stage hand and change the scenery."

"Make like a bakery truck and haul buns."

# General Studies Aptitude

Part One: *Multiple Choice* – Select the most accurate response. (Hint: all item responses are correct, applicable, and true, so pick the most undeniable.)

1. Which of the following were famous philosophers from ancient Greece or Rome?
   a. Phallus Erectus
   b. Testiclese
   c. Tittius Humongous
   d. Luscious Cunnilingus
   e. Homo and Ulezzes
   f. Play Dough
   g. Ludicrus Quirk, the Trype

2. Which is the correct definition of a honeymoon?
   a. When you moon your honey
   b. When your honey moons you
   c. Gazing at someone's derriere and finding it pleasing
   d. Luscious Cunnilingus

3. Which of the following are considered forms of drug abuse?
   a. Incinerating a brick of cocaine
   b. Poisoning a marijuana plant with herbicide
   c. Flushing barbiturates and/or amphetamines down the toilet
   d. Breaking a bottle of liquor on the pavement

4. Which of the following statements are true?
   a. A swap meet is where you swap your meat for that of another.
   b. A meat market is where you swat your meat against that of another.
   c. A swinging night club is also referred to as a swap market.
   d. A swinging night club is also referred to as a meat meet.

5. Which of the following would you find at a butcher shop *and* a bordello?
   a. Boneless round, beef trust, prime rib, flank, rump roast, hot links, salami
   b. Breast of chicken, gaming cocks, cornish hens, quail, dark and white meat
   c. Filet of fish, scum-sucker, barracuda, big mouth bass, red snapper, blubber, shrimp.
   d. Sow belly, sweat hog, ham hock, pork roast, peccary, loin chops, raw bacon.

6. Which of the following would you find at a tavern *and* a bordello?
   a. Men with high balls
   b. Women with cocktails
   c. John boy getting a Quickie
   d. Tom Collins slamming down Mexican Brandy
   e. A stiff shot of Seven on the rocks
   f. Pink Lady slurping Bailey's Cream

(6. Continued)
- g. Beef Eaters nursing their Peni Colladas
- h. A Colorado Bulldog downing a Bloody Mary
- i. A Jamaican guy holding his Banana Diquerie
- j. A Jamaican gal holding her Chocolate Cherry Cordial
- k. A Black Russian having a double shot of Southern Comfort
- l. Harvey Wallbanger passed out with Old Grandad
- m. Vintage '69 with Sherry in the wine cellar
- n. All of the below

7. How much wood would a woodchuck chuck if a woodchuck could chuck wood?
- a. He wouldn't
- b. The woodchuck would upchuck
- c. I believe the woodchuck would leave it to beaver
- d. The woodchuck had bad luck. He couldn't duck and was struck. He got stuck under the truck, and now he's a pile of yucky muck.

8. Was the following conversation recorded at a golf course *or* a bordello?

Duffer: Would you like to play a round?
Pro: I've played with all the other members here.
Duffer: How do you like my driver? It's the kind with the
      enlarged head, and the long, hard, stiff shaft.
Pro: That's the way I like them.
Duffer: I have a handicap. How many shots will you spot me?
Pro: Take as many strokes as you need. I'll let you score.
Duffer: You know, I've never made a hole-in-one.
Pro: It's easy. Just take a smooth, steady swipe at it; and
      don't forget to follow through.
Duffer: My balls usually bounce into the bushes.
Pro: I can teach you how to punch and pitch with my special wedge.
Duffer: I'll probably slam it right into the water hazard.
Pro: Just make sure you don't go out of bounds.
Duffer: I only have two balls in my bag.
Pro: You only need one to shoot with.
Duffer: I'm aiming for a sixty-nine so I can go pro.
Pro: Take a straight approach to the hole.
Duffer: Wow, what a great little niblick!
Pro: It's perfectly designed to get it up high.
Duffer: I like the mounds in these fairways and the elevated tee box.
Pro: Remember, the surface is very moist and slick, and the
      fringe has been shaved short so the balls will bite.
Duffer: Fore!
Pro: Drive on!
Duffer: Look at the size of that divot.

(8. Continued)
>       Pro: You landed in the bunker.
>       Duffer: I'm out of practice.
>       Pro: I'll hold the flagstick steady in the hole and you take your best shot.
>       Duffer: Wow, what a great lie.
>       Pro: That's par for the course.


## Part Two: *Fill in the Blank* – Provide the correct responses, demonstrating your knowledge of synonyms, antonyms, and homonyms.

1. Show what you know about synonyms by listing as many words or phrases as possible defining an obnoxious oldster.

_____

_____

_____

[*Excellent answers*: old bag, old bat, old biddy, old codger, old coot, old crow, old fart, old fogy, old fossil, old geezer, old mossback, old buzzard]
[*Acceptable answers*: ancient artifact, antique, decrepit dodo, medieval relic, meddling Methuselah, my parents, nagging neolith, rotting remains, senile senior citizen, zombie]

2. Show what you know about synonyms by listing as many words or phrases as possible defining an impetuous imp.

_____

_____

_____

[*Excellent answers*: brat, creep, cretin, dolt, dud, dunce, punk, puss, rascal, sprig, whelp, whipper-snapper, wimp, wuss, rapscallion]

3. Show what you know about antonyms by listing words or phrases that, by definition, are the opposite of the following:

ax, bird, decibel, huh, moose, plop, quack, rhumba, vampire, yucca, poop, crematorium, machinegun, menopause, croissant.

_____

_____

_____

[*Excellent answers*: Please refer to the next edition of this textbook.]

ninny

4. Show what you know about homonyms by listing as many words or phrases that sound like or rhyme with the following:

hieroglyphic, kayaking, prophylactic, ostriches, onomatopoeia, troubadour, curmudgeon, thermonuclear, redorange, formaldehyde.

_____

_____

_____

[*Excellent Answers*: Send $100 to the Dr. Zorch Foundation for answers to this test item.]

5. Bonus Item: Show what you know about homonyms by listing as many words or phrases that sound like or rhyme with the following:

Amerigo Vespucci, Zbigniew Brzezinski, Copernicus, Nairobian, Okefenokee, Zimbabwe, Appalachia, Zhangjiakou.

_____

_____

_____

[*Excellent Answers*: Send $1000 to the Dr. Zorch Foundation for answers to this test item.]

6. Extra Credit Item

   a. Give a homonym for antonym.
   b. Give an antonym for synonym.
   c. Give a synonym for antonym.
   d. Give a homonym for synonym.

_____

_____

_____

[*Excellent Answers*: (a) aunt done him; (b) antonym; (c) anti-name; (d) sinnin' hymn]

It's
Party
Time

# Science Aptitude

Part One: *Chemistry* – Demonstrate your knowledge of chemistry by answering these true-false questions. Each correct answer is worth 3.1416 points minus $\pi$ to the quantity sqared.

1. Only a sour puss should douche with sodium bicarbonate (baking soda for you non-nerds).

2. Only a sour puss douches with white vinegar.

3. When a woman is on her seventh period, her atomic weight goes up.

4. An organism that has no sex organs is made up exclusively of neutrons.

5. The correct chemical symbology for sodium bicarbonate is NaACpH.

6. The correct chemical symbology for calcium carbonate is Caca.

7. The correct chemical symbology for cobalt chloride is Cob Clyde.

8. A mixture of boron and neon would produce BoNe.

9. The air we breathe is a mixture of chemicals and gasses symbolized as NBC.

10. Gallium and sulfur (GaS) make up the common discharge known as flatulence.

11. Ag is the symbol for agriculture.

12. In the Mexican version of the periodic table of elements, silver is symbolized as Si, señor.

13. The symbol H refers to the element called heroin.

14. The hardest substance known to man is a compound made of carbon, oxygen, and tungsten, and is symbolized as COW.

15. The most powerful rare earth known to man, which can make a man keel over with one whiff, is symbolized as PU.

16. Lysergic acid diethyl-amide is the chemical compound most often prescribed by doctors for patients experiencing hallucinations and delusions.

17. LSD consists of a mixture of the following chemicals: Lococene, Spacetate, Deliriumite.

18. Tetra Hydra Cannabinol (ThC) is the antidote for overdoses of hashish.

19. Md is a chemical compound found only in Maryland.

20. Pb is the chemical compound known as puberty.

Bonus Item: Identify and write the elements listed below:

I Am N As  _____

U N He Ar O K _____

Ce Eu In Th Nd _____

And a good time was had by all at the Dance Macabre.

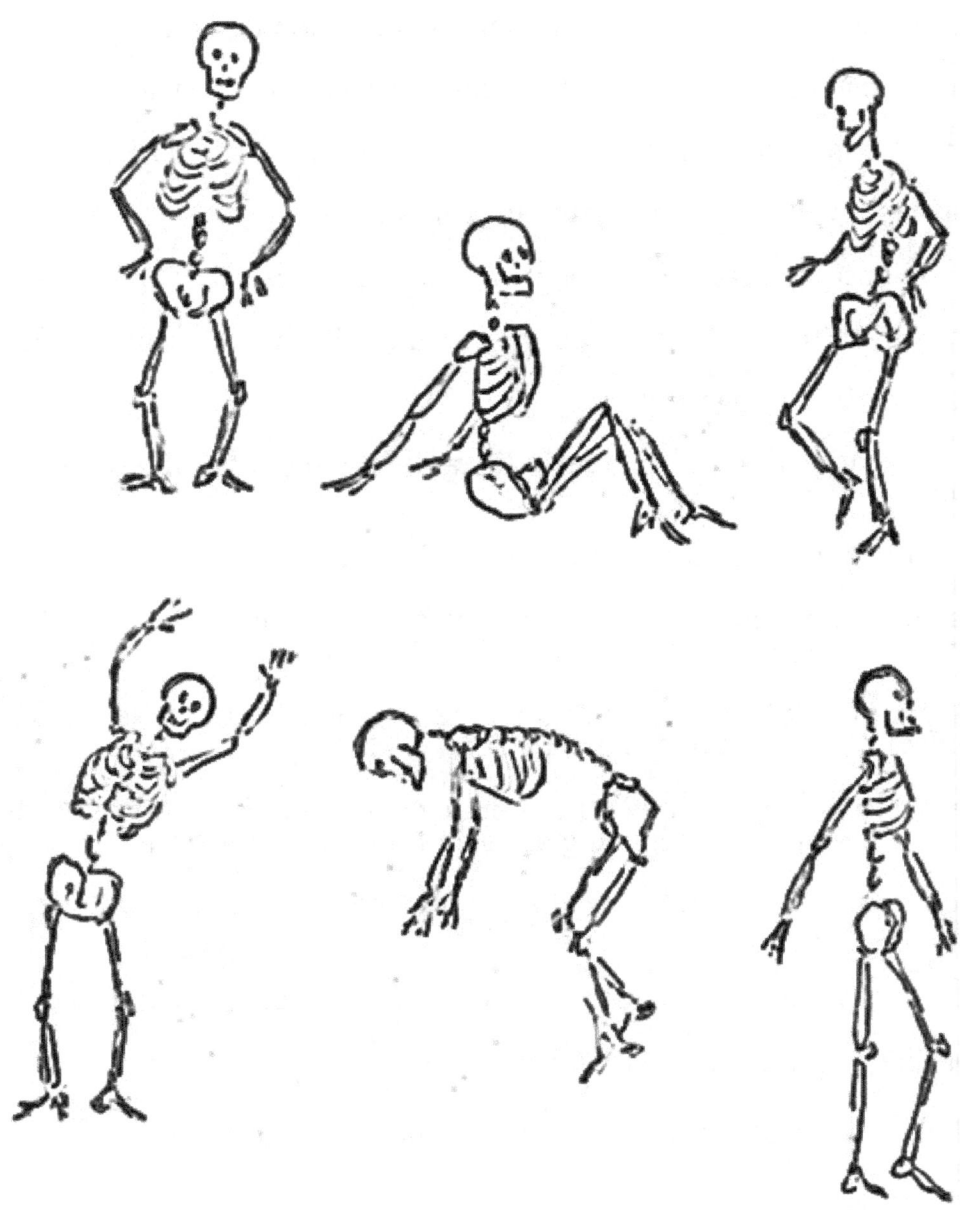

Part Two: *Basic Anatomy* – Identify the parts of the body from the multiple choice items.

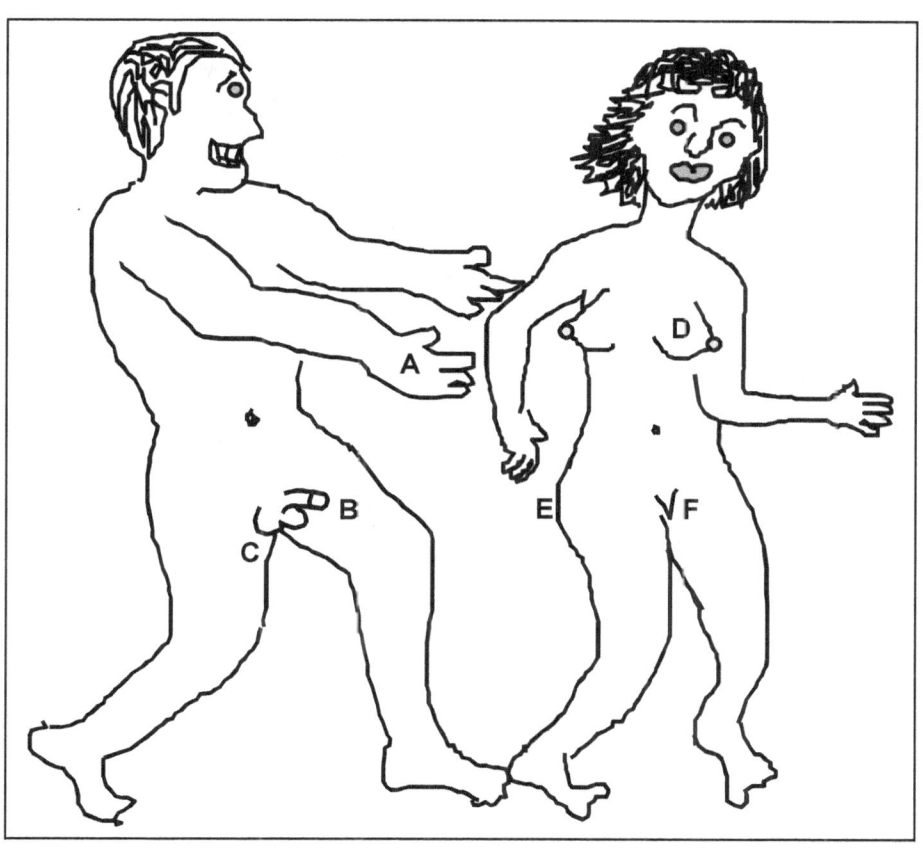

A    Jack
       Clutch
       Alternator
       Fuel Pump

D    Headlights
       Hubcaps
       Spark Plugs
       Tooters

B    Dip Stick
       Connecting Rod
       Universal Joint
       Drive Shaft

E    Tail Gate or Bumper
       Rear Shock Absorber
       Vibration Damper
       Engine Mounts

C    Ball Bearings
       Distributor
       Lower Ball Joints
       Pistons

F    Grease Fitting
       Intake Manifold
       Master Cylinder
       Crankcase

# Identify the parts of the body (Continued).

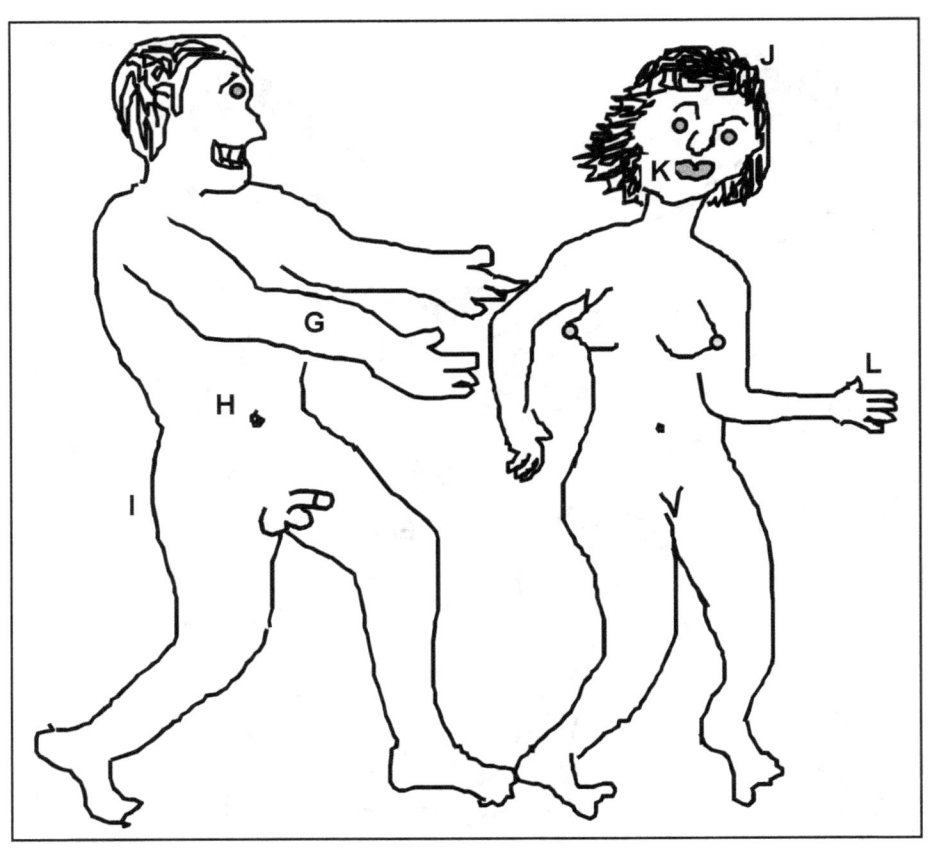

| G | Rocker Arm | J | Cylinder Head |
|---|---|---|---|
| | Front Stabilizer Bar | | Head Gasket |
| | Cam Shaft | | Timing Gear |
| | Throw-out Bearing | | Speedometer |
| | | | |
| H | Cylinder Block | K | Main Seal |
| | Steering Column | | Water Pump |
| | Suspension | | Catalytic Converter |
| | Frame | | Brake Fluid |
| | | | |
| I | Pos. Crankcase Ventilation | L | Circuit Breaker |
| | Exhaust Pipe | | Push Rods |
| | Vapor Line | | Sending Unit |
| | Odometer | | Throttle Linkage |

# Errata and Your Continuing Education

Here is a useful reference guide that provides you with the unforeseen mistakes that were deliberately made in the body of this document. It is your objective to study each item and determine which section in the book it belongs to; items are randomly presented to control for stupidity effects.

Next, in your continuing search for fallaciousness and feeblemindedness, restudy the appropriate section of the text where the missing item has been located. Did you notice the exponential increase in your frivolous figurations? This response is routinely required for remedial reparation of your repertory of ridiculous responses.

---

X. The conversation that follows is typical of which popular card game? Circle the correct choice(s).

Poker   Gin   21   Solitaire   Crazy-8   Slapjack   Spoons

a. All I've got is ten high.
b. I've go two pairs, crosses and reds!
c. My three black beauties have got you beat.
d. Well I'm totally straight, with a low placebo high.
e. Check out this purple microdot flush!
f. Full house, bennies over barbs.
g. That don't stand up to my four ludes.
h. Too bad, see my pretty royal white lines, straight in a row!
i. Read 'em and weep people, five dimes!

---

66. *Fill in the Blank.*

What flies use when they cast their lines: a ____ hook.

What freaks use when they form their lines: a ____ whore.

What whores give when they open their lines: a ____ shot.

What doing lines and shots with whores will get you: in deep ____.

9. Runner-up in the *Politics* category.

## The Tires

For a year and a day the commotion would stay,
And the world might never redress.
It began in a snap (I was taking a crap),
While the day was so great it was blessed.

From a Firestone fire there arose quite a tire
(The world unaware of the fear).
And the ranks were piled higher, by the banks of the mire,
With the Uniroyals down to Goodyear.

Later, Atlas galore, Big O, Kelly, much more;
B. F. Gooodrich was leading the way.
With all kidding aside, while they all multiplied,
It was three solid weeks of dark gray.

First they marched to L. A., up to Frisco, the bay,
Until all California was taken.
Over deserts, the Rockies, these wide-oval jockeys
Invaded; the West looked like bacon.

They rolled through the bayou, and up to Ohio,
Farther north as they smashed New York City.
Then the circular beast finally flattened the East,
And they left the whole nation in pity.

Every tire was in motion (I was lost to this notion).
They had driven the nation aside.
Then I found the solution:  This new type pollution
Would take the whole world for a ride.

Down to Europe and Greece (I just laughed and made peace)
As they flooded Taiwan and Malasia.
Further outward they spanned, they took China, Japan,
And eventually captured all Asia.

Next the tires doubled back, they took Australia black,
And then back to the place of their birth.
What with Africa gone, I just sat on the john
(For I knew they had conquered the earth).

Now that all foreign lands had obliged their demands,
(I just kicked back and played with my balls),
Every city and town had been trounced and squashed down
By retreads, and black or whitewalls.

# The Tires
## (continued)

The world had been branded. The roads were abandoned.
The cars, trucks, and bikes all lay still.
No-one wandered or roamed; everybody stayed home.
The tires rolled with a passion to kill.

Corrupted and vile they governed awhile,
But their politics: flat out no good.
I spent all my time drinkin' (there was no sense in thinkin'),
And I slept just as much as I could.

Then the steel-belted kind all at once changed their mind,
They decided to rule on their own.
But the radials lacked what it took to fight back,
And the tubes of their race were soon blown.

At the knowledge of this (I was taking a piss)
All the tires in the world seemed uptight.
They would sit back no more with this hard rubber door
Being shut, leaving them out of sight.

After being insulted, they finally revolted.
(The power had gone to their heads).
So they busted their chains and they left the remains
Of some hubcaps, ball bearings, and treads.

Well the tires, they were bold, but they couldn't keep hold,
So they met at the site that was chosen;
Where the heads of all brands said their prayers and joined hands;
And the reign of the tires was frozen.

A peace treaty was signed in the back of my mind,
And the wheels of the world resumed turning.
They returned to their place in society's race,
But I flat opted out of the journey.

---

Stay tuned for our newest variety show seen only on the Pubic Broad-Casting Network (PBCN): *The Didactic Dr. Demento and His Dynamic Double Donkey Dildo* Don't miss it if you can't.

DR. ZORCH'S IDIOCIES

-22. Did the following episode occur at a grocery store *or* a swinging nightclub?

To continue, I went to the meat market for a weekly swap meet. One couple was swapping their T-bone and filet of fish with another couples team. Singles were there to exchange peppered salami for breast of chicken. The butcher's bar had special cuts. At the poultry counter gaming cocks were traded for cornish hens; there were quail, goosers, different kinds and cuts of fowl. And what a variety of swine. A plump sow was negotiating for some ham hock; she was a real porker and he was a typical peccary. There also was quite a selection of beef. They had everything from calf's loins to prime rib, flank steak, rump roast, eye of round, hot sausage links, you name it.

I was a wildcat, just hanging out at the sushi bar, where that scum-sucking bottom-feeder accompanied the big-mouth bass who I identified previously. Three lesboes were swapping their red snapper and tuna for some whale blubber. I was distracted by a barracuda shaking her shrimp cocktail. Then I saw her: Miss Kitty wearing her high heel sneakers. I couldn't take it anymore, so I grabbed puss-in-boots and she split for me, yeah me. I would have given her a ride on my hotrod, but she turned out to be a real sourpuss.

---

## And now for a few words from our sponsors...

Please support: *Dogs for Africa.* Donate your condemned canines to this worthy cause and make a dent in world hunger. Wouldn't you like to fill the stomachs of starving children? Don't you have any compassion? After all, what else are we supposed to do with all those strays? You cannot permit them to get gassed and incinerated, while you can easily contribute just $5.00 a day and have them shipped to Africa, where some unfortunate individual will give them a good home. Feed your altruistic needs and the needy at the same time. Don't treat those deprived kids like dogs but give them doggie treats. You'll sleep better at night knowing that somewhere, somebody is nourished thanks to your generosity and a little dog meat. That's what we call dog food. So remember, one man's pooch is another man's lunch.

WANTED: A bright, aspiring entrepreneur to become an apprentice at my Fishing Tackle and Bait Shop. Learn all the tools of the trade and work your way up to the level of Master Baiter. Job requirements: Must be good with the hands and have excellent finger dexterity; must love the smell of fish and the taste of salt; must be willing to come on demand and work long shafts during peak seasons. Experienced hookers and seamen preferred. Contact: Doug Moe Graves, proprietor (call toll free: *1-888-EAT FISH*).

FYI, feed your intellect; try it for one week and see if it doesn't remove those bald spots on your brain. Who says you cannot grow hair on a billiard ball? Receive one month free if you order a twelve month supply now. Use the code-word THINK and reduce the price further by ten percent. A duplicate of the popular logo is provided below; you can attach it to your ceiling to remind you when it is time to reorder.

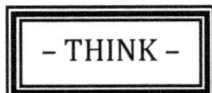

firs-neuf

# Famous Quotes
## (Name the famous philosopher-rapper who uttered this monologue.)

I met her in France. It only took a glance and I was under her trance. Like the blow from a lance, I was knocked askance by her advance, right out of my stance. My desire was enhanced so I asked her to dance; she offered no resistance. I put my hands on her gams as she rubbed against my pants. I felt a throbbing in my glans. We didn't want to prance, so we took a chance on this wild romance. But the fancy fantasy was soon canceled by her constant demands. How she raves and rants, seeking intermittent reassurance, as I near the end of my patience and endurance. In an instant I'll need some persistent sanative assistance, so please hand me a sanitary napkin.

---

## Number Nine. Where exactly *is* the peck of pickled peppers that Peter Piper picked?

a. Poor Peter was picked up by the police for packing a pistol, got in a peck of problems, and now he's got to pay the pied piper.
b. Peter peed on the plant and the peppers became pale and putrid, making Peter puke.
c. Contrary Mary gave them all to Larry, who gave one each to Terri, Barry, Harry, Perry, Gary, Carrie, and Jerry. Then Peter committed harakiri.
d. Horny Peter traded them to ornery Jack Horner for a worn and torn assortment of porn.

---

## .001 *Multiple Meanings*:
## Draw a line from the word to its correct meaning(s).

Coast   Fling   Match   Hunky-Dory   Creep   Hooters

Present   Pitch   Duck   Fall   Joint   Butt   Trick

- Tripping and landing on your butt during Autumn.
- Drunken riff-raff that crawls across the ground on their belly.
- Dodging a web-footed fowl flying towards your face.
- Two barn owls with big boobies.
- Getting bumped by a billy goat in the derriere.
- Throwing a couple of adulterers overboard.
- Tossing out a bucket of tar.
- Selling your body for sex during Halloween.
- Holding a reefer between your fingers while inside a jail cell.
- A fishing boat filled with big guys eating candy bars.
- Giving a gift to someone who is in attendance.
- Cruising along the shoreline on a bicycle without pedaling.
- Twins using phosphorous to light a fire at a tennis tournament.
- An item that doesn't belong because it has no relationship.

# Appendix and Coloring Book

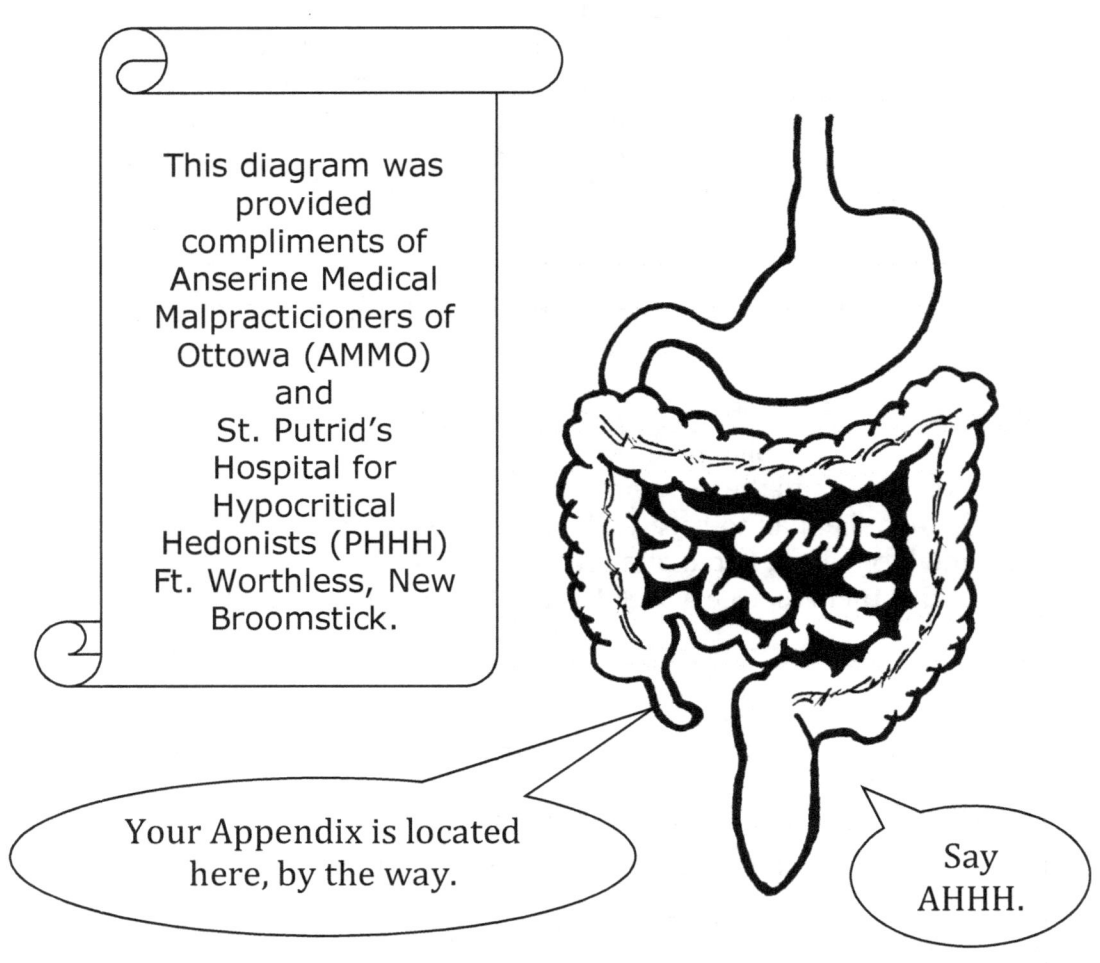

This diagram was provided compliments of Anserine Medical Malpracticioners of Ottowa (AMMO) and St. Putrid's Hospital for Hypocritical Hedonists (PHHH) Ft. Worthless, New Broomstick.

Your Appendix is located here, by the way.

Say AHHH.

We hope you have enjoyed your quest for density and we pray that you will continue in your endeavor to drain your brain of all that useless grey matter. Dr. Zorch would like to express his appreciation for your participation and enthusiasm. Aren't you glad that you don't have to deal with that dumb old attention span mess anymore?

As a final exercise, try to identify with the characters in the scenes that follow as you color the pictures. Make sure you finish coloring every picture in this book, and you will have completed the course successfully. Congratulations. Thank you, and good day.

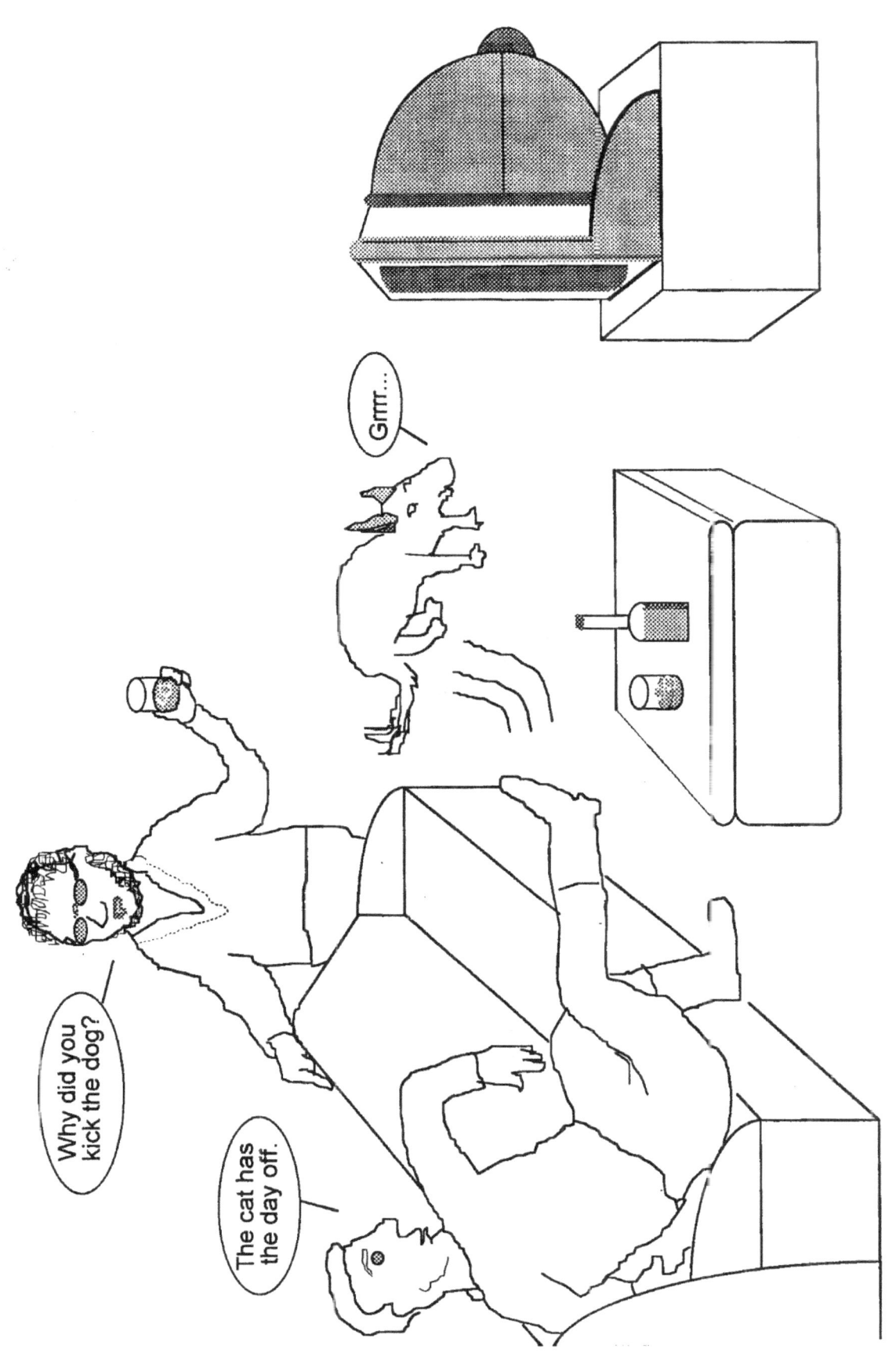

DR. ZORCH'S IDIOCIES

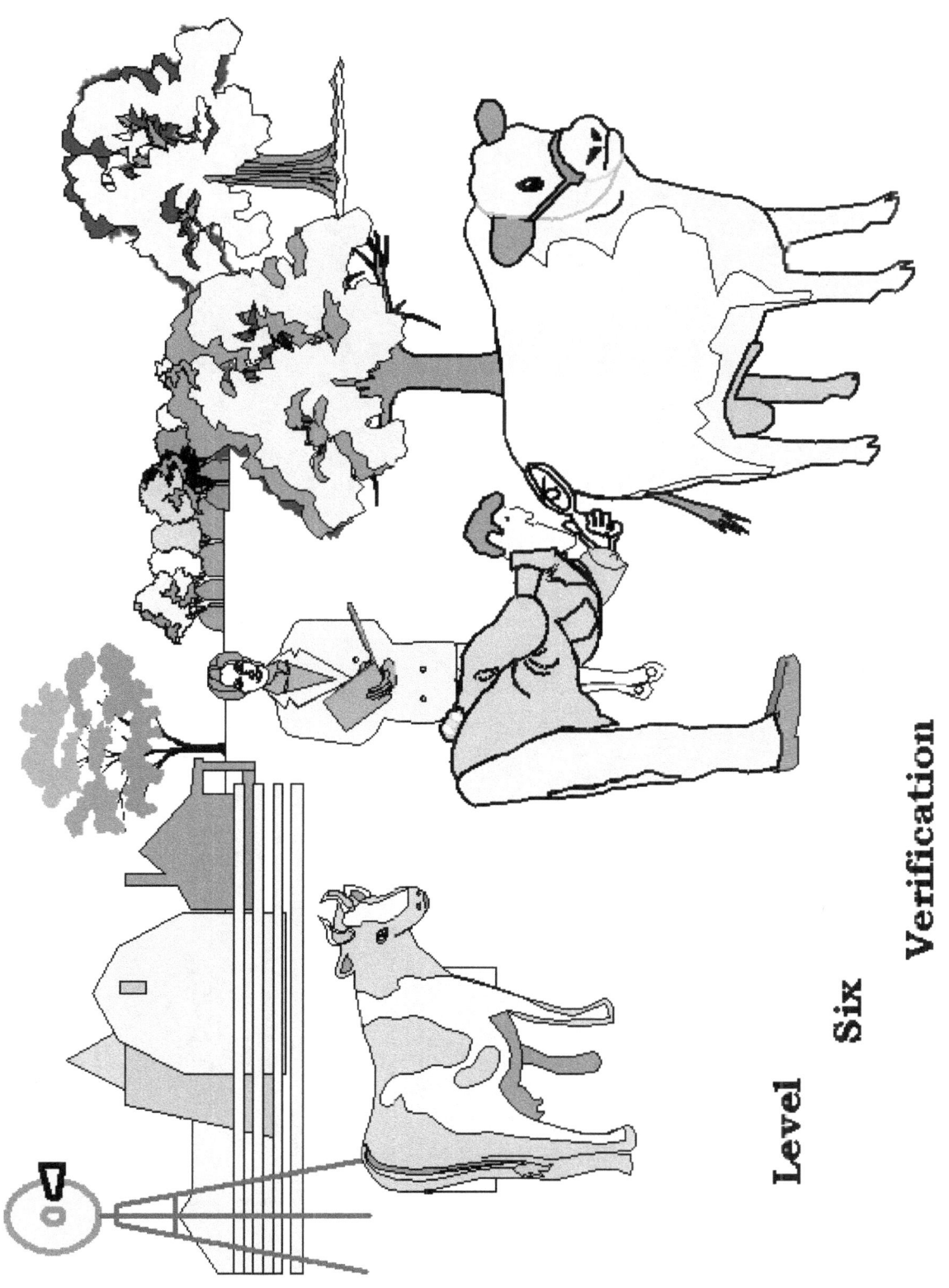

**Level Six Verification**

DR. ZORCH'S IDIOCIES

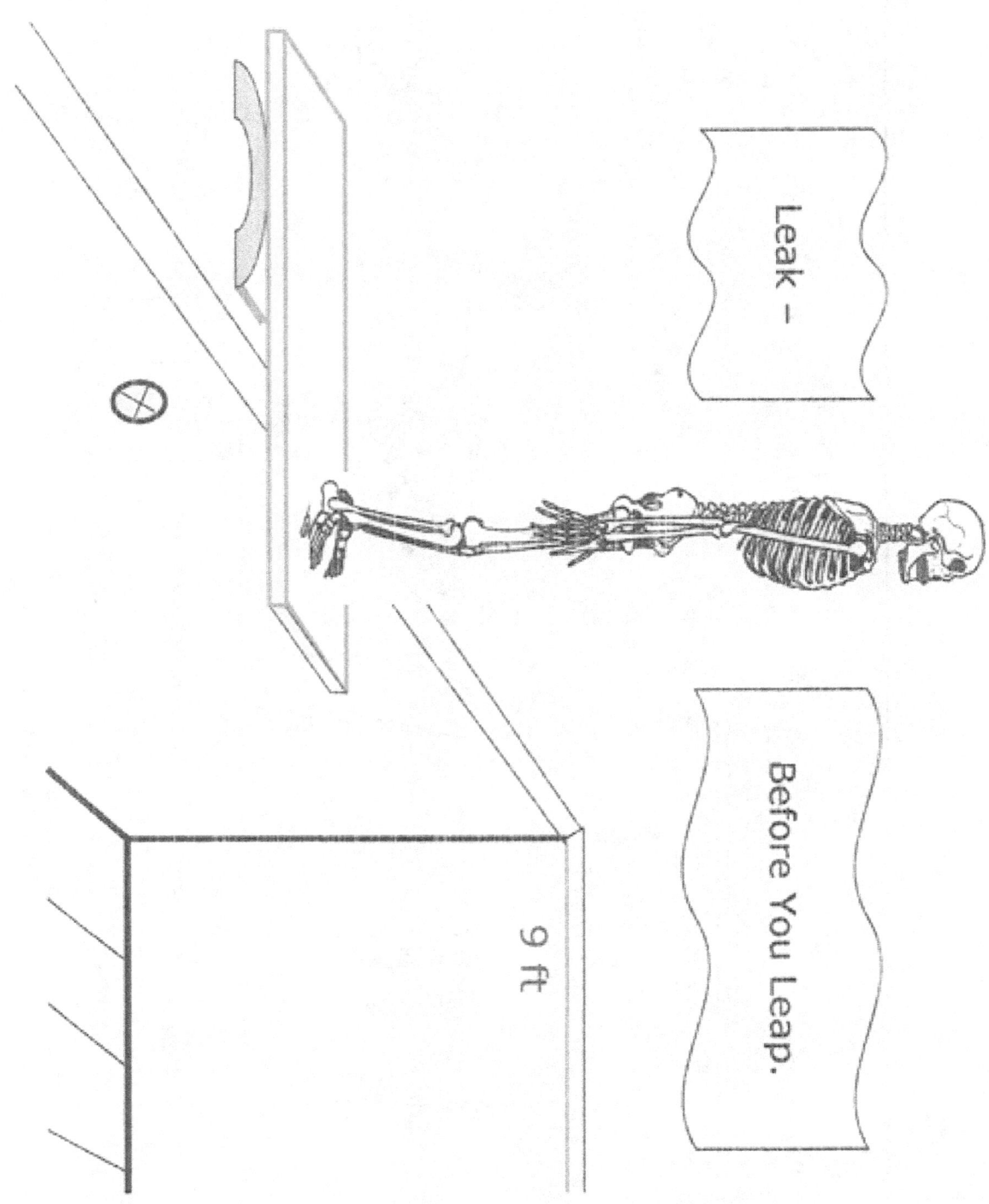

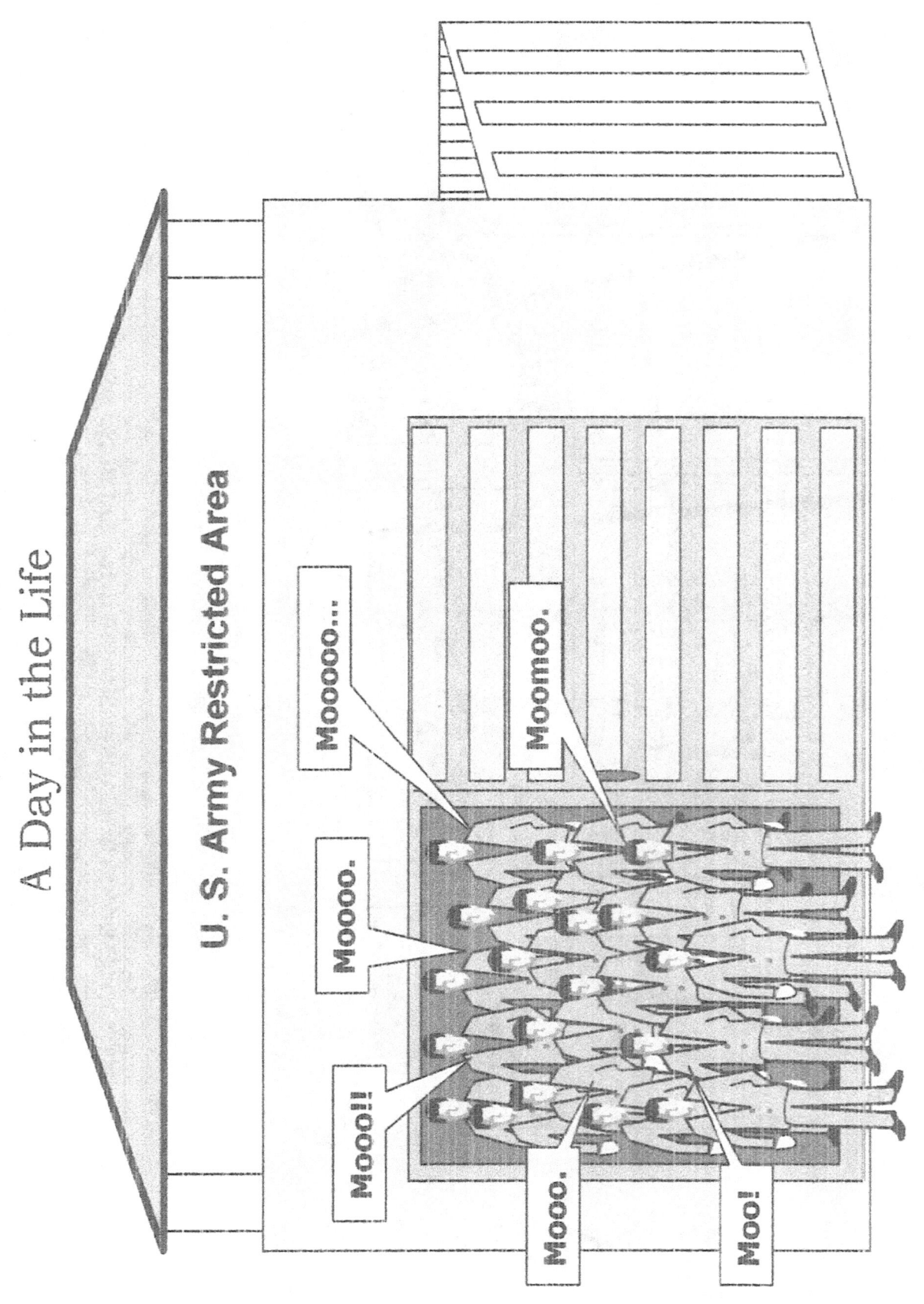

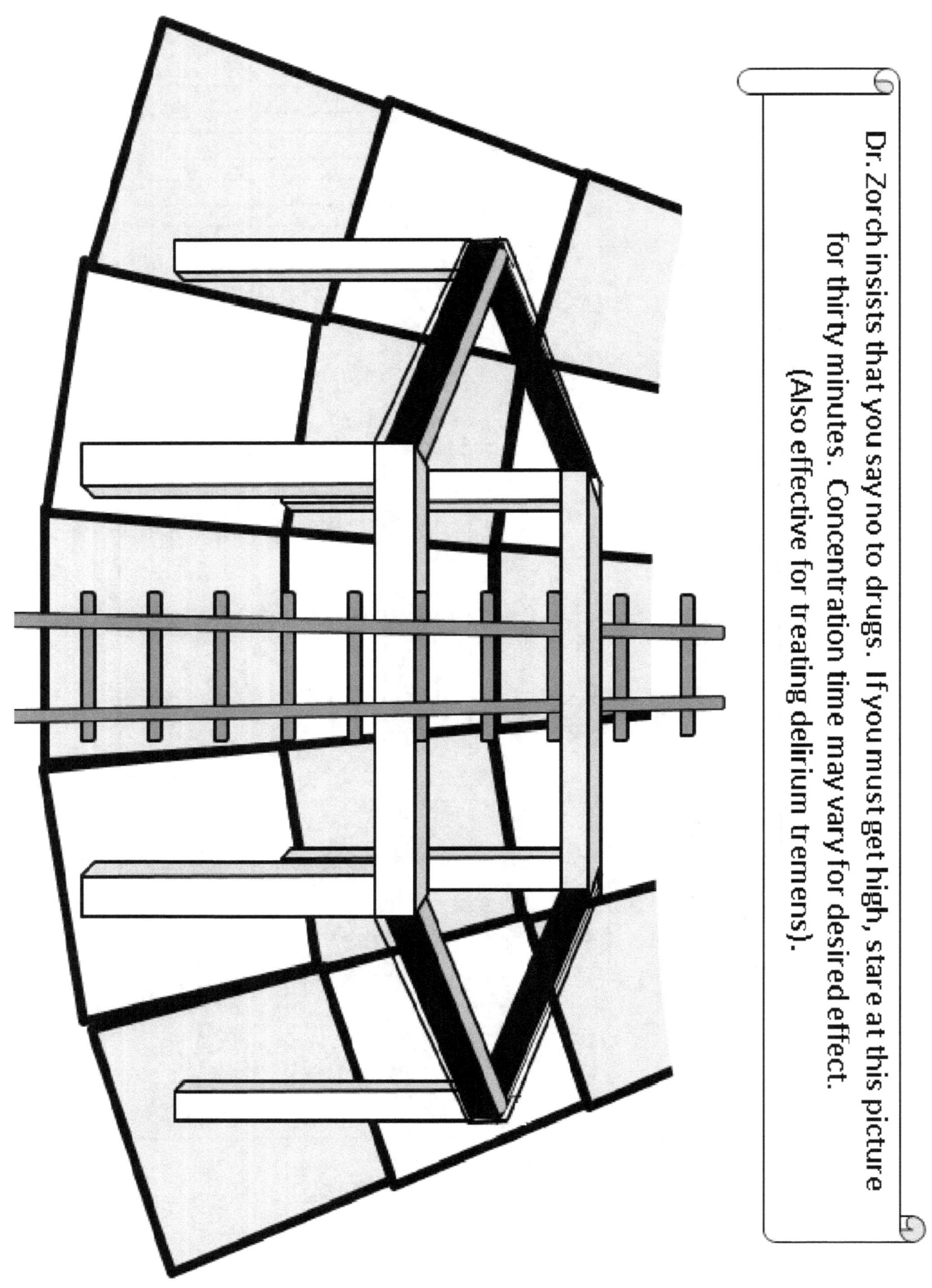

Dr. Zorch insists that you say no to drugs. If you must get high, stare at this picture for thirty minutes. Concentration time may vary for desired effect. (Also effective for treating delirium tremens).

You are what you drink.

Therefore, if you don't drink, you're a nobody.

So, drink Millionaire's Club blended bourbon, and you'll feel like a million bucks.

Robin and Minnie Stills, *Hoodoos & Spirits, Inc.* Back Woods County, TN.

DR. ZORCH'S IDIOCIES

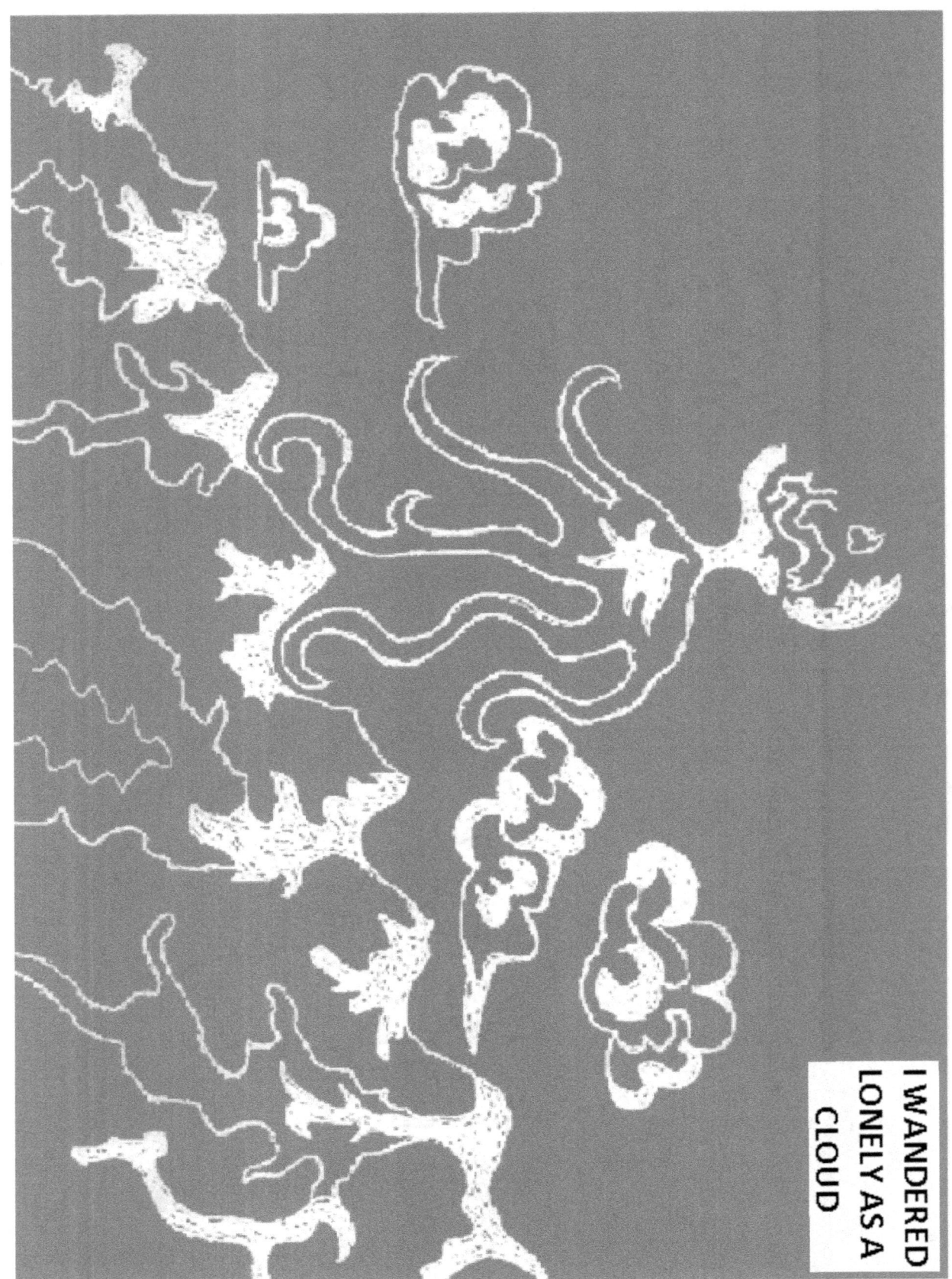

I WANDERED LONELY AS A CLOUD

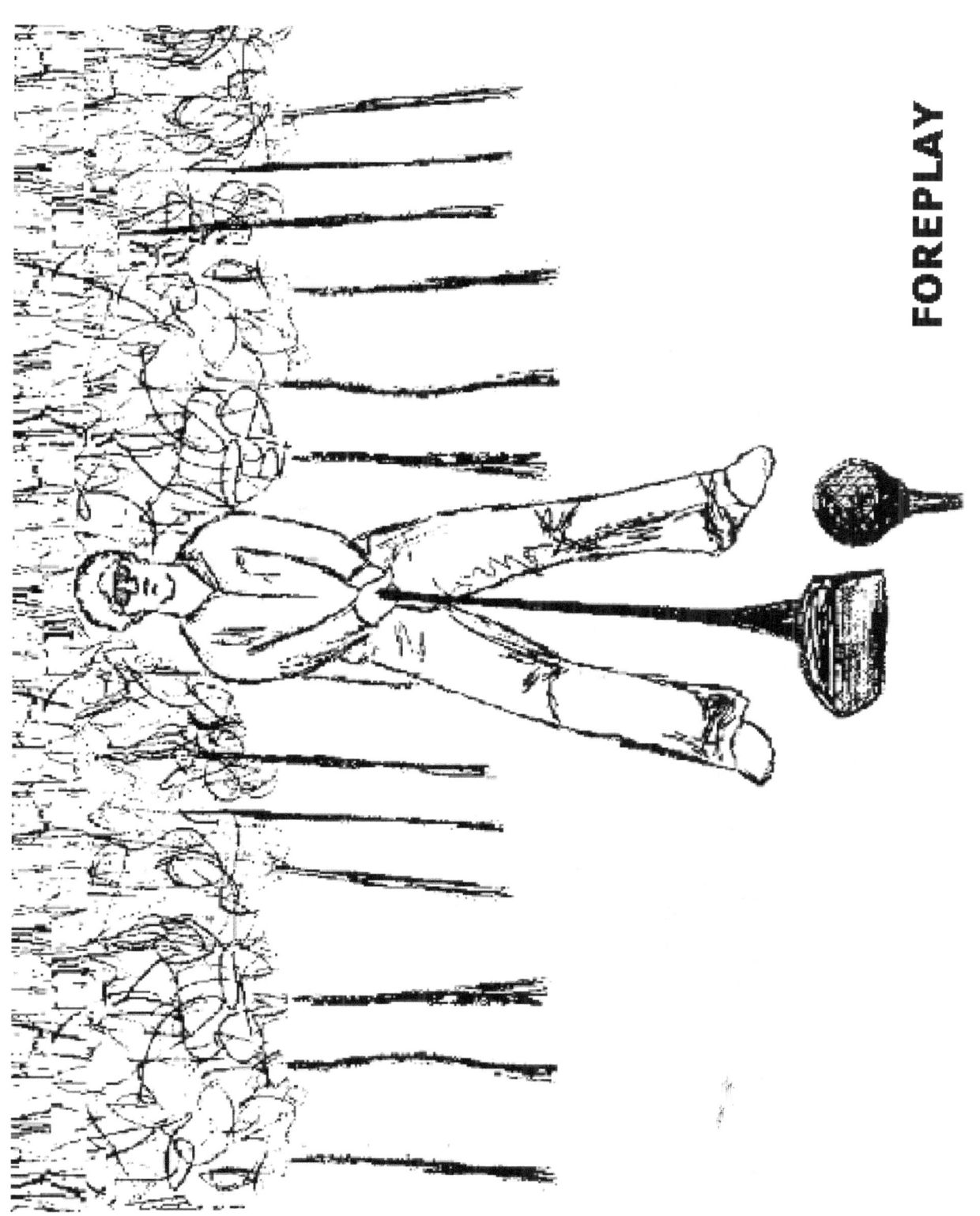

FOREPLAY

DR. ZORCH'S IDIOCIES

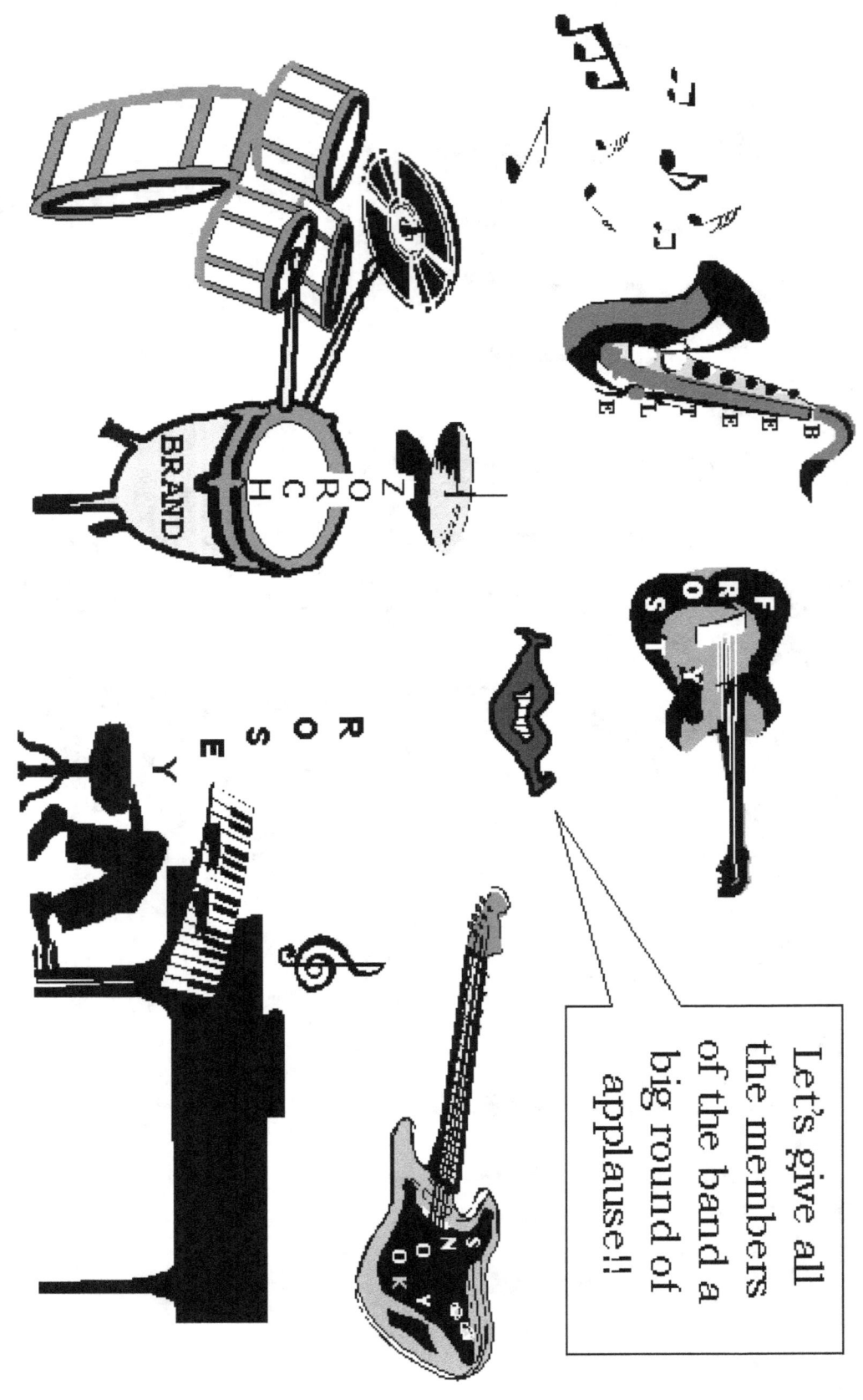

The hills can see, hear, smell, and feel. Can you?

All things are beautiful but deadly at the same time.

You will not breach the mountain without them.

They are there for us to use, but not to abuse.

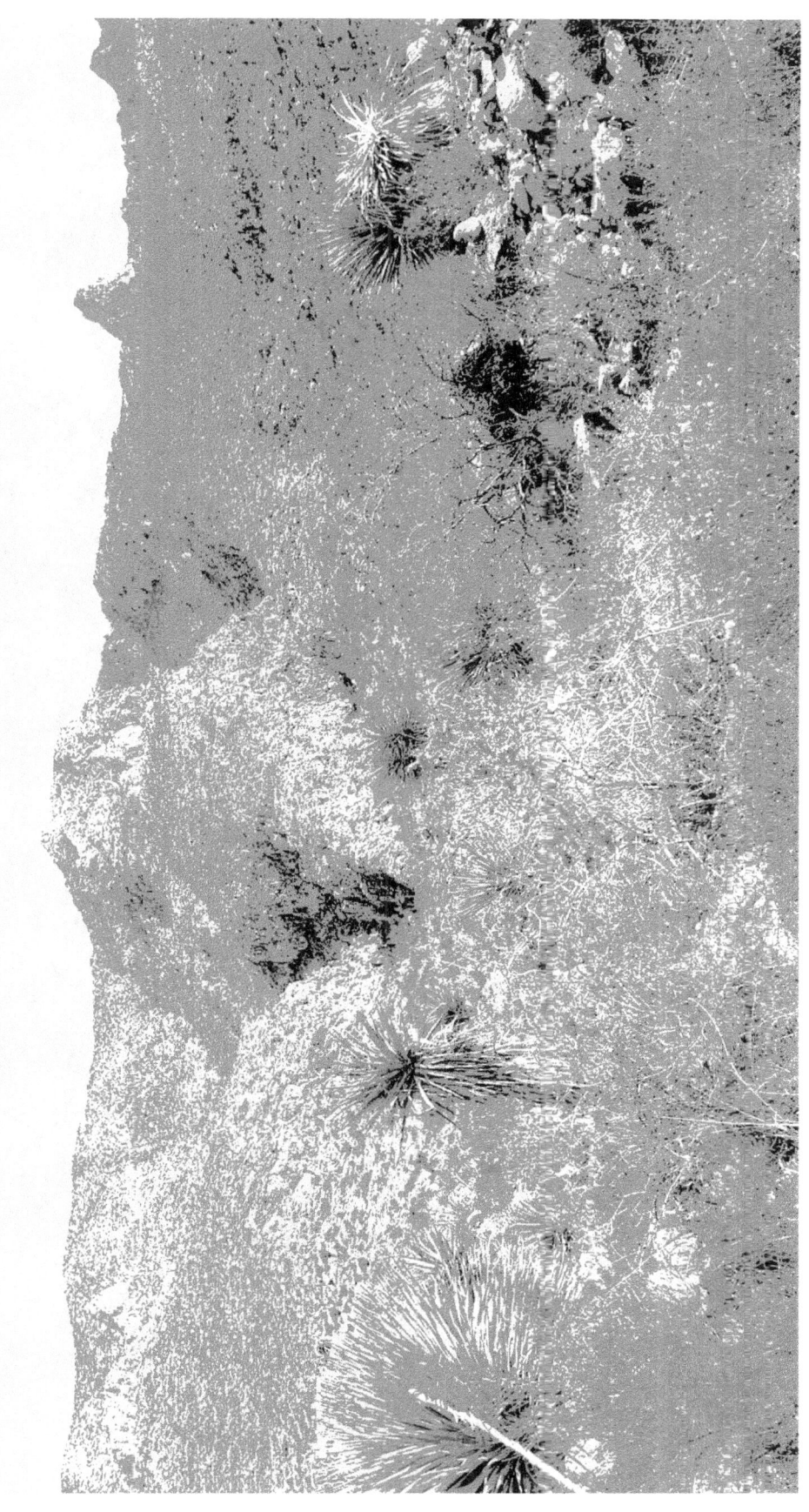

cem-dvacet-fyra

DR. ZORCH'S IDIOCIES

Your left, left, left, right, left...

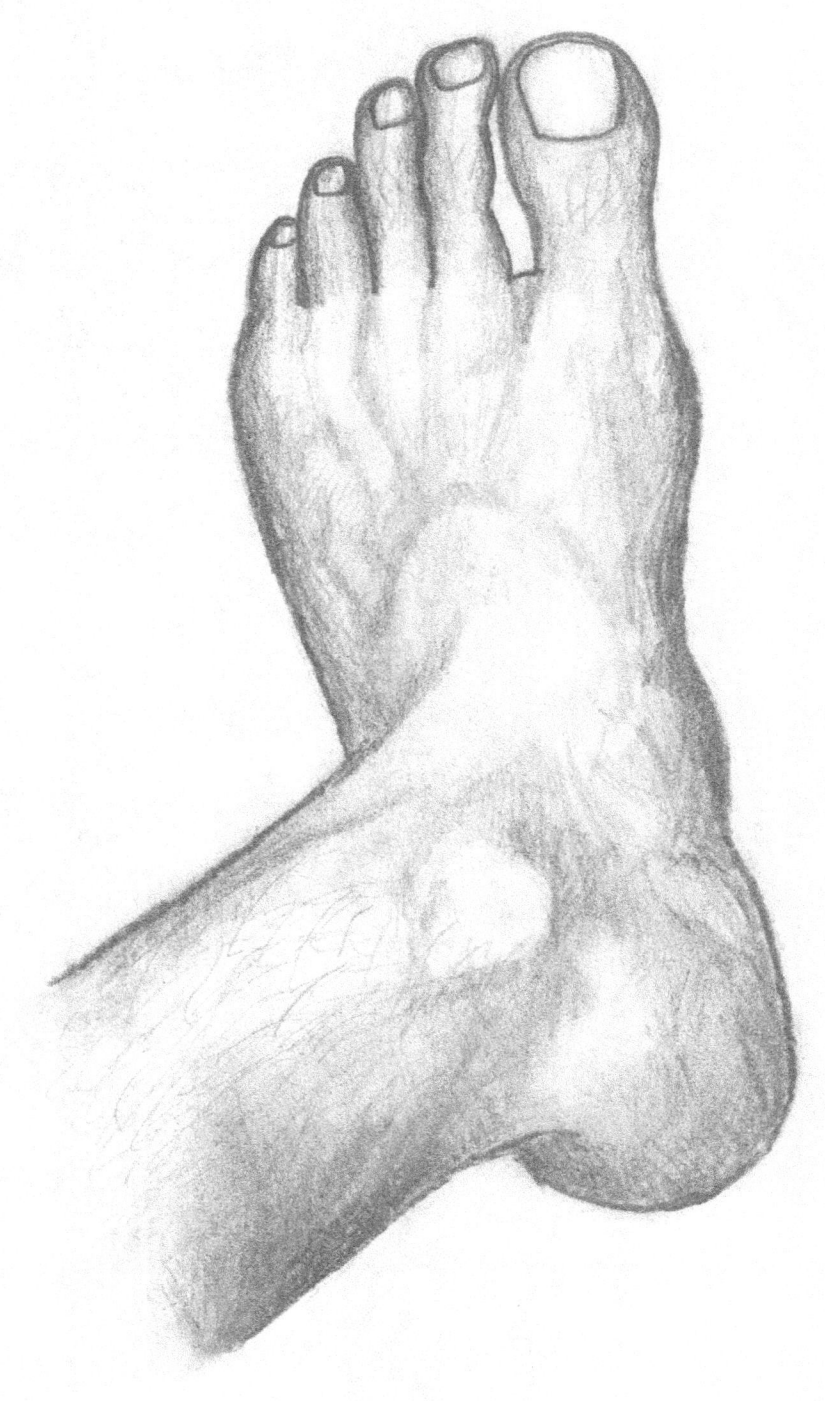

ANTHOLOGY                              bye-bye